# LOST
# ROYAL

## LILY WILDHART

Lost Royal
The Knights of Echoes Cove #2
Copyright © 2021 Lily Wildhart

Editor: David Hamilton
Proofreader: Sassi's Editing Services
Interior Design & Formatting: Wild Elegance Formatting

Lost Royal - 1st ed
ISBN-13 - 978-0-9957402-7-3

*Courage is grace under pressure*

**-Ernest Hemmingway**

# PLAYLIST

Playing with Fire - Sam Tinnesz

This Little Girl - Cady Groves

Cravin' - Stileto

Fake - The Tech Thieves

Serial Killer - Moncrieff

Back to You - Taylor Acorn

Middle Finger - Bohnes

Panic Room - Au/Ra

Control - Halsey

Uncomfortably Numb - Arrors in Action & Taylor Acorn

Prom Queen - Molly Kate Kestner

Partners in Crime - Set It Off

Saints - Echo

Dance in the Dark - Au/Ra

Who Am I - Besomorph

I Love You's - Hailee Steinfeld

I Fall Apart - Living in Fiction

The Diary of Jane - Breaking Benjamin

Wildest Dreams - Taylor Swift

Back to You - Taylor Acorn

*scan below to listen*

# ONE

## FINLEY

Some monsters live in the shadows. Some live in the depths of your soul. But mine… I keep mine close to the surface, just in case I need them.

For times like now.

The pounding from the body in my trunk sounds in time with my heartbeat.

I clench my hands on the steering wheel, my knuckles white as I try to calm myself down. Maverick just slips into that cold quiet he has.

It's a trait we share.

The killing quiet.

And this son of a bitch will be lucky if we kill him after

what he tried to do to Octavia. When Maverick declared her off-limits, he was being a dick, but he was also trying to protect her. Even if it was in that twisted way of his.

No one touches her but us.

No one.

Raleigh has been left to his own devices for too long. The Knights rarely go after their own, but I don't care if we're punished for this. He isn't a Knight, not yet. And he deserves to scream.

The same way he wanted to make her scream.

Luckily, I've never been the squeamish type. Probably not so lucky for him.

"Where are we heading?" Mav asks, piercing the silence. The dark of the night shrouds us, the perfect time for monsters to come out and play.

I glance over at him as he cracks his knuckles, the anger in his eyes reflected in the set of his shoulders and the tic in his jaw. "The Cage."

My lips curl at the edges just thinking about it, and he barks out a laugh. "Nothing less than what he deserves."

We drive through Echoes Cove, over the railroad tracks and into the vast wasteland of desert outside the city. Then I keep going. Way beyond the Kings' territory and into what I like to call the barren lands: stretches of open road with not a soul in sight for miles.

Nothing.

Except for the ruins that cover what is just one of many bases for the Knights.

This one in particular is a nice little hellscape they dreamed up. A headquarters of sorts with a nightmare basement. The Cage. It's usually reserved for initiation, but I'm pretty sure they won't mind us going off book.

Not that I'd give a fuck if they did.

The pounding in the trunk stops, and I let out a dry, sharp laugh.

Of course he gave up already.

If he thinks that will save him, he has another thing coming.

We already warned him. He thought that the Knights wanting his mom's connections would keep him safe.

I guess he's about to learn that here, you only get one warning.

I pull off the main road onto the dirt backroad, our dust a thick cloud as we make our way across the bumpy terrain. Shouts of pain from the trunk make Mav laugh, low and dangerous, as we drive the eight miles down the dirt road that brings the crumbling building into view.

I look over to Mav as I pull the car to a stop and turn off the engine. "Do not kill him."

"You spoil all my fun." He sighs before climbing from the car, practically skipping to the trunk. I meet him there. He's rubbing his hands together, the look of glee on his face like a kid at Christmas. He might be more than a little unhinged, but

I'd trust him with my life.

I push the button to unlock the trunk of the sedan, stepping back as it pops open. Raleigh's bound body comes into view, his eyes wide as he tries to shout around the gag in his mouth. I step forward and rip it away, letting him scream into the night.

Mav laughs beside me, his eyes dancing with excitement as he leans forward to speak to the piece of shit. "You can scream as much as you like. No one can hear you out here."

And just like that, the screams die out. "You guys can't do this."

"Watch us." I grab him by the hair and drag him from the trunk, dropping him face down in the dirt.

Raleigh scrambles on the ground, rolling himself over so he's looking up at us. He looks so afraid I think he might actually piss himself. Whatever buzz he was riding before has well and truly gone. One eye is already swollen shut and his lip is still bleeding from where Lincoln laid hands on him.

"What are you going to do to me?" His voice wobbles and I roll my eyes. Why is it that the entitled assholes who don't know how to take no for an answer are the first ones to crumble?

Mav reaches down and yanks him to his feet by the throat. "Oh, QB. I warned you once already about touching Octavia. What do you think I'm going to do to you for what you did?"

Raleigh pales as his eyes go wide, the reality of his situation sinking in. "You can't. My mom won't join. Not if something happens to me. The Knights need those connections."

"You think you're the only one with connections?" I ask, letting the silence of the night fill the space once I'm finished speaking. I learned long ago that there is power in silence. Words have more power when you use them less often. People fear noise, but there's something unsettling in silence that most can't handle; something that resonates with the darkest parts of our souls and brings them forward, reminding us that we *all* have those secret parts of ourselves that we try to hide away from the world.

"Please, you guys, I'll do whatever you want," he begs, and Mav grips his throat tighter until his breaths come in strangled, rattling gasps.

"Pathetic. If I wanted you to beg, I'd *tell* you to beg." He releases him, letting him drop to his knees before pulling his knife from its sheath at the small of his back. Raleigh whimpers in the dirt like a fucking coward as Mav crouches down. He cuts the rope at Raleigh's ankles before straightening and kicking him square in the chest.

Raleigh crumples to the ground, wheezing.

I look down at him, a sneer on my face, making sure to catch his gaze before speaking. "Get up. And if you even think about running, I'll slit your throat myself."

He whimpers and I turn my back on him, looking over at Mav who grins sadistically down at our toy. "He said get up!"

I head into the ruins, ignoring the wildlife that scatters as my footsteps echo through the cement and stone entry. Footsteps behind me let me know that Mav and Raleigh aren't far behind. I descend the crumbling spiral staircase, using the flashlight on my phone to illuminate the way down.

As I reach the lower floor, the lights flicker on, the lone hall illuminated in a sickly shade of yellow, leading to the only door down here.

The elevator.

The lights flicker in and out, buzzing like a fucking mosquito in my ear. I'm halfway down the hall when Raleigh stumbles onto the cement. I turn in time to see him faceplant and I'm not sure if he tripped or if Mav pushed him. Either way, I don't care. He whimpers. Once I reach the elevator, I push the button to call the car and try to shove away the memories of the first time I came here. It's hard to believe that it was nearly five years ago.

It was the day that changed my life and took away every hope and dream I ever had.

This is the place where dreams come to die.

The place where innocence is stripped and any semblance of freedom you thought you had is caged up and put on display as a mocking reminder of a life you once lived.

The weight of the guns in the shoulder holster under my jacket are yet another reminder of just how far I've come since I learned these tortured halls existed.

The ding of the elevator echoes in the space as the two of them finally catch up. I step into the car, turning to face them once I'm in. Raleigh has a bloody nose to add to his collection of minor lacerations and contusions, and the blood on Maverick's knuckles tells the rest of the story. I say nothing as I lean against the metal wall, waiting for them to join me.

"What is this place?" Raleigh stammers as Mav pushes him into the car without a word. He steps in and stands beside me, his arms at his sides, hands clenched as he bounces on the balls of his feet.

Mav was made for this world long before we ever knew about it. I've never figured out if his dad was intentionally merciful in never letting him know a life outside of this, or just a twisted sadist.

There's a reason we tried to keep Octavia from The Cove.

This place is just one of the many reasons we tried to protect her from this world, but I think we might be swimming out of our depths in trying to save her.

She was always our light, but even the brightest of lights fades in the depth of this darkness.

That's what the last five years have taught me.

Taught us all.

Raleigh's whimpers fill the silence as the elevator descends into the depths of hell. Six basement levels of pure nightmares.

But we're going to the base level, where I know no one will be, not at this time of night.

When the lift stops and the doors open, Raleigh pushes past us, trying to run, and Maverick barks out a laugh. "I love it when they run."

His eyes light up as he stalks after our prey. I stroll casually from the car, knowing that Raleigh isn't getting far. Even if I did doubt that Mav would catch him, there's no way out of here except the way we just came in.

The lights along the walls of the circular room flicker on, starting at the doors as they close behind us and slowly making their way to the opposite end of the expanse.

A strangled scream fills the room, followed by the crunch of bone, just as the last of the lights flicker on, illuminating Maverick standing over Raleigh's quivering body.

I move toward the single metal chair in the middle of the room, nodding to Mav who drags Raleigh toward it by an ankle that juts at an unnatural angle. I move to the left of the room, running my hand over the hidden panels in the wall to open the cubbies I want access to, and grab cable ties and lighter fluid before closing them.

Between the two of us, we have everything else we need already.

By the time I get back to them, Raleigh is trembling with his ass firmly planted in the chair. I throw the cable ties to Mav, who catches the pack in one hand, his sadistic smile widening. "Move again, and I'll cut you open and play with your insides while you watch."

I don't doubt Maverick would do it either. A smile plays on my lips at the squeak Raleigh lets out as Mav binds him to the chair. Mav steps back, admiring his handy work before nodding.

There's no way Raleigh is leaving here without us.

"It's not so fun being the one with no control, is it?"

I tilt my head as I ask the question, letting him see the monster I keep caged inside of me. He gulps audibly and I smile.

"I wasn't going to—"

"Ah, ah. Do not lie to us," Maverick says, waving the tip of his blade in Raleigh's face. "Digging for the truth is one of my favorite things to do."

He cuts through the QB's t-shirt until he's sitting topless, then does the same to his jeans so he's sitting bared to us.

That'll teach him to go commando.

Mav bounces giddily once he throws the cut up clothing across the room.

"What are you going to do to me?"

I move across the room to lean on the wall, letting Mav have his fun. I won't let it go too far. While the Knights might overlook us maiming him a little, I'm pretty sure the punishment for killing him is more than either of us are willing to pay.

"Nothing less than a rapist deserves," Mav replies, dragging his blade from the hollow of the worm's throat, down to the bottom of his abdomen, laughing as Raleigh roars in pain. "What's wrong? Don't like being defiled? Made to bleed? I told you she was off-limits, you should have listened."

I watch as Mav works his blade like a master. There really isn't much worse than death by a thousand cuts. Raleigh's skin peels open like butter under the knife, and blood runs from his wounds like a gloriously macabre waterfall, mixing with the pool of piss beneath the chair.

Some of these scars will fade, but not all of them. Maverick avoids his face—the Knights don't usually like it when you mess up the pretty faces that belong to them.

"Should I peel your dick like a banana? I bet my knife would enjoy that real good," Mav taunts before I tune him out and ignore the scene playing out before me. I don't enjoy this shit like he does, but I'm not about to hide from it either after what this asshole tried to do to V.

After a while, the screams Mav tears from him don't even really register. Except for when he pours on the lighter fluid and they get even more high-pitched. But when Raleigh falls silent and looks like he's going to pass out, I step in. "Enough."

Mav steps back, covered in almost as much blood as Raleigh. "I was barely getting into it." I quirk a brow at him and he barks out a laugh before shrugging. "At least let me finish what I started?"

He motions to the cuts on Raleigh's crotch, and I look, trying not to laugh. "Go on." I wave, encouraging him, and Raleigh cries out as Mav finishes carving the T of rapist into his skin.

Ink can be removed. Scars are forever if you cut deep enough.

When Mav is done, I pull one of the guns from the holster and point it at Raleigh's head. I smile as his screams turn hysterical. "You said you couldn't kill me. I heard you from the trunk. You said *he* couldn't kill me!"

"I guess I did, didn't I? Though I didn't say I couldn't kill you." I tilt my head and laugh before lowering the gun, levelling it at his dick and letting off a round. "That won't kill you at least."

His screams echo violently off the distant walls, almost matched in volume with Maverick's laughter.

"Next time you're warned... Pay fucking attention. Do not touch things that aren't yours. Especially when they're ours." I holster the gun as his head lolls to one side, his eyes unfocused and glassy, before heading back to the elevator with Maverick on my heels. When the car arrives, we climb in and I hit the number three.

We reach the third level and find Eleanor behind the front desk of the office-style space that's housed on this floor. There is someone here twenty-four seven, either Eleanor or Elisabeth. The Knights always have someone available.

Her lips twist when we step from the elevator toward her desk. "Finley, Maverick. What brings you here?"

"Clean up in the basement. He'll need a medic pretty quick so he doesn't bleed out." I grab a towel from the pile on a cart near her desk and throw it at Mav. "Clean up before we head out."

He nods and saunters down the hall to one of the many rooms at our disposal, and I lean against the desk. I don't bother with the cleanup—I didn't get any blood on me—whereas Mav looks like he took a blood shower.

"Who is it?" Eleanor asks with the phone to her ear.

"Raleigh Rittenhouse." Her eyes go wide before she looks down at the desk and calls for a medic. It doesn't take long for two of the doctors on the floor to rush past me to the elevator, not even sparing a glance in my direction.

"We'll need a car too. The one we arrived in was borrowed."

Maverick appears, freshly showered in clean jeans and t-shirt, a few minutes later. "We good?"

"I think so." I cut my eyes to Eleanor who nods. "Perfect. Let's head back."

We ride the elevator in silence to the first floor and when the doors open, Jerry—yet another cog in the machine that is The Knights Society—greets us with a set of keys hanging from his fingers. "Where to, gentlemen?"

My phone buzzes in my pocket as cell service returns and I see the message from Linc.

Linc

At V's. East is here.

I show Mav the message before pocketing the phone and turning to Jerry. He doesn't need to know where we're going and, right now, I've never been more grateful that Octavia moved back home. "To the Saints'."

Jerry drops us off at the gates to the Saint mansion, waiting until we're on the grounds with the gates shut before he drives off. I have no doubt that the Knights are watching us closely with V back in town.

Especially since I'm convinced they're the reason she's here at all. I'd put money on Stone's suicide being a cover up. The Knights specialize in fixing their problems. Even if the problems are of their own making.

I walk up the drive and head straight to the hidden gate between this property and V's. Maverick is hot on my heels. Neither of us has said a word since we left the base.

"Shit," I hiss, halting abruptly.

"What?" Mav asks, perplexed.

I tap my ear, then motion to his clothes. It only takes him a second to clue in to what I mean and he starts to strip out of the Knights-issued clothing. Bugs and trackers are implanted in pretty much everything they have. He grins as he stands in front of me, butt-ass naked, then walks the clothes to the trash cans before heading into the Saints' house. A few minutes later he reappears in another jeans and t-shirt combo, but this is one of his own.

Once he's ready, we make our way to the Royal house, heading in through the back doors to the kitchen where the lights are already on, illuminating the backyard. The alarm beeps as I open the door and I disable it. Mav closes the door then re-arms it. I'm pretty sure V doesn't know we have the codes, but in this instance, what she doesn't know won't hurt her.

We keep quiet as we remove our boots and pad through to the lounge, where we find Octavia asleep on the sofa, wrapped in a blanket, while Linc and East murmur quietly between them. Linc sees us hovering in the doorway and stands. East looks over his shoulder then follows his brother toward us and we head into the kitchen.

"How is she?" are the first words to fall from my lips. The rest of the world might think we hate her, but there are few secrets between the four of us.

Lincoln drops onto a stool at the island while Mav grabs us all sodas from the fridge. "As good as can be expected. She's sleeping off whatever he gave her. Is he dealt with?"

"He won't be raping anyone else." Mav grins as he hands out the drinks. "Finn shot his dick off."

I roll my eyes at the exaggeration and accept the drink, dropping into the stool opposite Linc. "I shot him in the dick after you carved rapist into his crotch, but yes, he's dealt with, we took him to The Cage, so the Knights are cleaning up."

"This was by the door when we got here," East says, dropping the black card onto the table.

*You're out of time, Miss Royal.*
*We're coming for you.*
*Ready or not.*

"Motherfuckers," Maverick hisses as he slams a fist on the table.

"Keep your fucking voice down. Do you have any idea how long it took for her to fall asleep?" Linc glares at him, that commanding tone of his biting. It's rare that we bicker between us, but when we do, it's usually because of her.

She has always been our weak spot.

"So what do we do?" I ask, looking to the brothers.

Lincoln always has a plan. He runs his hand through his dark hair and sighs. "I don't know. She won't leave, that much is obvious. Even after this, I don't know that we could drag her away with a herd of wild horses, so we need a new plan."

"I've been saying that for weeks," East grumbles as he gets up and walks back to the doorway to check on her. I turn my attention back to Lincoln, who glares at his brother.

The resentment that East is still here when he could've escaped is real, and while I have my own suspicions about the whole situation, I keep my mouth shut. They have their issues, but the bond between them is ironclad.

"As I was saying, we need a new plan of attack. She won't leave, and what we've been doing isn't working."

I lean back in the chair, watching him closely. "So what do you propose?"

A scream cuts through the air and I move without even thinking. My heart pounds in my chest until my eyes are on her. Tears stream down her face as she claws at her throat. I stride across the room, and lift her from the couch. I sit, placing her on my lap and hold her so she can't hurt herself anymore than she already has. "You're safe, V. I got you."

I murmur the same phrase to her until she calms, rocking her softly until she falls asleep again. The others are all standing around the room, just watching us.

I have zero doubt in my mind that any chance of us giving her up, of getting her out, went out the window when Raleigh attacked her.

That means we need to do the opposite of what we *were* doing.

"We need to keep her close. It's the only way to protect her now." My words aren't meant for anyone in particular, but Lincoln nods.

"He's right. We tried pushing her away, but the only way to keep her safe now is to keep her as close to us as possible."

East runs a hand through his hair and pulls his phone from his pocket. "I'm going to call Smithy. He needs to know what's happened." He leaves the room and I hold my breath as V shifts in my lap, clinging to me even in her sleep.

I'm not surprised Smithy has some clue of what's going on. You don't work for the Royals and not know about the Knights—they go hand-in-hand. The downside of being involved with a legacy—something I know all too much about. I'm not sure how much he knows about the finer details though.

As if reading my mind, Linc speaks up. "He can help us

keep her safe. We just need to bring him into the fold."

Mav shifts from foot to foot before crossing his arms over his chest. "This stuff isn't my strong suit. You point me in a direction and I'll make people bleed—to get them out of the way, or to keep her safe. I'm not the guy with the plan, but I'll do what needs to be done to keep her."

He doesn't give himself enough credit, but I nod anyway and Lincoln does the same.

"Now all we have to do is convince her that this is either the right plan of attack or the only option." I sigh.

Lincoln barks out a dry laugh before leveling me with a scowl. "Yeah, because she's not going to be stubborn about that at all."

"Can you blame her? Especially after these last few months. We just have to be more stubborn than she is. She'll come around eventually."

"If you say so," he murmurs, eyes fixed back on the girl in my arms. The girl we've all been in love with our entire lives. "You make it sound so easy."

I lean back, shifting to cover her with the blanket again. "Nothing has ever been easy when it comes to her."

He huffs and drops down into the armchair across from the sofa. "Maybe, but I'd do it all over again if I thought it would save her."

# TWO

## OCTAVIA

A scream rips from my throat, the remnant of a nightmare that clings to me as I struggle against the hold someone has on me.

"You're safe, V. You're safe."

East's voice soothes me a little. My heart hammers against my ribs, even as his grip loosens a bit, helping me to relax some more. I open my eyes and squint against the brightness. The sun is just starting to rise, and the light is filtering in through the windows.

For one moment, I feel a little peace before icy dread runs down my spine as broken memories of last night hit me. The fractured flashes make my stomach churn. "I'm going to be sick."

I scramble off of the couch to the downstairs bathroom, just managing to get my head over the bowl before the feeble contents of my stomach show themselves. My head pounds as memories of Raleigh continue to assault me, the images making the room spin. The back of my neck heats, so I look at the doorway, seeing Maverick standing there, watching me. I groan before my stomach churns again. He moves quickly, pulling back my hair and rubbing my back until the somersaults my insides are doing calm for a moment.

I lean my head on my forearm, trying to remember exactly what happened. How far Raleigh went. How the fuck I got back here, and why the hell East and Maverick are here.

My head pounds like my heart is in my fucking skull. I close my eyes, wishing the room wasn't so goddamn bright. The feel of a cold washcloth on the back of my neck makes me jump, but I groan in appreciation as the water trickles down my spine.

I should not be taking comfort in anything Maverick Riley does or says, but the world is spinning backward, my stomach is a rollercoaster, and I don't have the strength to tell him to get the fuck away from me. He waits with me until the puking and the dry heaving stops.

I take a few deep breaths, hoping that they'll help my stomach to stop flipping. When I'm fairly confident I have a handle on my upchuck reflex, I stand up and brush my teeth, ignoring the fact that Maverick is still in here with me. I'm still not entirely sure why he's here at all.

Once my mouth doesn't taste like a trash can, I splash cold water on my face to try and clear some of the cobwebs from my mind. I try not to panic about the black holes in my memory from last night; what I do remember is enough to make me not sleep for a week.

Last time something like this happened… well, I got justice. Kind of.

This time… this time I'm not really sure what happened. I know I'm going to have to ask them, even though I wish I didn't have to. I don't want to feel like I owe them anything. They've been such assholes to me the last few months, the last thing I want is to be indebted to them.

I glance at Maverick in the mirror. He's standing with his arms folded across his chest, watching me as he leans against the doorframe. His gaze is like a red-hot laser on my skin—it's so intense—his broody look as menacing as ever.

So much for the softer side of him I thought I might see.

"Are you done?" he asks, the softness of his voice a complete contrast to his demeanor.

I turn to face him and scrub a hand down my face, exhaustion sweeping through me despite the fact I *just* woke up. "I'm done. You can leave now."

"I'm not going anywhere." He pushes off the frame with his shoulders and opens it, ushering me out of the bathroom.

He stays on my tail as I head back toward the living room; where I find East still on the couch and Lincoln sitting in the arm chair, watching me as I come to a halt in the archway. Mav stops at my side and leans against the wall.

The sound of sizzling and a shout of "Fuck!"—which sounds very much like Finley—comes from the kitchen, drawing my attention. "You're all here?"

"Where else would we be?" Lincoln snaps, and I wrap my arms around myself.

Mav straightens up and moves closer to me. "Don't be an ass, Linc."

"Who's being an ass?" Finley asks as he appears in the doorway from the kitchen, a plate in each hand.

"You have to ask?" East sighs and stands, moving toward Finley. "I'll get the other plates."

Finley glares at Lincoln while I shift from foot to foot, wondering what fucking twilight zone I stepped into when I woke up this morning.

"What the hell is going on?" I don't ask anyone in particular, but Finley looks over at me before putting the two plates he's holding on the table in the far corner of the room. Lincoln rolls his eyes before standing and moving to the table. Mav follows suit, leaving me standing alone as Finley approaches me.

"Come and eat, you probably need something to line your stomach."

I twist my lips, stepping back as he reaches out to touch me. I don't want to be touched right now. What I really want is a shower and more sleep. "I'm not hungry."

"I'm sure you're not, but that doesn't mean you shouldn't eat."

I let out a sigh and run a hand through my hair. "Why are you here, Finley?"

His hand drops to his side and he smiles sadly at me. "Like Linc said, where else would we be? After what happened to you last night…"

He trails off, like he doesn't want to trigger me, but these guys being in my space is enough to do just that.

"What *did* happen tonight… last night?" I ask, pulling at the hem of my top.

All of them look at me, a mix of surprise and discomfort on their faces. "I mean… I remember some of it, but my memory is a little patchy." I swallow down the emotion that threatens to rise. I remember enough to know I'm going to roundhouse Raleigh's head off his shoulders if I ever see him again, but I *need* the holes filled in. I can't let the blank spots in my memory fester.

*I survived this before, I can survive again.*

I repeat the mantra in my head. Maybe if I say it enough, it'll be true.

"V," Finley starts, moving closer to me again. He raises a hand toward me, but seems to think better of it and lowers it again. "You eat first, then we can tell you whatever you're missing."

I move toward the table. I have zero intention of eating,

but maybe if I play along they'll just tell me what I want to know and leave. I sit at the end of the table, opposite Lincoln, and next to Maverick. Finley takes the seat on my other side as East reappears with the last of the plates. There is silence for a minute as East sits between Finley and Lincoln, and they all just stare at me.

It's so fucking suffocating.

I look down at my plate, the smell of the freshly baked croissants is beautiful, but my stomach protests. I know I should eat something, but the thought of it… just nope. Picking at the skin beside my thumb nail, feeling more vulnerable than I have since I got back to The Cove—which in itself speaks volumes—I try not to spin out about everything that's happened.

The silence hanging in the air is so fucking loud it's practically deafening.

"V," East starts, but doesn't say any more. I look up to find Linc glaring at him before he turns his stare to me.

"Raleigh drugged you and attempted to assault you. We stopped him, and brought you home."

I glare at him. Way to play it down. Here's me going through the worst possible scenarios and that's all he gives me. "I'm going to need more details than that."

His eyes harden, staring me down. "What else is there to know? He tried, we stopped him."

For just a moment, the darkness inside me is burned away by fiery rage. "What else is there to know? You're kidding me

30

right? It's my fucking body. I'm the one who was violated. You want me to just sit and imagine what happened? Wait for the memories to come back and knock the breath from my lungs? Tell me what the fuck happened."

"V—" East starts but I shut him down.

"No, I'm sick of whatever all of this is that you guys have been doing. So either tell me or get the hell out." I fold my arms across my chest, glancing between all of them, waiting for someone to speak.

"Ellis called me," Lincoln starts, and I sit in silence, waiting for him to continue. "He said you looked out of it, and that Raleigh was following you around like a bloodhound. Since he's known for being, well, a rapey asshole, we found you. When we did, you were telling him no, but you were topless and I'm pretty sure his hand was down your pants while he was slobbering all over you. I couldn't really make out for certain, because I was too busy getting him off of you. Is that what you want to hear? That he had his hands all over you?" Anger simmers just beneath the surface of every word, and I can't tell if that anger is directed at me or elsewhere, but whoever it's meant for, it's bleeding all over me.

"Of course it fucking isn't, but you know what's worse than knowing? Fucking imagining what happened!"

"He didn't do any more than that," Maverick adds, looking at me like I might break.

I don't want him to look at me like that, because then I might actually curl up and shatter rather than stuff it down and put it on a shelf like I've been doing since my dad died and I came back here. I've just been trying to survive this place so I could escape it. I'm pretty sure if I opened up the mental closet with all of my trauma, my mind would splinter.

Instead, I nod once and look down at my plate again. "Thank you for telling me."

The sounds of silverware against flatware fills the space and no one says another damn word. I don't even pretend to eat. I just sit and wait for them to leave, trying not to let everything swirling inside of me spill over.

*Not much longer.*

Once they're finished eating, I finally stand, my legs still shaking a little. "I'd like you all to leave now."

My voice comes out shaky but I jut out my chin, trying to feel a little like my usual self, and catch everyone's gaze one at a time.

East looks like he's going to object, but Linc interrupts him by standing from the table with a glare tossed in my direction, making me wince.

"Fine," he spits and heads out of the room toward the door.

Finley looks up at me with sad eyes. "V—"

I cut him off with a shake of my head. "I'd really just like to be alone. *Please.*" I stress the last word and it's only then, when my desperation to be alone so I can break comes through, that the three of them stand.

"You know where we are if you need us," East says before leaving. Maverick just looks at me like he wants to object more, but Finley shakes his head. At the move, Maverick follows East, leaving me alone with Finley.

He watches me closely in that assessing way that he has. "Are you sure you're going to be okay alone? What happened tonight… last night… I'm happy to stay."

I clutch my arms tighter around my stomach and step back, giving me some more space from him. While I'd probably feel safer with him here—which I'm aware is fucking moronic, all things considered—if he stays, he'll keep looking at me like he is now, and I can't cope with that. My dad raised me to deal with stuff on my own, so asking people for help isn't exactly the easiest thing for me. "I'd really just rather be alone."

He frowns, and I'm aware he doesn't agree, but why he thinks I'd feel safe with the four of them baffles me. East, I could understand, but him, Maverick, and Linc? Other than last night, they've not done one thing that tells me I can trust them. And I sure as hell am not about to forgive them just because they did what any decent human should have done.

Finley watches me closely and I guess that, despite me trying to keep my face passive, he can see everything I've tried to hide, because he just nods. "Okay. I'll be next door if you need anything."

He gathers the dishes and leaves the room. I stay where I am, staring out into the back yard until I hear the alarm arm and the door slam shut. Only then do I let the emotion out. Only then do I fall to the floor and clutch my knees to my chest, crying tears of violation, of devastation for everything that happened at that party last night.

This is the only time I'll let Raleigh Rittenhouse break me, after this, I'll put my armor against the world back on, but right now… right now I need to be broken.

I just hope I can put myself back together after.

After spending most of the morning breaking and drowning in the despair I try not to feel; showering to try and wash off the violation of everything and failing; then trying to sleep and failing; spiraling in my shame, I find myself down in the music room.

Composing was part of my healing process the last time something like this happened. The crazed fan that thought I was in love with him… I shudder as the memory assaults me.

*I survived this before, I can survive it again.*

I'd never been so scared in my entire life as when he grabbed me in that hall and I felt the needle plunge into my neck.

My memory of that night is all too vivid from when I came around, tied to a bed, with him standing over me, watching me. If it wasn't for Panda… no… it isn't worth thinking about. I shake my head, trying to chase away the memory, the pain, so I don't sink further.

My therapist encouraged music to help me heal, and it did. So while I might not have all my memories of last night like I did before, I'm pretty sure that it's still the best way for me to deal with everything that's whirring inside of me like a hurricane.

I sit down at the baby grand, but I can't bring myself to put my fingers on the ivory. I still feel dirty, and I don't want to taint the pureness of the keys. A shudder runs through me as I close my eyes, the feel of Raleigh's hands still on my skin.

It occurs to me that I should probably call the police. That I should do something. But I also wonder what the point would be. The police in this town have never done anything against people like him. His dad owns a Fortune 500 company, not to mention his mom's restaurant—fucking power couples—so even if the police did anything, his dad would just pay to get it swept away.

The corruption in the system, especially in The Cove, is disgusting.

Still, I wonder if it would stop him from doing it to someone else.

Or if I'm the only person he's done this to, did I do something to deserve it? Did I lead him on?

I close my eyes and tip my head back, trying to take deep breaths.

While, logically, I know that I don't deserve what he tried to do, the fact that this isn't the first time it's happened to me... it makes me question if I didn't bring this on myself? Was this my fault? What is it about me that makes people think something like that is okay?

I need to call the police.

Report what happened.

*Do something.*

Even if it's fruitless, at least I tried, and then maybe he won't try it with anyone else.

I stand, fixed in my decision, when I realize I haven't seen my phone since I woke up this morning. Heading back upstairs, I search everywhere for it and come up empty.

*What the actual fuck?*

I find my clothes from last night and go through the pockets, still nothing.

*Where the fuck is my phone?*

Trying to cast my mind back, I can't think of where I had it last, so I do the only thing I can think of.

I put on my hoodie and head next door.

It doesn't take more than a minute to head through the gate in the back yard to bang on the Saints' front door. Not thirty seconds later, it's ripped open and I find a half-naked Lincoln looking back at me. His jeans aren't even zipped up.

Who the fuck opens the door like that?

"Do you have my phone?" I ask before he can say a word, because my fragile state can not handle him being this new, cold version of Lincoln I've known since coming back. Right now,

I'd give just about anything to have my old friends back.

Which reminds me to call Indi as soon as I've spoken to the police.

God, I'm such a bad friend sometimes.

Lincoln just stares at me, and jams his hands in his pockets.

"Well?" I take a deep breath, trying not to get frustrated.

He nods and walks away from me, the muscles in his back flexing as he goes. I shift from foot to foot while I wait for him to return, trying not to look as awkward as I feel. The seconds seem to drag out and it feels like it's been at least an hour when he returns, though I know it was likely just a few minutes. At least he's done up his jeans now, even if he is still topless.

He hands me my phone and when I tap the screen, nothing happens. Of course it's dead, why wouldn't it be?

"Thanks," I say, smiling stiffly before turning and heading back the way I came.

"Octavia." I turn as he barks my name, and realize he's only a few steps behind me, barefoot on the paved ground. "Are you okay?"

A glimpse of the boy I used to know shines through for a moment, but I'm not foolish enough to think that the ghost I see is who Lincoln still is. Maybe, deep, deep down, my friend still exists, but I don't have the energy or the time to go hunting for him. Not right now.

I shrug at him and play with the cuffs of my hoodie. "I'll be fine. I've survived worse."

He looks confused for a minute but doesn't say anything else, so I turn back around and walk away from him. As I reach the gate between our properties, I find him still watching after me. I give him a tight smile and head home, determined to make a stand.

Once I'm back in my own space, I set the alarm before finding my charger to plug my phone in. The silence in this empty house is deafening, I hate it. I hit the tablet on the wall and start a playlist of low, classical music, just to fill the silence.

As I stare into nothingness, flashes of last night replay over and over in my mind until the buzzing of my phone brings me back to the present. I look down at my screen and see dozens of messages from Indi. I swipe them off the screen for the time being, determined to call the police without further distraction. I open up the phone app and my phone starts ringing in my hand. I don't know the number so I hesitate, just a few seconds, before answering anyway.

"Hello?"

"V?" I relax at Finley's voice. "I've been trying you on and off all day, I was starting to worry."

"What do you want, Finley?"

The line is silent for a moment and butterflies take flight in my stomach. "I need you to not call the police."

I practically hold my breath, wondering how he could've known and why he'd even ask that. "How? How did you know?"

"Because despite what you might think, I know you, Octavia

Royal. Always have, always will. Which is why I know you've wrestled with the decision of what to do, and you think this will help stop it from happening to anyone else. I need you to trust that it's been handled. There isn't anything the police can do that hasn't already been done."

My heart thumps in my chest at his words. "What does that even mean?"

"I'll tell you one day, when you're ready to know. Just know that it was handled."

I suck in a breath as I clutch the counter. My knees shake as I try to calm myself. None of this makes any sense to me. None of it.

"He won't hurt you ever again. No one will. He won't hurt anyone else either. I know you don't trust me, you have no reason to, but that will change. I promise you that much. Call me if you need anything." He pauses, and I'm stunned to silence. "I mean it, V. *Anything.*"

The line drops, and I stare down at my phone wondering exactly what just happened. I'm still tempted to call the police, but something in his voice makes me pause. I've nearly chewed through my lip, grappling internally with the decision before me, when my phone rings again and Indi's face fills my screen. The phone is barely to my ear when I hear her screech. "About fucking time!"

It didn't take long for Indi to ditch whatever she was doing once she realized I was conscious and home alone. Less than forty minutes later, she blasts through my front door like a hurricane on the warpath.

"Are you okay? That's a stupid question. Goddamn, I am still so angry I could murder!" She practically vibrates with rage the way she radiates negative energy.

I smile a little, for the first time since I woke up, and laugh softly at her. "I'm okay. Kind of. I *will* be okay, and that's what matters. What happened to you last night? The guys just said they got me home."

"Yeah, it was kind of hectic after everything happened. The party shut down pretty fast when Maverick and Finley hauled Raleigh out of there after Lincoln got you out." My eyes go wide at her words, and my earlier conversation with Finley rings out in my head.

*What did he do?*

She watches me closely with narrowed eyes. "They didn't tell you that bit I'm guessing?"

"No, no they definitely didn't. They just told me that Raleigh drugged me, and attempted to... yeah... that they stopped him, and brought me home. I was out cold and I still don't remember anything. All I know is that the four of them were here when I woke up this morning."

She huffs out a laugh. "That's definitely the condensed version. I tried to get you home myself, but Lincoln refused to let anyone else near you. Hell, he parted the crowd at that party like Moses parted the freaking sea."

"Enough about me, and all of that. I can't yet. I need some time to process. What happened with you last night? The last thing I remember properly, you were with Ellis Donovan?" I wag my eyebrows at her, feigning the excitement I want to have, because fake it till you make it, right?

A blush spills across her cheeks at his name and I smile a little wider. Apparently music therapy isn't the only thing to get me through the bad times. Especially when I have friends like Indi in my life.

"Spill!"

"Are you sure? I don't want to, like, sweep what happened to you under the rug. We should be outraged, angry, and all of the fucking things about what happened to you." That fire in her flares bright once again and my heart pangs that she cares for me so much.

"I'm sure. The last thing I want to do is focus on what happened. Finley told me it was handled. I have no reason to trust him fully, but I trust that much at least," I tell her with a shrug.

She goes a little pale and nods. "Girl, I would. You should have seen his face as he and Maverick hauled Raleigh out of there last night. I don't think I've ever seen him that angry. I would not want to be Raleigh."

I get comfortable on the couch and she joins me. "Moving

on… Ellis Donovan."

She blushes again, and I laugh softly. She throws a cushion at me and I grin harder.

"Ellis Donovan… is a long story. I told you I knew the brothers before, that I was friends with Scout…" She trails off while I sit, butterflies taking flight in my stomach. My excitement for her is the exact distraction I needed from my own freak show of a life. I curl up, pulling the cushion against my chest and hugging it while she spills the tea. "Well, I actually dated Ellis last year. And Ryker… and their friend Dylan."

My eyes go wide at her confession. "Holy shit, you've totally been holding out on me!"

She looks down at her hands, wringing them uncomfortably. "Yeah, not everyone is too open-minded about a girl dating three guys."

"Dude, I am so not that girl. Date seven of them if you want. Power to you! So, you and the three of them… what happened?"

She shrugs before looking back up at me. "I'm not really sure. We got halfway through the summer, and they told me it wasn't working anymore. That it was too dangerous for me to be with them."

I roll my eyes and lean back on the arm of the sofa. "Ugh, boys fucking suck sometimes. Why do they get to judge that shit?"

"Well, I mean, their brother runs The Kings… they're basically his seconds. Shit can get dangerous real quick in their world."

"The Kings?" I ask, beyond confused.

Her eyes go wide as she realizes I have no idea what she's on about. "I…I thought you knew. That's literally the rivalry between the Donovans and Lincoln and co." She blinks at me, squirming, while I sit waiting for her to continue. "I don't know everything, but I'll tell you what I do know."

She takes a deep breath, pausing as if trying to find the right words. "I'm not sure exactly what Lincoln and those guys are mixed up in, but I know that Ryker and Ellis got dragged into something last summer that they were a part of, and that's why the rivalry between the schools seemingly escalated."

"That explains the gun…" I trail off and she looks at me, jaw slack.

"Gun?"

"Yeah, Ryker was at the school one day a few weeks ago, talking with the guys, and pulled a gun on them."

"He did what?!" she shrieks, outraged, before taking a deep breath. "I swear to God, they might have been right. Their world is not anything I've ever experienced before. They kept me out of most of it, so I don't really know that much. All I know is that if something nefarious is happening in their side of The Cove, they probably know about it. Though, they didn't know about my car getting jacked. When they found out, they were pissed…" She trails off, blushing again.

"So are you back with them? Or just Ellis? Or?"

"Honestly? I have no fucking idea." She shrugs and I laugh softly again. "How did we end up dating—or not dating in your case—but still smack in the middle of the two biggest rivals in this not so big town?"

"That, my friend, is my luck. My curse. Whatever you want to call it." I sigh, trying to get comfortable. "All I've ever wanted is zero drama, yet that shit chases me like I'm its favorite main course."

"You don't have *that* much drama," she says, wincing a little, and I bark out a laugh.

"No, no, not that much. Just my dad turning my world upside down, putting me in the public eye, then making it so I have to come back here after he kills himself… only to find out that the people I thought were once my closest friends basically hate my guts. Let's not forget my only family in the world *also* hates my guts. And well, I mean, you've been around since I got back. You know the rest. Being stuck in the middle of their… what? Turf war? That doesn't feel like that much of a stretch at this point."

She stares at me, eyes wide, and starts laughing so hard she cries. "Man, and I thought I was the drama queen." She wipes at her eyes, trying to take a deep breath but just ends up laughing harder. I get caught up in it and end up laughing until I cry too.

What the fuck even is my life?

"But for reals, if the guys are willing to aim fucking guns at each other, we might have issues," I say, chewing on my lip.

"Boys are idiots. Way too much testosterone," she says with a shrug. "They can hate each other all they like, it's not going to fuck with us."

I nod, because well, I've never had a bestie before. I'd lay down my life for her at this point.

She grins at me, looking freaking devious as fuck. "Maybe they'll learn to love us enough that they can love each other."

I burst out laughing. "The chance of those four falling in love with me is pretty slim. Let's just hope for a truce?"

"Girl, you are straight up blind sometimes, but you didn't see their faces at that party either. They love you, whether any of you admit it or not." She spares me a sad smile for a moment before changing the subject. "Fuck boys... not literally, either. Crazy assholes. How does pizza and a movie sound?"

My stomach gurgles at her words and she giggles. I realize I haven't eaten since yesterday morning. That might explain the spaciness I've felt today. "That sounds like heaven."

She grins and fist pumps. "Perfect, you order the food, I'll pick the movie."

I grin back at her, glad that, even while everything else in my world feels up in the air, my bestie is my rock and my safe space. I might not have wanted any friends when I came back here, but I'm not sure I'd have survived here this long without her. I'm just thankful I won't have to find out.

The buzzer for the gate sounds and I grab my phone to check the security feed, my stomach twisting when I see what's waiting for me at the gate.

Yellow tulips. Dozens of them sprawled across my entire driveway.

That's when I remember the note from the night before, and fear flushes through me.

> *You're out of time, Miss Royal.*
> *We're coming for you.*
> *Ready or not.*

Out of time for what?

LOST ROYAL

# THREE

## OCTAVIA

A night with Indi was exactly what I needed. I ignored the flowers, and by the time the pizza arrived, they were gone. Which is a-okay with me. I do not want to know what is going on. I just want a quiet life, dammit. I knew coming back to Echoes Cove was going to be insane, but everything that's happened thus far is *so* beyond that.

By the time she left, after me practically forcing her out of the door, I'd learned even more about the Kings, and what sort of stuff they do. I'm more than a little shook by it all, but more really by the fact that she kept it from me; this huge part of her life.

On the one hand, I understand it, but on the other… I don't know. I guess I thought we were closer than that. Hell, I told her everything that has happened to me since I arrived here. *Everything.* I'm trying real hard not to be butt hurt about it.

Trying and not succeeding. I'm aware I'm likely hyper focusing on that to distract from the clusterfuck that has been my life this weekend, but still… it doesn't stop my illogical emotions running riot.

In my attempts to distract myself from the insanity playing on a loop in my mind, I'm trying to just live life as normally as freaking possible. I messaged Smithy when I woke up to check in with him, casually leaving out the events of my weekend, because I don't want him to worry. Now I'm attempting to cook breakfast.

Cooking has never really been my strong suit but I've got to earn points for trying.

Right?

I put the English muffins in the oven and decide to head outside to the mailbox. I haven't been out there for a few days, so lord only knows what's going to be in there. The fresh air of the morning is so cold that goosebumps rise on my arms as I step out of the house. I scurry down the drive and grab the various envelopes and magazines from the mailbox before practically running back into the house. I should've put on a hoodie today apparently.

I'm aware that it's November, but still, this is California. It shouldn't be this damn cold.

Once I'm back inside, I drop the mail on the counter in the

kitchen so I can go through it while I eat. I grab my hoodie and slide it over my head before I grab the eggs and bacon from the fridge. This cooking thing can't be *that* hard, right?

Wrong.

After butchering my attempt at simple meal preparation, I sit down at the counter to try and eat some of what I cooked. If I liked my eggs rubbery and my bacon charred, I'd have this cooking thing nailed. The only thing I managed to get right were the English muffins, and that's because they only had to go in the oven for ten minutes and I set a timer.

I give up on trying to eat the charred remains and pop a bagel in the toaster. That's got to be simpler... I grab the cream cheese from the fridge, smearing it over the bottom part of the bagel once it's done, then go about opening the mail. Bills and junk mail freaking galore. If it's not that, it's people wanting me to buy stuff.

I get toward the bottom of the pile and spot a manilla envelope. Just the sight of it makes my pulse race. I gingerly pick it up, my hands shaking as my mind flicks back to the last envelope like this I got. This is not how my morning was intended to go. I wanted a slice of normal, dammit.

I open the envelope and tip it up on the counter. A ton of photos cascade over the surface and my stomach turns.

They're from Friday night.

Pictures of me alone.

Ones with Raleigh. A red cross through his face.

Ones of Lincoln beating the crap out of Raleigh.

Of him putting me in his car.

Of Finley and Maverick putting Raleigh in the trunk of a car.

Others of just them with their faces scratched out, some of me just puttering around the house and in the yard. It's so fucking gross. Underneath them all, I find a note.

*They can't keep you safe. Not like I can.*
*You'll see.*

What the *fuck* is my life?

I grab my phone and dial the number Finley called me from yesterday. I'm aware I could just go next door to Lincoln or East, but I feel so exposed that I don't want to go back outside. I put the phone to my ear and Finley picks up on the first ring.

"V, what's wrong?"

I suck in a breath that that's his first assumption, hammering home that my life really has gone to hell in a handbasket since I came back here, but I might actually need to rely on them for help with this and not just sweep it under the rug, or put it on a shelf with the rest of the shit I don't want to deal with. It's not like I have the security team with me twenty-four seven anymore, and this isn't just bullies or paparazzi. I'm going to have to be the girl my dad raised me to be. The headstrong, smart and capable girl I was before I came back to The Cove.

Something about coming back here, whether my grief or not, had me putting my head in the sand, but the time for that is done.

The problem with that is I don't have the resources I used to, which means I need to rely on someone, and they're all I have right now whether I like it or not. And if I need their help, he needs to see these pictures. They all do. "More pictures turned up in my mailbox." I know I don't need to say any more than that for him to understand what I mean. Lincoln took the last set of photos that arrived, but there's no way he didn't share the news. My voice shakes more than I'd like as I speak, but considering this weekend has been a living fucking nightmare, I'm cutting myself some slack for being a little weak.

My life shouldn't be this insane. I don't know what I did to deserve it all but if I could repent, I would. I take a deep breath and realize he hasn't said a word but I can hear him moving around whatever room he's in.

"I'll be there in less than ten. Stay on the line with me till then."

"I don't have to—"

"Just humor me. Please?" Something in the way he says please makes me relent. I put the call on speakerphone and place it on the counter before going around and closing all the blinds and curtains. My skin crawls at the thought that someone has been watching me inside my house. It was bad enough when the last set arrived and they were me out and about, but I'm used to that, because, well, paparazzi. This is a little different.

I've dealt with a fully fledged stalker once before, and that's all I can assume this is. Except last time… last time I had round-the-clock security. Mac and Panda barely left my side. My dad might've wanted me to be capable and independent, but he also made sure I was safe… most of the time anyway. Last time, my dad and Mac kept most of it from me—which still pisses me off but I can't change the past—and it wasn't until I was taken that I had any idea there was something wrong.

The purr of the Lamborghini sounds down the line, and I let out a small breath of relief. I should not be relieved that he's on his way here, not after everything, but better the devil you know and all that.

"I texted the others. Everyone's on the way." Finley's voice is tight, and I let out a shriek when there's a bang on the back door. I spin to find Lincoln and East trying to get in the back door.

"What's wrong?" Finley's voice is urgent, and it takes me a second to speak as I try to calm my racing heart.

"Lincoln and East are here. They scared the shit out of me."

I move to let them in. I forgot I'd moved the spare key to the back door, but all things considered, it seems to be a good thing that I did. The door opens just as Finley responds.

"Okay, I'll hang up since they're there. I'll be two minutes. Open the gates for me."

I end the call and open the gates from the app on my phone. East locks the door once he's in and disables the beeping alarm.

I really need to work out just how many people have the code to that freaking thing. That, or figure out how to change them myself since these four all seem to have it.

Lincoln doesn't say a word as he moves to the counter and starts going through the pictures. East moves toward me, wrapping me up in his arms, and I sink into him. He's been one of the few shining lights I've had since I got back, so I take his offered comfort. "Are you okay?" he murmurs, squeezing me tighter before letting go.

"Not really. It's been a long few days, but I'll survive," I say, shrugging, just as the front door opens and slams closed. Seconds later, Finley and Maverick are in the kitchen with us.

Mav glances at me, like he's trying to work out just how unstable I am, before moving toward the counter with Lincoln. Finley assesses me quietly too, before stepping toward me. "We should reset the alarm, just in case. You secure the gates, and I'll do the house alarm."

I nod and do as he says, wishing my brain would function properly for a minute. That should have been a no-brainer. I look down at my phone and bring up the app to make sure the gate is locked and closed.

"Is this everything?" Lincoln asks, his voice harsh. My head snaps up to look at him and I find his face practically blank. Just his usual cold stare looking back at me. I nod, frozen on the inside from his chilly demeanor. It's the only thing that keeps my anger toward his dickhead behaviour in check.

Finley glares at him before ushering me onto a stool at the counter. He and East sit on either side of me, as if protecting me. Which is the funniest thing considering the hurt Finley has helped to cause the last few months.

"Yeah, that's everything that was in the envelope." I sigh, and sag a little. This is all too much. I don't understand any of it. I'm not usually the type to tuck tail and run—at least I never used to be, I used to face my shit head on—but that's all I want to do right now. Just to escape the madness surrounding me. "Is this linked to the note that was on my door when we got back here Friday night?"

They all glance at one another, and that gets my back up. What the fuck?

"What note?" Maverick asks, leaning back on the far counter and folding his arms across his chest.

"The note that was on the door when Lincoln got me home from the party," I deadpan, because what sort of question is that?

"There wasn't any note, Octavia," Lincoln finally says.

I pinch the bridge of my nose, trying not to be exasperated. Why would they lie about something like that? They obviously know something, and I don't understand why they're withholding details. Getting information from them is like trying to get blood from a fucking stone. "Enough with the gaslighting! Of course there was a note! I remember seeing it. It said I was out of time."

"There wasn't any note, Octavia. Maybe you dreamt it up. A lot happened that night." Lincoln shrugs and turns his attention back to the photos.

I close my eyes, trying to tamp down the anger that rises. "I don't know why I even bothered calling. You're not going to help me. I'm just going to call the police. There's nothing any of you can do. Just leave. I'll handle this alone. Like I've done with everything else."

"Octavia, don't be so fucking ridiculous. I already have a PI looking into the last pictures you gave me, I'll give him these too. Just leave it to us," Lincoln chastises, and I see red.

I have had enough.

"Don't be so ridiculous? Are you fucking kidding me? You come over here, chastise me, give me no information, and expect me to just what? Accept that shit? I don't know who the fuck you think I am, Lincoln, but I am not that girl. I was wrong to call you guys for help. I should've known better. Just fucking leave. I'll figure it all out on my own. And give me the other pictures back." I jump down from the stool and move to the back door to emphasize my point, but none of them move.

I take a deep breath but my anger is spinning out. I am so sick and tired of them treating me like this. Helping me on Friday does *not* make up for everything they've put me through up to this point. I'm sick of being this girl, I've let too much slide, and I am done. Shit is going to change. Starting right the fuck now. I hit the app on my phone, disabling the alarm before ripping the door open, refusing to have them in my space any longer than they already have been. "I said get the fuck out!"

This entire weekend has been too much. I've survived so much, powered through, stayed strong, but everything that's happened these last few days, the things I've learned… I thought I had a handle on it all until this morning. This stalker thing might just be what pushes me over the edge to the place I can't come back from.

I wish it was just the Raleigh thing. I've survived that before. I know I can do it again, but that on top of everything else? I don't think I can handle it all at once, but I don't have any other option. Nobody else is going to do it for me. I have to save myself.

My world is spinning off axis, and I feel so fucking alone. Not for the first time, my anger at my dad rears its head for leaving me to this cesspit. He might have raised me to deal with shit on my own, but maybe, just maybe I don't want to. I tried to deal with him spiraling alone and look where that got me. Back here, acting like someone I don't recognize. It's like losing him turned me back into that useless little girl I was before we left.

Sitting around in the dark probably isn't helping me deal with anything, but that's what I'm doing anyway. I thought coming to the theater room and putting on a movie might help me compartmentalize; I usually do it so well. But today… it's as if that part of my brain has just fully shut the hell down.

The absolute nothing I got from the boys this morning just has everything turned upside down. Telling them to get the fuck out was only the smallest part of what I wanted to do.

I can't tell if I'm angry, disappointed, or just so fucking sad.

I guess the only person I can really rely on is myself.

My phone beeps, the new security system letting me know one of the doors has opened. Got to love that nifty little upgrade. I flick to the cameras and see Finley walking through my entrance hall. What the hell is he doing back here?

He pauses, tilting his head as if trying to work out where I am, and then a small smile plays on his lips as he looks directly up at the camera. *'Found you'* he says to the camera, then disappears off screen. It's not long before the door to the theater room opens and his frame casts an imposing silhouette in the light spilling through the doorway.

I should probably feel angry that he's here, scared even after everything that's happened, but I just feel numb. "What do you want, Finn?"

His old nickname slips from my lips but I'm too tired to care. This man staring down at me is so far from the boy I used to call my friend. "I wanted to talk. Just the two of us."

"I'm not sure what there is to say." I sigh, tucking my knees up against my chest inside my oversized hoodie.

He shakes his head and steps forward, the door closing softly behind him as he approaches with his hands up in surrender. "This morning was a colossal fuckup. I didn't say much of anything, but what I should have said was, I'm sorry."

"You're sorry?" I let out a dry laugh, quirking a brow at him as he sits down next to me, turned so I can see his face clearly.

He nods, and as much as I hate to admit it, I can see just how sorry he is in his eyes. It's hard to describe, but it's just there for me to see. The guy who opens up to no one, showing me a part of himself. Just like he used to. "What exactly are you sorry for?"

"I'm sorry for hurting you. I know it won't make any sense to you, but I was trying to keep you safe. There's more going on here than you know but I can't tell you yet, and I'm sorry for that too." He takes a deep breath, scrubbing a hand down his face.

My heart pounds in my chest at that small bit of information. I knew there was something else going on. I knew I wasn't hallucinating. I cling to that tiny shred of information like it's a lifeline. "But why can't you tell me? If it affects me, I deserve to know what the hell is going on."

I'm sick of being left in the dark. If I'm really going to start taking charge of my own shit. I need to know what's happening around me.

"V, I wish I could tell you, but I can't."

I sigh, exasperated. What the fuck does that even mean? "That's a bullshit non-answer, Finley. I deserve to know what's happening. Especially when I'm supposedly the one in danger. You say you're trying to keep me safe, but I'd be safer if I knew what the hell is going on, and if you guys weren't such giant jackholes to me."

"I'm sorry for being an asshole, I am. If there was any other way... but I won't apologize for trying to keep you safe. I will never be sorry for that, but I'm sorry for the way we went about it. For the pain it caused you. I never wanted to hurt you... Not really. " He drops his head so he's looking at his clenched hands in his lap. I hate that I hurt for him, that he's obviously been through a lot, but I don't know how to move past this. "I'm mostly sorry for not getting to you sooner on Friday."

I let out a deep sigh and tuck my chin under the neckline of my hoodie too. "Friday wasn't your fault. You guys got me out of there before anything really happened. That much I should probably thank you for... but the rest of it? How am I supposed to believe that everything has changed between us? You won't tell me anything, you treated me like shit, attacked the people I love, hell, you nearly broke me... Keeping me in the dark isn't exactly the way to go about fixing things. I felt so alone after my dad died... the only bearable thing about being sent back here after that was that I might get to see you guys again, and honestly... you guys crushed me. If I didn't have other shit to keep me going..."

He swallows, his throat bobbing, and I know my words hit home. "I'm sorry—"

"Sorry doesn't fix everything, Finley," I snap, tired of the empty apology.

"I know," he says, nodding, "and you have no reason to trust me, but I'm still going to ask you to trust me on this one thing. I'm going to do everything I can to earn your trust back, V. Whatever it takes."

Biting the inside of my cheek, I consider his words. He seems genuine, and he's letting me see past his walls, but I still don't know what to do. That little voice inside my head tells me not to trust him, but my heart, my intuition, tells me he's on my side.

And holy fuck could I use someone on my side.

"Okay," I nod, "but earning my trust isn't going to be easy, Finn. You guys put me through *hell* these last few months. I'm not ready to forgive you yet, either, but we can have an actual truce or something."

"I'll take whatever you give me. But, V, I'm not going anywhere. I'm in this. I lost you once already, I tried to push you away and that didn't work, so you had better prepare yourself for having me in your life, because I'm not going anywhere ever again."

His declaration makes my heart race and I nod, because there isn't anything more I can do. I want to ask more questions, find out what is happening, but he already shut me down once.

"What are you watching?" He shifts around on the couch, getting comfortable.

I bite down on my lower lip, glancing up at the black screen. Maybe a distraction from all of this heavy shit will be good for me. "I was just watching musicals."

He grins at me, the first real grin I think I've seen on him since I returned back to The Cove. "You always did have a weak spot for them. Come on, get comfy with me and we'll put another one on."

I eye him skeptically as he pats the couch beside him.

"Come on, I don't bite. Not unless you ask nicely." He says it with such a serious look that I can't help but laugh a little, relaxing almost instantly.

I roll my eyes and untangle myself from my hoodie, scooting over beside him. I flick through the other musicals available and flick on *Wicked*. He doesn't say a word, just settles in and watches the screen with me.

You'd think, after everything, I'd be tense. On edge. Yet something inside of me never wanted to believe they hated me. That little girl who loved these boys more than almost anything is dancing a little bop inside of me as I start to relax.

I lose myself to the joy of love and friendship, of power and betrayal, and how much a person can sacrifice for their dreams before they're not themselves anymore. Not trying too hard to hide that I'm basically singing along, and trying not to smirk when I hear him humming beside me. I *might* have watched this more than a few times with him when we were younger. By the time we're halfway through the movie I start to relax a little more, leaning into his warmth. It's insane that I feel safer with him here, especially considering how they've treated me, but I try not to overthink it.

"You okay?" he murmurs into my ear, a shiver running down my spine at the feel of his breath on my skin. I turn to face him and his face is so close to mine that it causes my heart rate to spike. His gaze drops to my lips and before I can think anything of it his lips are on mine.

He kisses me like this might be the only chance he gets and it's filled with heat. Want. Need. Pulling me onto his lap, I'm helpless, lost in the pull of him. The logical part of my mind tells me I shouldn't be doing this. That this is absolutely not a path I should be going down, but my body is louder.

I place my hand on his shoulder and he stiffens a little before pulling back from the kiss.

"What's wrong?" I ask, confused, wondering yet again if this is all just a game.

He shakes his head and takes my hands in his. "Nothing. I just don't want to push you."

I can't help but frown at him. They've all been pushing me; just look at what happened in the pool house. He had no issues pushing me then. But I guess that was before…

"I'm sorry," I say, feeling weirdly ashamed as I start to climb off his lap.

He grabs my chin and forces me to look at him. "Hey, none of that. I didn't say I was done with you, just that I didn't want to push you. I'm not here for that." My eyes go wide at his words, and I feel more confused than ever. He grabs my hips, lifting me with ease, turns me around, and pulls me back onto his lap so my back is flush with his chest. "Let me look after you."

A shiver runs down my spine as his lips touch my neck. The screen before us goes dark, and music starts playing softly in the room. I stiffen a little at the move and he pauses, putting his hand in my hair, gripping firmly until I can see him. "Relax, V. I'm not going to hurt you or do anything you don't want to."

"Okay." The word comes out breathy and he releases my hair. In the next second, he has my hoodie up over my head and tosses it across the room, leaving me in my tank and leggings. His lips caress my shoulder as one hand wraps around my throat.

I suck in a breath and feel him smile against my skin as my heart rate increases. "I won't ever hurt you again, V. Do you trust me?"

I nod, trying to relax as his hand slips beneath my leggings and panties.

Inching down at a snail's pace, I barely register what's happening when the pad of his middle finger reaches my clit and he applies just enough pressure to make a shudder run down my spine. Contrary to before, this time my body's reaction is one of pleasure, not fear, and for that I'm grateful.

Finn scoots down just enough to spread his legs wider—opening my thighs to give him better access—then follows a path down to my slit. I can hear just how wet I am as his fingers slide up and down, in and out.

This is insane. I should be hating him and pushing him

away, but I don't. I can't. Something inside of me wants this, even though I know I shouldn't. When two of his fingers push in deep, I melt into his touch, feeling oddly secure—safe even—with his other hand firmly on my throat and pinning me down against his shoulder.

"Relax. I got you."

Easy for him to say.

His fingers at my throat tighten as he brings my cheek to his mouth, the warmth of his breath like a drug.

His tongue burns a path of lust from my jaw to the slope of my nose. It's so dirty and primal. It's filthy and animalistic. It's everything I should hate but don't.

In fact, I fucking love it. That simple act of dominance gets me even wetter and by the low chuckle he lets escape, I'm guessing he's figured it out too.

"Hmm, I licked you and now you're mine." I try not to laugh, because now is *so* not the time, but who says that? Feeling bold, I reach back to hold his head in my hand, but as quick as a snake, he's got my wrist trapped in his fingers before he brings it to his mouth and kisses the inside of my wrist softly.

In the following second, every bit of my attention hones in on just how obvious it is that I want him.

"Mmm," is all I'm capable of saying as he finger-fucks me like it's a punishment. Except the harder he goes, the more I want.

*I am definitely more than a little fucked up.*

Just when I think I'm about to come, when I feel like I'm going to fall off that cliff of ecstasy, he stops everything.

"What the fuck, Finley?" I untangle myself from him and stand so I can face him and give him a piece of my mind. Quickly realizing Finn has other—more twisted—plans when he grabs me.

I do end up facing him but instead of standing, Finn tugs at me, twisting around our positions so I'm somehow lying facedown on the couch, his big frame kneeling on the floor behind me. It's a good fucking thing this double decked couch is fucking huge or else my face would be smashed against the back of the couch.

"Give me your hands." I don't even hesitate—which, again, is fucked up—but I'm intrigued. Finley takes both of my wrists and places them behind my back, right where my ass begins.

I can't see what he's doing behind me but I hear the tell-tale sound of a belt sliding through the loops of his jeans right before I feel the leather strap imprisoning my forearms. "Is that okay?"

I think it over for a minute, all things considered I should probably be panicking right now, especially after everything that's happened recently, but weirdly, I'm okay. So I nod, and he starts to move again. He places his big hands on my thighs, guiding me to kneel with my ass up and out and at the perfect height for his mouth but—

"Holy shit." The words come out as a whisper when I realize what he's planning, except my legging are on so—

The slashing sound that breaks the silence and the sudden breeze of cool air at the apex of my thighs tells me my leggings are a thing of the past.

*RIP leggings.*

"What the fuck, Finn?" When I twist my neck just right to see what's going on, though, I'm even more pissed off. "A knife? You destroyed my fucking leggings and panties with a fucking knife? You could have hurt—"

My words and my anger dissipate in the seconds that follow when Finn lies beneath me, his shoulders keeping my legs spread and his mouth latches onto my pussy and all I can think about is how fucking good that feels.

Holy fucking shit.

With both of his hands on my thighs, spreading them impossibly wider, I forget about ripped leggings and knives at my pussy and just enjoy his very skilled tongue.

From clit to slit, he feasts on me like he's a man starved. He's never been one to express his feelings or... much of anything, really, but his moans and the occasional growl when his tongue intrudes inside me is enough to tell me he's enjoying this as much as I am.

My shoulders are tightly pinned back, so movement on my part is difficult, which makes the whole experience even hotter. All I can hear is the sound of Finn's mouth drinking up everything I have to give him. My heart pounds in my chest and I feel almost dizzy from it all.

I push back, seeking more—needing more—wanting to feel everything from his lips to his tongue to his cock.

It's like he can read my mind and in the next second, he's pushing two fingers inside me, curling them just right and reaching that perfect spot.

My entire body jolts up off the couch at the sensation. Fucking hell, he knows what he's doing.

I kind of hate that he does, it means he's got a whole hell of a lot of experience. That simple thought brings about a pang of jealousy that I'm not ready to analyze quite yet.

He curls his fingers once more, causing me to jolt again. His response is almost primal as he pulls me impossibly closer to his mouth, giving him a whole new level of access to my throbbing clit.

As his fingers relentlessly fuck me, his tongue fixates on my swollen nub. My blood begins to thrum, running through my body like uncontrollable fire, and I know I'm about to lose my mind with this orgasm.

With his free hand, Finn grabs the strap of the belt and pulls enough for my upper body to lift. My head tilts back, my hair spilling over my arms and ass. Finn is relentless. He fucks me with fingers and tongue, driving me toward the brink

I'm almost there. I can feel it taking over but it still feels just out of reach.

Then he curls his fingers and massages that sweet spot just as his teeth bite into my clit, and I'm a goner.

I don't recognize the sound that escapes me. It's both a cry for more and a scream to stop. It would be scary if it weren't for the intense pleasure burning through my veins. I can't breathe, I can't move. I'm frozen with the power of this tsunami of ecstasy that I don't know how to handle.

Finley doesn't let up. He laps up every fucking drop of my orgasm until I come again, the filthy sounds of his mouth another detonator to a smaller but equally intense orgasm.

It's only when he lets me fall back down on the couch that he gives me a single soft, lingering kiss on my clit before releasing my arms and unbuckling his belt.

I'm panting, trying to catch my breath to no avail, when he turns me back around, pulls my body closer to his, and bends down to lightly touch my lips with his.

I can taste myself on him, and that light kiss turns into a battle of lips and tongues. Just when I'm about to reach up to wrap my arms around his neck, he's gone. In the blink of an eye he's standing at the foot of the couch, looking down on me with longing in eyes and my orgasm on his mouth.

I want to think he doesn't regret what just happened, not while I'm lying here half naked and blissed out, but why else would he practically run from me? "Fin—"

I'm cut off by the ringing of his phone. He looks down and goes pale. "I have to go. I'm sorry." He looks torn as his gaze bounces between me and his screen. I just nod at him, open-mouthed, and he disappears from the room, looking back once before the door closes behind him. I watch him leave the house via the feed on my phone, hating how twisted up I feel about everything.

I flop down onto the couch, staring up at the ceiling. When will I learn?

He might say he won't hurt me and maybe he didn't mean to, but I should know better than to trust a damn thing any of them say.

# FOUR

## LINCOLN

I barely slept last night, tossing and turning over the tangled web we've found ourselves in. With each move we make to save Octavia, we end up deeper in the murky waters. At one point, my greatest hope was to escape the Knights… but it has become painfully clear that my fate is written. With each job they have me do, the monster inside of me grows. He feeds on the darkness that spills across my soul with every person I destroy. With every life I end.

I stare into the darkness, having given up on sleep shortly after three a.m.. Though I have no idea what time it is right now, the blackout everything—walls, shutters, tightly sealed doors— makes this room almost like a sensory deprivation chamber. Yet… I still can't find sleep.

The only time I've known peace and actual sleep recently, is when I slept with Octavia. I don't know what it is about her that soothes the demons writhing inside me, but I'm past questioning it.

I already know I can't have her, and I sure as fuck can't keep her, so I can't get attached.

None of us can.

I can see my brothers slipping under her spell, that glow of light that she radiates captivating them all and there's nothing I can do to stop it. The more I push, the harder they'll pull.

East might be my brother in DNA, and I can read *him* like a book, but the other two are my brothers in blood and we don't have many secrets from each other.

We all survived initiation, just barely, and we survived it together.

I'm not sure we'd have made it alone. Not all of us.

Memories from those weeks still haunt me, and I'll do anything I can to save Octavia from it. Even if it means sacrificing everything I thought I wanted and needed in life.

Stone tried to save her, he sacrificed more than most would, but in the end even that wasn't enough.

I'm still convinced they killed him. I just don't know why. Even Finley, the quiet genius that he is, hasn't been able to find any information from hacking into their files.

I just wish I knew what their end game was with all of this. I know we started the ball rolling by voting against the trafficking

being brought into town. They tried to justify it by claiming that
tourists get lost every year, so no one would notice, but still,
Echoes Cove isn't that big. Not really. Even with the number
of people on their take, someone somewhere would have
eventually worked it out.

My phone buzzes on the bedside table for the third time in
what's probably the last half hour, and I give up pretending I'm
going back to sleep. I roll over and flip my phone, the screen
illuminating the room, and groan when I see my father's name.

It stops buzzing while I'm trying to decide if it's worth the
headache to answer, saving me from making the decision. The
last thing I need right now is my father wading in. He is all
about the Saint way of life. Loyalty to the Knights is basically
his life blood. He doesn't even see how broken his belief system
is. He doesn't care who he hurts, or what he breaks, as long as
it benefits him.

Benefits the Knights.

The phone starts buzzing again and I groan, scrubbing a
hand down my face, trying to mentally prepare myself for this
conversation. "Harrison, what can I do for you this morning?"

I can practically hear his frown at the use of his name, but he
lost the right to be called Dad when I was thirteen. "Lincoln, you
and your friends have been making a mess, and it's becoming
something of a headache, all this nonsense with the Rittenhouse
boy. His father has been pitching a fit, and his mother is thinking
about taking her cartel connections elsewhere."

"He tried to rape Octavia." I don't say anything else, because I don't need to justify myself to him, and I'd do what we did all over again if needed.

Harrison scoffs down the line, like rape is nothing, and I suppose to a guy like him, it isn't. It could be worse.

"Regardless of what he did, it's causing me a headache. It needs to be dealt with."

His impatient tone makes me grind my teeth. This fucking guy. "What exactly is it that you want me to do?"

"I'm going to handle it, but you're going to owe me a favor." I take a deep breath as I pinch the bridge of my nose, trying to rein in my anger. Owing my father a favor is never a good thing. Never. I've tried to avoid it at all costs. The last time… well the last time wasn't pretty.

"I can handle it," I say, and I swear to fuck I can hear his smile stretch across his face.

"No, no, Son. I've got it covered." He laughs softly, and I can just picture him checking his watch, looking out over the skyline of whichever city he's in, lording over the population he rules, and they don't even know he exists. He's everything I fucking hate, and I despise that I'm destined to become him. "You'll just owe me."

"Fine," I grind out, because I don't want to prolong his joy. "Was there anything else?"

"There was. You and the boys are needed later today. Prepare yourselves and be ready for instruction." I grip my phone so hard

I'm a little worried it'll smash in my grasp, but take a deep breath and try to push past it.

I fucking hate The Knights Society.

"Anything else, Harrison?"

"I'll be home for Christmas. Make sure the house isn't trashed when I get back." The line goes dead. He has what he wants, so there's no need for him to stick around. That has been the story of my life.

I remember, once upon a time, I thought my dad hung the fucking moon. Then I got the slap of reality and I've never looked at him the same since.

I drop my phone and flop backward onto my pillows.

I wish this was the shittiest start to a day I've ever had, but compared to some, this is sunshine and fucking rainbows. Gritting my teeth against the urge to scream out at the injustice of this entire fucking thing, I fist my hands into the comforter and count back from ten.

*My father won't break me.*

I repeat the mantra that has kept me going for the last five years and focus on one thing: Doing what needs to be done to keep Octavia safe.

I've spent this entire godforsaken afternoon in my basement gym trying to work out my frustration; yet, it doesn't matter how hard

I run, how much weight I lift, or how hard I hit the bag, my anger only grows.

I wish I could tell her the truth, but if she knew… it would just put her in more danger. There is also no way she would believe me. Hell, I wouldn't believe me if I were her. It all sounds like something out of a movie.

I wish it was a fucking movie, at least then there would be a happy ending, but there is no happy ending in this. Not for me anyway.

This is exactly why I wanted her gone from here. This place is toxic. Twisted. It will eat you alive if you let it.

Fuck knows it tainted all of us.

My phone pings on the floor, so I step back from the punching bag, wishing my wrapped hands were the only pain I felt anymore. I pick up my phone and shut off the music when I see the message.

Unknown

> You're up. Mission details will meet you at the drop.

Fuck my fucking life. Could this day get any fucking worse?

I pull up the thread with Finn and Mav, sending a message of my own.

Me

> You get the message?

Mav

> Yep. You driving?

Me

Sure. Be here in ten.

We've always been sent on these missions together. They tried sending us separately to begin with, but we all went together no matter what, so eventually the Board decided this was easier for them. One small tick in our column of wins.

I wait for Finn to respond, frowning when it doesn't come through. It doesn't usually take him more than a few seconds when we get hit up by the Knights.

Finn

Yeah. Be there in a few.

I grab my towel from the weight bench and dry off before putting my tank back on and heading upstairs. I snatch a bottle of water from the fridge in the kitchen and drop onto the couch to wait for the others.

East has no idea how lucky he is that he's not a part of this fucking shit. I still don't know why Harrison chose me instead of him, but sometimes, it's hard not to resent him for it. Especially when he chooses to stay here when he could go anywhere in the world. He is free from their clutches. Well, as free as anyone can be. He isn't a slave to them.

Not like we are.

I'm pulled from the spiraling darkness by Finley walking through the front door. He looks about as happy as I feel. Most people wouldn't be able to see the nuances, he doesn't really show much emotion, but the set of his jaw, the tightness of his shoulders… let's just say when you've been through what we have together, you notice the small things. He nods at me and heads straight for the bathroom. I turn back on the couch just as the door opens again and Mav strolls in, rubbing his hands together.

The guy is twisted.

We all are, really.

"Any idea what this is about?" Mav asks as he jumps the back of the couch and drops onto the seat beside me.

I finish my bottle of water, just as Finn reappears. "Not a fucking clue, but where's the surprise there?"

Finley takes a seat in the arm chair opposite the couch and runs a hand through his hair. Something isn't right with him. "What's wrong?"

He looks at me, his stare cold, almost calculating. "We need to tell V about the Knights."

"We've had this conversation, her not knowing is the best way to keep her safe." I sigh, wishing that our lives were different. That this wasn't our reality, and that we didn't have to shoulder everything we do. But the more she knows, the more danger she's in. I don't understand why they haven't realized that. I know her, and she's like a dog with a bone. If we give her even a little, she'll dig until she gets to the heart of it, and then it'll be too late. Then there will be no saving her, and I couldn't live with myself if she became like the rest of them.

"I don't agree. Not anymore. You saw that note, they're going to come for her. She'll be better prepared if we tell her. Even if we just tell her a little."

I sit up straight and pin him with a look while Mav just glances between us. The three of us have never argued, not since initiation. But since V came back, things have been different. "You think she'd believe us? You think she'd think it was anything more than another ploy to run her out of town? If we tell her now, she'll brush it off, and that'll probably just put her in more danger. We need her to trust us first. So we keep her safe. We do what we can to keep her with us, to build back what we once had, and then we can tell her."

"She'll think we betrayed her," he counters, and I run a hand through my hair.

"Maybe, but she's also not stupid enough to not see that we did it to keep her safe." I lean back on the couch and look up at the ceiling. "The hardest part is going to be getting her to trust us first. Finding out who the fuck is stalking her and dealing with them will help, but we did a lot of damage in the last few months."

My phone buzzes in my pocket, and theirs ping at the same time.

Unknown

Be at the drop in twenty minutes.

"We need to table this for now and deal with whatever bullshit they're throwing at us today."

Finn looks torn and I don't blame him. He hates the chokehold we're in as much as I do. "What if we didn't?"

"Then they'll use her against us. That was their plan all along. Now she's here, and we know they can get to her easily, they already know we'll do what we have to in order to keep her safe."

"This is bullshit. I still don't get why they wouldn't just accept Blair and Nate to take over the Royal seats. Then Octavia would still be blissfully ignorant, a world away from here." He hisses and stands. "Let's get this shit done. Where is East? Someone needs to be with V while Smithy is still away."

"I have no fucking clue." I drop him a message to let him know we're heading out and ask him to keep an eye on V before grabbing my keys. "Let's head out. The quicker we get going, the quicker we get back."

"If only that were true." Mav laughs. "Remember that one time a job took us out for three fucking days? Let's hope that's not the case tonight. I like 'em quick and dirty."

I clap his shoulder and belt a laugh. "Oh, we know, buddy."

He shoves me, grinning. "Asshole."

We head into the garage and pile into my Cayenne. I hit the clicker to open the garage door, half hoping we get another text cancelling this little outing, but I know it's not going to happen. Most of my hope has been beaten out of me at this point. It's only the thought that we can keep Octavia safe that keeps my head above water.

I drive on autopilot toward the drop. I hate that my body remembers the way because I've driven it so many times. I'm not stupid, I know that they send us on more missions than the others because of our reluctance, our free will, the unwillingness to buckle under their thumb, but I'll be fucked if they ever take that fight from me.

The difference between us and those who submit easily is we have something else, *someone* else, that we're fighting for. Even when she wasn't here, when Stone had her away from us, when he did what he could to keep her from this, we fought for her. Even if she didn't know it.

I hope she never has to.

We drive through the pitch black of night, no moon in sight, and a shiver runs through my body. It feels like the darkness is an omen of what is to come. The Knights have made us do some fucked up shit, do things I never thought I'd be able to do to another human, but when it comes to survival, I'm always going to pick me and mine.

I pull up in front of the office building on Main Street and idle at the curb while Finn jumps from the car and enters the dark building. He's only gone for a few seconds before he returns with the envelope and three bags. Once he's back in the car, he opens the envelope and shows it to Mav and I.

*Dominic Taylor*
*3465 Crest Crescent*
*Sand Bay*
*A debt unpaid. Bring him to the Snake Pit.*

"He must owe Diesel money," Mav pipes up from the back, putting voice to my thoughts. "But if he hasn't paid Diesel, tonight is going to be bloody."

Finn hands Mav and I a bag each. Black clothes, boots, untraceable guns. The usual kit. All of which will be bugged to the high heavens.

*Fuck, I hate this shit.*

"Let's hope we're just the delivery system this time," I say, shoving my bag in the back and settling back into my seat while Finn puts the address in the GPS. A glance at the screen tells me tonight is going to be a long night. This address is two cities over.

*How the fuck did this guy get on Diesel's bad side?*

Diesel, one of the Knights, runs the Snake Pit. A den of underground fighting, and so much worse. Things that, despite everything I've done, still make my skin crawl. Things I will never condone.

Since we have legacy votes, we've managed to oppose some newer things—which is exactly what brought Octavia to the attention of the Knights in the first place—but some shit was already established and getting that stomped out will take more juice than the three of us have alone.

Money and blood make the world go round, and we're drowning in both.

We head around the building and enter through the back door after I punch in the code and change into the contents of the bags. I feel like one of the fucking X-Men in this get up. So fucking ridiculous.

It doesn't take long and I stash my clothes back in the bag before we head back out to the car. We throw the bags in the trunk. I already know we're going to need the back seat for transport, so this is just efficient for later.

Once we're all sorted, I climb in and start the engine, taking a small piece of joy from the purr of the car. Just one moment, one sliver of a speck of light in the dark, before I throw myself into the oblivion of what's to come.

Mav and Finn talk quietly for most of the drive, and I sit in silence, mentally preparing myself for whatever we're about to walk into. I'd like to hope he'll come quietly, but they never do. Mav's favorite thing is when they run. He really does run the gauntlet of psychopathy, though really he's just a product of his father's twisted ways.

The same could be said for us all.

They groomed us from a young age to be ready for when the Knights would come calling, but it was done in such a subtle way we never saw it coming.

I shake my head to clear out the memories. That is not a dark hole I need to go down. Not now. Not ever.

I focus back on the road, the dark of the night split only by the headlights of the car. Before I realize just how much time has passed, the GPS has me pulling into a fairly upscale suburb in Sand Bay. We come to a stop in front of a two-story house with a white picket fence.

The children's toys in the front yard make my stomach churn.

I don't hurt kids. None of us do.

It's a hard and fast rule.

"Fuck," Mav mutters when he sees what I do. "What do we do?"

I swallow against the lump in my throat as they both look to me for direction. I hate that I have to be the shot caller, but it's always been this way. "We do this quietly. We don't wake the wife or the kids. We get in, we grab him, we get out."

They both nod and we climb from the car, blending into the shadows. Finn heads up front, the guy can get past any lock or alarm system. He's a goddamn magician. He pulls the small tablet he never leaves home without from his back pocket before nodding back to us. The door is open and he heads straight for the alarm.

In less than a minute he reappears in the doorway. "We're in."

We move through the house quietly, making sure not to stand on, or trip over, any of the toys strewn across the floor. I'm just thankful that the stairs don't creak as we climb them.

"Linc," I pause, turning to see Finn at the bottom of the stairs, staring at the photos that line the wall there. "I think he's a single dad."

Fuck.

"Call Ellie, she's the closest person we have to this place," I tell him and head back up the stairs as he heads outside to make the call. This changes everything. Thankfully, we've had some time to build our own network of people outside of the Knights, so we have contingencies for shit like this. I grit my teeth, trying to swallow down my frustration as I head down the hall. I pause at the kid's room—obvious from the rainbow wood letters on the door spelling out 'Sofie'—hating that if this goes wrong we're going to rip away her innocence the same way ours was.

I fucking hate this bullshit.

But if I have to sacrifice this kid to keep the Knights' sights away from Octavia… It's not a competition.

I continue toward the master, opening the other doors as I go to make sure there isn't anyone else here.

Mav is on my heels as I enter the master and find Dominic fast asleep. I grab the guy's phone from the dresser and pocket it. Best way to avoid any accidental texts or calls. Mav pulls his gun and points it at Dominic's head as he covers the guy's mouth with his free hand.

"Dominic," I bark out, and his eyes open instantly. They go wide with fear as he takes in the gun and Mav hovering over him. "You've been summoned by the Knights to the Snake Pit. If you shout, or try to evade us, we'll have to kill you. I'd really rather not, especially with Sofie down the hall. So let's do this like men, shall we?"

I hate using the girl against him, but this will go better for us all if it happens quietly.

Dominic nods once and Mav releases his mouth. "I already asked for an extension, Diesel granted it. Why are you doing this?"

"We're following orders. Now get out of bed, slowly. My friend is a little trigger happy," I say, as Mav smiles maniacally at him. The shiver that racks Dominic's body is almost audible, it's so visceral. He climbs out slowly, in his pajama pants and tank top. At least he's dressed.

That makes this easier.

We head out of the room, Dominic first with Mav behind him, gun pointed at his back, and I follow them out.

When we reach the ground floor, Finn joins us and ties Dominic's hands and feet with zip ties before gagging him. I look at Mav who nods, holsters his gun, and fireman-carries the guy out to the car, leaving me with Finn.

"Ellie is on her way."

"Good," I say, nodding. "You stay here till she arrives. I'll take him to the pit and stay to make sure he leaves alive, even if not in one piece. The less that little girl knows about all of this the better. Meet us there when Ellie arrives. Use her car, we know that it doesn't have a tracker."

He nods once and I turn, knowing he'll handle things here while I deal with whatever horrors await us at the Snake Pit.

I just hope I can live up to my word and keep this guy alive for that little girl. No kid deserves to grow up without their parents, and I'm going to try my damnedest to ensure she doesn't end up an orphan.

My alarm goes off and I groan as I hit the screen of my phone, bleary-eyed. I take in the time and groan again. I barely got an hour of sleep after last night's activities.

While I'm pissed I barely slept, I'm glad I managed to ensure that the guy got home to his kid, even if he was more than a little bloody. Diesel isn't a guy you want to cross, and apparently Dominic tried to extend one too many times. I get the feeling if I hadn't insisted on staying, he'd probably be in a shallow grave somewhere this morning. The advantages of being a legacy and not just a pawn piece.

I roll out of bed and into the shower in my ensuite. I keep the spray ice cold, trying to shock myself into some semblance of consciousness, and run a hand over my face in an effort to wipe away the last of the sleep before turning the temperature up. I stand under the hot spray and try to wash away the stains last night left on my soul.

I already know I'm beyond saving, I lost hope of that a long time ago, but I try to counter the dark shit with things like looking after that little girl as much as I can. The world is too broken. I know I can't fix it all, but if I can keep some people from the darkness that's overtaken my life, then I will.

After spending too long in the shower, I rush through my morning routine and head to school. By the time I pull into my space in the lot, I'm exhausted and caffeine deprived.

Today is not going to be a good day.

Mav pulls in on his bike as I'm climbing from my Porsche, and Finn is already waiting, leaning against the door of his Aventador. At least some things never change.

They meet me at the hood of my car, each of them looking as exhausted as I feel. Not that anyone here would dare say a word.

"Lincoln!" I wince at the screech of my name, turning to see Blair practically skipping in our direction. I hate that we tried to make a deal with her—not that she knows it was all to help Octavia—especially now that she thinks we're friends. Maybe once upon a time, but the person she's become just isn't someone I want to associate with. Her thirst for what the Knights can offer her and her family tells me all I need to know, and it's enough to know that she isn't my kind of people.

"What do you want, Blair?" I snap, too tired to deal with her bullshit today.

She flinches, her step faltering a little, but only for a second before shaking it off and squaring her shoulders as she stops in front of us. "I want to know what your next steps are? I heard about Friday. This is the perfect thing to get her gone."

"We're done, Blair. Plan's changed." I don't mean to be a giant asshole, but it's a switch that got stuck on a long time ago and just won't turn off anymore. "Back off of Octavia."

She jolts back, looking like I just hit her. "But we had a deal. I need this, Lincoln. You can't just change your mind!" She stomps her foot and I roll my eyes. She looks like a toddler having a tantrum. The quiver of her lip doesn't escape me, but she's deluded if she thinks that's going to work.

"Shit happens." I shrug and lean back against my car, folding my arms across my chest.

It takes her a moment as her gaze bounces from me to Finn to Mav to realize that I'm being serious. Once she does, that cold, calculating bitch stare washes over her features. There's the Blair I know she is deep down. She really would have done well with the Knights.

I just wish I knew why they rejected the suggestion of her and Nate replacing Octavia. There has to be more to it than just keeping us three in line. "You're going to regret this."

She flicks her hair before turning and stomping away from us. Mav starts to laugh beside me while Finn shakes his head. "We should head inside; I need coffee."

"Sounds good," Finn says, grabbing his bag from his car.

"Can I throw my shit in your trunk?" Mav asks. I nod, unlocking the car with the key fob. He puts his jacket, helmet, and boots in my car, changing into the shoes in his bag before throwing that in there too. "Let's do this."

I lead the way up the stairs with both of them flanking me, and the sheep part like they'll shrivel up and die if they get too close to us. Almost no one here knows about the Knights, but everyone still seems to be able to sense the danger that rolls off us in waves.

Even Blair's friends don't know what she was trying to get wrapped up in.

If only she knew the true cost, I'm not sure she'd be so eager to join the sect.

We head to my locker, banners everywhere for the upcoming Homecoming dance, and I roll my eyes. I am so done with this dance bullshit already. Listening to the girls in this school titter on about it for the last few weeks, about who will be homecoming queen... I'm so over it. As I close my locker, having grabbed my books for the morning, I notice Indi, Octavia's new friend, saunter past us and head to her locker. I look around, but Octavia isn't anywhere to be seen. "Either of you know where Octavia is?"

Mav shakes his head. "No, I haven't seen her since she kicked us out of her place over the weekend."

Finn shakes his head once and glances down at his phone. I feel like I'm missing something with him, but I'm sure it won't be long until he spills whatever's on his mind. I move across the hall to where Indi stands at her locker and lean against the one beside hers.

She sees me standing there and turns to face me, crossing her arms over her chest. "You were supposed to look after her after Friday. Not piss her off more."

I guess they really do share everything.

"Wasn't my intention, Octavia just has a way of getting under my skin," I tell her honestly. No point in hiding from her, especially if she's dating the twins again. Chances are, she knows more than she's meant to. Between them and Octavia, she probably knows more than most.

"Well try harder," she says, slamming her locker shut. "Was there something you wanted?"

"Where is Octavia?"

She quirks a brow at me before barking out a laugh. Apparently Octavia really is rubbing off on her new friend. Awesome. "She's staying home today. After Friday she didn't care to face the student body. Especially since Raleigh was posting over social media that he'd be back in today. I guess whatever your boys did to him wasn't enough to keep him down for long."

I glance over my shoulder at Finley and Mav, who look about as shocked as I feel at the news. They worked him over pretty well, so the fact that he'll be back today... not something I expected.

"Thank you for telling me."

She nods once before heading down the hall toward her class. The other two join me as I let out a deep sigh. "Apparently, she's staying home today."

Mav claps his hands together, smiling. "So we're skipping too? With everything going on, it's not safe for her to be home alone all day. Not with all four of us here."

I nod, because there's no way in hell I'm leaving her vulnerable like that. Finn looks like he's going to say something, but thinks better of it, "We should grab coffee and breakfast on the way."

"Sounds good to me. You get breakfast, I'll get coffee?" He nods. "Awesome. Mav, you head straight to her place. The less time she's alone the better."

He grins like a Cheshire fucking cat at the command. "Oh goodie. Octavia in the morning is fun to play with."

# FIVE

## OCTAVIA

I swear I ache worse today than I have all weekend. It could be a delayed reaction from Friday, or it could be that I beat myself stupid in the gym yesterday as penance for succumbing to Finley's pretty words.

I should know better by now that actions speak louder than words. And his actions are hot and cold as fuck. I'm not beating myself up about messing around with him—a girl has needs—and he *is* a talented motherfucker with his hands and tongue. Even if I did fuck around with Mav a few weeks ago. No one is about to shame me for what I do with my body. I am not about that life.

Am I more fucked up about the fact that I did that with Finley so soon after what happened with Raleigh? Yes, that bit

I'm a little conflicted over, but we all deal with trauma in our own way, so I'm not about to beat myself up over that either.

What I *am* going to beat myself up over is believing his words to me and then saying nothing when he disappeared. I haven't heard a peep from him since either.

Like I said, actions over words.

I flop down onto the couch, having resigned myself to taking a few days from school. While I might be able to compartmentalize my trauma pretty well, the thought of facing Raleigh today while dealing with Blair and her bitch squad too, just no. I might be strong, but I know when to give myself a minute.

So I pull the blanket off the back of the couch and turn on the TV. A sofa day is exactly what I need in my life. A sofa day *alone*. That is the key part here. A day alone, dealing with my thoughts so I can steel myself and prepare to face the masses. It might be worse because I skipped a few days, but fuck it. I'm not letting the opinions of a bunch of virtual strangers rule my life. I never have before, I'm not about to start today.

It's only a few weeks until break. I'm sure I can survive till then. I just don't really want to see Raleigh if I can help it. I hate what he did to me, and I need enough space to build some emotional walls before I can handle seeing him again. Plus I need to deal with the anger I have building toward him, otherwise I'm going to land my ass back in jail on assault charges again.

I flick through the channels on the TV and settle on some

mindless comedy show to pass the time. Something I can get lost in and not have to think too hard about . Usually I'd use the day to watch my true crime documentaries, but I'm not sure watching about how to get away with murder would be great for my mental health at present.

I snuggle beneath the blankets, preparing for a long day of absolutely nothing, when the buzzer on my gate sounds. Picking up my phone, I check the camera and see Maverick sitting on his bike. He pushes the buzzer again and doesn't let up.

God, he knows how to literally push my buttons.

"I know you're in there, V. Let me in." His voice comes through the speaker and I groan, hitting the button on my app to respond to him.

"No."

"Come on, V. I just want to talk."

"Are you going to answer some of my questions about shit that's going on?" I ask and am met with silence. "Exactly. So no."

"Don't make me come in the side gate. We both know I can."

I hit the button to speak, my rage flooding back. "Why are you such a fucking asshole?"

"I'll tell you if you open the gate."

I scream into a cushion, relenting because he's going to get in here one way or another. As much as I don't want to deal with him right now, at least this is kind of on my terms. Plus it's easier to hear him out and get him to leave than to try and ignore him. Maverick is the kind of guy who will sit there all day with his finger on that goddamn buzzer just to piss me off.

I hear the roar of his bike as he pulls up in front of the house, and laugh when he tries to walk in and I hear the *bang* as he walks into the door with the full force of his body weight behind him.

Smooth. So smooth.

I cackle to myself as I walk across the room and unlock the door, opening it a fraction before moving back to my spot on the couch. I don't know why he's here, but if he thinks I'm giving up my spot he has another thing coming.

He closes the front door before kicking off his boots. He puts his helmet on the table by the door and hangs his jacket up, like he's almost a civilized human. He wags his brows at me, smiling as he asks, "Want company under that blanket?"

I roll my eyes as I snuggle down. "Get your own damn blanket."

He takes me literally and jumps the back of the couch, grabbing the blanket draped there as he does, and settles in opposite me.

"What are you doing here?" I stare over at him and wait for his response. Sometimes I wish I could fight him and the others as hard as they've fought me since I got back here, but a piece of me still belongs to them, even though I've denied it since my return.

The bond between us might be frazzled and frayed, but it's still very much there. No matter how much I might not want it to be.

I don't think I'm alone in feeling it though. Not if I look at their actions over the last few weeks. Even with them being assholes, there have been small glimpses of the boys I used to know.

"You weren't at school," he says, finally answering my question.

"No shit, Sherlock. That doesn't explain why you're here." I sigh, rolling my eyes again.

"Of course it does." He shrugs and steals the remote from the table, flipping over to some football game replay that's on from last night. I pick up my phone, realizing I didn't close the gate, just to see Finley's Lamborghini pulling up the drive as Lincoln's Porsche slides in behind him.

Awesome, the whole gang is here. Well, almost. I guess being a teacher makes skipping a little harder.

I hit the button on my app to close the gate once their cars are clear, accepting my fate and preparing myself for a day with the boys, whether I want them here or not. Better to resign myself to it and get them out of here as soon as possible than fight it. I get the feeling that fighting them isn't the best way to get the information I want from them. This way, at least I can find out what they want without draining myself emotionally. I don't have much reserve left to fight them, so I'm hoping they're not here to argue with me.

Seconds later, Finley and Lincoln enter the house, the smells of coffee and food hitting me almost instantly. My stomach grumbles at the smell and I realize I've barely eaten all weekend.

Oops.

Usually food isn't far from me, but I'm a terrible cook and I'm out of pretty much everything. I've also been a little preoccupied.

Finley looks over at me, and I don't know how, but just like I know Lincoln hasn't shared that he's been hopping in and out of my bed at night, I know that Finley hasn't shared what happened over the weekend. The same way I'm pretty sure Maverick never divulged what happened between us.

These boys hurt my fucking head.

"We brought breakfast," Lincoln says, holding up a tray of coffees in his hand as he strolls past me into the kitchen. Finley follows him with a brown bag that smells like heaven while Maverick just seems to wait for me to move.

I follow quickly. I'm hungry and it smells too freaking good to pass up. I'm going to have to learn to pick my battles with them eventually and now seems as good a time as any. If they want to feed me, who am I to deny them that? Totally not a battle I mind forgoing.

Heading into the kitchen with Maverick hot on my heels, I grab plates for everyone as Finley unpacks the bags. "I got some of everything. Pancakes, eggs, breakfast burritos—"

"Dibs on the burrito!" I interrupt as I jump onto the stool at the island where the rest of them are standing. They all just stare at me as I grab the burrito and do a little jig in my seat. Mav barks out a laugh while a small smile plays on Finn's lips. I let out a groan as I take my first bite, because goddamn that shit is good.

Thanks to breakfasty goodness, I can almost forgive them for barging in on my morning.

"So, other than feeding me, why are you guys here?" I ask once I'm done having my happy dance, then swiftly take another bite, groaning all over again.

Mav coughs and just watches me. "V, you keep making those noises, we're going to have another moment."

"Moment? Are you referring to taking my virginity, Maverick Riley? Because that was definitely some moment. However my happy groans about food should probably not take your mind to the same place." He pales, and Lincoln's hands turn to fists on the counter.

"Virginity? But there was no blood…" Mav's eyes go wide, gulping as he sits. "V, I didn't… I didn't know. Why didn't you say something?"

I just shrug and take another bite. "It was a good orgasm, why should me being a virgin get in the way of that?"

"Mav, do you maybe want to explain what the fuck she's talking about?" Lincoln practically growls. Not going to lie, it makes my kitty flutter a little, but I mentally tell her to calm the fuck down. We're playing happy times with too many of these assholes as it is, we do not need to add another one to the mix.

Mav just looks from me to Linc, looking like I just junk punched him. Not my problem he didn't tell them we fucked. Him not knowing about the virginity thing might be my fault, but since it's not a big deal to me, it shouldn't be to him either.

"Calm down your growliness." I grin up at Lincoln after swallowing my last bite and grabbing another one, because apparently I am hungry as hell. "We fucked. We're both grown-ups. No harm, no foul." I shrug, but let out a squeak when Lincoln flies across the counter and hits Maverick.

Well shit.

Did not see that coming.

Nope.

I look at Finley who is just watching the two of them beat the shit out of each other as they roll across the fucking room. "Will you do something?"

He looks at me a little worried before glancing back at them.

"Mav took my virginity, and Finn ate me out in my theater room!" I shout, and the fighting on the floor stops momentarily. "Boom, all three of you had a peek at my kitty; it's really no big deal. Now can we stop with your macho bullshit please?"

Apparently Indi's sassy bullshit is rubbing off on me, but that was too much fun to shout at them. "The food is going cold."

Personally, I don't get the fighting. It's not like Linc didn't eat me out all those weeks ago in the pool house.

God, that seems like a fucking lifetime ago.

They get up off the floor and Lincoln brushes himself off before taking the seat opposite me. They all glare at each other as the other two sit down and start eating in silence, too.

*Well this is fun.*

I finish my second burrito, refusing to let their stupid boy bullshit fuck with my little slice of happy. Once I'm finished, I rinse off my plate and put it in the dishwasher before sitting back at the island. "Which coffee is which?"

"Yours has your name on it," Finley says softly, passing me a cup. I take a sip, black and sweet. Freaking heaven. It might not be the floofy goodness Indi has taught me to love, but I love it like this just as much. I sigh happily into the bitter liquid gold that makes me feel more human and Maverick looks at me again before dropping his head into his hands.

"Okay, so, does anyone want to enlighten me as to why you crashed my morning? There I was, all set up for my pity party for one, and now you're here when a few weeks ago you'd have rather been anywhere but here." I lean back in the chair, sipping at my coffee as I look between them.

"Why didn't you tell us you were a virgin at the pool house?" Maverick asks, and I level him with a look.

"Would it have made a difference? You guys had those strangers manhandle me, and watched while they did it. You didn't give a shit about what they were doing to me, what you all did after, virgin or not."

He looks down his lap like he's almost ashamed, and good. They were assholes. Not that I didn't enjoy Lincoln going down on me while Mav watched and Finn whispered dirty nothings to me, but still. That kind of isn't the point. Not right now anyway.

I look to Lincoln who just stares at me. "Would it have stopped you from telling Mr. Peters that I didn't do our assignment? Do you know what he tried to do to me when he kept me back?" I pause, looking at each of them, waiting for an answer that I know I won't get. "Did you know he'd ask me to suck his dick to pass his class? Did you know he'd get his dick out, right there in class, and threaten me with it, telling me how no one would believe a word I said because of that sex tape? Did you even care?"

"He did what?" Mav roars, his emotions doing a full one-eighty. Shame replaced by blazing anger.

"It's done," I tell him with a shrug. I've moved past it and put it in the column of things I can't change, so I'm letting go. I just wish there wasn't so much in that column lately.

"We need to tell her," Finley says, looking at Lincoln. "She needs to know why."

"Does why even matter?" I sigh, gulping down the last dregs of my coffee. "What could you possibly say to excuse it? What could *possibly* be a good enough explanation for anything you did to me? I know you guys did me a solid on Friday with Raleigh, and you looked after me, but I'm not ready to forgive any of you. I have absolutely no reason to. And you still haven't told me why you're here."

"I told you I was sorry," Finn says quietly. "If I'd have known…"

"It probably wouldn't have changed a thing." I shrug and let out a deep sigh. "Now what is it you need to tell me? I have TV to watch, and I'd rather be alone to do it."

"Octavia…" Lincoln starts, scrubbing a hand down his face. "I don't even know where to begin. Or even how, but everything we did was to try and keep you safe. I won't apologize for that."

I roll my eyes, because of course that's his answer. "Wow, such a way with words. You gave me so much insight there. Bravo."

Finley's eyes narrow as he looks toward Lincoln, and I swear to fuck, if they start brawling in my house, too, I'm going somewhere fucking else.

"There's so much you don't know," Lincoln says, almost resigned. "And plenty more you won't believe."

I lean forward and rest my elbows on the counter, resting my chin in my hands. "Why don't you just try me?"

"We did what we did to make you leave," he starts, and I bark out a laugh.

"No shit, Sherlock. I caught onto that bit. But you're still not answering any of my goddamn questions. If you're not going to let me in on what's going on, you might as well go back to school."

He glares at me and I roll my eyes. If he's going to be Captain Obvious, then I'm going to give him shit for it.

"Well, what you obviously didn't catch on to was just how much danger you're in by being here in Echoes Cove. Which is exactly why we wanted you gone."

My eyes go wide at that little tidbit. "You want me to believe you were doing all of this *for* me? Give me a fucking break. That would require you giving a fuck, which you have very clearly shown you don't. Doing this shit for me because I'm in danger. I mean, fucking really?" I scoff.

"I told you she wouldn't believe me. What's the point?" Lincoln huffs and stands, looking back at me. "You're obviously not going anywhere, so we're changing tactics. You won't believe me about the rest, and I don't want to waste my breath trying to force you to hear me, so just don't expect a whole lot of privacy anytime soon. You're in danger, we can help. *That's* why we're here."

He grabs his coffee and leaves the room, putting his phone to his ear. I'm more surprised he didn't have something more to say about all three of them having got me off in one way or another, especially after his outburst earlier, but I shrug it off.

I don't claim to know anything about him anymore. He's confusing as fuck.

I look back at the other two who look conflicted as hell. "Do either of you have anything to add to his sparkling insight as to why you've all been such giant assholes since I returned? Or has the king spoken?"

My challenge hangs in the air, met with nothing but silence. Of course they're not going to tell me shit if Lincoln doesn't sign off on it.

"I figured as much. You should all just leave. You talk about keeping me safe, but the only thing I can see that I need protecting from is you three."

And maybe a stalker, but who's counting?

After successfully clearing my house of those who seem to love to hate me, I decide my mental health can take the backseat and get lost in a documentary on cults and killers—the blood and gore is a welcome change from the jumpy shit I've been dreaming up—which is perfect to distract me from the insanity of my own life. I might have made everything worse by letting it slide the last few months, and that has to stop, but I'm going to give myself today to ignore it all.

Well, kind of anyway.

My phone pings with an alert from my security app, and I groan, wondering which of those fuckheads is coming back to mess with my zen some more. It's only when the door opens and I see Smithy that my mood lifts. I jump from the sofa, letting out a squeal as I run across the room.

Wrapping my arms around the old man, who I've missed

way too much, he chuckles as he drops his bags and hugs me back. "Good morning to you, Miss Octavia. I didn't expect you to be home."

"I didn't expect you home today! I'd have made a cake or something!" I gush, happier than I thought I would be to have him back.

"Miss Octavia, I wouldn't wish that fate on my kitchen," he chuckles. "But I appreciate the sentiment. Now, why are you not at school?"

I pull back as he frowns down at me, though a small smile still plays on his lips. "It was a rough weekend. I needed an extra day."

His frown deepens, but he shakes it off. "Well, okay. Just this once it won't hurt, I suppose. What are your plans for today?"

"Honestly?" I say and pull at the bottom of my hoodie. "TV day."

I grin up at him and he shakes his head, smiling softly. "But of course. Well, how about I get these unpacked, then make us both a milkshake, and you can introduce me to whatever it is that has you so fascinated you can watch it for a whole day."

"Sounds perfect! Do you want some help?"

"No, no, Miss Octavia." He pats my shoulder gently. "You go get comfortable. I won't be long. Will Miss Indi or Master Saint be joining us this evening?"

"The Saints most definitely are *not* joining us, but Indi might. I'll drop her a text now."

He nods and grabs his bags before heading down the hall to his room. I feel lighter than I have in weeks as I bounce back over to the couch, get comfy, and find the crime documentary we started watching together a few weeks ago. Picking up my phone, I check in with Indi.

Me

How is your day going, sunshine?

Indi

It's weird. You missed it, Raleigh's schedule has been changed and he blew up first thing this morning about it. He's on crutches though. The football team is raging. Blair seems to be on the warpath again oo. So... Typical day at ECP.

Me

I'm sorry you're out there alone. I'll be back tomorrow.

Indi

You sure you've taken enough time?

Me

I'm not going to know if I stay hidden away. Smithy just got home. He asked if you were coming for dinner?

Indi

Is he cooking mac and cheese?

I grin down at my phone. I tried to warn her before she ate it the first time that it was addictive.

Me

I can ask.

Indi

I am soooo there. We both know that adorable man won't deny you a thing.

Me

Awesome, I'll see you in a few hours. Good luck and may the odds be ever in your favor.

Indi

I love you, ya big nerd. See you in a bit.

I laugh at her message just as Smithy appears in the kitchen and starts making milkshakes.

"So how is your sister doing, anyway? Everything okay back home?"

He stops as he pulls the ice cream from the freezer and smiles at me. "She's doing much better, thank you, Miss Octavia. Now that she's situated everything is much better. We managed to arrange for some home care for her until she's fully back on her feet too."

Guilt spikes my stomach, knowing that he came back here for me, rather than looking after her. "You could've stayed longer if you'd needed to. I would've been okay." I chew my lip because I'm not sure how true that statement actually is, but I hate that I'm the reason he had to leave her.

"Nonsense, Miss Octavia. I was going a little stir crazy there. There is only so long a person can be around their family before they need to be with the people who are truly their family." He winks at me before starting the blender for the milkshakes. He pours chocolate sauce on the inside of the milkshake glasses before adding more chocolate chips to the blender.

My mouth waters at the thought of how good that's going to taste.

He brings the two glasses over and gets comfortable on the other side of the sofa. "So what did I miss while I was gone?"

I take a sip of thick, chocolaty goodness to give me a second to think of how to answer that question, groaning as the sweetness hits my tastebuds. There's no way I can tell him everything that's going on, but a small part of me wonders if he knows more about what's happening here than I do. He's lived in The Cove while I've been gone. He obviously kept an eye on the Saints, surely he wouldn't keep secrets from me if they put me in danger, right? So I decide to counter his question with one of my own. "Do you know why the boys want me out of Echoes Cove?"

His eyes go wide quickly, and he turns to face me, putting his milkshake down on the table. "Not exactly."

My heart sinks. He does know something, and he kept it from me. I thought I could trust him.

"I knew they weren't all happy about your return, but I didn't know they wanted you out of here. I hope they haven't been too persistent." He frowns, guilt shining in his eyes, but I say nothing. If he isn't aware of what I've been going through, I'm not about to add to his obvious guilt. "I've worked for your family for a long time. For your grandfather before your father. You don't work with a Royal for as long as I have and not know that everything isn't what it seems. I know enough to keep myself out of what they were wrapped up in, enough to know that the boys are likely trying to keep you safe. The same way I am. As for the exact details, I don't know much. I'm sorry I didn't tell you this before, but I assumed your father would have passed the details on. You are his legacy after all." He pauses, and I wait for him to continue as my heart pounds in my chest. "What I do know is that your family has been wrapped up in the darkness that beats under the surface of Echoes Cove since the beginning. They were a founding family here, the same as the Saints, the Knights, and the Rileys, and it wasn't long before they became tangled up in the web of The Knights Society."

"The Knights Society?" I blink, trying to take it all in. So much information—and so little—all at once. And it still sounds so unbelievable. I don't think he'd lie to me, but how can any of this be real?

He nods before glancing around the room. "They are more dangerous than you can imagine, Miss Octavia. There's a darkness prowling just beneath the surface of Echoes Cove. Sometimes The Knights are there to fight it back, but more often than not, they're the ones ushering it to the surface. From what

I understand, it's been that way for close to two hundred years. I've kept my head down and stayed off their radar. I don't know for certain exactly what they are, but I know that nothing good can come from being tangled up with them.

"They had their claws in your father at one point, but I assumed he broke free when he left this place, though it was never confirmed, not to me at least. He took you from here for a reason, and I'd lay my life down to say it was to get you away from the Knights. And if I had to make a bet, I'd say the boys were trying to protect you from it all too. The same way they protected you when you were younger. "

My brain about implodes with that little nugget and I lean back in my chair, taking in his words. I'd put money on this being what Lincoln thought I wouldn't believe. What Finley wanted to tell me. My mind works overtime going over everything that's happened since I arrived back here.

The only thing I know for sure anymore is that nothing is what I thought it was.

# SIX

## OCTAVIA

I've been stewing over what Smithy said to me all week, and in the end, I decided to take most of the week off. When I woke up this morning, I knew that today was the day I'd bite the bullet and head back into school. It's a Friday, so it's only one day to suffer through before the weekend.

I can totally do this.

I just need to work out how to face the guys without asking them a million questions. I know them better than they realize. Going in for the kill isn't the way to get the answers I want. I tried to ask Smithy more, but with the amount of fear he seemed to have about it all, I dialed it back. Giving him a heart attack really isn't on my to-do list.

Even if I'm still not really over the fact that he withheld

information from me.

On the one hand, I get it. If this is a legacy thing, my dad really should've said something. I can't help but wonder if this is why I had to come back here. If that's why he killed himself; to be free of them. But if that's the case, why would he leave me at their mercy?

I put on my last swipe of mascara and fluff up my hair, shaking off the thoughts. I've been lost to this train of thought way too much the last few days, but without more information I'm just going around in circles. I really need to get some fucking answers, I just haven't worked out the best way to go about it yet. Finley and Maverick obviously won't say anything if Lincoln doesn't approve, and Lincoln is a tight-lipped motherfucker. So I need to think of something to get them to open up a bit. East might be an option, but I'm not even sure how much he'll say without Lincoln.

My phone pings on my dresser and I smile when I see Indi's name on the screen. My one silver lining in all of this is that I'm pretty sure Indi isn't in on this Knight bullshit. She's new to the city, and she already told me about Ryker and Ellis. I'd like to think if she knew about any of this, she'd have told me then.

I hope, anyway.

Indi

> Yes bitch! You're back. I'll have coffee waiting for you on the steps!

Me

You're the best. See you soon!

Butterflies kick up in my stomach, more than just nerves about seeing Raleigh again. I'm a little nervous about seeing the guys. Including East. He is the biggest enigma to me so far, because if Lincoln knows about all of this shit, then surely East does. So if he wanted me gone too, why be so nice to me?

I pinch the bridge of my nose, my head aching from the swirling thoughts, all of the questions that I don't have answers to. I intend to get some answers, and soon.

I head downstairs and find the four of them waiting for me in the foyer. I eye them suspiciously as I reach the bottom of the staircase. "What are you guys doing here?"

East steps forward, smiling sadly at me. "Smithy called me last night. Said you'd had questions that maybe we were better off answering."

*Oh he did, did he?* Old man is suspiciously absent, too. So much for my plans to get answers my own way. Once I reach the ground floor, I walk past them into the kitchen and grab a bottle of water from the refrigerator. "So, talk."

Lincoln eyes me, like he doesn't want to say a goddamn thing, which is exactly what I expected. No one else says a word.

*Of course they fucking don't.*

"We have to tell her," Finley says, and I quirk a brow. Finally, some movement.

Lincoln shakes his head and folds his arms over his chest.

"If you don't tell her, I will," Finley argues, and Lincoln levels him with a look.

"Seriously?"

"I told you Lincoln, I won't hurt her again. Keeping all of this from her is going to get her hurt." Finley stares Lincoln down until Lincoln runs a hand through his hair.

"Fine. Fuck." He glances over at me, as icy as ever. "Sit down. We have a lot to talk through."

I move back to the counter and take a seat, waiting for someone to start talking.

"Was I right? Is this about the photos?"

Lincoln takes a seat as Maverick opens the fridge, grabbing water for the rest of them before joining us. "Okay, so let's start with the photos. No, the photos have nothing to do with everything else as far as we know. They're a problem all on their own. This is obviously a stalker of some sort. I already told you I have someone looking into it, so I'll give them this information, too, but currently we're coming up empty. If you have any ideas about who would be stalking you, anyone who seemed overly interested, anything suspicious, let me know."

I nod at him, letting the words sink in. Of course I have a stalker. Awesome. "The only one who's been overly interested is Raleigh, and considering the photos, I'm going to say it's not him."

East squeezes my thigh and Lincoln nods at me.

"Okay, well I'll keep digging."

I look around at each of them, waiting for someone to start talking, but I'm met with deafening silence. "What about the note?"

"The note…" Lincoln starts, before looking up to the ceiling as if looking for the right words. I knew there was a fucking note! I knew it. Asshole. "The note, the flowers, the dress… They're all from the same people."

I think back to all of the things I've received with the black cards. "Right? But that doesn't explain much. Why am I out of time? Out of time for what? I feel like I'm missing a huge chunk of information here."

"The people who sent you all those things are part of the same organization. They want you to join their ranks. You're a legacy, and legacies don't escape them." He looks me directly in the eye and I see a glimpse of the boy I once knew, but then the shutters come down. In a blink he's back to this new version of himself. "They are the reason we tried to make you leave. The reason we did everything we've done since you arrived. You're not safe here. Stalker or not. The Knights Society is the bigger threat to you right now."

"The Knights Society?" I laugh, glancing around at their somber faces. That's what Smithy called them too, and as much as I want to believe him, believe them, it still all just sounds made up. Like something out of a movie. "Are you fucking with me right now? Trying to get me to forget, or figure, that you've all been giant assholes the last few months with a made up what? Secret society? I'm a lot of things, Lincoln, but stupid isn't one of them."

He looks from me to East and then Finley. "This is why I said there was no point in telling her." He pushes back his stool and paces the floor. "The Knights Society is very real. I wish for all our sakes this was some elaborate ruse, that I was making it up, that it was all a ploy to fuck with you some more, but it's not. You should be thankful Stone made the deal he did before you left. It's the only thing that's bought you this much time."

It's like the room sucks in a breath at his words. "My dad? What are you talking about, Lincoln?"

He pauses to stand and stare at me for a minute before clenching his hands into fists at his sides. "Your dad was a part of TKS. So was your mom. Just like all of our parents. We're all legacies. Three other families in The Cove make up the board for the sect here, but their reach spans, at least, nationwide. They are the chess players behind everything that happens. They are the real monsters in your closet, the demons that live under your bed, and even though you think you're free, I promise you… they've had more control over your life than you can ever think possible. They are everywhere, and once they have their claws in you, you can never escape."

I clasp my throat, trying to take what he's saying seriously. He certainly believes what he's saying, and from the looks around the room, so do the others. There's no way my dad would have been wrapped up in something like this.

This can't be real, right? Secret societies or whatever this is are just crazy things you read about in books.

"Okay, so what do I do?" I ask, trying to work out what it is they're not saying.

Lincoln looks me dead in the eye and puts his hands in his pockets. "You do what we've been trying to make you do all along. You leave."

I throw my hands up in the air, exasperated. This all ties into what Smithy said, but it's just so hard to believe. "And this, right here, is exactly why I don't believe what you're saying. You've wanted me gone since I got back here, this is just another ploy."

"Why else would we want you gone?" Lincoln yells, and I startle.

"Lincoln, enough," East says, touching my arm as if trying to soothe me.

Lincoln turns his cold look on his brother and narrows his eyes. "You don't get to say when it's enough. You're already out. You chose that, remember?"

I'm obviously missing something, because Lincoln's rage seems to grow as East deflates next to me. "You're not a Knight?"

"No," he says, and it looks like it hurts him to say it, so I decide not to ask any more questions on that for right now. I look over to Maverick. He's still standing in the same position he was in earlier, watching everything play out, ready to throw hands if it's needed. But he seems happy enough to sit back and observe.

Finley on the other hand, looks like he's close to breaking point. I don't think I've ever seen him look like that.

"Let's just dial it back a little, shall we?" Finley says to Lincoln who throws his hands in the air and leaves the room. Mav follows him after a nod from Finley, leaving me with just him and East.

"This is just madness." I drop my head into my hands, trying to work out which way is up. How everything got so twisted. How exactly it is that my life ended up at this crux.

"Octavia, I know it's hard to believe," East says softly. "But Lincoln is telling you the truth."

I look up at him, and I wish I saw something that made me think he was lying, but East hasn't lied to me yet. Not that I know of. "None of this makes any sense, let alone sounds believable. Surely if they were this all-knowing, all-powerful, terrifying whatever it is they are, they'd just do what they want?"

"The Knights live by a code. It might be a fucked-up code, but it's still a code. To break it is to betray the Society," Finley says quietly. "That is why they do what they do, the way they do it. We still don't know exactly what they want from you, but trust me, it's better to be out and not know."

He clenches his fist as he stops speaking, and an icy drop of dread runs down my spine. They all seem so... scared. Which isn't something I'd have thought I'd ever use to describe any of them.

"My dad really knew about all of this?"

East nods in response to my question, and my heart breaks a little more. I didn't realize that was possible. "These knuckleheads have been trying to get you to leave to keep you safe."

A quiet rage pools in my stomach at his words as a realization comes to me. "You knew what they were doing?"

His eyes go wide and he leans back, pulling away from me. "I mean... not exactly. I didn't want any part of it, but yes, I knew they were going to try to do something to keep you safe. To make you leave."

"You have got to be fucking kidding me," I hiss and start pacing back and forth. Just when I thought I could trust him, that he wouldn't lie to me. "This is so fucked up. And while we're just laying out the truth bombs, I'm just going to be straight with you guys—which is more decency than any of you have shown me, I might add—I can't leave," I grind out through clenched teeth, trying not to hulk out over that little revelation.

Finley turns to me and I take a deep breath to try and focus my thoughts.

"Why not?"

I debate telling him the truth, whether they'll just use it against me later, but at this point, what more could go wrong?

"My father's will states that in order to have access to my inheritance, I must graduate from ECP with at least a 4.0 GPA. That, and stay living with one of my guardians until I'm of age."

"Those motherfuckers," Finley hisses before slamming a hand down on the table as Lincoln and Mav re-enter the room. Finley looks up at them, a quiet rage washing over him. "They brought her here. I'd put money on it."

"It's what we thought," Lincoln says with a shrug. "They had a hand to play, a pawn on the board to move, so they did. The question is, what do we do about it now?"

"Wait! Will you all just wait a freaking minute?" I stand up to put some distance between us. This is all getting too much, and I've had about as much of their cryptic bullshit as I can take.

"You tormented me, bullied me, rallied the whole fucking student body against me. My car was trashed, my home was broken into. *Smithy was put in the fucking hospital.*" I suck in a breath, trying not to go nuclear and failing. "My best friend had her car hijacked, YOU MADE A FUCKING DEEPFAKE SEX TAPE, and you're trying to tell me you did all of that shit, and more, *to keep me safe?* From a supposed secret society. And then you talk about it like it's nothing more than another breezy Monday morning. You have got to be fucking kidding me."

They all just stare at me, not saying a word. Not trying to deny a thing. I look at East, and rage fills me further. "And you did nothing to stop them! You're as bad as they are!"

"V…" East starts, standing to move toward me. I put my

126

arm out in front of me to stop him.

"No. Don't you 'V' me. My dad fucking died. I came here to get the resolution I needed so I can get on with my life, and you made these last few months *hell*. Do you have any idea what I've been going through? Then, on top of that, I have some fucking psycho stalker, and someone I thought was my friend tried to rape me. I am so done. You all need to leave." I pull at my hair and turn my back on them. "Fucking secret society," I mutter. "What a bunch of horse shit."

I spin back around when nothing but silence greets me. "I said get the fuck out!"

They stand in unison and leave without a word, leaving me with more questions than answers.

What a fucking joke.

This morning was a mess, and by the time I pull up to school, my anger hasn't really subsided. What an absolute mind fuck of a few days. Hell, my entire time since I came back has been a shit storm. So I make a pact with myself to buck the fuck up. I need to shake some of my grief off and start thinking clearly.

Letting stuff happen around me, *to me*, isn't helping anything and it's become very apparent that if I don't demand answers, or look into stuff myself, I'm never going to get anywhere. Everything I've discovered so far is about as useful as trying to travel on a paper airplane.

Indi bounces down the steps to the front of my car as I take a deep breath. She doesn't deserve bitchy me. She's done nothing but be my friend. I just wish I wasn't so jaded. I was convinced she had no idea, but everything in my life is tipped upside down.

I grab my bag and climb from the car, painting on a smile as I come face-to-face with my new bestie. She thrusts the ice-cold coffee topped with cream and chocolate sauce in my face. "I know fall is here, but I'm holding onto my iced coffee like it's a lifeline. We can move over to hot coffee next week."

My smile widens genuinely. I could kick myself for doubting her. She's too good, too genuine, to have known and not said anything. "Thank you," I say, linking my arm through hers. "Now, let's go and survive this day, shall we?"

"We've so got this." She grins and we head up the steps into the school. I pretend like everyone isn't looking at me like a lion at the zoo. I flick my hair over my shoulder and walk through the hall with Indi, heading to my locker.

"So what did I miss?" I ask as I empty the contents of my bag into my locker and grab my book for English. "Anything juicy?"

"Not really. Raleigh is off the football team. Well, benched anyway. He broke his ankle Friday night." Her eyes dart across the hall to where Maverick is leaning against the lockers, watching us.

Not creepy at all. Nope.

I roll my eyes and bring my attention back to her. "Wannabe rapists get what they deserve."

She nods reverently. "Yes, yes they do. Also, that creepy hall on the far side of town burned down. It's been all over the news."

"Nestwood?"

"That's the one. Place gives me the creeps everytime I drive past."

I bark out a laugh. "Dude, *same.*" I make a mental note that that means I'm totally free and clear of that stupid gala invite and do a mental fist pump.

We head over to her locker, dodging Maverick as we go, as she fills me in on all of the other drama that has filled the school this week. "And the best one yet, which I'm not sure anyone has told you about... but er... you've been nominated for homecoming queen."

"I've been what?!" I screech. I groan and bury my face in my hands.

She just laughs that twinkly laugh of hers as she closes her locker. "Yeah I knew you'd be happy about it. The dance is next week, later than usual, but something to do with vandalism. At least now we have an excuse to go shopping again?"

"You want to go to the dance?" I ask, shocked, as the bell rings.

She shrugs as we head toward English. "I've never been to a dance before. I figure you haven't either, what with homeschooling. It could be fun, right?"

I suck in a breath before letting it out slowly. "Sure, why not get all dressed up to spend more time with people who hate me?"

"Yes!" She does a fist pump, twirling as she enters the classroom for English. "I knew you'd be on board. We could head up to Santa Monica tomorrow, do some shopping, hang out on the pier. Do normal teenage girl shit."

"You're not hanging with the twins?" I ask as I slide into my desk, wagging my brows at her.

She rolls her eyes at me as she takes her seat. "No, I am not. I have zero idea what's going on with them right now. I've barely heard from them all week, so fuck them. I'm not going to do the chasing thing. Especially after the whole thing with Jackson. I am done running around after boys. If they want to speak to me, they know where to find me."

I smile softly, feeling a little proud of her. "Good, you deserve better than chasing around after boys who don't know what they want."

"Speaking of boys who don't know what they want." I look up at her words, and find three of the four of them watching me from outside the class. "Any idea what's going on with them and their total turn around since Friday?"

I open my mouth to speak, having no idea how to even begin to tell her about what happened, as Miss Summers breezes into the room, closing the door behind her. I've never been more glad for not having to answer a question. "Good morning, all. Let's finish this week with a bang, shall we? I declare today debate day!"

A groan sounds across the room and I smile.

Maybe this day will turn around after all.

I somehow managed to evade everyone I didn't want to see yesterday. No Raleigh, no Blair, even the guys kept their distance—though that could've been them trying to avoid any more of my questions. It was a nice change and a pretty easy day to settle back in with. Admittedly, we went off campus for lunch, heading back to Penny's. It's hard to believe it's already been three months since we set foot in there.

The day is unusually hot for November, apparently we're getting a last minute dash of summer sunshine, and I'm totally not opposed to it. I pull on my cutoffs, pair them with my knee-high Chucks and a crop top, finishing the look with my leather jacket. My waves cascade down my back and I check my face once more in the mirror before I head to pick up Indi.

I still can't get over this whole homecoming thing. Not going to lie, I've been completely oblivious to all of the posters lining the walls of the school, but it's not like I didn't have enough going on to distract me. Apparently I've been oblivious to a lot since I got back to The Cove.

I grab my keys, phone, and purse before I head downstairs, calling out a goodbye to Smithy before skipping out to my car. Sliding on my aviators, I connect my phone to the sound system, blasting *This Little Girl* by Cady Groves as I drive out of the gate and through the center of town. I can't help but smile at the lyrics of the song because they're so freaking true.

I pull up in front of Indi's house just as she skips down the front sidewalk. "Morningggg!" she sings as she slides into the car and buckles in.

"New hair?" I ask, taking in the vivid violet, somehow darker yet brighter than the purple she had when I first met her. I have no idea how she always makes it so bright and shiny, or how she suits every freaking color, but I love it.

"I fancied a change again. The rainbow is fun for a minute, but the root touch up is murder. Plus, how awesome are these extensions?" She grins as she steals my phone, flicking through the playlists.

"They are all kinds of beautiful, I'd never know it wasn't your hair." The curls wave down her petite frame to just below her boobs, the perfect compliment to her thickly lined eyes and deep purple lipstick.

"My hair woman is a freaking genius with extensions. Now then, are we ready for all of the shopping?"

I grin at her, shaking my head as I pull away from the curb. "Not even a little. Homecoming dresses aren't exactly my usual repertoire."

"I mean, mine either, but it's got to be fun right? It's a 007 Casino theme. We can be Pussy Galore."

I burst out laughing while she just grins at me, trying not to laugh, "You, my friend, definitely know how to cheer a girl up."

"That's what besties are for. You know I'm here if you want to talk it out." I grin over at her before looking back at the road. As much as I'd like to unburden myself, I don't really know much yet. And the last thing I want to do is drag her into this bullshit. If she's free and clear, I'd like to keep it that way.

"Thank you." I pull out onto the PCH and head up toward Santa Monica. We spend most of the journey singing at the top of our lungs.

It's so nice, just driving with the windows down, wind in our hair, singing, acting like the seventeen-year-olds we are. Everything going on in my life makes it easy to forget I'm still allowed to be a teenager sometimes.

I pull into the parking lot at the pier once we reach Santa Monica and turn to face Indi once I'm parked. "So, are you going to tell me more about the twins and... Dylan, was it?"

She lets out a deep breath, blowing her hair out of her face. "What do you want to know?"

"How did you guys all meet?" She looks a little shocked, like she thought I was going to go for the jugular, but that's not my style. Plus, I adore her, I'm not going to judge her for a goddamn thing.

She smiles softly as she looks out at the water. "It was the first summer I moved here. I had no idea who the hell anyone was, so I just kind of did my own thing. I met some people at the beach that invited me to a party. The party was at the Donovans'. I actually met Scout first. She accepted me instantly, the twins were such giant assholes—mostly Ryker, but Ellis stands by his brother in pretty much everything—but Scout and I got along really well. I hung out with her a lot at the start of the summer, but then… I still don't know exactly what happened, but it was like Scout couldn't go anywhere without one of her brothers or Dylan present. So I got to know them all slowly too."

"That's kind of adorable," I tell her, and she sticks her tongue out at me, making me laugh.

She climbs from the car and I follow suit, double checking I have everything, before locking it up and dropping my keys in my purse.

"It was. Ellis was attentive, Ryker was a little dangerous, and Dylan… well, he was their perfect balance. They were so freaking loyal, but that was part of the problem. The Kings came first. And I get it. Kind of. But being second priority, or even fourth, because of their dedication to each other… it just got to be too much. I tried to ride it out, and it was harder with me coming to Prep and them going to High, but we were doing okay. Then, at the end of the summer this year—after an entire year, I might add—they dropped me like a hot freaking penny, telling me it was for my own safety. Boys." She rolls her eyes and loops her arm through mine.

Her words trigger a memory… Ryker out in front of the school, talking to the guys, mentioning the Knights. My eyes go wide as my heart pounds in my chest. Maybe they really were trying to keep her safe. I keep it to myself and shove the emotion down. That's another question for Lincoln and the others, when I can finally pry open the treasure trove of information I know they have. Today is about having a day with my bestie and shaking off this week. I can deal with the other bullshit later.

Assuming it doesn't catch up with me first.

# SEVEN

## EAST

This week has been fucking torture. Between arguing with Lincoln, dealing with my goddamn father, trying to look into this stalker with the PI Linc and I hired, and kind of coming clean with V then her icing me out… I'm beyond ready for it to be done.

I also need to try and find a way to apologize to V. I'm not sure she wants to see me. She iced me during class yesterday, only speaking when absolutely necessary, and I haven't heard from her otherwise.

Not that I blame her; I'd be pissed if I was her too. I might not have played a part in what sounds like the torture those little fuckers put her through, but I knew they were trying to make her leave, and I didn't do anything to try and stop them.

I'd like to say that I was just trying to keep her safe—that because I'm not a Knight, I wasn't as involved—but that's just a bullshit cop-out. I might not be a Knight, but that doesn't mean I don't know almost as much about them as Linc and the others. It also doesn't mean that I couldn't have fought the others harder when they came up with their little plan.

I hate my father for having put us in this position, for making me keep even more fucking secrets. I hate this place and everything it stands for. But mostly, I hate that I don't think I'm going to be able to get Lincoln, or any of them, free and clear from the grasps of those controlling them.

That was my plan once upon a time; once I discovered I wouldn't be taking the Saint seat at the table, when I learned there might be a way out, I wanted to get us all out.

Then Stone took Octavia away, and I thought I could really do it. I thought if he could find a way, so could I.

And then the boys were taken.

That's when I knew I was too late.

The Knights already had them. By the time they came home two weeks later, none of them were the same. I knew they never would be again.

None of them ever spoke about what happened while they were gone, but I knew it was the Knights.

I stare back down at the mountains of pictures that have been delivered to V, trying to work out if there's anything that could give away who is stalking her. There are so many more than she's seen because Linc started intercepting them before she could.

I know at first he took them because he thought he was fucking with her. But when he saw what was inside the envelope he took, he pulled me in on it and we called Lucas, a PI we discovered that has zero ties to the Knights. Not the easiest person to find, especially with their reach being as wide as it is, but there are some advantages to me not being a member. This was one of them. I'm not watched. Well, not as closely as Linc is anyway.

Fuck this. I'm not getting anywhere just staring at these pictures.

I need to speak to Smithy. I need to know if he's seen anything, but I don't want to bring him in any further than he already is. The last thing I want is anything else happening to him. Her house being broken into and Smithy ending up in the hospital wasn't the boys, that much I know, which means it was the Knights. Likely a warning for him to remember his place.

I wouldn't be surprised if they were the reason for his sister being in the hospital either. Their reach is wide, and crossing them isn't typically a wise move. I'm not sure what Smithy did to end up on their radar the way he did, but maybe he saw something that connects to this and he hasn't said anything just in case.

God, that sounded convoluted even in my own head.

I head over to the Royals' house, half hoping I'll get the

chance to speak to V, but also not holding my breath. She's nothing if not stubborn. Not that I blame her, but how can I make it better if she won't let me explain?

That is a problem for later. Right now, I need to focus on dealing with the sicko hunting her. She has enough psychopaths in her life already, she doesn't need any more.

I head through the back gate between the properties and find Smithy in the garden, tending to the flower beds by the kitchen. "Smithy, my man! Good to see you."

"Master Saint!" he exclaims, squinting up at me as the sun beats down on my back in the late afternoon. He stands, brushing himself off. "What brings you here?"

"I wondered if you had a few minutes to talk about Octavia."

He frowns at me, and I swear I feel like a kid again, being scolded by him for touching the cookies when they were still cooling. "I'm afraid, Master Saint, that she is rather displeased with you. Well, all of you, really. She's out with Miss Indi today."

My smile falters, but I put it back on. I might not be a Knight, but I'm still a Saint, and I'm all too familiar with wearing a mask of emotion. "That's fine. I need to speak to you about her anyway. It's probably best she isn't here for this."

"Okay then, let's head inside and I'll sort some refreshments. Iced tea?"

I nod, my smile a little more genuine this time. "Sounds great."

Following him inside, I close the door, enjoying the cool air from the a/c as it washes over me. I lean on the counter while he pours the drinks, trying to sort out everything in my mind. Do I just tell him all about the stalker, ensure that he's as aware as we are, or keep him safe and just ask questions?

The bigger question is, which option will keep V safest? Because as much as I love Smithy, she is my priority. Even if she doesn't know it yet.

The guys all pile into the kitchen this morning as Mrs. Potts is serving up breakfast. "Don't forget I'm not around much this week. I've put dinners in the fridge for you for the week, but other than that and breakfast tomorrow before school, you'll need to fend for yourselves."

"We got this, Mrs. P." Mav grins cheekily as he drops a kiss into her hairline, taking the plates from her hands and sitting down at the table with me. She mothers over him, clucking as he charms the socks off of her—the little psychopath—before disappearing into the laundry room.

I dig into my eggs as they all sit down. "You guys got in late last night."

"Don't we know it," Linc grumbles. "We were out on an errand that ran long."

Well, that explains it. They don't talk much to me about what it is they do for the Knights, but I know Lincoln doesn't sleep much anymore. Though, from what I've managed to piece together about the Knights, I'm not sure I would either.

Guilt slams into me once more over him being the one carrying the mantle. Not that I had much choice about it—a secret I am prepared to take to my grave, even if he resents me for it. It's better than him knowing the truth.

"Something big happened though. Not sure what's going on, but all recruitment has been paused," Linc adds, and my eyes go wide. "Means V should be safe for a little longer, but Dad was flipping his shit last night. Apparently being the head honcho of our sect isn't all roses right now."

"Serves him right for being a giant fucking cunt." Mav shrugs before plowing into his food—you'd think he'd never eaten before, Jesus fucking Christ. He isn't wrong though.

"Well, I'm not going to be sad about it. If things stay down for long enough, maybe you guys will catch a break." I look around at them, each of them nodding while they eat.

Lincoln stays quiet while Mav snorts. "Gives me time to dream something up for Mr. Peters."

I groan. "What does that mean?"

"He got his dick out in front of V. Told her he'd pass her if she would play with him."

My jaw drops seconds before the burning anger takes root in the pit of my stomach. "He did fucking what?"

Mav shrugs while Linc fills me in. "It's our own fault. Everything we did to get her to leave. The tape, the attacks.

Everything. But we tidy up our messes."

"Attacks?" I ask, raising an eyebrow. "I think maybe it's time you guys fill me in on just what you've been doing so there are no more surprises."

Sitting back, I fold my arms, my gaze bouncing between them. Finn and Mav look to Linc, unsurprising really, but this means there's likely something I'm going to be pissed about. We don't usually keep secrets, but these last few months, I've known less and less of what they've been doing. Both with the Knights and V. I get it. I'm not one of them, but we've always been close. I hate that there's so much I don't know now, things I can't help them with.

Lincoln starts talking, and I clench my fists as I try not to blow up. I manage to keep my cool through most of it. The car jacking, the sex tape, Mav's threats—but when he finally admits to locking her in the closet, I lose my shit.

"Are you out of your goddamn minds?! Why would you do that to her? I know you were trying to protect her, but fuck! That shit was too far. Did you see what you did to her? How broken she was? Fuck you all." I seethe quietly, trying to calm myself, while they all sit there looking thoroughly guilty.

"I hadn't thought it was so bad till it was listed out like that," Mav says sheepishly, rubbing the back of his neck. "No wonder she won't forgive any of us."

I pinch the bridge of my nose. Sometimes it's easy to forget that he's only seventeen. That Linc and Finn are only eighteen.

Hell, that I'm barely twenty-two. Our lives are so fucked up. I take a deep breath, trying to remember everything V has told me about so far this year, when something pings in my mind. "What about the break-in at her house? The attack on Smithy. You didn't mention that. Was that you?"

Linc shakes his head. "No. I think that was the Knights. She was ignoring them. That, or Smithy learned something he shouldn't."

"I'd had the same thought," I say, nodding. "We really need to work out what it is they want from her. I know I'm not officially a Knight, but I don't think keeping secrets is going to help anyone. I don't give a shit if something happens to me. We just need to keep her safe."

"Agreed." Finn nods. "Her safety comes first."

"Any luck with the stalker shit?" Linc asks, and I shake my head, hating that the answer is no.

"I haven't heard from Lucas yet either. It's on my list of calls to make today."

"Okay, well you do that. We didn't get much sleep last night, so I'm heading back to bed. Any idea what V is doing today?" Lincoln asks, glancing around the team.

"I volunteer as tribute!" Mav grins as he drops his fork on the table, "Maybe I can get her to forgive me for the whole taking her virginity thing."

"I'm sorry, what?" I growl. The punches just keep rolling today.

Mav shrugs, standing before moving to the counter to grab his crap. "Shit happens. We all know any one of us would be happy to carry that ticket. Don't be pissed 'cause it was me. I just need to get her to forgive me so I can do it again. I like that no one else has had her."

He leaves out the back, leaving me gawking after him, wondering what the fuck just happened.

After a somewhat friendlier gym class today than I was expecting, I call out Octavia's name as everyone else leaves the gym. I watch her hesitate for a second before saying goodbye to Indi. I know they came in together today, not that I'm stalking her or whatever, I just happened to see Indi pick her up as I was heading to my car this morning.

*Yeah right, stalker.*

She turns and struts toward me, looking hotter than anyone should, especially in that outfit.

*Down boy, now is not the time.*

She juts her hip out as she stops to face me, arms folded across her chest. "Yes?"

"I'm sorry." The words fall from my lips, and she deflates a little. "I never meant to hurt you, and I know that not telling you things, and letting Linc and the others do what they thought was right, was the wrong thing to do but I didn't know what else to do. There's still a lot you don't know, but I'm basically powerless. I just wanted to keep you safe, and I went about it in the wrong way."

She runs a hand through her long, dark hair and lets out a sigh. "East, I just… I feel betrayed, ya know? I thought you were the one person who hadn't changed. Who was still on my side."

"But I was on your side! I *am* on your side, V. I might have gone about it the wrong way, but I will always be on your side. Just let me make it up to you." I don't even care that I sound like I'm begging. I wish I could say I haven't loved her my entire life, but I'd be straight up lying.

"I guess."

"Let me drive you home, we can talk some more?"

She looks over her shoulder, like she's expecting to see someone, but turns back and smiles sadly at me. "Sure, why not? I came in with Indi today, but this will save her going out of her way to take me home."

"Thank you."

She nods before scurrying out of the gym, and I take a few deep breaths to calm myself.

*You're not forgiven yet. Don't get ahead of yourself.*

I tear through my office, getting everything I need as quickly as I can so I don't keep her waiting.

Heading out through the back, I jump in my car and pull it around to the front of the school just in time to watch her coming out of the front doors with Indi. She waves goodbye to her friend and heads for the car, a wary smile on her face.

This is progress, I just need to remember that. Baby steps, East. If we rush this, we're going to fuck it up.

Once she's in, she buckles up and I cruise out of the lot slowly. No need to draw more attention to us than necessary. I'm just a guy giving a girl a ride home. It can't be any more than that right now, even if I want it to be. The thought of being blackmailed, and having that hurt her in the long run… a shiver runs down my spine at the thought of it.

I won't be another bad guy in her story, and I refuse to be the reason she ends up pushed into a corner.

I'm pretty sure that at twenty-two, being blackmailed isn't supposed to be the thing I'm thinking about when the girl I've loved my entire life is in my car, but here we are. Echoes Cove warps fucking everything.

She connects her phone to the bluetooth and starts playing *Who Am I* by Besomorph, and I frown a little. "You doing okay, V?"

Her brown eyes look more than a little lost when she looks over at me. "I'm fine. I'm just tired of everything already, and I get the feeling that this is just the beginning."

"I'm sorry. I wish there was something I could do to help you."

"Is there any way out?"

I clench the steering wheel until my knuckles turn white,

trying to find the words.

"You managed it, right?"

I glance over at her, at how hopeful she looks, and hate that I'm going to be the one to crush that hope in her. "Yes and no. I didn't have a choice. It was my father's choice, but trust me, just because I'm not in, doesn't mean I'm out."

"Do any of you ever not speak in riddles?" She sighs as she flops back in the seat just as we pull onto our street.

I consider her words. "We do, it's just something of a minefield with all of this. Things with you are so different than usual. Nobody knows exactly what the Knights want with you. It could be something to do with Stone, it could be something entirely different. It's more about not saying the wrong thing."

Trying to be as honest as I can while not putting my foot in anything is harder than I imagined it would be.

"How about we spend the night just hanging out, and forget about all of this bullshit. One night of normal?" The suggestion is mostly for her, but I'd really like to have just a little bit of normal with her.

A smile plays on her lips as we pull through her gate and up to the front door. "Sure thing. It's been a while since I kicked your ass on the Xbox."

"Those be fighting words."

She laughs softly and climbs from the car as I shut off the engine before moving to follow her out, but I pause as I try not to stare at her ass in that skirt. I don't even notice the uniform on anyone else, but Octavia Royal is undeniable.

I close my eyes, taking a deep breath, trying to picture things that aren't her in that skirt so my dick isn't obvious as I walk into her house. She's already through the front door before I even climb from the car. If nothing else, tonight will test my strength of will.

I head inside, closing the door and kicking off my shoes.

"Smithy isn't here. He's shopping," she calls from the kitchen, so I head in that direction. I find her with her head in the fridge, ass cheeks hanging out of her skirt.

Being her teacher never felt like such a bad idea, even if I am just the gym teacher.

"Water?" she asks, pulling a bottle from the fridge, and I nod, catching the bottle she throws at me.

"Stop delaying the inevitable." I grin, trying to push back any nefarious thoughts. "I promised you an ass kicking."

"Bring it on." She laughs as she sashays past me, flicking her hair over her shoulder. Following her into the living room, I drop onto the couch beside her, taking the offered controller. I'm looking forward to this more than I should be. It's been a hot minute since I had just a normal evening.

We settle into playing Apex, and surprise, surprise, she kicks my ass, just like she did last time. I'm not really sad about it though. Seeing her relax and let go, just enjoy herself, has been reward enough.

God, I'm turning into a sappy shit.

She throws her hands in the air and starts a dance that takes her to her feet as she celebrates winning. I can't help but laugh at her. Right up until she trips. I rush to stop her from face-planting the floor, catching her in my arms, her face barely an inch from mine.

She looks up at me, like I'm the guy that can save her.

Then she looks at my lips and everything changes. I know I shouldn't be doing this.

Despite knowing it, I find myself leaning forward and brushing my lips against hers. Her fingers tighten in my hair as she takes the kiss deeper.

Groaning, I pull back. I make sure she's steady on her feet before I let go of her and drop back onto the couch.

She sits down beside me, looking down at her hands. I don't want her to feel like I don't want her, but I'm pretty sure this isn't a line we should cross. She has enough going on in her life that she doesn't need any more complications.

I sit, white-knuckled, on the couch as she inches closer and closer to me. I've just about managed to restrain myself tonight, other than that one slip, but denying myself isn't really in my nature. That doesn't stop me being aware of the fact that she's seventeen, and technically she's my student. That's what I need to keep reminding myself.

But putting her off-limits just makes me want her even more, and I didn't think that was possible.

I take a deep breath, trying to calm myself down, but she

stands back up and turns to look at me. Her skirt flares a little as she spins, and sweet baby Jesus, that skirt. She puts her hands on her hips as she looks down at me.

"Really?"

I swallow, blinking up at her. "What?"

She rolls her eyes and faster than I can object, she steps forward and literally drops onto my lap. Straddling me, looking down at me from where she's seated. I try to count back from ten, to focus on anything but the fact that she's right there, her hands on my chest, looking at me like I'm the only thing in the world she wants.

If someone found out about this…

My cock strains against my sweatpants as she wiggles on my lap. If she keeps that up, I'm going to turn into a goddamn teenage boy and come right in my fucking pants. I grasp her hips to keep her still, and she smiles at me.

"Vixen."

She grins again and grinds against me.

Leaning forward until she's pressed against me, she touches her lips to mine and my resistance snaps.

My arms band around her, pulling her closer against me, and I kiss her like she's all I need to breathe.

I'm acutely aware of everything about her. Her scent— sweet vanilla and honey—creeps up my nose and weakens my already precarious control. Her hands are on the back of the couch just inches from my head, and her tits press against me, but I restrain myself, making sure to keep my hands clasped around her waist.

Mostly, it's the heat coming from what I'm imagining is a seriously wet fucking pussy. I can't think of a better way to die than this, but fuck my life, I don't want to until I've at least had a taste of her. As delicious as her mouth is right now, I want to know what her pussy tastes like. I want to bury my tongue deep inside her and kiss her there just as I'm kissing her mouth.

My fingers curl tighter around her waist and without consciously thinking about it, I pull her closer, kiss her deeper, and moan a little louder from the feel of her all around me.

Faster and faster, V rubs against me like a cat needing release, and I'm the only asshole in this place with a conscience who refuses to touch her.

My dick hurts from how hard I am, from the friction of her all over me, from the need I won't allow myself to indulge. It all hurts. This fucking situation, this reality we have to live in, every fucking thing about this life sucks ass, and not in a good way.

Fuck, now I'm thinking about her ass and this is not good. Not fucking good at all.

"East, please."

Christ, how am I supposed to deny her? Her lips are gliding from one corner of my mouth to the other, her begging words a mere whisper across my kiss-swollen lips.

"I can't, V. I want to, but I can't."

If I thought she'd back off, maybe give me a little breathing room so I don't fucking come in my sweats, I was dead wrong. Instead, this little minx doesn't relent and rubs even harder, her resolve a clear message.

She wants me to make her come.

Fine.

Just because I refuse to take advantage of her, doesn't mean she can't have pleasure, right?

*Right?*

With one hand at her waist holding her down and close to my aching cock, I bury my other in her hair, fisting her long, dark locks right at her nape. She's trapped in my grasp, my prisoner in this very precarious moment. Yet her breathing kicks up, her thighs squeeze mine, and her breaths against my mouth are shallow and quick.

All the signs are there—she wants me as much as I need her—but I will not be a selfish asshole, not for this.

Our mouths slam back together, our tongues fighting out our baser instincts. We are just lust and chemistry, our bodies calling one to the other while my mind tries to slam on the brakes to no avail.

"Please, East. I want you so bad."

Fuck my fucking life.

"I can't, V. I just... I can't." Jesus Christ, how did I get myself into this mess? This perfect, irresistible mess.

Instead of hearing my silent pleas, the universe decides to

up the ante. Octavia fucking Royal doubles down and starts grinding my already painful cock like she's trying to get off on that alone.

My head is leaning against the back of the couch, her mouth no longer on mine, and when I open my eyes, the sight before me is nothing short of spectacular. The hand at her nape falls to her waist, and I watch in utter awe as she transforms into a full-blown woman with carnal needs.

Head thrown back—her throat deliciously exposed—her face bathed in pleasure as her clothed pussy rubs freely around the hard ridge of my dick. She looks every inch the queen I've always known she would become.

My resolve is holding on by a thin, frayed thread that could snap any second, but instead of doing the right thing and pushing her off of me, I lift my hips just a tiny bit and give her the pressure she needs. This is fine, right? I'm not technically doing anything wrong. She's getting herself off, I'm just the means to her own end.

Until, that is, she snaps her head back up, fists her hand in my black t-shirt, and rests her forehead on mine before she says the words that nearly break me.

"With or without your help, I'm gonna come very soon. Please, East, make me feel good."

Fuck. This. Shit.

V is every man's dirty little fantasy. My ultimate fantasy, wearing a schoolgirl uniform and begging to be fucked. How

I'm resisting her is beyond my comprehension.

Sliding one hand down her pleated skirt and up her silky thigh, I expect to find cotton underwear, something that acts as some kind of barrier, helping me to backtrack from what I'm about to do.

I should have known better because what my fingers feel is a whole new temptation.

Satin.

Smooth, hot, and wet. She's been doing such a good job using my covered dick as her own personal toy that she's soaked her silk panties.

Fucking soaked.

Christ, I'm not going to survive this.

Using one finger to pull aside her panties, I allow myself to slide my index finger along the smooth lips of her pussy, gathering her wetness and using it to rub her clit around and around.

Fuck, I can smell her. Her need and her want. I'm doing this to her, and it gives me a sense of power I've never felt before.

"Yes, East. God yes."

This is for her. It's all for her.

V keeps grinding up against my cock while I rub even circles around her clit, watching her breathing grow shallow, her chest rising and falling with every intake and exhalation of air. Her eyes fluttering closed as her lashes caress her cheeks.

Her mouth, her fucking mouth—with swollen lips from my

fucking kisses—parts just enough for me to imagine my dick sliding inside and coming right down her throat.

"Fuck!" My dick hurts in all the best ways.

"Yes!" That one word breathing out from between her lips is like a fucking detonator.

"Don't stop, East, please don't..." As V accelerates her movements over the hard length of my cock, she chants out my name over and over again until I can feel the tingling in my lower stomach that tells me I'm about to fucking lose it.

But I resist. I'm no thirteen-year-old watching porn for the first time, I can control myself.

That is until she grabs my hand and pushes two of my fingers and one of hers inside her pussy, fucking our joint hands like she's about to lose her ever loving mind.

Which is exactly what I do when I feel her walls constrict around my fingers and her juices coating my skin.

I gasp as my hips instinctively thrust up like I'm fucking her, my fingers doing the job my dick would much rather be doing.

As her moans turn into a cry of ecstasy, I feel my own wetness coat my dick.

So much for control.

It would seem that when it comes to Octavia fucking Royal, I have none.

# EIGHT

## OCTAVIA

This week, so far, has been strangely quiet. I still haven't seen Blair or Raleigh, and happy as I am about it, I'm suspicious as fuck. I swear I keep ducking around corners, waiting for someone to jump out at me and attack.

I don't know if the guys finally managed to call Blair and the bitch squad off, or if Blair just isn't around this week, but considering it's homecoming week, I can't imagine she'd miss it. Especially since I was nominated for Queen.

I'm half expecting her to tar and feather me, if I'm being honest. Even if I can't think of anything worse than being crowned homecoming queen, being the center of attention like that… just nope. I've had enough attention to span a few lifetimes. I'm done with it. I'd happily fade into the background for the rest of time, please and thank you.

I head to my locker after my Stats class and find Indi waiting there for me. I smile as I open it, sliding my books in before grabbing my purse. "Cafeteria or Penny's?"

She grins at me. "I would love to say Penny's, but I need to hit the library. I have a test after lunch, so swing by the cafeteria then study?"

"Sounds good to me. God knows I've got plenty to catch up on." I bite my lip, mentally going over what I need to hand in before Thanksgiving break in a couple weeks. Fuck my life. I'm basically going to do nothing but study between now and then.

It could be worse, I guess.

I just wish I didn't have everything else crowding my mind. Focusing on school and keeping my grades up is proving hard enough as it is. We head to the cafeteria as Indi tells me about her morning. She opens the door and steps inside before pausing. I almost run into the back of her. About to ask her why she stopped, I look up and realize why.

The cafeteria is in full homecoming mode.

"As you all know, the court will be present at the football game on Friday night, remember to get your votes in for your King and Queen. This might just be the most important decision you make all year."

I snort a laugh at the declaration and everyone turns to stare at us. Apparently laughing when it's this quiet was a bad idea. Mikayla glares at me from the makeshift stage she has set up in here. Apparently the bitch squad *is* at school. I've just missed them.

Definitely not sad about that.

I nudge Indi forward, looping my arm through hers as I drag her to the line so we can grab food and escape as quickly as possible. Everyone stares at us until Mikayla starts droning on about the dance again.

"Remind me why we thought going to homecoming with these assholes would be fun."

"You're going to homecoming?" I jump at the sound of Maverick's voice, groaning when I turn and see the grin on his face.

I turn back to get food as quickly as I can, and Indi follows suit.

"Don't make me ask again, princess," Mav growls slowly as he moves into my space, his front flush with my back. I can hardly breathe, and I don't even have to look around to know that every set of eyes in the room is on us. I can fucking feel them.

"I don't have to answer your questions. You sure as hell never answer any of mine." I say it quietly enough that I know he heard it, but it's unlikely anyone else did. He growls in my ear and grips my arm, but I tear it free.

"Yes, we, as in Indi and I, are going to homecoming." I sigh, deciding this isn't worth the attention it's garnering as I pay for my sandwich, chips, and soda before moving out of the line to wait for Indi.

Maverick steps back from me, the room still so quiet you could hear a pin drop, as he drops to his knees. "Octavia Royal, will you go with me to homecoming?"

That cheeky glint in his eye matched with his smile makes me want to laugh. Especially after everything we spoke about over the weekend. There's no way he can be serious.

"Not a chance in hell. I told you, I already have a date."

At my rejection, the whispers start in the room and Maverick almost looks sad. I didn't know psychopaths could feel sadness. I link arms with Indi and head out of the cafeteria as she giggles beside me, looking back over our shoulders.

"Well, that was definitely something."

I look behind us and see him still on his knees, grinning at me sadistically. "It was, though I might have just poked the bear."

I smile internally, because maybe this is the way to get answers? Play them at their own game? I'm clutching at straws, so it's probably a terrible idea, but I tuck it away as an unlikely maybe.

We stop by our lockers before heading to the library and I fill her in on my Sunday morning with Mav, lazing around the pool enjoying the last of the summer sun that the weekend brought, even though the grounds guy was around cleaning the pool and stuff. I definitely took advantage of him offering to do my lotion and parading around half naked. Even if it did look like he'd had only about an hour's sleep.

Funnily, I feel closer to him than I do the others. Maybe it's 'cause we messed around, just hung out like I'd thought we would when I came back, but there was something just… different about him. He seemed lighter, and I felt safe around him.

Not something I thought I would say a few months ago. Especially not after the whole knife incident. With everything else going on, I'm leaning toward just letting some stuff go. Lord knows my plate is piling high enough without holding onto anger. Yes he did some bad shit and I still want answers, but it was fun to just hang out with him and not have a million things hanging over us. Forgiveness has never come easy to me, but it's time to put my big girl panties on and just get on with shit.

"He made it more than obvious he's not opposed to jumping into bed together again, too." I laugh as we sit at our usual table in the library.

Indi exhales a drawn out "Oooh," as she sits and I laugh.

"Well, I mean, you did say it was the best orgasm ever." She grins as a smile dances on my lips.

She's not wrong. I did say that. Though, after sampling what the others had to offer too…

I get lost in my own mind, letting that dumb horny bitch part of my brain take over and only return to the real world when she snaps her fingers in my face.

"You've been holding out on me haven't you? That was the

face of a well-pleased woman."

I shush her as I feel a blush spill across my cheeks. "Maybe."

"Girl, you had better spill."

"We're supposed to be studying," I say, trying to wave her off as the librarian glares at us from across the room. "Later," I mouth to her, and she gives me a look that says that's a conversation she isn't going to let slide.

I pull my Business text book from my bag and drop it on the table with a thud. Might as well take the time to catch up while I can. Especially with that F still looming over my head.

Mr. Peters can eat his own dick, 'cause I'm sure as hell not going to.

I cannot believe it's Saturday already and that tonight is homecoming. This week has been a whirlwind. I swear it was only Monday yesterday. I honestly don't know where the days have gone.

Indi is due over any minute. We have a full day of full-scale pamper treatments planned. Smithy is cooking as we speak, he has sparkling apple juice for us because, bless his heart, he didn't think champagne was suitable. He is just too precious. I booked someone to come and do mani-pedis for us, hair and makeup. The whole nine yards.

I might not be that bothered about this whole homecoming

thing, but Indi has practically bounced with excitement all week. I still can't quite believe she's never been to a dance before.

What I do know is that there's no way I won't be seeing Raleigh or Blair tonight. They're both also in the homecoming court which, considering he tried to rape me, is a fucking joke. But I guess that's just Echoes Cove Prep tied up in a bow, really.

I bounce down the stairs in my robe, only shorts and a tank beneath the fluffy goodness, and head into the kitchen where Smithy is in full chef mode.

"Morning, Smithy!"

"Good morning, Miss Octavia. How are we feeling today?"

"We are bright and sunshiny. Ready to spend the day with Indi getting our girl on."

He chuckles at me, shaking his head, "You do say some of the darndest things, Miss Octavia. I also spoke to Master Saint, who asked me to let you know that your ride to the dance tonight is sorted."

That motherfucker.

I don't let my smile drop though; Smithy wasn't to know and I refuse to let those boys rain on my parade today. "Which Saint?"

The words are practically dripping with saccharine sweetness as I flutter my lashes up at him. He gets a little flustered and heads back to the stove. "Master Lincoln."

"Thank you for letting me know."

"Of course, I'm just glad that you seem to have made up

with them all. It's not good for a girl to be alone so much and an old man like me isn't the best of company."

I move to stand beside him, nudging his arm with my shoulder.

"Best old man I know." I smile up at him and he blushes a little. "Oh! I knew I had to ask you something. Do you have plans for Thanksgiving?"

"Not yet, Miss Octavia, though I suppose I should start thinking about it since it's only just under a week away!" He seems flustered all over again, which definitely wasn't my intention.

"Well, if you're going to be home, I was wondering if you'd mind if I invited some friends over. People from the tour. People who knew Dad. I thought it would be a nice way to celebrate this year."

He gazes down at me warmly before wrapping an arm around my shoulders and hugging me tightly. "That sounds perfect. Just let me know numbers, and I'll begin the preparations."

"You're the best, Smithy. Thank you."

"Anything for you, Miss Octavia. How long until Miss Indi arrives? The bagel boats are nearly done."

I practically drool at the sound of that. I don't know what a bagel boat is, but I am here for it. I check my phone and see a message from Indi.

Indi

On my way! Driving in pj's is weird AF!

I laugh at the message and see it was sent a few minutes ago. "She'll be here any second," I tell him, and he smiles, nodding as he pulls the bagels from the oven.

My God, they smell divine.

The bagel bread is squished to the sides to make a little river inside, filled with egg, cheese, bacon, green onion and then topped with more cheese, baked until they're gooey breakfast beautifulness.

I really am so very lucky to have him in my life, and not just because of the amazing food he keeps feeding me. Without him, I'd still be stuck with my aunt and uncle. I can't think of a fate much worse.

The buzzer at the gate goes off, and I hit the button on my app to let Indi in. I do a little dance as I skip to the door.

"It's dance day, bitches!" she squeals as she bounds up the stairs, her dress bag in hand. She hugs me tight before bouncing into the foyer.

"If you want to hang your dress in there," I say, pointing to the security room, "Smithy is just serving up breakfast."

"Smithy is a *GOD!* Is that what smells so good?"

"Yes, yes it is." I grin and she drops her dress in the security room and runs past me into the kitchen. I hear her squeal again as she says hello to him and laugh softly as I hit the button to close the gate before following her.

We enjoy breakfast and the sparkling apple juice just in time for the mani-pedi girls to arrive. The morning of pampering is divine and I adore just how much Indi is loving it. She is my little ball of happiness, and I am here for it all.

When our mani-pedis are done, Smithy reappears. "Afternoon tea, anyone?"

He holds two cake tiers full of tiny cakes and sandwiches. It's freaking adorable.

"You are my favorite person ever!" Indi beams at him as he brings the tiers in and places them on the coffee table. He disappears and returns with a tray of tea cups, a teapot, sugar cubes, and a little jug of cream.

"You didn't have to do this!" I exclaim, though I am not so secretly loving it.

He just waves me off. "This is just an easy lunch. Enjoy, girls, let me know if you need me."

"You can join us if you like," I offer but he shakes his head.

"I've got a few errands to run, but I'm just at the end of the phone. I'll be back before you leave for the dance." He waves before heading back into the kitchen and we dig in.

"Dude, these tiny sandwiches are so soft." Indi grins as she shoves another one in her mouth and I start laughing.

"I wouldn't know. These tiny white chocolate and raspberry blondies are freaking divine and I don't plan on sampling your adult food. Give me dessert or give me death." I stuff another one in my mouth to prove my point. "You sure you wanna go to this thing tonight? I'm pretty sure Smithy will feed us all day long if we really want."

"Hush," she says, waving me off. "We are going to that dance, dammit. We are going to be the belles of the ball, and you are going to be queen."

I groan at the thought, "Please do not tempt fate."

"I can feel it in the air. Octavia Royal, Queen of Echoes Cove Prep." She grins as I groan again.

Someone please save me.

The day passes in a blur of happiness. Of stupid antics and laughter. By the time I'm slipping into my dark-green dress, I find myself wondering where the day has gone. I walk out of my bathroom and find Indi struggling with the strings of the corset on her dress. "Want a hand?"

She spins and gasps when she sees me. "Girl, you are *fire*!"

I laugh at her assessment and motion for her to turn around so I can do her up. "You're not exactly the pumpkin of this ball, yourself."

She grins at me in the mirror as I help her and do the strings on her corset-topped tutu dress. "Oh yeah, we'd totally get it."

I burst out laughing at her assessment, though she isn't wrong. When we went shopping for these dresses, I was just having fun with it, but we definitely made some choices that brought out the best in us. Her vivid locks are a shocking contrast to her pale skin and dark dress. Put together with a vampy eye and dark purple lipstick, she's rocking that emo chic look most girls would kill to pull off.

"What shoes are you wearing?" I ask as I smooth down the front of my emerald satin dress. I check my hair once more. The front is pinned away from my face and the rest of my dark locks cascade down my spine in curls, brushing against the bare skin of my back. This dress makes me thankful for tit tape, because without it I'd never pull it off.

"Docs, of course." She grins and I turn my attention back to her, barking out a laugh. "A girl needs some comfort."

"Yes, yes she does." I pull out a pair of Choos from my closet. They're not so high that I'll break my neck, and they're so freaking pretty. I grab a black clutch to match the shoes before turning back to Indi. "Okay, I'm ready. You good?"

"Hell yes I am, let's get our dance on!" She throws her hands in the air and does a little jig on the spot before leading us from the room. She dances all the way down the hall but pauses at the top of the stairs. "Umm… V?"

I come to stand beside her and see why she stopped.

Four very delicious, and mostly unwanted, guys stand in the foyer of the house fully suited and booted.

Well *shit*.

All eyes are on me as I descend the stairs, trying not to scowl at the four of them. I turn to Mav first. "I thought I told you no."

I fold my arms over my chest, quirking a brow at him, just as Indi lands beside me.

"You did. I chose not to listen." He grins at me. "And damn am I glad I did. You look good enough to eat, princess."

I glance from him to Finn who smiles softly, to East who looks more than a little sheepish, then to Linc who just looks bored.

"Are you ready to go? The car is waiting," Linc says, his tone as bored as his countenance.

I roll my eyes at him and turn to Indi. "You good riding with them? If not, I'll just drive like we planned."

"No, no. I'm good." She grins, so I bend down and slip my shoes on. The boys head outside and Indi grabs my arm to hold me back. "If they don't want a peek of your kitty cat in that dress, I'll eat my own damn kitty cat."

I burst out laughing at her and the guys turn to face us, making her blush.

"Well, they can just keep wanting," I say, winking at her. "Let's go!"

I take her hand and yell out a goodbye to Smithy before heading out. Finley offers me a hand to help me step into the limo, kissing the inside of my wrist as I take it. His lips are a scorching heat on my skin.

I slide into the car and Indi climbs in behind me, followed by the guys.

They talk quietly amongst themselves during the drive. If they were going to ignore us, why even bother asking us to ride with them? They seem to be arguing, so I turn the music up and have a mini party in the backseat with Indi instead. Tonight is not about them or the chaos we seem to be tangled up in. Tonight is about a night with my bestie.

When we pull up at the school, it's like there's been a freaking transformation outside of the gym. The trees that line the back steps up to the entryway are wrapped with twinkle lights and music spills through the doors. Indi practically vibrates in her chair as someone opens the door and she slides out.

"Thanks for the ride." I wink at Mav and follow Indi out, taking her hand once I'm standing straight again. "Let's go rock this, shall we?"

We strut inside, and it really is a full transformation. There's a makeshift stage that holds a few guitars, a drum set, a keyboard, and a couple of horns, while a DJ plays from his decks. There are all sorts of tables in here, living up to the 007 casino theme. There's poker, blackjack, craps, and a ton of other stuff I don't recognize.

"Dance or gamble?" I ask Indi. She stares longingly at the dance floor. "Dance it is!"

After dancing until my feet feel like they're going to fall off, I tap Indi's shoulder and prepare to slink over to a free table. These shoes might be beautiful, but they are not built for dancing, that much is for sure.

I start to move away from Indi just as a hush settles across the room, despite the music. Looking over to the main doors, my jaw drops.

"Umm, Indi?" I grab her and turn her so she can see what I see: the three drop dead gorgeous bad boys dressed up in suits that just crashed our dance. "Isn't that…"

She nods, gulping. "Yes, yes it is."

I look at her, my eyes wide. "Well, I guess the message about you not doing the chasing was fully received."

She smiles at me, blushing a little.

"And fuck anyone who says a thing. Trust me on this, whoever says shit is just jealous as fuck." I push her in their direction just a little. She glances over her shoulder at me and I motion for her to go to them as they walk toward us. Ryker leads them, Ellis and, who I assume is Dylan, flanking him on either side.

If she wasn't my bestie, I might almost be jealous. Instead, I am just insanely happy for her.

I drop into one of the chairs at my recently claimed table as the song changes and everyone loses their minds as the bass drops. I kick off my shoes and discreetly rub one of my feet under the table.

"You having fun?" I look up as East slides into the chair beside me.

"Should you be seen talking to me?" I tease. He frowns.

"I'm technically a chaperone. I can talk to whoever I want.

Just like I talk to you in class."

I roll my eyes at him. I get he's on edge about what we did, but it's not like I'm going to tell anyone. I just wish he wasn't acting like he regretted it. He's barely spoken to me all week, even in class. "I was joking. You know, giving you shit?"

I get up and head to the drinks table where Maverick finds me. "I wouldn't touch the punch if I were you." He smiles down at me, wrapping an arm over my shoulders. "Want to get out of here?"

"Maverick Riley, what on earth makes you think I want to leave this dance, and with you of all people?" His grin widens at my words.

He stoops down to whisper in my ear, "Oh I can think of a lot of reasons, princess."

I blush a little at his insinuation.

"Did I tell you yet that you look good enough to eat?"

I cough, trying not to laugh at just how cheesy he is. "Yes, you did. But all women like to be told they're pretty, so thank you."

His hand brushes across the bottom of my back, skimming just above where the material of my dress sits above my ass, sending a shiver down my spine.

Nope. Not today, Satan.

And definitely not here.

I remove myself from his grasp and take a step back. "What are you doing?"

"Being friendly," he says, wagging his eyebrows at me.

I roll my eyes at him, because despite the good day we had over the weekend… I'm still not ready to forgive him. "We're not friends, Maverick. You made sure of that."

"We could be friends though. You're going to forgive me one day."

"Maybe." I shrug. "But today is not that day and I am not that bitch. And until you guys start answering my questions, or even just fucking respecting me, that isn't going to change."

I walk away from him and head to the bathroom, catching a glimpse of Indi dancing like a loon on the dance floor as I leave.

The bathroom is empty when I enter, so I close the door to the stall and just lean back against it, trying to catch my breath. These boys are going to give me whiplash if they keep going back and forth like they are.

Lincoln might drive me to insanity, but at least he's mostly consistent with his iceman routine. He's even stopped sneaking into my bed since that night with Raleigh. I don't pretend to know what's going on in that head of his.

When I came back, I wanted nothing more than to reconnect with them. But too much has happened now, and I'm not sure that's what I want anymore. Beyond the occasional mind-blowing orgasm anyway.

How does a girl get over the things they've done?

I don't even know for sure exactly which bits were them and which bits weren't. But the bits I know for certain are already enough for me to have reservations about ever forgiving them. No matter how much I might want to at times.

I hate how back and forth I am about this; I need to just make a fucking decision and stick to it.

The door to the bathroom opens and the click of heels echoes throughout the room.

Time to head back out I guess.

I'm trying not to regret coming tonight, because Indi is having so much fun, but I was right. School dances really aren't my thing. Taking a deep breath, I head out of the stall and come face to face with Blair, Mikayla, Serena, and Emma.

Oh awesome. Just what I needed to make this night better. If I had to guess, I'll find Brittany outside the door. I try to move past them, but they block the way to the door. "What do you want?"

"I warned you, Octavia. I warned you on your first day of school. Do you remember what I said?" Blair's shrill voice fills the silence of the room, and I wince at just how hysterical she sounds.

I resist rolling my eyes at her, and let out a sigh. "No, Blair, I don't remember what you said. It was a hot minute ago."

Despite the truth of my words, they just seem to anger her further. She clenches her fists at her sides, practically vibrating with rage. "I told you that this was my school. That I was queen, and that you had better remember it."

"Oh that." I sigh, "I don't want your school or your crown,

Blair. You can have them. Now if I can just leave, please. I'll get out of your hair."

She smiles at me, looking almost possessed and maniacal as her eyes go wide. "I have a better idea in mind."

The four of them rush at me and we all go down in a tangle of limbs. I try to fight them off, but apparently being cheer barbie gives you more muscles than my pathetic attempts at working out recently.

"Get the fuck off me!" I shout, and Blair just laughs again as she basically sits on my chest while the others hold my arms and legs.

This is fucking insane.

"I'll teach you to take what is mine. It was all meant to be mine. *They* were meant to be mine but you just ruined everything! And now I'm going to ruin you!" She pulls a pair of scissors from her clutch, and my eyes go wide before I struggle against them even harder.

She cackles before grabbing a handful of my hair and starts snipping. I scream until my throat is hoarse, but no one comes to help me. I don't give a fucking inch though.

"You're going to regret this, Blair," I shout as she makes her last cut.

She laughs dryly as she drops the scissors and pulls a Sharpie from her purse. "There isn't anything left that you can do to me. I already lost everything."

She grabs my cheeks and uses the Sharpie to write on my

forehead before slapping me on the face twice.

"Suck on that, homecoming queen."

They clamber off of me and I scream, jumping up and lunging after them, but they yell and run from the room. I growl in frustration as they reach the gym and enter as if nothing happened. I storm back to the bathroom to grab my bag so I can get my phone, and I get a look at the damage they've done. I lock the door before turning to face the mirror, not wanting to be interrupted while I bathe in my shame.

My long, dark locks hang in uneven lengths around my shoulders, the word 'Slut' smeared across my forehead. I blink back tears of anger because I refuse to cry.

There is no way they will see me fucking cry.

I try to call Indi, but it goes to voicemail so I send her a text instead. I hate pulling her from her guys right now, but selfishly, I need my bestie.

Me

SOS. Bitch Squad got me. I need to head home.

I try to scrub the marker from my forehead but it won't come off. I bark out a dry laugh. Of course it won't. My phone pings on the counter and Indi's name flashes on the screen.

"Where are you?" she asks the second I answer.

"In the bathroom."

I hear her footsteps down the line as she walks through the empty halls. "Let me in," she says as a knock sounds on the door.

I end the call and open the door. She gasps when she sees me, covering her mouth with her hand. "Oh, V."

"I know. I just… I need to go home," I say, my throat thick with emotion, still trying not to cry because it seems ridiculous that this is the thing to push me over the edge. So I do what I vowed I wouldn't and shove it down for the time being.

She wraps me in a hug, but I shake her off. If I let her hug me, I'll cry. "Okay, come on. Let's go. I swear to fucking God, I'm going to burn those bitches to the ground."

I try to smile, because I love how feisty she gets when she's mad, but I just feel beaten.

"I'm sorry, I don't want to ruin your night…" I trail off and she pulls me to a stop making me face her.

"V, boys will come and go, but best bitches are for life. You have nothing to be sorry for. I'm sorry I wasn't here to help you."

A lump forms in my throat as I shake my head, trying to tell her that she has nothing to be sorry for, but words don't come. I managed to stay strong through so much. I thought I could survive it all, but I was wrong. I thought I'd finally made it past everything. I was beginning to have hope, and now…

I open the door and come face to face with Lincoln, whose gaze scours me from head to toe.

That's when a tear slips down my cheek. I wipe it away quickly, not wanting him to see me cry, but when his eyes narrow, I know I wasn't fast enough.

"Who?"

The one world fills the space between us, but I don't have to say a word. I see it on his face when it comes to him.

Another tear falls and he reaches forward to wipe it away, caressing my cheek. Without another word, he turns on his heel and walks away from me, shoulders rigid as he heads back toward the gym.

Maybe one day Blair will get what's coming to her, but I doubt today will be that day. Regardless, she's officially pushed me over the edge. A war is coming, and whether she thinks she has nothing to lose or not…

I'm going to show her that there is always something more to lose.

# NINE

## OCTAVIA

I take a deep breath as I stare at my reflection in my bathroom mirror. Gracie—Indi's hair woman—is a fucking magician. You can't even really tell I was butchered at the dance. If anything, the extensions just make it look like I had a few layers put into my hair.

Looking the same doesn't stop my simmering rage though. I'm not even sure exactly what I did for Blair to hate me so much; we used to be so close. Our history doesn't stop me from wanting to watch her world crumble. Not at this point.

I am so done being the victim in her story. She started this, but I'm sure as fuck going to end it. I just need to bide my time and work out what is going to hurt her the most.

I finish getting ready for school and head downstairs. As I

go to open the fridge, I notice a note from Smithy, telling me he's gone grocery shopping and he'll see me later. Inside, I find a smoothie along with a berry box waiting for me.

He is too good to me.

I notice the time and practically inhale my breakfast before rushing out of the house. I drive like a crazy person to make sure I get to school on time, finding Indi standing beside her Wrangler in her usual spot. I pull into my space, practically jumping from the car, flustered. Not exactly how I wanted to start the day.

*Just three days until Thanksgiving break. We've got this.*

She beams at me and hands me my coffee. "Your hair looks fucking amazing. I'm so glad that Gracie did such a good job for you."

"Me too." I smile before taking a sip of the hot mocha goodness. "I never put myself down as a vain person, but apparently I was wrong."

We head into school and come face to face with Blair and her bitch squad. I put on my fiercest smile, enjoying the shock on their faces when I'm not the hot mess they expected me to be this morning. We breeze past them and I give them a little finger wave while Indi giggles beside me.

Okay, so that might not be the revenge I'm craving, but it definitely felt good. I don't even care if it's petty as fuck. "Do you have any plans tonight?"

She looks up at me from her phone and shakes her head,

"No, I saw the guys yesterday while you were with Gracie, so my night is free and clear. What did you have in mind?"

"We are one hundred percent coming back to you and the guys in a moment, don't think you're getting off the hook with that, missy," I tease, and she blushes a little, "but I was thinking of an all night homework and cram session to prepare for all the things we have to hand in this week before break. I'm so freaking behind. I swear, next semester, drama or not, I *need* to put my school work first."

She nods as I grab my books. "Sounds good. I've got a ton to do, too."

"Perfection."

We make our way down the hall to her locker so she can grab her things before heading to English, where Miss Summers is already waiting for us.

"Morning, girls!" She beams at us as we enter the room.

We head to the back of the room and take our seats. The bell hasn't rung yet, so I take the opportunity to interrogate her. "So. Boys. Weekend. Spill the tea."

She blushes again, hiding her face behind her hair. "Well, after they showed up at the dance and basically begged my forgiveness, we decided to just hang out on Sunday. It was weird being their main focus again. I forgot how intense they can be."

I fan my face and she laughs. "Yeah, but the best kind of intense I bet."

"You could say that." She sighs happily, and I smile.

"Hey, as long as you're happy, I'm happy. But if they hurt you, I'll bring the shovels. I know how to get rid of a body or three."

She bursts out laughing just as the bell sounds and we turn our attention to Miss Summers, who starts talking about our exam coming up before Christmas break next month. Groans chorus around the room and I try to calm the spike of anxiety that makes my heart pound in my chest.

I've fallen so behind with all of my school work thanks to everything that's been going on. Despite my stubbornness that I wasn't going to let any of it mess with me... it already has. I try to focus on Miss Summers as she talks about what's going to be covered on the exam, but my mind goes down the rabbit hole of just how much shit I have to get done to not just pass my classes, but also meet the terms of my dad's will.

Usually the money thing wouldn't bother me too much, but the thought of losing the house, of Smithy being without, of potentially no college—nothing—until I turn twenty-five is enough to have me spinning out. When I first heard the terms of the will, I wasn't too deterred. I've never had a problem with my grades. But with everything that's happened, alongside adjusting to freaking mainstream schooling, it hasn't been great.

I'm so fucked.

I spiral for so long that the bell rings before I realize the class is even over.

Fuck my life.

"Please tell me you took notes," I hiss to Indi, who nods, looking more than a little concerned. "Awesome. Time to go face Mr. Peters."

"I still think you should report him." She frowns as I shudder, thinking about his gross proposal.

"There's no point, who would believe me?" I shrug, hating that he'll get away with it. That he might do it to someone else. But he hadn't been wrong about that part: no one would believe me.

She looks like she wants to say more, but as we leave the class, I almost run straight into Lincoln, Maverick, and Finley.

"I'll see you at lunch?" I say to Indi, who nods, her gaze bouncing between me and them. I smile at her, trying to reassure her that I'll be okay. She turns and heads down the hall in the opposite direction I need to go. "Can I help you?"

I move out of the doorway and head toward Business when none of them respond. They trail behind me like guard dogs and everyone scurries out of our path as we make our way to the class. It's not even unnerving.

God, the sarcasm in my own head needs to come down a notch.

I enter the classroom for Business and come face-to-face with Mr. Peters. I've managed to avoid being alone with him, or even in close contact, since that day. This is the closest I've been to him since he practically waved his dick at me like a flag.

"Miss Royal," he says, his eyes raking over my body,

making me feel as dirty as I would if I'd bathed in blood and dirt.

I feel the heat at my back as the guys catch up with me. Mr. Peters' eyes go wide and he takes a step back, as if he's flustered. I don't even care that he did that purely because of their arrival, there has to be some upsides of these assholes hovering around me. I take advantage of the situation and scurry over to my desk. Once I'm seated, I look up and find Mr. Peters is caught in a battle of wills with Lincoln and they're staring each other down.

Mr. Peters looks away first, and I smile as I look down at my text book. I hate that Lincoln is a giant asshole ninety-nine percent of the time, but just this once, I kind of love it.

The bell rings again and they finally move, allowing the rest of our class to filter into the room once they take their seats.

I guess someone did believe me after all.

I pull up at home, grinning wide. Last night was a whirlwind of catching up and essay writing, and today has been a day of avoiding the guys, Blair, and… well, everyone that isn't Indi, as much as possible.

Now school is almost done for the week and we have a long weekend to look forward to, I just need to survive tomorrow, then I'm free for four whole days.

I am too excited to see everyone. Jenna messaged me

yesterday to confirm that the whole gang is definitely still coming. Smithy has been rushing around like a crazy person to get everything ready, even though I offered to have it catered.

He looked like I stomped on his puppy at the suggestion, so I didn't bring it up again.

It might only be Tuesday, but the thought of having all of my found family together under my roof is too exciting. Indi even managed to persuade her mom to let her stay here over the next few days, rather than heading back east with them to see their family.

I just need to finish setting up the guest room for her.

I bounce into the house, excited butterflies taking flight in my stomach. "I'm home!"

"In the kitchen," Smithy hollers back, and I grin as I head in the direction of his voice. With how much time the man spends in here, I'm beginning to think he sleeps under the table.

I find him arm deep in pie crust, with five pie dishes already lined with pastry. "Do we have enough pie?"

"Well, I thought I'd do pecan, but nut allergies, so I did key lime, which led me to pumpkin. Then I remembered lemon meringue is your favorite, so I added that too, and well... I added a lemon tart and a chocolate and raspberry torte to the menu too. Because why not?" He grins at me like this is truly his happy place. Who am I to stop a man keeping me stocked in pie?

"I'm sure it'll be amazing. Do you need me to do anything?"

He shakes his head. "Not a thing. My kitchen doesn't need

that sort of punishment," he teases and I laugh. "Plus, I might have invited the Saint boys over since Mrs. Potts is away for the long weekend and their father... well, let's not discuss him, shall we? Mrs. Potts is going to help me prep some more dishes tomorrow before she leaves. I hope you don't mind."

"No, it's fine," I say, my heart sinking just a little. I suck it up though, because he doesn't ask for much, and despite my topsy turvy feelings toward the brothers, it'll be nice to have a full house. "Indi will be heading over Thursday morning and she'll be with us until Sunday night."

"Sounds perfect, Miss Octavia. Do you have many plans for tonight?"

"Just finishing up some more school work, so I'll be around if you need me." I smile at him and take my bag to the living room. I take a quick detour to my room to change before settling in on the floor and spreading my books out over the coffee table.

I work for about an hour until the smells get so distracting that I'm practically drooling over my Business textbook.

The buzzer for the gate sounds, officially pulling me from my studies. "I'll get it!" I yell to Smithy and grab my phone. I frown when I open the app and an empty drive appears on the screen.

Weird.

Getting up, I pad over to the front door and open it to see if there's just something wrong with the camera, but there's still no one at the gate.

Probably just kids fucking around.

Stepping back to close the door, something catches my eye and I freeze. There, at the bottom of the steps, is a small parcel wrapped in manilla paper with my name written on the top.

My stomach churns as my heart pounds. Everything else that comes in that shade of package has been from that creepy stalker fuck, but this isn't an envelope.

My hand shakes as I rush down the steps and reach for the box. I stop before I pick it up, an icy drop of fear running down my spine.

What if it's something that could hurt me?

I take a deep breath and do something I really don't want to do.

I call Lincoln.

He picks up on the third ring, sounding out of breath. I'm too freaked out to think about why. "Lincoln. I'm sorry, I didn't want to call…"

"What's wrong?"

"There's a box on my steps. I don't suppose you guys are playing another weird-ass prank or something are you? 'Cause if not, someone got through my gates. Again."

"I'll be there in two minutes."

The line disconnects and I bounce from one foot to the other, wishing I was wearing something on my feet. I use the cold ground to try to distract myself from whatever could be in the box.

Less than a minute later, he's jogging toward me with the other three hot on his heels. All of them in various states of workout gear or half naked, and I'll be damned if I don't find myself suddenly *very* distracted.

Definitely not the time to ogle them, but it's better that than focusing on the stupid box.

Finn heads straight to me and wraps me up in his arms. "You okay, V?"

"I'm fine, just a little freaked out. Plus Smithy is inside, and I haven't told him about any of this. I didn't want him wrapped up in it all. But I don't know what's in there, and I'm spiraling a little."

He nods before stepping away from me and crouching down to look at the box. Mav hands him a knife which he uses to cut the brown string on the box and the manilla paper falls away, revealing a nondescript white postage box. He cuts through the tape and opens the box.

The lid falls away and I gasp at the contents.

A bloody knife inside a plastic bag, and a note. I reach past Finley to pick up the paper and regret it immediately.

*They can't keep you safe. Not like I can.*
*You'll see*

x

I think I'm going to be sick.

"Whose blood could that be?" Lincoln asks, and I shake my head.

"I have no idea. I have no fucking clue about any of this." I hand him the note and wrap my arms around my waist.

Lincoln turns to East and they murmur between the two of them while Mav strides over to me and runs his hands up and down my arms. "We'll find whoever this sicko is and deal with it. I swear."

I nod, because what else can I do? "I feel like I should be doing something to help find out who it is, rather than sitting around waiting for something to happen."

"I get it, feeling helpless fucking sucks. I'm right there with you, princess, but for now, Lincoln is on it. You know he's like a dog with a bone when it comes to a mystery. He won't let it evade him for long."

I chew on my lip as I consider his words. Maybe I really should go to the police? Or speak to Smithy. He has friends in all sorts of weird and wonderful places.

But what if that makes him a target too?

Lincoln turns and motions to Finley, who picks up the box and heads over to the brothers.

"Come on, let's get you inside. These guys will deal with it. I'll stay with you for a bit."

This might be the softest side to Mav I've seen since I got back, but there's still a hardness behind it, like he's just trying to protect me, and that sets me off balance all on its own.

"We'll be in touch soon," Lincoln says as Mav starts to usher me inside, and I nod, feeling more than a little numb.

Maybe one day my life will be normal, but at this point, I think that's nothing but a dream.

After Smithy's delight at having Maverick around for the evening, we ate, and the two of them chatted up a storm like two friends who had been separated for years. I left them to it and grabbed a shower, throwing on a pair of cutoffs and a hoodie, because comfort is key right now.

I make my way back to my room and find Maverick sprawled out on my bed, grinning wickedly at me.

I definitely shouldn't be thinking about how good he looks, but right now he looks like the perfect kind of escape. He's taken so much from me at this point that I don't even feel bad about taking something for myself.

Especially when I want to feel something other than fear.

I know I shouldn't want him, and I know I definitely shouldn't forgive him, but there is something about Maverick Riley that makes me weak. He makes me feel brazen, like I can take on the world and come out swinging on the other side.

Having him lie there, on my bed, in my space, makes me bold.

I might not have completely forgiven him yet, but that

doesn't mean we can't have fun. I only just lost my virginity, and while I put absolutely zero stock in the whole virgin thing, maybe I shouldn't be messing around with three different guys? I've never had any issues with women owning their sexuality, but I can't help but second guess myself. Especially when it's *these* guys I'm messing around with. Pretty sure I should be avoiding them at all costs. Or at least put up more of a fight. Retaliate against everything they've done… make them work a little harder, or at least give me some of what I want.

"Get out of your head, princess. I know what you're thinking, and trust me everyone is okay with sharing as long as we get to have you. Now, crawl up on this bed with me." The devilish smirk on his face promises even more than the fantasies his words trigger in my mind, and it sparks a fire in me. The challenge in his eyes emboldens me.

Fuck overthinking it.

I sashay across the room, compartmentalizing the events of the evening as I go, and crawl up the bed like he instructed until he's caged in beneath me. Not that I'm taking that for granted. Caging Maverick Riley is like caging a tiger—dangerous as fuck.

He captures my lips with his, pulling me down on top of him until our bodies are flush. "Tell me what you want, princess."

I bite the inside of my lip, considering his words.

"I want to suck your dick."

His eyes go wide at my words, and then he grins that

signature smirk of his. "If you think I'm going to turn that down, you are out of your damn mind."

The next thing I know, Mav has deftly swapped our positions and *I'm* now caged beneath *him*, his eyes burning with what I can only describe as dangerous lust. Unhinged desire. A beast cornering his prey, playing with them, before going in for the kill.

It's exhilarating.

Maybe something is wrong with me. Maybe my fight or flight instinct really is broken. But that look in his eye has me so fucking excited that butterflies take flight in my stomach.

"Just remember, princess, you asked for it."

It's my turn to grin up at him, because fuck it. "Bring it on."

There's a moment, no more than a heartbeat, where I'm almost afraid I've gotten myself into a heap of trouble. Then he leans in and captures my mouth like I'm the last piece of his complicated puzzle. Our tongues battle, each of us fighting for dominance, but it takes less than a second for me to know it's a fight I'm not going to win. He's leading the charge. He's got a plan and it's all I can do to stay caught up. My hands fly up to his black t-shirt and fist the fabric like it'll be able to keep me on solid ground as Mav kisses the breath out of me. His hands hold me so tightly I know he'll leave behind the imprint of his fingers before long. While I know I shouldn't like it, a sharp thrill runs through me at the thought.

When he's done kissing me to the brink of unconsciousness,

he doesn't just stop. No, that would be too normal. Instead, he traps my bottom lip between his teeth and slowly, like time is on his clock, sinks his teeth deep into my flesh until I can taste the iron of my own blood.

It's when he sucks and licks my blood that I admit to myself that Maverick Riley is a man apart from all others.

Maybe my vampire fantasies and all the Anne Rice books I read on the road have finally caught up to me.

As I'm contemplating the situation at hand, I feel Mav's hand gliding beneath the leg of one of my cutoffs before he grabs a handful of ass cheek and winks. Not a flirty wink, though. This one is more of a promise that I might end up regretting what I wished for.

He leans over me and kisses my throat, discarding my shirt as he works his way down, biting, licking, and kissing my flesh, marking me further as he goes. When he pulls back and sees the still-faint line from the cut he made on my chest, his eyes go wide and his pupils dilate.

He likes seeing his marks on my skin.

Goosebumps break out over my entire body under the heat of his blazing stare. "Lie sideways on the bed."

That's it. Those are his only instructions before he's off the bed and standing with one hand at the button of his jeans, his muscles contracting beneath the layers of ink across his skin.

I turn sideways, my feet hanging off the side and my head turned toward the end of the bed, following him as he makes his way to me, unzipping and grinning like he knows a secret and won't tell until the timing is perfect.

His fly is open, revealing *just* enough of his thick cock begging to come out and play.

My mouth waters at the thought and I wonder how he'll taste. Salty or tangy. Will he make me swallow? Would I even consider it?

Mav leans over me, both of his hands on either side of my head, and kisses me upside down. It's strange and different and nothing fits the way it's supposed to. Then again, when it comes to Maverick, nothing ever has.

With one long, lingering swipe of his tongue across my lips, he puts both of his hands on my waist and hauls me up closer until my head is hanging off the side of the bed.

Well, this is weird. And a little uncomfortable, if I'm honest.

"When I fuck your mouth, I want to see my dick in your throat."

Oh.

Maybe I should have thought this through a little more.

"Don't be afraid, princess. You'll love it, I'll make sure of it."

I relax a little. Despite his unhinged tendencies, for some reason, I trust Maverick when it comes to this. Which says more about my state of mind than it does about his.

"Okay."

"Hmm, now open up and show me how much you want my

cock." God, I love his filthy mouth.

With my hair touching the bedroom floor and my fists clenching the bed, I watch Mav from my position as he meticulously takes out his cock then rubs the head across my parted lips.

"Such a pretty, dirty mouth you have." He's watching himself paint my lips with his precum, going round and round like the sight mesmerizes him. "A dirty, filthy mouth fit for a princess. Now, open nice and wide while I fuck the filth right out of it."

I do as I'm told and he slowly—almost delicately—pushes his dick into my mouth. At first he dips in and out in shallow pumps, but I want more.

More of him, of this power that I feel as I watch his eyes turn molten with undeniable fire. The sight of me with my mouth full of his cock is turning him on like nothing else I've seen.

He humors me by pushing a little bit more and staying in a little bit longer.

My gag reflex is starting to work, and I'm afraid I won't be able to go as far as he'd like.

"Breathe through your nose and open up your throat for me, princess."

I try to follow his instructions and soon enough, I've got tears streaming into my hairline. Mav picks one up with his thumb and brings it to his mouth, making a whole production of licking it up.

"Hmm, even your tears are delicious. Now, be a good girl and swallow my dick." Without further warning, he presses the rest of the way forward. Just when I think I'm going to tap out, he places his open palm over my throat and squeezes, practically choking me.

I should be afraid—I should be freaking the fuck out—instead, I'm strangely comforted by his dominance. Like he knows what's best and if I don't fight him, I'll be okay.

We'll be okay.

When he pulls back out of my mouth, his hand squeezes just a little bit tighter around my throat, making my pussy clench with need.

"You like that, don't you? You're fucking soaked for me."

I don't answer, I'm not sure there's even anything to say to that because he's one hundred percent correct.

"The next time I'm fucking your throat, I want you to play with your clit."

"But I don't know if I can—"

"Don't talk back, princess. Do what I tell you."

He's back to circling my lips with his cock just as he leans in to unbutton my shorts and lower the zipper.

"Off."

I shimmy my shorts off and take my underwear with them so that I'm bare when he moves back into position.

The feeling of the blood rushing to my head is making me even hornier, a tingling sensation overtaking my entire bloodstream.

Mav taps the head of his cock on my lips, and I take that as my cue to open up.

Next thing I know, I'm reaching for my clit as Mav's dick is slowly pushed in and down, his hand back at my throat, squeezing even harder.

I concentrate on my breathing, getting used to the feeling of being completely full.

And then he starts to fuck my mouth.

Like, seriously. I can feel everything. Every inch of him as he slides down, the pressure of his palm when he reaches as far as he can go. His balls slapping my face. His scent. Holy shit, his scent is everywhere.

My fingers are frantically working over my clit and my orgasm is about to fucking explode like a furious volcano.

"Goddamn, your fucking mouth. I knew it'd be good, but fucking hell, V."

I can't talk, I can't nod, I can't fucking think.

"I'm gonna come, V. You better fucking swallow every goddamn drop."

My hips fly off the bed at his words, my climax taking over my entire body just as he comes straight down my throat.

I think I'm choking when he pulls his cock out, one hand pumping the last remnants of his cum onto my chin, the other holding me down by the throat.

My body is trembling and my hands fall to my sides as my eyes drift shut, heavy from the effort my orgasm demanded of me.

I swallow everything down as I was instructed, and although I was afraid of this moment, I enjoy every single second of it. So much so that I hungrily swirl my tongue around his thumb when he brushes it across my chin and presses it into my mouth, ensuring I don't waste a single drop.

He's salty and thick and all fucking male.

Breathing heavily like I've just run a marathon, I take a second to get my heart rate down.

Without bothering to tuck himself in, Mav picks me up and cradles me in his arms as he makes his way to the middle of my bed.

After being the beast in my dirtiest fantasies, he becomes the prince who protects me from himself.

Resting my head against his chest as we lie there in silence, I wonder what other parts of himself he's hiding from me.

# TEN

## MAVERICK

I wake up bleary-eyed, having slept deeper than I ever remember doing. I usually only manage about three hours a night, at best, and they're broken as fuck. Blinking against the light spilling into the room as the sun rises, I try to orient myself. I'm so fucking warm I'm practically sweating. I blink a couple more times and realize why as the haze finally lifts from my mind.

V is curled up on my chest, snoring softly. She sounds like a fucking kitten. Except her claws are much sharper than that.

I try not to take too much pride in the marks on her skin. Proof that she is mine. Just seeing it reminds me of the first time I marked her. Dragging my knife between her tits. Just thinking about it makes me hard again.

Extracting myself from her hold is easier than I thought it would be, but leaving her isn't. I don't know what sick motherfucker is messing with her like this, but when I get my hands on him, he's going to regret every decision he's ever made to this point. And if he doesn't, I'll make him bleed until he does.

I glance back at her once as I slip my sneakers back on and head out of the room before jogging through the house. Smithy is sitting in the kitchen sipping a cup of tea as I walk in. He looks up at me over his newspaper, an eyebrow raised. "Master Riley."

"Morning, Smithy," I say, raising a hand and smiling sheepishly. I'm not used to getting caught making a great escape, though usually I don't sleep over. "I'll just, uhm, see myself out."

He grumbles quietly, before looking back down at his paper. I take the opportunity to duck out of the back door. Thankfully the alarm is already disabled. Jogging through the back yard over to Linc's only takes a minute and I check my phone as I let myself in through his kitchen door. I didn't look at it once after I left them to chill with V last night. There's just one message from Linc waiting for me.

Linc

Knife handed over to Lucas. I'll update you when you're back.

Oops.

I shrug and slide the phone back in my pocket as I grab the orange juice from the refrigerator.

"You better not drink that from the carton." East's sleep-filled voice breaks through the silence of the room, and I grin as I lift it to my lips and take a swig. "You're a fucking heathen."

I swallow the juice and replace the lid before putting it back in the fridge. "Tell me something I don't know."

I jump up on the counter as he grabs the eggs from the fridge and pulls a pan from the hooks on the wall. "How was V?"

"Satisfied and sleeping when I left." I grin as he glares at me. "Hey, I know you went there too. We already vowed we'd be open about everything when it comes to her."

"You really think last night was the time?" he scolds, waving a spatula in my direction. He hands me the bread and I drop a few slices in the toaster as he cracks the eggs into the pan and starts to scramble them.

"She seemed to think so. I'm done with trying to think I know what's best for her. I'll leave that to the rest of you."

He mumbles in response, but I'm not surprised. I'm not wrong and he knows it.

"Where's Mrs. Potts? Why are you trying to kill us off with your cooking?"

He glares at me again. "She's sleeping in. She's helping Smithy with Thanksgiving prep today before she leaves for the weekend."

Ahhh Thanksgiving. The one holiday when my parents try

to pretend we're a big happy family. "What are you guys doing for the day? Feel free to come crash Happy Days at my house."

"We're going to V's." My jaw drops at his response.

*The fuck they are.*

I guess my parents are going to be real pissed off this year, because that isn't a day I'm missing. "Count me in, sounds like fun."

"That wasn't an invitation," he growls, just as Linc and Finn enter the room.

"What wasn't?" Finn asks as he sits down at the table.

"These fuckers are spending Thanksgiving with Smithy and V, so I invited myself along." I jump down from the counter as Linc rolls his eyes at me.

"I guess we'll let Smithy know to add two more," Linc says, turning to Finn. "I assume you'll be coming too?"

Finn pauses for a second as if, like me, he's wondering just how much shit he'll get for not being home. But, his parents are worse than mine. Though they don't usually try to pretend like mine do. "Yeah, count me in."

"Awesome." I grin as I drop down next to him at the table. "Now what did I miss last night?"

Linc starts the coffee brewing before he speaks. I swear his veins hold caffeine not blood. Though, he usually sleeps about as much as I do, so it's not surprising. Once he's holding a mug of coffee in his hands, he turns back to face us. "Lucas has the knife; he's running it for prints and DNA to see if this asshole left any traces behind. He's also running the blood to see if we know who that belongs to."

"It's probably pig's blood," I offer. "That's what I'd do if I wanted to freak someone out."

"Maybe," Linc says, nodding, "But for now, we need to play our cards close to our chest. How was she last night?"

East cuts his eyes to me at the question, so I shoot him a shit eating grin before turning back to the others. "She was shook up, but that's to be expected. She's tougher than we give her credit for though. She handled it with more grace than most people we know would."

Lincoln sits at the table as East plates up the eggs. He brings them and the toast over to the table, and I dig in. Linc looks at the food like it offends him. I went without food often enough that I learned to eat when food is there. Whether the eggs taste like rubber or not.

"That's good. Hopefully it's not just a trauma response from something we don't know about. She seems to compartmentalize like a pro," East offers, and Finley frowns at him.

"Do you know something we don't?"

"No, we said we'd be open and transparent about everything to do with her going forward. You know what I do," East says with a sigh. Getting over the secrets we kept from each other these last few months is taking a minute. Everyone's so goddamn possessive and protective when it comes to V, which makes it difficult.

"She knows we all know by the way," I chime in, and they look at me. "She was feeling squirrely about fucking around with all of us." I look at Linc and grin. "Well, most of us. So I told her we were all chill about it. Do *not* make me a liar."

"And what if one of us wants her to ourselves?" East asks, an eyebrow raised.

"We don't make her make that decision," Lincoln adds. "If you're not okay with sharing her, then you don't get her. Unless she makes the decision on her own."

"Dude, you're not even trying with her. Who says you make the rules?" I challenge. I mean, Linc usually makes the rules, but with V, everything is different.

"I never said I was trying with her," he says gruffly, "I said that no one puts that pressure on her. None of us get to keep her anyway."

"I'm chill with that. I mean, I'd like her to myself, but I'd rather have her and share than not at all," Finley agrees before getting up and pouring himself a glass of milk.

"Fine," East says, basically pouting. Sucks to be him, but that's what happens when you hand the mantle of power down to your little brother, I guess. You lose the power that should've been yours. "I'm going to go and get ready. Are you assholes going to school today?"

"Yeah, we'll see you there," Linc says, and it's my turn to frown. I am very much looking forward to never having to go to school ever again. Though I do have one thing on my agenda today. I feel a sadistic smile stretch out across my face.

A day with blood on my hands is always better than one without.

I follow my prey out of the school parking lot on my Ducati when the school day ends, excitement making my heart race. I spent the entire day dreaming up ways to punish this motherfucker for what he did to Octavia.

You could say that others have done worse shit to her, me included, but I'm working on ways to make up for that. Plus, I did what I did *for* her. This asshole crossed a line purely for himself, taking advantage of her situation and exploiting it.

I'm going to make sure he knows he fucked up… and that he can never do it again. To V, or to anyone.

I follow him to his home, glad that he lives his pathetic existence alone, because that's going to make my life easier. Even better that he lives outside of town in the middle of nowhere. The joys of living on a teacher's wage, I guess.

I ride past his house as he pulls in the drive, and circle back around. There aren't many places to tuck myself out of the way, but I want to wait until the sun sets before I enter his house. Just to make sure there isn't anyone else in there.

Shutting off the engine, I take off my helmet and place it at my feet before shrugging my backpack off. I went home at lunch just to make sure I had everything I needed to deal with this scumbag. Dad just smiled when he saw me getting my collection.

I'm not sure what it says about me that he seemed proud. I guess it's why people think I'm such a psycho. Clinically speaking, I might not be a psychopath, but it's easy enough for me to slip into that state of mind where emotion doesn't exist that I'm probably toeing a line or two. My dad made sure of that from a young age.

I shudder at the memory before shutting it away and going to that quiet part of my mind. The part that lets me enjoy the pain I inflict. The part that stops me feeling even one drop of remorse for my actions.

I watch the house for hours until the sun sets, and once I'm confident there's no one but Mr. Peters in the house, I make my approach. The silence of the night makes me grin. Everyone likes to believe it's the things that go bump in the night that they're afraid of, but in reality, it's the oppressive silence that gets to most people. If you can find a home in the shadows and silence, that's when you know you can truly claim the title of monster.

Unfortunately for Mr. Peters, I embraced the monster inside of me a long time ago.

I drop a text to Eric before I creep in through the back door of the small house. He was more than on board for tonight. Pedophiles are his favorite type of victim. The sounds of the

TV filter through the house and his laughter at whatever drivel is showing grates on me like nails on a chalkboard. I palm my knives, one in each hand.

The others prefer guns, but I like to be up close with the pain I inflict. There's just something more personal about drawing blood with a blade than with a bullet.

This way, I can coat myself in their blood as I revel in their screams.

I have some special humiliation planned for Mr. Peters. I just want to have some fun with him on my own first.

Try and humiliate my girl and you'll regret it.

I slink into the living room and find him in the lone recliner in front of the TV. Moving silently up behind him, I place my blade at his throat. "Surprise."

He squeaks, jumping at the word and causing the steel to split flesh where the two meet, widening my smile. I move around the chair, keeping the blade at his throat.

"M…M…Maverick? What are you doing here?" he splutters, beads of sweat rolling down his face.

I grin at him and crouch, adrenaline rushing through me, the thrill of having prey at my mercy making my heart pound. "Did you really think your predatory ways would go unnoticed? In our school? Did you not understand that *we* are the apex predators?"

His eyes go wider and I genuinely think he might piss his pants. Fucking pathetic.

"I didn't… I don't… Nothing happened."

My grin widens. At least he didn't try to lie to me. Not about this time anyway. There is no way that this is the first time it's happened, and while it wouldn't be on my radar if it weren't for V, like I told him… *we* are the apex predators.

We bathed in blood and walked through fire to claim that right.

Literally.

"What are you going to do?" he whines, his sweaty skin turning the color of a tomato.

My grin widens at his question. "What do you think I should do?"

He sputters, trying to answer, and jumps when my phone dings, scoring another bloody mark across his throat in the process. I pull it from my pocket with my free hand and glance down at the screen.

Eric

Be there soon.

"Oh, Mikey boy, you really should've kept your hands and cock to yourself." I laugh harshly, and he starts to cry a little.

"I wouldn't do that if I were you. Tears aren't exactly a deterrent. Not to me, and especially not to my friend. He really likes tears." I tilt my head a little before standing. "Get up."

I walk him to the lone chair at the dining table and zip tie him to it.

"It's not so fun being the powerless one, is it?" I use my

blades to slice through his clothes, making sure to nick his skin as I go. His small squeaks just make my heart pound harder.

If he thinks being weak will make me stop, he's sorely mistaken. I appreciate strength. Even a quiet strength. Weakness just disgusts me.

I drag my knife from his throat down to his exposed tiny fucking dick. "Should I just cut it off? You'll survive it, plenty do. Then you couldn't try to use it as a weapon against people, could you?"

He starts to cry harder, and I roll my eyes.

"Cry some more and I'll cut it off just because you're being a fucking pussy, so you may as well have one of your own."

He sucks in a breath, trying to stop the tears, but the pathetic fucking weasel just continues to whimper. "Don't say I didn't warn you."

I push my knife into the soft flesh between his dick and his thigh, reveling in the scream he lets out. I mirror the cut on the opposite side, and sobs rack his body.

If he thinks this is the worst part of his night, he has no idea what's in store for him. I'm just the warm-up act.

The thought makes me grin.

I take my time, carving into his skin. I have a thing for branding people with their sins. Which is exactly why I use my blade to carve the word *pedo* into the skin on his chest, basking in his screams as his blood flows like a waterfall, coating my own skin as I go.

Headlights break through the darkness, and I see the hope in his eyes. Like someone is coming to rescue him. Butterflies take flight in my stomach, because watching that light go out in his eyes is going to be too much fun.

I continue drawing screams from his lips as his blood begins to pool at our feet. I haven't really got started with punishing him as much as I'd like to, but also, killing him isn't a part of my plan. If I lose myself to the bloodlust, to the anger of what he tried with V, then that's exactly what's going to happen.

The light in his eyes grows as his gaze continues to dart to the front door. Like he's waiting for someone to save him.

I almost laugh, but manage to refrain.

Seconds later, when his front door bursts open, my desire to watch the hope in his eyes die is fulfilled. I watch as relief briefly washes over him as his would-be rescuer steps through the doorway, his eyes lighting up like his prayers to a deaf God have been answered. Then his brain processes the behemoth of a man that is Eric.

"Jesus, kid, I thought you were going to hold back until I got here."

I bark out a laugh, watching as panic floods Michael Peters and he tries to fight against his bindings. "This *is* me going easy," I tell him with a shrug, and he shakes his head.

"I guess it's no less than he deserves." Eric's grin is almost as sadistic as mine when he laughs. "So this fuck likes to shove his dick at little girls and make them choke on it?" He looks

Michael up and down and laughs again. "Well, choke on it might be a stretch."

I snicker as the pathetic lump of skin that is my teacher freaks the fuck out in the chair.

"I'll show you how to choke on a dick." Eric smiles. "Maybe then you'll be more hesitant in the future. You got your camera, kid?"

I don't even bristle at being called kid—it's just part of who Eric is. I pull my phone from my pocket and wave it at him.

"Oh, good," he says as he unzips his jeans. I step back, giving him the space he needs to deal with Mr. Peters. I hadn't quite planned this bit, but who am I to stop him meting out his own form of justice. After what happened to his daughter, after she took her own life because of it, Eric has always held a special place for pedo rapists. Wannabes or not. It's almost hilarious that he's one of the Knights, considering the other… proclivities of some of the other Knights, my father included. But I guess that's just life. A total double standard of a mind fuck.

"Ready to choke on a real dick?" Eric asks Mr. Peters, who starts crying in earnest. I disassociate myself from it, just turning on the video function on my phone. Our own insurance that Mr. Peters won't say a word to anyone. Not that it would do him any good. Unfortunately for him, the police in this town are as corrupt as they come.

It's only when Eric comes over Mr. Peters' face, laughing at him and calling him a scumbag, that I shut the camera off.

"You're good to leave, kid. I'll make sure that he knows the game."

I nod, pocketing my phone and grabbing my kit. I'll clean my blades once I get home. Mr. Peters sits quietly in the chair he's tied to, the cum mixing with the blood as it runs down his chest.

"I'll see you in class after the holiday," I say, saluting the room before heading back to my bike.

Maybe next time he'll think twice about fucking with people at my school.

I wake up Thanksgiving morning, groaning as I roll over. The music blasting through the house makes me want to crack heads. I had the delightful conversation with my mother yesterday about missing dinner today—which went about as well as expected—but after sharing the details of my little detour on the way home last night, Dad was too proud to say no.

I'm not sure who's more twisted: him or me. Either way, there's no denying I am definitely a product of my father.

I jump in the shower and let my mind wander to the last time I saw V. I swear every time I think about her, I end up with a raging fucking hard-on. I palm my dick, because I might as well start the day off right. I picture those firm-as-fuck tits of hers, the way she gasps when I squeeze her throat just a little too tight, the way her pulse races under my touch, the way her skin bruises in my grasp.

Everything about her makes me like a fucking prepubescent boy and I come way too fast for my own liking. Fuck it, maybe I can convince her to fuck me again later.

I finish up my shower and throw on sweats and a t-shirt before heading downstairs to see what sort of masochism my mom has dreamt up for the day. I might not be sticking around, but that doesn't mean this house won't be the usual fanfare of dinner followed by the worst kinds of debauchery.

"There he is," my mom coos as I enter the kitchen. From the outside she looks like your typical, overbearing PTA mom-ager type. Don't let that fool you though. She'd gut you like a fish and giggle about it if you knocked over one of her vases.

I learned that the hard way, and I have the scars to prove it. Not that you can see many of them anymore; they hide beneath my ink the same way she hides behind her mask.

"What time are you heading out? Do you want breakfast?" she practically sings. I'm going to guess she was with one of her toys last night. That's the only time she's this cheery.

"I'm good, I'm heading out in a few, just came down to say hello before I leave."

"Okay, sweetheart." She grins at me, and that's when I notice the speckles of blood on her throat. Yep, she was with one of her toys last night. She blows me a kiss and I head back upstairs, practically jogging in anticipation of escape.

While I might be basically immune to my parents' brand of dysfunction these days, that doesn't mean I want to be here any more than I need to be. There's a reason my father is one of the top members of the sect of the Knights in The Cove. He's ruthless and has almost no limits. You do not fuck with Edward Riley. While he's happy with me right now, his moods are mercurial as fuck and I do not want to be here when the switch flips.

I get to the top of the stairs and head for my room, when the roar sounds. I wince on reflex.

I knew Mom was too happy. The morning was going too well.

I hurry into my room, but I know there's no real escape from his anger. Even if he's not pissed at me.

His shouts echo through the house, the walls shaking as he slams doors. The smash of glass reaches me as I lean against my bedroom door.

Shit.

This right here is why I need out of Echoes Cove. I might revel in the shadows, playing with my monster, but my monster is a creature of necessity. One born of fear to help me survive the horrors my parents put me through.

I close my eyes and take a deep breath. I can face almost any other monster and not think twice about it. Hell, I won't even break a sweat, but my father...

He's a whole other type of darkness.

I grab my phone and drop Finn an SOS. He and Lincoln are the only two people who know the truth of my father and his... extra curriculars.

Finn lives closer.

While I'm not confident of my chances to escape here on my own, two against one ups the odds. They're still not odds I like though.

Usually I wouldn't even think about including the boys in my shit, but I need to tell them about yesterday, and I'm pretty sure that turning up to Thanksgiving at V's half dead might be questioned.

My phone buzzes in my hand and I see Finn's name, letting out a small breath of relief.

Finn

On way.

No more than those two words are needed. Hell, even if he just distracts my dad long enough for me to sneak out of my window, I'll owe him one.

Shit.

I hate feeling this weak. Like that scared little twelve-year-old boy again.

Finley and Lincoln were right there with me when we were taken for initiation. My father's playground. Just thinking about it makes my mouth water like I'm going to vomit.

My mother screams like a banshee and it breaks something in me.

They hurt each other all the time, but not like this.

Fuck.

I can't listen to that.

I take a deep breath before leaving the sanctuary of my room and charging down the stairs, trying to amp myself up to take on the biggest monster in my world.

I find them in the kitchen, him holding her against the wall by her fucking throat.

Fuck my life.

I look around the room and grab the first thing I see.

A goddamn rolling pin. Not my usual weapon of choice, but it's all I've got. I swing it as hard as I can at the back of his head. The crack it makes on impact reverberates down my arm, and I jump back, preparing for his attack. He drops my mom, who crumples in a pile on the floor, and turns to me, practically foaming at the mouth.

He lifts a hand to the back of his head, his fingers come away red, and his look of anger turns into a twisted smile.

Shit. Shit. Shit.

"There he is. The little boy who thinks he's a big man. Want to come and play with the grown-ups do we? You're nothing but a pathetic little worm." He steps toward me and it takes every ounce of strength I have to stay in place, even if my hands do shake a little. "You think you can go up against me and win? Because you dealt with a pathetic fuck last night? You, boy, are about to learn a fucking lesson."

He unbuckles his belt and steps toward me again, but still I hold my position. I've cowered from him my entire fucking life. I am sick of it.

My dad pauses, and for a second, I think it's because of me. But his gaze goes over my shoulder and his eyes widen quickly as he smiles. "Now, that is how you deal with a problem."

I turn and find Finley standing behind me with a gun leveled at my dad's head.

I don't say a word. There's no point. Instead I move to stand shoulder to shoulder with Finn who walks backwards as we leave the house, never lowering the gun. I don't want to leave my mom behind, but I've tried to get her to leave him before. There's no use. She's as bad as he is, and I think that she feeds on the pain he puts her through. Hopefully he got his anger out on me, and she won't suffer any more of his bullshit.

Once the front door is closed, we run down the drive and jump in his Aventador, which is parked on the street. "Thanks, man."

He nods, no other words needing to pass between us. This isn't the first time, and I doubt it'll be the last.

Hopefully the rest of our day is less eventful.

# ELEVEN

## OCTAVIA

I wake up in a thunderstorm of a mood. I've been so excited about everyone being here, that it was easy to push away the fact that this will be my first Thanksgiving without my dad. But now that it's here, I wish I hadn't arranged anything. Even with learning more of the truth of who he was and what he was mixed up in, none of that takes away from the fact that he was a fucking awesome dad, and that I miss him.

You don't have to be a great person to be a great dad. Though I find it almost impossible to merge the version of him that the guys have with the man I knew.

All I want to do is sit in the bottom of the shower, cry, and eat ice cream until my chest doesn't hurt anymore, but I promised myself that I wouldn't bury my head in the sand anymore. I've done enough of that. While I don't want to see anyone, especially those people who are going to remind me of my dad—it's going to be so much more obvious that he isn't here with them all around—I know that seeing them is exactly what I need to heal.

I've been tossing and turning since the ass crack of dawn, toying with the idea of pretending to be sick, but the thought of letting everyone down when they've come all this way to spend the day here makes me feel even worse.

It's going to be one of those "Suck it up, buttercup" kind of days.

My phone pings on the nightstand for the eleven millionth time so I roll over and pick it up.

Indi

I'll be over soon, do you need me to bring anything?

Indi

V?

Indi

Helllllooooooo

Indi

Did you die? I swear TG if you died and you don't haunt me, imma be pissed.

Indi

Worrying just a little. Are you okay?

The corners of my mouth tug up. Thank God for my little ball of joy.

Me

I'm here, sorry, slept in. We don't need you to bring anything but you. Just jumping in the shower now.

Smiling at just how lucky I am to have her in my life, I send her another message with the code for the gate so she can get in if I'm in the shower or Smithy is busy then climb out of bed. I glance over at the Saints' house through the glass doors in my room, wondering what today will bring. I know Smithy said they were both coming, but where two of those boys are, the others will surely be.

They're like a pack of wolves in that they rarely travel alone.

Closing my eyes, I take a deep breath and head into the bathroom, trying to psych myself up for this day. I don't want to be the storm cloud that rains on everyone's parade.

Turning on the shower, I step under the hot spray and try to wash off the funk that I woke up in.

I hurry through my usual routine, knowing that Indi will be here soon, and quickly sort my hair and dress once I'm done.

Smithy already has the house in full freaking swing by the time I make it downstairs. There are decorations everywhere and my mood lifts a little. This season is my favorite, and he has not forgotten, apparently.

A smile tugs at my lips as I follow the delightful smells

coming from the kitchen and find Smithy working away. "Good morning, Miss Octavia! Happy Thanksgiving!"

"Happy Thanksgiving! This all smells amazing already. What can I do to help?"

He looks at me in horror. "Oh no you don't. You don't need to do anything at all. I already told you about this poor kitchen."

I laugh at him because I can tell he's deadly serious. "Okay, if you're sure. What's the plan for the day?"

"Well, once everyone arrives, I have light appetizers prepped for everyone while dinner finishes cooking. I'm hoping we'll sit down at two. You're sure nobody has any allergies or dietary requirements?"

"Nope," I say, popping my *p*. "For a bunch of roadies and rockstars, everyone is really chill apparently."

"Good, good," he mumbles and goes back to whatever it was he was doing before I came down. I pour myself a glass of orange juice, skipping breakfast to save space for later. Hell, I even wore stretchy jeans in preparation for *all* of the food goodness.

The front door bursts open, making me jump. "I'm here, bitches!" Indi yells and I laugh, the last remnant of my funk lifting. She's like a walking, talking happy pill.

She bounces into the room and wraps me up in a hug as she does. "Morning, pumpkin, are we ready for today?" I laugh as she pulls on the waistband of her leggings.

*Great minds think alike.*

"I think so." I smile, hoping it comes across as genuine.

She bounds toward Smithy, who hands her a cookie.

"Where's *my* goddamn cookie?" I ask in fake outrage.

Indi sticks her tongue out at me before taking a bite. "*Mmmm,* so good."

"Miss Indi requested snickerdoodles, and since I made you your pie, I made her snickerdoodles," Smithy says as he laughs softly. "Now out of here, both of you. I have a lot to get done."

He hands me a cookie and I grin wide. "Thank youuuuu."

Indi and I head into the living room and drop onto the sofa. I haven't told her about the stalker thing yet, and I don't intend on bringing down the mood, so I decide I'll fill her in tomorrow.

"We're putting the game on today, right?" she asks hopefully, looking up at me with those big green eyes of hers.

I just laugh softly, because while I won't tar all football players with the Raleigh-is-a-douchecanoe brush, I totally hadn't thought about it. "Sure, why not? I'm sure you won't be the only one who wants to watch since Smithy invited the Saints over."

"He did what?" she asks, eyes wide.

"You heard me. Mrs. Potts is going out of town, and their dad isn't around."

"Oh," she says, like her heart hurts for the sad, poor, lost puppies that they most definitely aren't. "I mean, you've started to forgive them, right? Kind of? It won't be so bad, maybe?"

"No, sometimes I think I've started to forgive them and then they do something to fuck it up, so I've not forgiven them. Not really. In fact, I had an idea that I could use your help with." I feel a little devious even suggesting it, and I know the look on my face is as devious as I feel because she shakes her head at me.

"Oh, Lord. Save us all. Tell me everything."

"Not yet, tomorrow, when everyone is gone. People should be arriving soon, and well... this will take time to plan." I laugh a little, the idea born from a dream I had a few nights ago. At first it seemed silly—maybe even a little petty—but the more I think about it, the easier it becomes for me to convince myself that it isn't petty at all. Who knows, I might change my mind a dozen times between now and tomorrow.

"Are you okay?" she asks, and I realise I totally spaced.

"I'm good, just missing my dad," I tell her with a small smile.

"I get that," she says, squeezing me with a one-armed hug. "It's okay to miss him, just don't miss out on the joy still around you."

Indi manages to keep me plenty distracted from spiraling thoughts of my dad with her uniquely magical ways until everyone else starts arriving.

It's not long before the house is a hive of activity. Mac, Panda, and a ton of the other crew arrive with Jenna B and the other Midnight Blue girls. The guys are inside watching the football game while Smithy cooks, since he banned us all from the kitchen. I'm outside, sitting beside the pool with the girls and Panda, drinking mimosas and laughing as we talk about shit from tours of the past.

It's only when the gate to the Saints' house opens that the jovial conversation comes to a halt. Lincoln leads the pack in his black shirt and suit pants, followed by East, Finn, and Mav all in various states of formal shirt and pants.

Jenna looks back at me and winks. "You're drooling," she whispers, trying not to laugh. I stick my tongue out at her before turning back to the boys.

"Afternoon," I call out, lifting my glass. "Drinks?"

They head toward us, and it's only then that I notice Panda's change in demeanor. His shoulders are stiff, his eyes glued to Lincoln as he approaches.

"Everything okay?" I ask him, nudging him with my shoulder.

He looks at me, conflicted, before glancing back at the boys. "I'm sorry," is all he says.

"What does that mean?" I ask, wondering what the fuck else it is I'm missing. And how the fuck does he know Lincoln? He doesn't get a chance to speak again before Lincoln and the others are standing before us.

"Happy Thanksgiving, V," East says, and I stand to give him a hug, being passed from him to Finley, before Maverick lifts me from my feet, spinning me around before putting me back down. I give Lincoln an awkward wave, because hugging just isn't a thing we do.

"You guys, this is Lincoln, Maverick, Finley, and Easton," I tell the others, making all of the introductions needed. When Lincoln moves toward Panda I'm still unsure what is going on.

"Evan, it's been a while."

My stomach flips as my heart races. I lean in to Maverick and ask, "How the fuck does Lincoln know Panda?"

Panda stands, offering his hand to Lincoln who looks at it before shaking. P looks at me quickly before settling his gaze back on Lincoln and nodding. "It has."

"What am I missing here?" I ask the two of them, and Indi jumps to her feet beside me.

"Drinks, anyone? Let's go harass Smithy for more, shall we?" She ushers everyone else inside, leaving me with the five guys who all look as guilty as the next.

Once everyone else is inside and the doors close, I fold my arms over my chest, waiting for someone to explain whatever the fuck is going on.

"V... I'm sorry. I should've said something before now," Panda starts, and Mav begins to laugh.

"Said something about what?" I huff, already tired of the lack of fucking answers yet again.

"You didn't tell her? Oh man." Mav drops into one of the just vacated chairs and kicks back like he's watching a goddamn show.

Panda's eyes go wide as his gaze bounces from Mav to me.

"I didn't know how—"

"Tell me what, exactly?" I demand, and Linc's smile turns dark, his eyes glinting with something sinister, reminding me of how he looked at me a few months ago.

"Evan here," Linc says, turning to face me, "is a Knight."

He is?

They've got to be fucking with me. I know Panda. He isn't anything like them. He's fun and laid-back. He's had my back more times than I can count.

"No he isn't. He's a roadie." I try to deny it, and it sounds stupid even as I say it but the way P looks at me tells me I'm only lying to myself.

"I was sent on tour to make sure nothing happened to you," he confesses, stepping toward me as I step backward, away from him. I clasp my throat as I shake my head.

This can't be happening.

*Why does everyone lie?*

Panda steps closer to me, and Finn shoulder checks him, putting himself between us. "V, I'm sorry. Will you let me explain?"

"What is there to explain?" I utter, shock making me stupid, but it does occur to me that maybe he will answer some of my questions. I open my mouth to speak but Lincoln beats me to it.

"Were you spying on her or Stone?" Lincoln asks, and I'm shook stupid again. I didn't even consider that. This Knight shit is so out of this goddamn world. I was still half convinced—half hoping—that it was some bullshit, but everything seems to lead back to this shit. "Are you responsible for Stone's death?"

I suck in a breath and the world tilts. My knees feel like they're about to give out as ice fills my veins, and I grab Finn's arm to keep myself upright

As much as I want answers, this is too much. I was having enough issues getting through today without wondering if my friend killed my dad. I can't go down that rabbit hole right now. If I ask and he tells me something I don't want to hear, I'm going to spin out.

"I didn't!" His eyes go wide in panic, and he tries to move toward me, but Lincoln stops him. "You have to believe me. V, you know me! You have to know I wouldn't do that."

"Do I? I can't do this right now, but, P, you and I are apparently due for a conversation. This isn't over." Leaving them to get the answers they're obviously seeking, I step back into the house. Leaning back on the door, I take a deep breath. I want answers, hell, I crave them, but am I really strong enough to hear the answer to that question?

I find the game on in the lounge, which is where everyone moved to while we were outside talking. Indi glances over to me, looking a little worried, but I shake my head, and give her a watery smile. Now is so not the time. I take another deep breath, deciding to join everyone when I see that Smithy has the formal tables all pulled together in here too.

Then I notice the tablecloth.

My throat thickens as tears prick my eyes. This is too much right now. This entire day is too fucking much. I rub the heel of my palm against my chest, trying to ease some of the pain that tears through me, praying for the strength to get through today without breaking.

Smithy enters the room, looking more than a little concerned when he sees me. "Miss Octavia, what's wrong?"

"The tablecloth…you remembered?"

He smiles softly before moving toward me and hugging me. "Of course I did. It's tradition. I figured we'd keep it up, especially with so many of your friends here."

He rubs my back up and down before releasing me. I move toward the table, barely able to stop the tears from falling as I take it all in.

The messages from my dad from the last Thanksgiving we spent at home. It was a silly tradition my nana started when I was young. Each year at Thanksgiving, we'd write what we were thankful for on the table cloth and sign our name with the year until that cloth was full, and then we'd start another.

Trailing my fingers against my father's spider-like writing makes the tears fall down my face.

*I am thankful to be surrounded by the people I love. To be graced with a daughter as talented as she is graceful, and a wife who loves us both so much.*

I wipe the tears from my face as I feel someone at my back.

"Are you okay?" Finley asks, and I lean back on him, just for a second while I compose myself, stealing some of his quiet strength.

"I'll be fine," I whisper, taking a deep breath just as Smithy announces that the food is ready.

As I take my seat, Finley moves to sit in the chair to my right as my found family take their places around the table. I know that, despite everything, I have a lot to be thankful for. Selfishly, I just wish for more.

Indi sits to my left and clasps my hand, squeezing tight. She has no idea what's wrong, but I know she's there for me no matter what.

Smithy, East, and Mav appear, carrying dishes to start loading up the table and laughter sounds at the other end where Mac and some of the other roadies are sitting. The corners of my mouth lift in a watery smile and I close my eyes, thanking my dad for giving me these people, even if he can't be here with me.

Life might not always be sunshine and rainbows, but today, I'm going to be thankful for all of the grace in my life. Starting with these people.

Even the ones that lied to me.

After the emotional whirlwind of a day on Thursday, Indi and

I relaxed for the rest of the long weekend. At least until her parents came home a day early. I swear all we've done is eat the entire time she's been here. I'm going to need to run every day this week just to recover from it. I'm not opposed to some extra curve on my ass, but damn, eating this much pie and not running is going to ruin me.

Indi left here yesterday afternoon, giving me my Sunday to myself. Which is exactly why I'm still in my pj's, curled on the sofa under blankets with Smithy, watching crime documentaries. What else is to be done over the weekend but chill after eating my own weight in turkey and all the trimmings? That and putting off calling P. Stupid move I know, but I need to process the shit that Thanksgiving brought back to the surface before I dive into that cesspit. That and the thought of him not answering my questions or lying to me again isn't something I'm sure I can handle right now with my grief gripping me just beneath the surface.

I'm not ready to discover if our entire friendship was one giant lie. Not yet.

A knock at the back door has me pausing the TV and Smithy gets up to see who's there. Since it's the back door, I can only imagine it's one of four people. Everyone else is civilized and uses the front.

I take a deep breath and prepare myself to deal with whichever one of them it is. I haven't spoken to any of them since Thursday.

"Master Saint! What brings you by?" Smithy's voice carries through, making me turn on the couch, just as a sweater-and-jean-clad Lincoln enters my house.

What the fuck have these boys been eating, and why do they look edible in fucking everything?

Why are the assholes always so pretty?

And why does my kooch seem louder than logic sometimes?

"I was hoping Octavia would be free. I was going to head to the range, and I figured with everything going on, she could probably use the extra practice."

Goddamn, why does he have to be so well-mannered to Smithy. Manners cost nothing and are fucking hot, too.

"She's just in the living room. We were, as you youngsters call it, binging television." His footsteps echo on the wooden flooring as he walks toward me, and I pull my blanket up a little higher. He might *think* I can use a refresher. Little does he know that going to the range is something my dad and Mac insisted we do weekly.

He steps into the room, hands in his pockets, and stares at me. I smile at him, batting my lashes while trying not to laugh. He rolls his eyes at me before speaking. "Well?"

"Well what?"

"Do you want to come to the range?"

Usually, spending any time with just him would make me want to be a little sick, but the thought of going to the gun range makes butterflies take flight in my stomach. It's been too long since I went, and Dad would be super disappointed in me for not keeping it up. Much like all of my defense stuff.

I make a promise to myself to start up my training again in the new year before jumping up from the sofa. "Give me ten to get dressed, then sure."

He nods in response and I practically skip up the stairs. I am not a gun nut, but there is something about holding a firearm that makes a girl feel powerful. And after everything that's gone on since I've been back here, I could use a little dose of that. Plus, this might be the perfect opportunity to pepper him with questions.

I grab a pair of jeans, a tank, slip on a V-neck sweater, and pull on my boots. I flip my head upside down and gather my hair in a messy ponytail, trying to make sure my extensions aren't too visible before heading back downstairs, where I find Lincoln watching my crime show with Smithy.

I smirk to myself. I knew the old man was secretly loving this show.

"Ready," I call out before I hit the bottom stair and bounce into the room. I grab my leather jacket from the security room where I left it and head back through to the living room where Lincoln is waiting.

He looks me up and down and nods when he apparently decides I meet his standards.

Asshole.

"I'll catch you later, Smithy." I lean down and kiss the old man's cheek as I grab my phone and keys from the coffee table.

"Have fun, both of you. Let me know if you'll be out late, please."

I grin at just how paternal he can be sometimes. "Sure thing. Have fun!"

I give him a finger wave before following Lincoln out the back of the house and through the gate to where his Porsche sits in his drive.

He might be a douchebag, but I still love his car.

I slide into the passenger side once he unlocks it, sinking into the cloud-like seat, just as soft and comfortable as I remember it being.

He starts the car without saying a word and we make the drive in silence. I stare out of the windows as he drives me out past the other side of town and just keeps driving. "Should I be worried that you're driving me out into the middle of nowhere to kill me without a trace?"

He looks over at me and smirks. "You've been watching too many crime documentaries. Anyway, if I was going to kill you, I'd have done it before now. And Smithy wouldn't know you were with me either."

"Reassuring, Lincoln, really reassuring." I sigh, shaking my head. "So where are we going?"

"A private shooting range that a friend owns."

I quirk a brow. What is it with him and just giving a little bit of the information but never really answering the question? "A

Knight friend?"

"So you're finally starting to believe the Knights are real, rather than a ploy then?"

"Did you really just answer a question with a question?" I counter, and he barks out a laugh, relaxing a little.

Point one for me I guess. Ice man finally melts a little.

He shakes his head, glancing at me before answering, gripping the steering wheel a little tighter. "No, the friend isn't a Knight. I wouldn't take you to a Knight freehold unless there was a gun to your head."

I ruminate on his words and decide to answer his question too. "Yes, I'm starting to believe it, even though it's entirely *un*believable. I mean, I believe they're real, but I don't think I believe that I'm in any danger from them. A few bouquets of flowers and a dress don't exactly scream danger."

"The most dangerous of things are usually unsuspecting."

I mean, he's not wrong. Silent but deadly isn't a phrase for no reason.

Deciding this is as good a time as any, I deliberate where to start. "Will you tell me more about the Knights? About what's going on with you guys? It's hard to just trust blindly, you know?"

"Octavia," he groans. "Really?"

"Yes really. You guys haven't told me much of anything, and I'm tired of being in the dark. I'm tired of reacting rather than actually being proactive. I'm aware I've walked around in a bit of a daze since my dad died, but that's not who I am."

He nods, and I feel a glimmer of hope. "You get three questions."

Hell yes! I mentally do a fist pump, and try to decide which questions to ask since I only get three.

Holy shit this is harder than I thought it would be.

"Okay," I start. "Three questions. First one… Who is in control of the Knights?"

He side-eyes me, letting out a deep breath. "I don't know."

"Oh for fuck's sake!" I shout, throwing my hands in the air. "I should've known you wouldn't have answered my questions. What is the point in asking me to trust you when it obviously doesn't go both ways?"

His knuckles go white as he clenches the steering wheel. "It's not that I don't trust you, Octavia. It's that I really don't know. I'm just a junior, that means my knowledge, while vast, is still limited. I can tell you that the sect in Echoes Cove is run by the seven senior members of the Conclave. But the Conclave is overseen by the Regent. My father."

My eyes go wide. I was not expecting that. Not even a little. Holy shit.

"Okay, so what does that mean for you? What do they make you guys do?" I pick at the skin by my thumbnail while I wait for him to answer. His jaw clenches, and that vein in his neck pulses as the silence grows thicker.

"That's two questions," he huffs. "But I'll give you them as one. For me, it means my entire life is mapped out, whether I want it to be or not. I'm the Regent Heir, and as such, in charge of the junior Conclave. Not that I have any real power, Harrison wouldn't allow that. As for what they make us do… It depends."

I try not to get excited about the fact that he's actually giving me information. My heart wars in my chest between glee at finding some answers and pain for him. But knowing Harrison could be the key to all of this could help. I don't know how yet, but every little bit has to help. "On what?"

"That's another question," he says, quirking his brow. "But it depends on what they need. Sometimes we're errand boys, collecting people, goods, and basically acting like mules for them. Others, it can be getting information…other times, it's wiping a board clean while drowning it in blood."

"Killing people?"

"Killing, maiming, torturing. All the things in life we really want for you."

I look down at my hands folded in my lap, trying to process everything he's told me, even with the sarcasm dripping from his last words. It's good, getting information, it means I'm no longer walking around in the dark completely blindfolded, but I know this is just scratching the surface. But I'm going to take the win, because with Linc, this is a big win.

I contemplate a million different questions running through my mind, aware that I've had my three, but trying again anyway. "Are all legacies bound to them?"

"Yes. Usually." He hits the blinker, taking the turn when the lights on the road allow before continuing. "I haven't heard of any legacy getting out. Not until the deal your father made to get you free, and before you ask, I don't know all the details of the deal either. All I know is that he made a deal, gave up his place, and in exchange, you were supposed to be out."

I sit quietly, going over all of that in my head. What exactly did my dad do, give up, for me to be free? Just another question to add to my ever-growing list.

"Thank you," I say quietly and he nods, not speaking any further.

We continue the drive in a weird but comfortable silence. I flick the stereo on, the radio helping to pass the time. It's only when we pull into Sand Bay and head further into the city, that I relax a little. We weave our way through the city and finally, on the other side, he drives down a dirt road. A few minutes later, I see the building come into view and relax even further.

He pulls to a stop out front, silence filling the space between us.

"Come on, let's go see if you're any good with a gun, shall we?" He smirks again, like he thinks I'm going to be useless. I just nod, not bothering to tell him otherwise. Following him inside, I gaze around the front; it's basically a gun store with a range out back.

"Will, good to see you," Linc calls out, doing that weird guy chin-tilt nod thing to the guy behind the counter.

"It's been a while, Linc, my man. And who is this pretty little thing?" His southern drawl makes my insides go funny. Damn, I love me a southern accent.

Lincoln looks back at me before scowling at his friend. "That is Octavia Royal, and no, you can't play with her."

"Says who?" I challenge, quirking a brow.

"Oh I like her." Will grins, looking me up and down before turning back to Lincoln. "You need anything?"

"No, I've got everything in my locker. I'll yell if I need you."

He motions with his head for me to follow him before going through a door in the back of the room that has a sign reading 'Range' above it.

I follow him out back to his locker, which is basically a giant metal trunk. He unlocks the padlock on it and lifts the lid, showcasing enough guns to equip a small army, I'm sure. "We'll start you with something small since, you know, you're small, and see how you get on."

"Sure thing." I smirk at him, letting him go through the motions, taking the ear muffs when he hands them over before leading me to the very empty shooting range.

He walks me through my stance and how to hold the gun he hands me. I have to admit, Lincoln is a very good teacher. He has more patience than I'd have expected. I follow his instruction without question, and as he wraps his arms around me to help me bring the gun level with the target, I almost hold my breath.

"Relax, aim, and shoot."

He releases me, but my entire body feels like it's on fire. I shake my head, trying to shake off the feeling, and pull the trigger, the kickback reverberating up my arms.

"Good," is all he says before moving to the target beside me. He moves into position and empties the clip of his gun into the target.

"Show off." I grin as he turns to look at me with an eyebrow raised.

"You'll get there."

I laugh. "Oh I know." I raise my arm at my target, gun in hand, while keeping my eyes locked on his before letting off three rounds.

His eyes go wide as he takes in the target, and I bark out a laugh. Turning to my paper target, I grin. Apparently I haven't gone rusty.

Head.

Chest.

Dick.

Just like Dad taught me.

"Thank God this semester is over! You have much planned for Christmas?" Indi asks as we head out of school. The last few weeks since Thanksgiving have been a whirlwind of exams, handing in papers, and trying like fuck to catch up with all the work I had fallen behind on. I think I might have just got everything done by the skin of my teeth.

The sub in place of Mr. Peters in Business even offered me a make-up paper for what I missed at the beginning of the year. Things might finally be looking up for me. Especially if Mr. Peters' sudden trip away stays permanent.

"No, we're keeping it low key this year," I tell her with a smile as we reach my Impala. I open the trunk and grab the gift bag I stored there. "But this, my friend, is for you. Merry Christmas."

She grins wide as she takes the bag, bouncing on the balls of her feet. "You totally didn't have to, but thank you! I'd rip it open right now if I didn't think my mom would withhold Christmas dinner for breaking tradition."

"As she should." I laugh. "It's not Christmas for three more days."

"But I love gifts. Speaking of..." She pauses before bounding to her Wrangler and opening the back door. "This is for you."

She almost falls over as she pulls a giant-ass box from the back, decorated with ribbons, bows, and so much more. I rush over to give her a hand, wondering how the hell she got it in her car. "What on earth is in there?"

I lean back and open the passenger door to the Impala and help her slide the box in. "You'll find out Christmas morning," she says, sticking her tongue out. I close the door and she hugs me tight. "We're hanging out on New Year's, right?"

"You know it." I grin at her and wave before climbing in the car. The last few weeks have been quiet. Too quiet. And I still haven't seen Raleigh. The school isn't that big, so I have no idea how. I almost want to just get it out of the way, but since school is done for two weeks now, I don't have to worry about it too much.

I start up the car, hooking my phone up and playing *Prom Queen* by Molly Kate Kestner, my latest song obsession. Just as I go to buckle up, I see Finley jogging toward my car.

Since the shooting range, those three have been strangely MIA, too. In fact, other than for gym, I've barely seen East either.

Of course, the second I start to accept that we might be becoming friends, that this whole Knight thing is real and I might want some more answers, they all pretty much drop off the face of the Earth. I've gone from not being able to get rid of them when I didn't want to see them, to them never being around. Finley didn't even respond to the text I sent him.

Weird as fuck, but I'm not sure why I expected anything different. These guys are never what I expect.

I roll down the window and Finley leans forward, his arms on top of the car. "I was hoping I'd catch you."

I bite down on my lip, waiting for him to speak.

"How are you doing?" he asks, almost awkwardly.

Letting out a dry laugh I look up at him. "I'm fine. What do you want, Finley?"

He lets out a deep sigh and stands, rubbing the back of his neck. "Do you have some time to talk?"

"So now you want to talk?" I quirk a brow at him, and he at least has the decency to look sorry.

"I know, I'm sorry. We've had some shit to deal with. Mav…" He shakes his head. "It doesn't matter, not my story to tell. Do you have some time?"

I consider his words. I'd noticed that Maverick wasn't really himself on Thanksgiving, even though he put on a good show. He's been oddly quiet around school since then, too. Eventually, I nod. "Yeah, I have time."

I shut the engine off and go to unbuckle, but he leans back down. "I'll follow you home."

"Okay." I nod, starting the car back up again. He moves back and heads over to his car. I can't see Maverick's bike in the lot, but Lincoln's Porsche is gone, too, so I might have just missed them I guess. I drop Smithy a quick message to let him know that Finley is heading back with me, and he responds almost instantly to let me know he's out shopping this evening.

Little sneak.

I remind him we said no gifts, knowing full well I have at least five for him tucked away, before pulling out of the lot and driving home through the very festively decorated streets of Echoes Cove. The world would probably come to an end if it snowed in southern California, but apparently no one here cares. It's fake snow galore.

Finley follows me the entire way and enters the gate behind me as I pull onto the drive.

Jumping out of the car, I head to the passenger side to grab the box from Indi, but Finley catches up to me and lugs it out instead. "What the hell is in this thing?"

"I asked the same thing." I laugh as I open the front door, pausing when I take in what Smithy has obviously been up to while I was at school today. The giant tree in the living room, decorations freaking galore.

I guess my quiet Christmas plan isn't what he had in mind. Hell, I was even going to skip the big tree thing. "I'll put this under the tree."

"Okay, thanks. Do you want a drink?" I ask as he heads across the room before placing the giant box beneath the tree where there are already more gifts than I care to count.

"Sure." He smiles softly at me and follows me to the kitchen. *Why does this feel so awkward?*

"So what did you want to talk about?" I ask as I stick my head in the fridge, grabbing a couple of sodas before handing one to him.

He sits at the counter, taking a swig of his drink before looking at me. If I didn't know better, I'd think he was stalling.

"About the Knights." I nod and take a seat across from him, waiting for him to continue. "Lincoln told us that you were finally starting to believe us, that he gave you some answers when you went to the range. And I know your friend being one of us was something of a shock. Plus, we haven't been around much."

I take a sip of my drink, waiting for him to get to the point. I hate it when they talk in circles. Finley isn't usually one to use this many words so I know he's a little uncomfortable, which is exactly why I don't interrupt him.

"I wanted to know if you had any more questions. I can't promise you answers to all of them, but if I can answer, I will."

My eyes go wide at his words. He's really going to give me information.

Well, color me shocked.

Except, of course now that the opportunity is here, the thousand questions I've had on the tip of my tongue jumble up inside my brain and tie my tongue in knots. Why are you guys so interested in saving me from these people? How come I've never heard about this before if I'm supposed to be a legacy? What's so special about the society and why is it such a big secret? If the Knights are such a big deal, why did my dad run and what do they want with me after all these years of being away? Are there benefits to me being involved with them?

But when I try to speak the words, they turn to ash and I have nothing.

"You asked Panda about my dad's death. Why would you guys ask him that? What did he say after I left?" The question spills from my mouth even though I'm not sure I want the answer to it. I've still been too scared to ask Panda myself, mostly because I can't take him lying to me any more.

"He said again and again that he had nothing to do with it. That he was put on the tour to look after you. It had nothing to do with your dad." He looks me in the eye as he answers, and it's the only reason I believe him. "And we asked him, because he's a Knight and we thought he could be linked to it. We told you we don't think your dad committed suicide, but Evan didn't have any other answers for us either."

"That doesn't make any sense. I don't understand any of this." I sigh, dropping my chin into my hand. "Does it make sense to you?"

"No, it doesn't, but we're trying to find out as much as we can. We've just had a few… obstacles pop up the last few weeks."

"The Maverick thing?" I ask, and he nods, "Is there anything I can do?"

He smiles softly but shakes his head. "No, but thank you. Just do me a favor?"

I raise an eyebrow but stay quiet and wait for him to continue. "Something big is happening with the Knights and I don't know if it's good or bad, but please, don't go anywhere alone for a while."

My stomach drops at the thought of being in more danger. Just what I wanted for Christmas.

"I'll try my best," I offer, because that's all I've got right now. "Do we have any information on my stalker?"

He grins wide at me. "Now that… that I have good news about." His phone chimes in his hand, and his smile drops. "Except I'm going to have to come back to it. I have to run. I'm sorry, V."

"You have got to be kidding me." I sigh, throwing my hands up in frustration. This hot and cold, push and pull bullshit is getting old.

He steps forward and kisses me, like it's an everyday occurrence. I hold onto his waist as he kisses me like he needs me to breathe. He pulls back, resting his forehead on mine. "I'll come back. I swear. Just… be patient with us. Please."

It's the "please" that gets me, and I nod before he pulls back and jogs out of my house.

I have no idea which way is up, but I do know that I'm getting a little tired of everyone picking me up and putting me down like a doll. These people need to learn that I am more capable than they realize.

# TWELVE

## OCTAVIA

Christmas with my dad was always a giant affair. Even on the years when we were traveling the world, he made a huge deal of it. Going through all of these firsts without him is more painful than I could've ever imagined.

More pain than I'd wish on anyone.

That's why I spent the last few weeks just focusing on school, on my friends, rather than on Christmas itself.

I also didn't want to be Scrooge McDuck because well... who wants that?

Before this year, I had always loved Christmas. The joy of being around the people who loved you, making the day entirely about family. Yes, we did the same on Thanksgiving, but that was always extended family and just *all* of the people.

Christmas was about the people we loved the most.

I remember Christmases as a kid-- we'd have giant dinners at our house: the Saints, the Rileys, the Knights. Every year we'd be in each other's pockets. I'm not sure if my friendship with the boys came first, or if our parents' friendships did. All I remember is that's how it was.

For a while anyway.

Until Mom left.

I never knew why things went sideways after that. Dad still made a big deal of Christmas even though she wasn't here, but we didn't spend it with the others. I don't remember asking why, or being told why, but after she left my whole world was upside down, so I guess I never really questioned it.

This Christmas reminds me of the first one that Mom wasn't here. Except it hurts more. I was never as close to her as I was my dad.

A knock sounds at the door, pulling me from the dreary thoughts keeping me company under my comforter. "Miss Octavia, are you awake? Your guests are arriving."

Did he just say guests?

I throw the sheets off and scurry to the door, opening it a fraction. "What guests?"

"Miss Octavia, you're not even dressed! It's nearly ten in the morning. The Saint boys are already here; I have breakfast in the warmer. Master Riley and Master Knight will be here soon according to them. I assumed you had something planned with them."

I grind my teeth, leaning my head against the side of the door. "No, no I did not."

"Well, now then, we can't be rude. It's Christmas after all. You get dressed and I'll start serving breakfast. It almost feels like the Christmases of old." He smiles so wide, joy practically radiating from him, and I don't have the heart to tell him I don't want to human today. Instead, I nod and close the door, groaning as I lean against it.

Just what I wanted for Christmas... those four idiots.

Fuck it. Smithy seemed happy, so I'm going to suck it up, push down the dark and twisties haunting me, and put on a smile all damn day if that's what it takes.

I refuse to ruin his Christmas. Even if I would rather just climb back into bed.

I head to my closet, grabbing a pair of jeggings, a tank, and a hoodie. No one said I couldn't be comfortable, even if we do have company. I finish grabbing everything I need and get ready for the day quickly, thankful I washed my hair the night before.

I plod downstairs in my thick, fluffy socks, hearing laughter coming from the kitchen.

Is that... Lincoln Saint laughing? Be still my heart. I didn't think that was even possible these days. I pause on the stairs, sitting down to listen to them laughing and joking. Because I know the moment I go in there, it'll stop. Something about me seems to put him on edge, and it's Christmas. I don't want to ruin his joy. Not today anyway.

The front door opens, and I'm caught red-handed, very obviously eavesdropping, by Finley and Maverick. "Fancy seeing you here." Maverick smirks up at me. I let out a sigh and stand, heading down to them.

"Merry Christmas," Maverick says as he sweeps me up in his arms and spins me around. I can't help but laugh, squealing as he continues to spin me. "Not too mad we're here?" he whispers into my ear when he stills.

"I suppose not," I breathe back as he lowers me down, holding me tight so I feel every part of him on my descent. He tucks my hair behind my ear before capturing my lips in a kiss so hot it makes my toes curl. I lose myself to the feel of him, curling my fingers in his hair, enjoying every second of the surprise.

It's only when he pulls back and I spot Finley watching us over his shoulder that I blush. Mav sees the red on my cheeks and grins before releasing me. "I'll go find the others." He moves past me, slapping my ass as he goes, making me squeak again as his laughs echo around the giant space.

Turning to face Finley, my blush deepens. The heat in his eyes does things to me that it definitely shouldn't. Especially when I was just locking lips with his bestie. "Merry Christmas." It comes out more as a question as he stalks toward me, until he's less than a hair's distance from me.

"Merry Christmas, V." He runs a finger down my face, until

he cups my chin. I stand frozen, unsure of where this is going right now. The last time I saw him, he kissed me, and then bolted at Lincoln's beckoning. I've not heard from him since then and I'm still kind of pissed about it, but I don't want to cause a scene at Christmas. Mostly for Smithy's sake. But I can't help but get caught up in him and the way he looks at me.

"There you are!" East's voice shatters the moment, and Finley takes a step back, putting distance between us. He turns to face East, a small smile on his face, before heading in the direction the voice came from.

I have no idea why these boys are here, but I have a feeling today is going to be a very long day. Heading through to the kitchen, I find Lincoln, East, and Maverick sitting at a table I've never seen before with Finley as Smithy hums Christmas carols while he cooks.

I hate how the smile on Lincoln's face fades with my approach. Mostly because I don't understand it. I don't know what it is I could have possibly done to make him continuously react to me like this.

I thought after our day at the range that things might turn around for us. I've seen glimpses of the boy I used to know since I got back. The one with a slightly softer side. I say slightly because he's never really been soft, though he was at least compassionate… empathetic… Whoever it is he grew up to be doesn't seem to like being that person anymore. I'm beginning to wonder if I'll ever know this version of him at all.

"Miss Octavia, please, sit, breakfast is just being served, and then we get to do my favorite part of the day." Smithy's eyes sparkle as he speaks. "Gifts!"

It occurs to me that there are four people here I hadn't planned on seeing today. Even though I may or may not have picked up something for each of them during my shopping trip with Indi because I have *zero* impulse control and couldn't stop myself. What they don't know, and I'll likely never admit, is that I have gifts for them for every Christmas we were apart.

As much as I've tried to convince myself otherwise, these boys have been a part of me for as long as I remember. I doubt that will ever change.

Even if they do try to push me away.

I take a seat at the table between Finley and the empty space, which I'm hoping Smithy will take. The man in question drops plates in front of the boys loaded with stacks upon stacks of pancakes with bacon and syrup. I look up at Lincoln, the corners of his mouth tilted up a little.

This always was his favorite.

I don't know what's going on with him, but apparently Smithy noticed the sadness about him too. He always made Lincoln pancakes when he'd come here seeking refuge from the chaos at home. Smithy takes his seat beside me as he hands me my plate, no syrup and bacon for me. Chocolate chips with whipped cream and berries. Just how I like them.

"Thank you." I grin up at him.

He claps his hands together, smiling at the people at the table. "It's been quite some time since we did Christmas here, so dig in, please."

Guilt pangs in my stomach at the thought of how lonely it must've been here for Smithy while Dad and I were away.

"Eat," he says, looking at me pointedly, so I chow down, staying quiet as the five of them talk about the football game that's on today. I swear, I don't remember football being such a big thing here before I left, but I guess a lot changed while I was gone. That or I was more oblivious that I realized.

"Are you okay?" Finley asks quietly while the others debate back and forth about who's going to win today's game.

"I'm okay. Just another big day without Dad." I shrug a little and he nudges me with his shoulder. "I'll be fine."

"You will, that's exactly why we're here," he says quietly. "And we have a few more surprises in store too."

He pulls back from me, leaving me hanging, and rejoins the conversation with the others.

What the fuck does he mean surprises?

I shake it off and try to join in on the conversation even though I have zero clue about football. It quickly becomes painfully obvious I'm out of my depth.

"I'll clear the table," East says, standing once everyone is done. He quirks a brow at Smithy when he tries to object, and it's amusing seeing him told. Smithy leads the others into the living room, literally as happy as I remember seeing him, while

I help East clear the table and load the dishwasher.

We work in silence, which is weird and awkward as fuck, but it's been a minute since we've even spoke, let alone had a private moment together.

I close the door to the dishwasher, making sure I haven't missed anything before pressing the start button.

"V…"

I look up at East, who looks at me with those puppy dog eyes, and I just know he's about to take a wrecking ball to what's left of the wall I put up between us.

"I'm sorry," he says softly. "I'm sorry I've been so MIA and so fucking weird since the Raleigh thing. I didn't want to push, and then… shit happened, plus homecoming… and then it'd been a minute since we'd spoke just the two of us. I hadn't heard from you, and I know that's not an excuse, I just… I didn't know what to do. If you wanted space, if you wanted me around--especially since things are better with the others."

He pauses, like he didn't mean to word vomit all over me, and I let out a sigh. "Honestly, I get it. I haven't exactly been present since Halloween. And with everything after homecoming too… I retreated. I swear there's been so much going on lately, I feel like I've barely been able to catch my breath. Some days I don't even recognize myself. So it's fine, I get it. But even if things are getting better with those knuckleheads, that doesn't mean that I don't want you around."

He smiles at me, the joy reaching his eyes, and it's like a little weight I hadn't realized was there lifts from my shoulders. He wraps me in a hug, squeezing me tight, and I relax against him. Here was me thinking that after fooling around he had second thoughts about everything, even if I hadn't put voice to those thoughts. He rubs his hand up and down my back, and I relax into him, more than I've relaxed in weeks. "Come on, let's go join the others. But first…"

He lets go of me and pulls a long, thin box from his back pocket. "This is for you."

I open the black velvet box, and inside is a charm bracelet, with just one charm. A music note. "East… this is…"

"To be completed. I figured I can add to it, as I intend on being around for a long fucking time. V, I lost you once, I don't want to ever lose you again." He cups my cheek and kisses me softly. "Want a hand putting it on?"

I nod, still unable to speak properly from the emotion cloying my throat. It's so fucking thoughtful. No one has ever bought me jewelry before. He takes the box and lifts the silver chain out, joining the clasp around my wrist. "It's perfect."

He grins down at me and kisses my hand. "I'm glad you like it. Now we should probably head in there before Smithy gets impatient about gifts. You know how he gets."

I laugh because he's not wrong. Maybe this Christmas won't be as dark and twisty as I thought it would be. We find the others all sitting around the base of the tree where there are way too many presents. "Did you guys move your entire Christmas here?"

"They did." Smithy grins. "And I, for one, am more than happy about it. Now come on over and take your seat so I can play Santa. Do you know how long it's been since I got to play Santa?" His joy is infectious, and I sit down with East close beside me.

"Oh wait!" I say, scrambling back to my feet. I run upstairs and head to my closet. I grab the gift bags that I stashed back here. I figured these would just go on the pile of other gifts that I bought and never actually gave to them, but I guess this year is going to be different. I chew my lip, considering whether or not this is a good idea. I get that they've been helping me, and that, well... other than Linc, I've gotten a lot closer to them again, but I'm also aware that I haven't exactly forgiven them yet. Fuck it. It's Christmas. Today, we can put it all aside and just enjoy the day.

I head downstairs, bags in hand, and slip them under the tree. I already put the ones for Smithy under there. Plonking myself back down where I was, Smithy starts handing out the gifts, and the shock on his face makes me laugh every time he grabs a gift for himself.

I watch the boys open their gifts from their families and I can't help but wonder why they're not with them today. Not that I'd take this joy from Smithy, but I'd give pretty much anything to be with my dad today.

I laugh as I unwrap the ridiculously big box from Indi, to discover it contains another box. I continue to unwrap them and when I get to the final one, I blush furiously, trying to hide the gift. I pull out the gift tag in the box.

*For you to explore with your guys. Love you, boo.*
*Merry fucking Christmas - see what I did there? Ha!*

I cannot believe she got me sex toys and fucking restraints. And didn't warn me not to open it with company. I move the box to one side, trying to keep my composure, but Maverick winks at me and I know he saw my fluster.

Dammit.

Well, they have their secrets, this can be one of mine.

I move to open one of the boxes in front of me and feel the burning intensity of Linc's stare as I look at the tag. It's from him.

Undoing the gray ribbon from the flat black box, a weird sensation of anticipation and dread fills me. Please don't let him use this as another way to hurt me. I lift the lid and find a leather-bound notebook sitting inside.

It's freaking beautiful.

I lift it from the box, and open it, admiring the handwriting on the first page.


*V,*

*Sometimes it's hard to say the right things, but putting it on*
*paper makes the darkness not so bleak.*
*Maybe this can be your light in the dark.*

*L*

I blink back the tears. How does he always know the best ways to break me? This might not have been meant to break me, but it did.

For once, being broken doesn't seem so bad.

After an emotional Christmas and several days of even more emotional down time as the black hole I've been running from finally caught up with me, today, I decided to get out of bed. I missed New Year's Eve, but Indi was super chill about it. I'm kind of glad she has her boys back, because as much as I love her, I really needed those days to wallow.

Today though, I'm washing off my funk. I'm starting this new year right, and dammit, something has to go better than it has the last six months.

I finish putting on my sports bra and leggings, tying the laces on my sneakers and putting my hair up in a ponytail. Glancing out of the doors to my balcony, I contemplate taking my jacket. I decide against it and pull on the armband for my phone, picking up my AirPods before heading downstairs.

"I'm heading out for a run!" I call out to Smithy as I slide one pod in.

"Be careful, Miss Octavia! I'll have breakfast ready for your return." I smile and slip the other pod in, hitting play on my running playlist. I stretch out a little before jogging down to the gate, enjoying the brisk morning air.

There's nothing quite like the icy bite of winter air filling your lungs to start the day. I hadn't realized how much I missed starting my day like this, but now I'm here, I promise myself that I won't lose my routine again. No matter how much crazy shit I have going on. This helps me physically and mentally.

I can't stay afloat through all the crazy if I'm already drowning in my own.

I hit the pavement, the sounds of *Partners in Crime* by Set It Off blasting through my pods. A grin spreads across my face as my lungs start to burn in the most delicious way. I lose focus on everything but the wind on my face, the beat in my ears, and the ache in my muscles from not having run in so long.

It's only when I reach the pier and take a few seconds to suck in lungfuls of air that I spot Lincoln about fifty yards away, jogging in shorts and a sleeveless t-shirt.

I head to the stall selling drinks at the edge of the pier and grab two bottles of water. Thank God for contactless. When Lincoln catches up, I wave the water bottle at him and he comes toward me as I take a drink from my own.

He takes the bottle and drinks half of it in one go, splashing some on his face when he's done. I try my hardest not to smile, but fail. Without even trying, he's like something off a goddamn commercial. His golden skin glistens, even in the winter sun, the water merely emphasizing it.

"Were you following me?" I ask, and he looks at me like

I'm ridiculous. And I might be, but I'm pretty certain I've never seen him out running.

He finishes his water before answering. "Maybe. But I mean, who goes out running alone when they have a stalker?" He raises his brow and I bite my lip. Sometimes I wonder if I have any sense of self-preservation at all, because I definitely hadn't considered that when I decided to run today.

"Right. That… Thanks."

He shakes his head, muttering something under his breath I can't make out. "Are you heading back?"

I check the tracker on my phone. It's only about half of my usual distance. "Yeah, we can head back."

He quirks a brow at me, crossing his arms. "Were you done?"

"No, but it's fine. I should've thought. I'll just hit the treadmill later or something."

"Octavia, I swear…" He trails off, pinching the bridge of his nose. I try not to feel like a scolded little girl and tamper the sass that rises in response. "Just run your normal route. I'll be fine, this was barely a warm-up."

I bite the inside of my cheek, wondering if he's just being polite or if his ire is from something else. I shrug, deciding that he's big enough to make his own decisions and if he says we can still run, then I'm going to keep running. I might as well start my new routine properly if I want to keep it up.

"Okay, then let's go." I slip my AirPod back in, the music

starting up automatically as I finish my water and drop the bottle in the recycling bin before taking off up the promenade. I only ran this route a few times before Halloween, but it's the perfect loop. And at this time of day it's beautiful, the sunrise spilling orange and pink over the horizon. There's something hopeful about it that makes me feel better about my day.

I take off at a steady pace, trying not to go too fast in case Lincoln was exaggerating, but after another half mile I get restless and pick up the pace.

There's something freeing about the burn of running.

After another half mile, Lincoln runs basically beside me, looking bored, like this really isn't a challenge for him. I have no idea why that riles me, but it does.

*Keep up with this, buddy.*

It's another four miles back home but I pick up my pace, pushing as hard as I can. It's stupid, foolish, and childish, but I grin inside through the pain. I know I'm going to regret pushing this hard on day one back out, but I can't help myself.

When we're about a mile from home, I look behind me to find Lincoln keeping back, maybe two strides behind me. The asshole grins at me. He fucking grins. Like my lungs aren't burning to the point where I think I might combust.

Then the asshole has the sheer audacity to increase his pace, so that he's running ahead of me. The sight might not be a bad one, but it gripes me nonetheless, and I push harder so we're running shoulder to shoulder.

When we finally reach the gates to the house, I hit the code, and basically crumple on the lawn on the other side.

"That was fun. Nice warm up before I hit the gym." He grins down at me, and I flip him the bird from where I'm lying face down on the lawn.

Asshole.

I take a deep breath as we pull into the parking lot at school, clutching Indi's coffee as she pulls into my usual space. My Impala isn't loving the cold snap we seem to be having, but I have the world's greatest bestie because she rescued me from having to come in with Lincoln.

"Are you okay?" she asks, glancing at me with a furrowed brow once she's parked.

I bite my lip, trying to think of how to explain it. "There's just this pit in my stomach, like something bad is going to happen today. Usually I'd ignore it, put it down to weird dreams or some shit... but with everything that happened here last semester, I can't help but wonder if my intuition is kicking in or something."

She pinches her lips together, like she's thinking over my words real hard. "I mean, you called a truce with Lincoln and the others... and you're definitely reaping the rewards of that, right?"

I nod, trying not to roll my eyes. As unconventional as it might be dating more than one person, my bestie is rocking it and she's all for me playing the field with these guys. "Yeah, well not with Linc, but yeah."

"Okay, well then they're clear from the board at least."

"Yeah." I sigh. "That just leaves the rest of the student body. Awesome."

She squeezes my hand, trying to reassure me. "Most of them will back off now that the Saint Squad have pulled back. That just leaves Blair and her bitch squad."

"And Raleigh," I tag on. I swear, I had no idea it was possible to avoid someone in this school for as long as it's been since I've seen him, but whatever Finley and Maverick did to him, he's avoided me like the plague since.

Somehow that's made it worse. The anticipation and anxiety of seeing him has built up into this big thing. Because I know I'll see him again. Except now I've had the time to dream up a million different variations of what that looks like.

It might sound silly, but if I could stop it, I would. My brain isn't always the kindest to me.

"We got this. I will stick to you like glue all day if it helps." I shake my head at her offer, sweet as it is.

"Thank you, I love you for offering. I just need to pull up my Bridget Jones and get on with it." I take a sip from my mocha as she grabs her bag and nods.

We climb from the car just as Maverick and Finley pull into

the lot, one after the other. They park in the spaces beside us, leaving one between them for Lincoln. I pull down the beanie on my head, my curls flowing down my back beneath it as I huddle into my coat. I swear it almost feels as cold as the winter I spent in London right now.

I can happily say I've adjusted back to California weather, and this cold is so not appreciated. Especially when I still have to wear this goddamn skirt. Even if the socks are cute and warm.

"Morning." Mav grins at me as he pulls off his helmet, his dark hair flicking back as he climbs from his bike.

I smile back, waving at him and Finn before scurrying inside with Indi. I haven't seen either of them much since Christmas, but Maverick does at least seem back to his usual self. On the outside anyway. I know as well as most that a mask is easily worn.

We head into the main hall, moving toward my locker, when we're stopped by Blair and her bitch squad.

I let out a sigh, moving myself just a little in front of Indi, because I'll be fucked if they mess with her too. "What do you want now, Blair?"

I feel heat at my back moments before hearing, "Yes, Blair. What do you want?"

I bite back my grin at Maverick's voice. Looking back, I see the three of them flanking Indi and I. Not going to lie, having that power at my back feels good. It feels like coming home. Almost like I have my friends back, even if I'm still not fully convinced they're entirely in my corner.

Her eyes go wide as she takes them in behind me and, I swear to God, actually stomps her foot. "I'd heard you were all slumming with the whore, but I figured it was just a rumor. I guess spreading your legs finally got you somewhere, Octavia. I hope you boys wrapped up, because she's nothing but a dirty skank."

"You listen here, you two-bit trash," Indi starts, jumping in front of me like she's about to throw down. Mav grabs her around the waist and pulls her back.

"Calm down, Cujo. We got this." He winks down at her, and I swear my ice heart melts a little more for him.

"Blair, just because I wouldn't put my dick in your shriveled-up bucket, doesn't mean I'm fucking your cousin," Linc says so bitingly even I wince a little. "Even if I did, it would have absolutely fuck all to do with you. So I'll ask again, slowly this time so you can comprehend. What the fuck do you want?"

He steps closer so I'm practically leaning against his chest, Finn on my other side, while Mav stays with Indi.

"I came to tell this skank that some of her shit was delivered to the house over the weekend if you must know. I didn't realize that she had guard dogs watching her every move. At least now I'll know for future reference."

"I'd keep an eye on that future of yours, Blair. We both know how much hangs in the balance. It would be so easy for everything to fall down around you," Lincoln says, and she pales. I have no idea what the fuck he's going on about but whatever it is, he obviously hit a nerve.

She lets out a humph and spins on her heel, storming away, her little band of bitches scurrying along behind her. I turn to face the guys, trying not to smile too wide. "Thank you, you totally didn't need to come to my rescue, but I appreciate it."

"We always had your back before," Mav says, making Indi snort. "Well, not before, but before before. And we told you over break that things would change. We meant it."

Lincoln nods, just as the bell rings. "We'll see you later."

He and Finley head up the hall as Mav kisses my cheek before he bounces along behind them.

"Well. That's a weird new kind of normal." Indi laughs as we rush to my locker.

"Tell me about it." I throw my stuff in my locker before we dive to hers.

"I get the feeling I missed out on some stuff that happened over break, so this weekend you and I are having a catch up date."

I grin at her, because I am so down for that. "It's totally a date."

I walk into the cafeteria with Indi at my side and freeze when I hear his laugh. My blood turns to ice in my veins as I turn and see Raleigh laughing and joking with the football team at their table. Blair and her bitch squad flitting around them like a hive of bitch bees.

"Oh look, it's the girl who cried rape!" Blair's voice echoes around me, and I feel like I've been plunged under an ice cold wave. The laughter that sounds around the room makes me want to be sick.

"Come on, we don't need to be here," Indi says, tugging at my arm, but it's like my feet are made of lead and I can't move. I thought his timetable changed; he wasn't meant to have lunch with us anymore.

Raleigh saunters toward me, with Blair clinging to his side. Now is so not the time to freeze, but I can't make my fucking body respond, despite my mind screaming at me to get the fuck out of here.

"You didn't really think I wanted you, did you, new girl? I guess points for not giving it up as easily as your friend did to my boy. But crying rape when you were just a little tipsy is a bit much, don't you think?"

Indi sucks in a breath, and I see the tears fill her eyes. Anger rushes through me and I clench my fists, turning to face Raleigh when a blur moves past me. The crack as Maverick's fist connects with Raleigh's jaw is enough to turn my stomach. He rails on him as Blair starts squawking. She turns to me, practically spitting, "Call off your fucking guard dog!"

I take two steps toward her, and despite what happened

last time, I slap her petty fucking face, making sure to curl my fingers so I scratch down her cheek. It's not even close to what I want to do to her after everything, but for now, it's all I can do.

I smirk, and she screams as blood trickles down her cheek. "You bitch!"

"I'm the bitch? Blair, you've done nothing but be an absolute asshole since I got back here and I have no idea why." She charges at me, looking almost fucking possessed. She tackles me to the ground, screaming like a banshee, and it's all I can do to stop her blows from landing.

She's fucking insane.

I get the feeling insane is the only way I'm going to get out of this, so I go limp for a second and then headbutt her as hard as I can. My head spins but damn it feels good, and her scream is like music to my fucking ears.

She's lifted from me, and I notice Finn carting her away as Lincoln pulls Mav from Raleigh's fucked-up form on the ground before turning back to Indi, who looks frozen stiff with watery eyes.

"Come on," I tell her, mouthing a thank you to Finley as he deals with the mess I leave behind.

"I think I'm going to bail," Indi says, her voice shaking. I swear I want to go back and nut stomp Raleigh for announcing her business the way he just did. How I ever thought he was a good guy is baffling. She pulls her phone from her pocket, tapping on the screen. I feel useless and furious.

"Is there anything I can do?"

She shakes her head, wiping at her face as we reach her locker. "No, it's fine. I think I'm just going to go and chill with Ryker and Ellis. They're not back at school till tomorrow anyway."

"Okay, I'm sorry my shit keeps spilling over onto you."

She looks at me, more fierce than I think I've ever seen her. "Don't you dare. None of this is on you. He's just a giant fucking asshole, and I hope Maverick cuts off his fucking dick."

I laugh because, well, that'd be hilarious. But also, I'm not convinced he wouldn't do it.

"I love you. I'll see you tomorrow," I say as I hug her.

"Thank you, I'm sorry for leaving you stranded."

I wave her off, because hell no is she going to worry about me right now. "I'll find my way, we're good. You go chill with the guys and I'll see you in the morning?"

"You will," she says, squeezing me once more before grabbing her stuff from her locker and bolting for the doors.

I head for my own locker, my stomach rumbling despite the chaos. Times like this I wish I still stashed granola bars everywhere.

"You want to get out of here?"

I turn and find a bloody-knuckled Maverick grinning at me.

"I am definitely not opposed to the idea," I say, smiling back at him. My GPA is pretty healthy right now. I can totally cut the afternoon. Especially after what just happened. I'd rather be anywhere but here.

"Awesome, let's go grab some food and chill." He puts an arm out and I grab my jacket, bag, and beanie from my locker before sidling up beside him.

"Thank you for that. You didn't have to."

He tucks me under his arm and leads me outside. Thankfully, the sun is back and it's no longer bitingly cold out here anymore. "You don't have to thank me, princess. He hurt you, and what he said about Rainbow… shit's out of line." I smile at his apparent nickname for Indi. It does suit her though. "Plus, I have a lot to make up to you. I'm not the guy to fix things with fancy words, or give you the answers I know you crave. But I am the guy that can make your enemies bleed and wish they were never born."

A shiver runs down my spine when he smiles at me. His version of romance is drenched in blood and brutality, but with everything I've learned lately, I can't be too surprised. Plus it's kind of sweet in a Maverick kind of way.

He heads to Lincoln's Porsche and opens it with a fob on his keys, grabbing his jacket and two helmets from the back. "I keep a spare back here just in case." He winks, handing it to me. I look longingly at the bike, then down at my skirt.

Fuck it.

I pull my jacket on, slinging my bag across my body before pulling my beanie on and putting the helmet on over the top. He gazes at me, groaning. "You shouldn't look that good in a fucking helmet," he grumbles, and I laugh.

He climbs onto the bike and I swing my leg over, sliding in behind him on what might be the tiniest seat I've seen in my life. "Hold on tight, princess. I'll take you for a ride."

I can't help but laugh at his teasing tone as I wrap my arms around him. This isn't exactly how I saw my day going, but I'm not sad about it.

The bike vibrates beneath me when he starts it up, and my grin widens. I shouldn't feel this good right now, but I'm not going to question it. We head out of the parking lot and he opens her up, pulling a squeal from my lips as he does. His torso shakes, telling me he heard the squeal, too.

I am having too much fun, so when Mav steers the bike away from home, I don't bother to object. I hold on tight, literally just along for the ride. I lose track of time, enjoying the escape. I know I've forgiven him—even if I probably shouldn't—even though he hasn't apologized yet.

There is just something about him that calls to me.

Like calls to like I guess. It just means we're both more broken than I ever realized.

We ride to the other side of town before he heads into one of the parks around The Cove. He pulls the bike to a stop at the side of the lake and takes his helmet off. "I thought you might want to decompress a little before you go home."

I take my helmet off and climb from the bike to set it on the ground. I take Mav's and place it next to mine, trying not to smile. I guess he does have a softer side after all. He doesn't step from the bike, so I raise a hand above my eyes to see him properly, to take a guess at what's going through his mind.

I take a step forward and he grabs me by the hips, lifting me with ease, and puts me on his lap, facing him. My heart races as I cling to him and the asshole just smirks. "Isn't this a little dangerous?"

"You telling me you don't like a little danger, princess?"

His hands run up my bare thighs and under my skirt. I squirm under his touch. "Someone could be here, anywhere. They could see."

"If you didn't catch it last time, that doesn't exactly faze me. If anything…" He trails off as I roll my eyes at him. His fingers toy with my pussy through the lace of my panties, and I bite the inside of my cheek to stop from groaning. "But if you don't want to play…"

Without a word, I slap my hand on his wandering one and press it hard against my thigh, encouraging him to inch forward. The tank behind me isn't exactly comfortable but I balance myself on him, not wanting him to stop.

Leaning in, his lips brush up against mine with a tenderness so shocking it takes my breath away. It's only when he sinks his teeth into my flesh that I remember who I'm dealing with.

Mav swallows my gasp like that bite of pain is his own personal oxygen.

"Why do you do that?" I lick my bottom lip, sampling the coppery taste it leaves behind. Meanwhile, he's staring at my mouth, his chest rising and falling with each breath and his dick getting impossibly harder by the second.

"Do what, princess?"

I roll my eyes at him and his devilish smile. I'm not opposed to a little pain with my pleasure, but I can't help but wonder about him making me bleed. "Bite me until I bleed."

Slowly, the corners of his mouth rise into a sinister, albeit sexy as fuck, grin and his eyes drag up from my mouth to my eyes.

"Because I can." As if to accentuate his words, he pushes one long finger into my pussy and curls it up to a place that makes me jump closer to him.

The strength he must have in his thigh muscles impresses me as he keeps his Ducati stable, even though I'm writhing from his touch.

Dragging his finger out, he brings it to my mouth, coats it from side to side, pushes it between my lips, and says, "Suck."

With zero hesitation, I do as I'm told and feel an electric satisfaction at the pleased look in his eyes.

But it's when he brings his finger to his own mouth that I feel myself getting exponentially wetter.

"I'm going to fuck you, princess, and this bike's not gonna work for the things I have planned."

In seconds, he flicks down the kickstand and lifts me as he swings off the bike. I wrap myself around him, trying not to fall as he moves. He grins at me as he walks us to a small patch of soft grass. The hard length of his cock is pushing against my aching pussy and every step he takes makes me rub against him.

I suck in a breath when he lowers me to the ground. Anyone could see us.

Fear spikes through me at the thought. I look up at him and he grins. He gets off on this shit. The risk. The power. Being watched.

"Mav," I start, and he stops my words with his lips.

"I'm about to show you just how much fun it can be, taking risks." He winks at me as he kneels between my spread thighs. He grabs his cock through his jeans and gives me a lascivious grin. I can't help but laugh outright at him.

"Shut up and do something or I'm walking home."

His expression goes from lighthearted to feral in half a second.

Leaning down, he rips open my button-down shirt and sinks his teeth into the smooth skin right above my nipple. "You're not going any-fucking-where."

My hips jolt off the ground at the sting of his teeth, moaning out loud at the pain as my pussy gets slicker.

Apparently my appreciation for pain with pleasure goes deeper than I thought.

I lick my lips, wondering exactly where this is going as he looks at me with a heated gaze.

He trails his tongue around my nipple, licking his way up to my neck before he unzips his jeans enough to get his dick out just as he reaches the soft space right beneath my ear.

"Every bite I take is me claiming you, princess. And you best believe that's exactly what you are. Mine." Just as he promised, he first sucks on my tender skin and then bites hard enough to make me whimper.

Fuck.

That's going to leave a mark.

Another one.

When he pulls away, I watch him as he stares at what I'm guessing is the red patch on my throat. The look on his face is fucking priceless and without conscious thought, my thighs spread even wider, a silent invitation.

Flipping up my skirt, he pushes my panties aside and in one determined thrust, pushes his dick inside me to the hilt.

We both groan, the fullness a stark reminder of just how big he is; how perfectly he stretches me. He pauses for just a moment, barely a breath of time, before he lifts my legs, my ankles resting on his shoulders and one hand at his favorite place: my throat. With his free hand holding the weight of his body, he pulls out slowly and then slams right back inside me.

Again.

And again.

And fucking again.

Each time he buries himself inside me, the force of it pushes the air right out of my lungs. Every time he pulls out, he squeezes my neck hard enough that I worry he might cut off my oxygen but I relax when I realize he's obviously not a beginner at this and I can breathe just fine. I bet he'll leave a mark there, though.

I'm a little fuck toy to this man. This animal that gets off on the control he wields. This savage who gets off on my pain. This lover who probably doesn't even know what love feels like.

It's when he turns his head—all the while keeping his intense stare on me—and sinks his teeth into my calf that I realize just how true my thoughts are. He's the predator and even though he's got his prey right where he wants it, he's not done. He wants to keep playing with me before going for the kill.

With every thrust of his hips, my body slides on the ground. If not for the tight hold of his hand wrapped around my neck— one finger gently caressing the new bite mark—I would be moving all over the place.

He angles his body just a little differently—positioning his groin to rub perfectly against my clit—and my entire body lights up with my building orgasm.

"That's it, princess. You're about to come all over me, aren't you? You like it when I hurt you? When I squeeze my fingers enough to cut off your oxygen? When I make you bleed?" He squeezes my throat harder, and it's like my entire world lights up.

I fall over the edge as he pushes me into oblivion. I cry out, no longer caring who might see or hear us, but almost no sound comes out around his grasp.

My eyes roll back and my fingers dig into the grass, trying

to keep myself grounded because I feel like I might fly off somewhere into the ether. Everything is heightened. The sound of the water, the smell of a California winter creeping up on us, the feel of him overpowering me. It's too much.

Pinning me down and basically choking the air out of me, he slams one last time inside me, biting my other calf as he comes.

We don't move for what feels like an eternity. I'm trying to gasp but he's still cutting off my air. My chest is rising and falling, fighting for breath, and it's only when I reach up and claw at his wrist that he opens his eyes back up—giving me his signature crazy-as-fuck grin—and releases my throat.

"You fucker! You almost killed me."

"Nah, I know what I'm doing. You had plenty of time left," he says, winking at me. Fucking winking. "Fuck, V. That orgasm was fucking intense."

Then he kisses me, like I'm his only tether to the earth, and any frustration I had melts away.

He might infuriate me, but Maverick Riley is worming his way back underneath my skin, and I'm not sure I have the desire—or power—to stop him.

# THIRTEEN

## FINLEY

*I* hide in my closet as my father's roars shake the house. I know I shouldn't hide from him. I know he'll make me play like he always does. But I don't want to play tonight. Every time his special friends come over…

I don't want to play.

I never want to play.

But they always make me.

One day, when I'm bigger, stronger, they won't be able to make me play.

If I can just hide until then, maybe I'll be okay.

Mom always says this time will be the last, but it's never the last. She just laughs as she breathes in the white powder, telling me it will be okay.

*But it's not okay.*

*And I can't even tell anyone. Dad told me he'd make it hurt more if I told.*

*I don't want it to hurt anymore.*

*Maybe if I run to Lincoln's house or Octavia's house, I won't have to play tonight.*

*Holding my breath so I don't make any noise, I push the door of my closet open a little. He's not in here yet. I creep from my hiding spot, crawling across the room.*

*I make it to the window, trying to push it up, but it squeaks so loud as it moves. Fear spikes through my heart as it pounds in my chest, hammering against my ribs, and my vision goes funny from holding my breath.*

*He's going to find me.*

*I dive under the bed, hoping that gives me enough time to hide from him, that he looks somewhere else.*

*I scream as I'm dragged from under the bed by my ankle, trying to grab onto the floor to stop him from getting me.*

*"You little shit!" Dad screams as he pulls me to my feet. I ball my hands into fists, trying not to cry.*

*"I'm sorry," I say, my voice wobbling. We don't cry in this house. Knights don't cry. If I cry, he'll make it hurt worse.*

*"You will be sorry if you ruin this for me. I'll make your mother pay for it too. Do you understand?" He spits in my face, and I shake so hard as I nod. "Get fucking dressed. Our guest will be here in ten minutes. Do not disappoint me. You know*

*what happens when you disappoint me."*

*He storms from the room, and I run to my bathroom and throw up.*

*My mom used to read me fairy tales and tell me about princes and saving people, but I don't think anyone is coming to save me.*

I wake up from the nightmare in a cold sweat. Those nightmares haven't haunted me for a long time, but considering what today is, I'm not exactly surprised they've unburied themselves from my subconscious.

I've visited my mom in her 'wellness center' this weekend every year since I committed her. It's the only time I visit her, and even then it's more out of guilt than anything else. I'm aware that she is a terrible human, and the worst kind of mom, but she is still my mom and we both suffered at my father's whims.

The only reason I still stay in this house of fucking horrors is because my father is all too aware that he doesn't own me any longer. This is not my home and my father uses the place as his own fucking pleasure den these days. He runs all sorts of shit from here, and on those nights I make sure I'm anywhere else.

His lessons taught me many things: that using words beyond reason will get you nowhere, that actions mean far more than words ever could, that being the smartest guy in the room is vital, and that listening to what people are *actually* saying when they talk is the smartest thing you can do.

Nothing is ever black and white. We live within the shades of gray.

The difference between my father and I, is that my monster has limits, and his… his does not. If it's for the bigger picture—whatever the fuck he convinces himself *that* looks like at the time—it's justified. No matter what.

I will never be the man—or the monster—my father wants me to be, and I am perfectly fine with that. The only thing that will see me truly happy is when he's six feet under by my own hand. Anything else will feel like it was stolen from me.

One day I'll taste my revenge in the form of his blood. Until then, I will bide my time, clinging to the small hope that the one true light in my life can be saved.

Another reason for today's visit.

We need some answers and my mom is likely the only person able to give them. Assuming she's actually coherent. Turns out, years of drugs and physical abuse fucks a person up to the point that they just check out of real life.

Committing her on my sixteenth birthday was a real hoot. Especially after I found her trying to slice open her wrists after one of my dad's bouts.

Happy fucking birthday to me.

I roll out of bed and head straight for my bathroom. I need a shower to wash off the haunted remains of my nightmares. I crank the shower to a glacial temperature and step beneath the icy spray, gritting my teeth against the sting as it jets onto my skin.

Once I'm fully awake and free of the lingering memories of my personal hell, I turn the temperature up and rush through the rest of my shower. Do I want to go and visit my mom today? Absolutely not. Am I going to? Yes, because despite the lifetime of trauma, I'd walk through the fires of hell for V if that's what she needed from me. Even if she has no clue where my mom is—or that I'm even going, for that matter.

I finish getting ready for the day, dressing as I'd be expected to at the center: slacks, button-down, and polished, scuff-free shoes. It's a fucking care facility, but God forbid I tarnish the Knight name by turning up in jeans and sneakers. I learned early on that it's easier to pick my battles, and dress-code isn't one worth fighting.

Heading downstairs as quietly as I can so as not to draw the attention of my father, I grab a granola bar and a bottle of water before heading out to my car.

Why he thought that buying me a car would make up for the fact that I was forced to commit my own mother on my birthday, I will never fucking know. Given the fact that he's lorded it over me every day since then, I could never forget it even if I wanted to. To this day he's still bitter that I cracked the careful façade he'd worked so hard to build over the ugliest parts of our family.

If only the world knew the reality of what happens behind

the closed doors of this house.

I mean, my father's closest friends know, but to everybody else, he's just a well-respected businessman. No depravity or filth on his gleaming record.

I'm not sure how many outside of his inner circle know the true depths of what he's capable of, but it doesn't matter. It's exactly why the Knights keep him around. That and the whole legacy thing. God forbid anyone ever be free of them.

Yet, I still cling to the hope that we can get Octavia clear of it all.

I jump in my Aventador, the purr of the engine soothing me when I start it up. Driving well above the speed limit, I head down the freeway toward the inner-city center my mom is still at. She moved here over the summer from the stricter facility I had originally put her in. On paper, it's because she's doing so much better. In reality, it's that the new facility is owned by the Knights and they can keep her under their thumb here.

Gripping the steering wheel tight, I remind myself why I'm making the trip today.

My mom has answers. She has to. She lived through everything, even if it was in a haze.

In less than an hour, I pull up to the front of the gleaming white stone building that's way too fucking bright in the winter sun. I take a deep breath before parking in the open space opposite the main entrance.

Gritting my teeth, I paste a smile on my face, the mask too

easy to slip into, and head inside the building. "Namaste, Mr. Knight. It's so lovely to have you back with us. Your mom will be so pleased to see you."

I glance at the blonde's name tag. Candy. Of course.

"Thank you. Is she in her room?" I ask, acting the part of the polite, dutiful son that I'm expected to be.

"I believe she's actually in the yoga center. If you'd like to have a seat, I'll check for you."

I nod, taking a seat, before grabbing my phone. I scroll mindlessly through my social media apps to pass the time. I haven't heard anything back from Mav or Linc yet, and as much as I want to message V, I don't want to get distracted, which is exactly what would happen.

Instead, I slip my phone back into my pocket and lean my head against the wall. This charming persona is draining as fuck. I am so not this guy--the guy who works the room. I leave that to Lincoln. He's the people person. Me, I revel in being the strong silent type. Or… well, just the one people don't talk to.

I'm much happier when it's that way.

"Mr. Knight, your mother is this way, please." The peppy voice pulls me from the darkness of my musings and back to this way-too-bright space, the contrast between the two stark to the point of painful.

I follow her through the halls lined with floor-to-ceiling windows, the winter sun filtering through down to the visitors' room.

The yellow space has big gray couches scattered throughout, a few tables surrounded by stylish, uncomfortable chairs, and a lone TV on the wall.

"There he is, my beautiful boy." I turn toward the sound of my mother's voice, and she strides across the room toward me. Dressed in all white, her blonde hair shining, she wraps her arms around me and I stiffen. This woman lost the right to this sort of greeting a while back, but I grit my teeth and briefly embrace her. Fuck knows who is watching.

"Mother. You're looking well."

We move to sit at a table in the far corner of the room, away from the few other people in here. There isn't much privacy, but if she thinks this is a good place to talk, then I'll have to trust her. I grab my phone as we sit, putting it on silent, and turning on the jammer app I installed the moment I got it. If I can protect this conversation, then I'm going to.

She sits opposite me, her eyes glassy and her gaze somewhere far beyond the walls of her cage, and smiles absently until she tries to grasp my hand and I pull it away from her. "What brings you here? It's been so long since I've seen you."

"Octavia is back." I keep my words to a minimum. She doesn't need more than that to know why I'm here. She might be off her fucking rocker, but even *she* has to realize I'm here for answers.

Her eyes go wide, and she leans back in the chair. "Oh."

"I need to know how Lincoln's mom got out. How Octavia's

mom got out." A small grin plays on her lips and a sadistic glint briefly flashes in her eyes before she turns back into the new-and-improved Stepford version of herself. For just a moment, I got to see the woman who raised me, the funhouse reflection of herself that my father warped her into. Hell, maybe she was always that person, and my dad just brought out the worst in her. Fucked if I know.

"They didn't get out, Finley dear." Her voice lilts at the end, like I made a joke. Gritting my teeth, I take a deep breath.

"Don't fuck with me. I need answers and I know you have them." Her eyes glaze over, like whatever drugs she's on have taken hold. "Mom!"

She blinks, turning her attention back to me, but it's like she's an entirely different person. This is the mother who would hear my screams and laugh. She rolls her eyes, before leaning forward, resting her forearms on the table. "You always were besotted with the Royal girl. Following her around like a sad, lost little puppy. You and the other two. It was like she was the flame and you the moth. She was always going to be your demise and, mark my words, she will be if you keep chasing her the way you seem to be. The fact that you're even here tells me that you're already on the road to your own destruction."

I roll my eyes and let out a sigh. "You always were one for dramatics. This was a waste of my time. I don't know why I even bothered."

She blinks again, her eyes glassy. "Oh Finley, no. Don't

leave. Please."

I pinch the bridge of my nose, trying not to lose my shit. I'm getting whiplash from her multiple personalities. "I need information, Mom. Can you help me?"

She pats my hand, looking at me like a doting mother. "I can try, but the Knights… well, it's not something you can fight against. My poor little boy, all grown up. Fighting them is like swimming against the tide. You're likely to get tired and slip up. But there was that one time… she skitted away like a butterfly, beautiful and never seen again… she might help. Though his dad always did have an obsession with her, he might be willing to help."

I sigh as she smiles at me, looking at me like I'm a freaking unicorn. "I don't know what any of that means, Mom."

"It means, sweet boy, that if you grow wings, you can fly away too. You just need to become so powerful that they can't clip them."

This trip was a waste of time. I'd really hoped that she would've been able to help. But I have no idea what she's talking about.

"You should speak to his guard dog, maybe he got her out. Though he might've clipped her wings too."

"Speak to who?"

She looks almost afraid and shakes her head, covering her mouth like she just said something that might get her killed.

"No, no… nothing, sweet boy. Nothing at all. It's Christmas

soon, right? Will you come and see me? I have something to give you." She pats my cheek, her finger tracing the faded scar that's there. She fixates on it, but I pull out of her grip.

That isn't a memory lane I want to walk down.

"Why don't you give it to me now, Mom?"

She shakes her head, looking all around as if we're being watched. I should really speak to someone about whatever it is she's on. Though they're probably keeping her on a concoction so she can't speak out about shit. "No, no. Not yet. It isn't time yet. If they knew you had the key… no. The King kept it safe, and now it's yours. She has the key too. Pretty little thing. But it's yours, really. Maybe then your wings will grow."

"This isn't helping me find a way out, Mom."

I sigh and move to stand but she grabs my wrist, her nails digging in hard enough that I feel my skin break beneath them. "Don't you get it?" Her eyes are clear and sharp, glinting with the all-too-familiar malice I had grown up with. "Once you're in, you're in. There is no escape. The only way out is if they don't want you in to begin with, and if you were already in, the only way out is in a box."

"But they got out!" I hiss as I rip my wrist from her grasp, blood trickling down onto my hand. Fucking crazy.

She laughs, the sound cold and hard. "If you think that, then you're a fool." Her voice softens and she lazily picks at an invisible spot on the table. "No one makes it out of this alive."

I wait with Lincoln and Maverick in the corner of the room, hands in my pockets. My visit with my mom was a bust and tonight isn't going to make this day any better.

The quarterly dick measuring meeting held by The Knights Society. It's not just for the inner sanctum or those of us who have a ruling vote. No, tonight is for a wider audience. For those in the second and third rings of hell. The Bishops. Those with enough skin in the game that they're important enough to rub shoulders with the Conclave. In our case, the Conclave are the seven founding families of The Cove.

Along with the prospects: a.k.a. the Rooks: people who want in, who believe they have something to offer. Though, just by being here they're already one foot in the grave. If it wasn't damn-near to a guarantee they'd be in, they wouldn't have set foot on the property. Taking care of people who see more than they should has proven time and time again to be too much of a hassle to accept the risk. It's just easier to run a tight ship and keep our circles small.

The military-grade security outfit also helps.

There's everyone here from drug and human traffickers to gun runners. From politicians to presidential candidates. Cartel bosses to CEOs of household-name brands. And that's just people in this sect.

I'm just glad I'm not deemed important enough to have to show my face when the senior members of the Conclave get together.

Not yet anyway.

For now, I'll take my junior status and run the fuck with it. The less I have to do with this fucking hellscape the better.

"So your mom had no details?" Lincoln asks, picking at the lint on his jacket, looking as nonchalant as expected.

I shake my head and swig back the whiskey in my glass—the only upside of these bullshit meetings. "Not a thing. She said no one gets out alive."

"Which is bullshit, because Fiona is currently sunning herself in the Caribbean with a beach boy." Lincoln rolls his eyes, referring to his mother. "There is very little chance my father would just let that happen if she wasn't out and completely unattached."

Maverick laughs dryly, just before a shadow appears over my shoulder. I turn and find Harrison, Lincoln's dad, standing just behind me. "Boys. Being sociable as usual I see."

I step sideways, not wanting him at my back. I make a habit of not letting anyone I don't trust be there.

Not anymore.

"Harrison." Lincoln smirks at his father. "What's on the schedule for tonight's display of debauchery?"

Harrison laughs, though it doesn't quite reach his eyes. "You'll see. I have a feeling that tonight's piece is going to be something that the three of you might finally pay attention to. After the fire at Nestwood before Christmas, we put together a plan of attack on certain holdings of the Conclave. Tonight... well, you'll see."

An icy drop of dread runs down my spine, but I don't let it show on my face. The key to survival here is to be entirely devoid of any emotion. Anything that can be used against you will be. It's partially why we were such assholes to Octavia when she arrived; we had hoped that the sect's Conclave would think she couldn't be used against us.

Unfortunately for her—and us—that plan didn't exactly prove successful. In fact, it was so *un*successful they even dropped their plans to start trafficking drugs through The Cove. It's all just a little too suspect if you ask me. It puts me on edge.

Harrison leaves us alone after dropping his little breadcrumb of what the night holds and goes back to his guests. And they are *his* guests since he's the head of the Board for our sect, making him a Regent: one of the few with a seat at the round table that makes up the inner sanctum of The Knights Society.

The night drags on, rubbing elbows with people whose names and faces I store for future use, just in case. As of right now, they mean absolutely nothing to me. But this place is a pit of vipers, and only the strongest and smartest survive. So I stay on edge, making sure I'm aware of our surroundings, the three of us never separating. We learned a long time ago that there's safety in numbers.

I get pulled in a dozen different directions, never too far from the boys, but I swear I've never been so fucking bored and on edge at the same time. Everyone in here is drenched in whatever fragrance they deem to be the one that makes them seem the wealthiest. No one in here is in anything less than designer, dripping with jewels and it's more than a little obscene. The only reason I'm in this monkey suit is because I'd bleed if I wasn't.

I tune back into the conversation between some of the Bishops, showboating because I'm a legacy. "Did you hear about the shipment of girls we sold to the Russians last month? Made an absolute fortune. Got at least twice what they were worth. Dirty, homeless bitches all hopped up on whichever drug was cheapest at the time. Thirty mil for six girls. Got to love how much they go for when they're young."

It takes a lot to keep the sneer from my face as the others laugh at this nameless idiot's boasting.

"Well, I was shocked to see Erica here, especially after that scandal. Twenty pounds of cocaine in her daughter's car. I mean really, who would be so sloppy."

"I heard that Michael swept it under the rug for her."

"He's out of prison?"

"Yes, good behaviour. Twenty-five years for one little explosion was a bit over the top if you ask me."

God, I might go to prison if it means escaping this fucking conversation.

"Well he did kill, what was it, five people?"

"Yes, but I was his lawyer. Here's my card if you need me." Their snooty laughter grates on my nerve endings, but I keep my stony mask in place as they pat my shoulder, and smile at me like I hold the cards to the rest of their lives.

Just when I think I can't take it any more, that I might just massacre the entire room to escape this posturing bullshit, the lights dim, and Harrison's voice booms around the room. "Members of the sect, welcome to tonight's quarterly get-together. It has been a pleasure to speak to you all." He pauses for applause which, of course, he is given. The sycophants here want a piece of him. Some would rather that piece be his head on a platter, but all must kneel before the King. "Tonight, as promised, we are unveiling things to come. Things that we know you want to be a part of, and for the Rooks of the room, a little taster of what is to come should we allow you to join us."

I stifle a yawn, because a beating from my father isn't on my agenda for the night, especially with school on Monday. Bruises don't fade in a day, unfortunately for most people in this room. I drown out Harrison's drivel, trying to work out more about what these assholes could want with Octavia.

We're all pretty certain her dad didn't commit suicide, which means either the Knights took him out, or someone wanting a seat in the Conclave did. Except, why leave Octavia alive if that's the case? My first suspect was Nate, especially with the way Blair came sniffing around us like a bloodhound.

She wanted that seat at the table real bad. Too bad for her, the senior members shot that down.

Pretty much everyone in this room is a suspect. Not a soul in attendance is innocent. Every one of them has done something that lands them on the wrong side of the moral scale. You don't get in this room by having clean hands.

"Fuck," Lincoln hisses, bringing my attention back to the room, applause sounding again.

"What? What did I miss?" I ask, looking between the two of them, each looking as angry as the other.

I turn back to where Harrison was standing when neither of them respond and I get my answer.

*Fuck.*

# FOURTEEN

## OCTAVIA

Pulling up to school on a Monday morning is never any fun. But pulling up *this* Monday morning sucks on a whole new level.

I find Blair hanging off of Raleigh on the steps of the school, along with most of the football team and cheer squad, plus the rest of their cronies. All of them watch me as I pull into my space.

That I could cope with. Being watched isn't anything new to me.

It's the taunts as I climb from my car that piss me off. If I thought Blair teamed up with Lincoln was bad… well, let's just say things can *always* get worse.

I can deal with the usual shouts.

*Whore.*

*Slut.*

*Skank.*

Words like that are water.

It's the "girl who cried rape" and "liar" that cuts me.

Keeping my head held high, I try to push through the crowd because there's no way around them. I climb the steps, but its so fucking claustrophobic as I try to reach the doors. People surround me on all sides, pushing in around me as they yell their taunts.

It's only when I reach the top step, coming face to face with Blair that it lets up and I can breathe. I try to shoulder past my cousin, but with Raleigh behind her, she's immovable. She laughs in my face as both of her palms connect with my chest and I fall backwards. Shock envelops me as I fall down the stairs, but the noise stops and before I hit the hard ground, a pair of massive arms catch me.

"We've got to stop meeting like this, princess." I blink up into Maverick's easy smile. He helps me back to my feet and the smile falls from his face as he looks at the congregation on the steps. "Did you all enjoy that? I warned you once, you were put on notice. Octavia Royal is ours. That means our protection. Consider this your last warning, and thank her for even getting a warning, because we all know if it was up to me, this would be dealt with here and now. Do *not* make me come for you. You know I won't come alone."

Without another word, everyone but Raleigh and Blair disperses as Lincoln and Finley arrive and flank me on each side.

Blair sneers at me before leaning into Raleigh. "Come on, babe, we don't need to waste any more of our morning on this trash." She looks back at us, gazing over my shoulder to Lincoln. "You picked the wrong Royal. You'll see."

"Blair, your desperation is showing," Lincoln says dryly.

Stifling my laugh at the look on her face, I turn toward the sound of laughter as Indi approaches us, hearing the end of what feels like a way-too-long morning already. Blair flicks her blonde locks over her shoulder and practically drags Raleigh into the building. His gaze cuts to me before he goes, the scorching hatred shining in his eyes is enough to steal my breath.

He has fuck-all reason to hate me. Anything that may or may not have happened to him is fully a consequence of his own actions. Nobody forced him to try and drug me, to try and rape me. I'm just lucky that Lincoln and the others arrived when they did.

I'm all kinds of confused about how I exactly feel about them all. I don't feel like I've forgiven them, yet there are moments when that's exactly what it feels like. Then, the next second I'm so spitting mad at them, I don't think I could ever forgive them. It's giving me fucking whiplash trying to keep up with it all.

But now is not the time to examine my emotions too closely.

I apparently have no respite from my cousin this semester, which means that even with the guys having backed off, this place is still likely to be a fucking nightmare.

Awesome.

"What did I miss?" Indi asks as she reaches my side, bumping Lincoln out of the way to loop her arm through mine as she hands me a cup of sweet nectar. I mouth a thank you before taking a sip. I sigh as the caffeine goodness hits my tongue. *Hello, liquid gold*.

"Just Blair's latest attempt to show me how much she hates me. Oh, and she's apparently simping over Raleigh now." I roll my eyes as I speak, only laughing a little as her jaw drops open.

"She is a crazy son of a bitch."

I lift my coffee in a salute. "That she is, my friend." Turning back to the boys who are all whispering between themselves, I quirk a brow. "Thank you for the save."

Mav grins at me before strutting forward and capturing my lips with his. I lose my mind at the heat of the kiss, curling my free hand into the lapel of his blazer as he overwhelms me entirely. "All in a day's work, princess. What else are dark knights for?" He winks at me before heading into school and the other two look at me with so much fire in their eyes that I feel like I'm going to combust on the spot before they follow behind him without a word.

"So that happened…" Indi says, laughing as I blink at her. That's when I notice the sheer number of people standing out here just watching us, and a blush creeps up my neck. "I guess it must be official now."

Looping her arm back through mine, she pulls me from the stairs and into the school.

"Nothing is official. Fucking Maverick. He might have an almost-magical dick, but he'll be lucky if I don't cut it off if he doesn't quit his shit."

She laughs loudly as we head toward my locker. "Dude, we don't maim magical dick unless it's absolutely vital to our survival. Maim other, less important, body parts."

I grumble under my breath as I sort the combination on my lock and open the door. "Yeah, yeah."

"So are things any better between you guys?" she asks, and I realize we still haven't had a chance to have a proper catch up. Life is totally kicking my ass at the minute. It feels like I've barely had a chance to catch my breath, let alone catch up with my bestie.

I shake my head as I sort out my books and slide my jacket into my locker. "Kind of but not really. They're starting to open up, and they've told me some stuff, but I still feel like I know basically nothing. Like I wish I could just lock them in a room with me until they tell me everything I want to know. That being said, I need some boy-free time. Want to hang out this weekend? I could use some bestie time. I feel like I've barely seen you since Thanksgiving."

"Hell yes. Life has been chaos. With Ryker and the others

stealing so much of my time, I know exactly what you mean. I need me some bestie time. What did you have in mind?"

"Sleep over, pj's, ice cream, the whole nine yards." I grin and she returns it with one just as wide.

"You had me at pj's." I close my locker and follow her over to hers. "I'll tell the guys that I'm MIA this weekend. I am too excited. I'm not even that far behind on school work, so if we have a study night this week too, I'm clear."

"Perfect. I've got a paper due for French and another for Statistics by Friday, so unless I get something else this week, I'm good too. Study night Wednesday?"

She nods as she grabs her books. "Perfection. Now let's just hope Miss Summers doesn't pile a ton of shit on today."

I loop my arm back through hers and finish the coffee she brought me, dropping the cup in the trash can just before we enter the class. It's still empty since the bell hasn't rung yet, so we head to our corner in the back.

"How are things going with *your* guys?" I ask, flashing her a knowing grin.

She blushes furiously as she slides into her chair. "They're definitely going. Apparently them deciding I was better off without them is a thing of the past and they're… erm… making up for lost time."

"Good for you!" I grin, wagging my brows at her. "I'm just glad you're happy, but if they don't treat you well this time, I'm not afraid of them. I will break them all."

"I have no doubt, but I think we're good. Something's changed since they broke it off. I don't know what yet, they don't talk much about that stuff with me, but there's definitely something."

I chew on my lip, wondering just how tied up they are in this Knight bullshit. I really need to pin Lincoln down and ask some actual questions. I know I'm not likely to get much from the other three: East, because I'm not sure how much he knows, and the other two because... well, Lincoln is the answers guy.

"Are we still going to work on your list?" Indi asks quietly as a few other people start to filter in the room. "Because I had a few ideas."

She smiles darkly and, well, color me intrigued. "I don't know, but I think so. I think they deserve to feel a little pain after everything. I'm just not sure how far I want to take it. Especially with things being so up in the air with them as they are at the minute. That reminds me, I need to tell you—" The bell interrupts my words, and Miss Summers floats into the room.

"Later," she whispers, and I nod. It's nothing that won't keep.

"Good morning, ladies and gents. I hope you shrugged off those back-to-school blues last week, because today we ramp it up. How does everyone feel about Shakespeare?"

Groans sound throughout the room, including one of my own. I am all for the classics, but Shakespeare has always been a bit much for me. Give me a remake any day of the week.

Sacrilegious words to some, I know, but there's something about modern retellings that's absurdly enjoyable to me.

"Glad to hear you're all so enthusiastic this Monday, but I guess it sucks to be you guys, doesn't it? Let's get this going, shall we?"

The days this week are passing slowly, but I'm not too sad about it. There has been minimal drama, minimal crazy, and I am here for it. I never did get any information from Finley about the knife that was delivered to my house, but it's on my list of questions to pepper Lincoln with when I manage to pin him down again.

Literally, if need be this time. I'm still convinced he only gave me those questions because he had nowhere else to escape to.

East's whistle blows and I finish my circuits, sucking in lungfuls of air. My morning runs with Lincoln have become a thing, and it's been so nice working out regularly again, but there is something about circuits that fucks me up every time. I can run for miles, but ask me to do aerobics and I crumble.

Indi dramatically wilts to the floor beside me and I laugh at her as she puts the back of her palm to her forehead as if she's a damsel from a fifties movie. She flips me the bird, making me laugh again before East shouts, stealing my attention.

He's been more than a little distant at school lately. I get it.

He's my teacher, but it still stings a bit. He certainly didn't mind getting up close and personal with me at home and it's only since then that he's been so off. I thought we'd worked shit out over the holidays, but I guess not. Just because I get it, doesn't mean it hurts less when he barely so much as glances at me during school hours now.

I've hardly spent any time with him alone since then. It's like he's gone from being my pillar of reliable strength to full-scale ghosting me unless the others are around.

"We're changing it up as of next week, ladies, so enjoy the circuits while they last. Next week won't be so easy. That's it for today. Get out of here." He blows his whistle again and people start to filter from the room.

Indi groans from where she's still lying on the floor. "Want a hand?" I offer her one, which she takes, and pull her to her feet.

"We still studying tonight?" she asks as she bends in half, hands on her knees.

"You know it. Smithy already promised milkshakes when we get in. He made you more cookies, too." Her grin is instantaneous, and it's like she is renewed.

"That man is a goddamn *saint.*"

I nod, because he absolutely is. "Come on, let's get changed and get you to the sugary heaven that awaits."

"V, do you have a minute?" East calls just as we start to head toward the locker room. I pause, biting down on my lip and glancing at Indi. She nods and heads out, leaving me alone with him in the gym.

"What's up?" I ask, sounding far lighter than I feel. I'm not sure when things got so weird and tense between us, but I'm putting that fully on him and his ghosting tactics.

He rubs the back of his neck, those stormy eyes of his seeming darker than usual. "I wanted to apologize…" He trails off as I stand awkwardly in front of him.

"Right?"

"I mean… damn… I don't want what happened between us to change shit. I don't want to rush you, or push you… and I'm your teacher, you're so much younger and despite how I feel about you… I just… I'm sorry." He looks so sad, so lost, that all of the weirdness I've felt about everything with him, all of the not-quite resentment, just melts away.

I move toward him, and wrap my arms around him, holding him tight, not giving a fuck who might see. "You have nothing to be sorry about. I'm sorry I've been a shitty friend. You've been there for me since I got back here and I hadn't even considered the sort of position all of this put you in. I'm the one who should be sorry."

He bands his arms around me and lets out a deep sigh as I melt against him. There is something about being in his arms that just feels safe. Like coming home after being out in a storm. He is solid, and reliable, and everything I need.

We stay like that for a few minutes, his face buried in my hair as I rest against him, until the bell rings again, breaking the moment between us. I untangle myself from him and tuck the loose strands of my hair behind my ear. "I should probably go and change, but we should talk soon. Just the two of us."

He nods, looking a little less sad but still just as lost. I wonder what's going on with him that I don't know, because it can't just be whatever this is between us that has him looking like that. My heart hurts for him. "I'm here if you want to talk."

"Thanks, V." The corners of his lips turn up as I grab the handle to the door. I want to say more but I'm not sure what I *can* say that will make any difference.

Another thing to add to my list of things to work out.

I head out to the locker room, changing without showering. I can do that once I'm home.

"Is it cool if I swing by home and then head over?" Indi asks as I finish changing.

I nod with a smile. "Sounds good. I need to shower anyway."

"Okay. All okay with that?" she asks, motioning in the direction of the gym with her head.

I shrug, wishing I had a better answer. "I think so?"

"Okay, we'll talk more in a bit," she says and I nod, conscious of the number of other people still in here with us. She heads out as I finish putting my gym clothes in my bag and generally sorting my shit out. By the time I'm done, the locker room has mostly emptied out and I head to my car with no issues.

I drive home with *Uncomfortably Numb* by Arrows in Action blasting through my speakers. It speaks to me way more than it probably should, but I lose myself to the lyrics and the melody, letting out some of the emotions I've been stuffing down lately. There is something about singing at the top of your lungs when you're on your own in the car that is so fucking therapeutic. I have yet to find anything else in the world that feels as good as belting out your feelings to a windshield.

I pull into the garage, glad that hump day is basically over and looking forward to my study night with Indi. Trying not to focus on the half-conversation I had with East, I climb from the car and head into the house, going straight up to my room. I take longer than I probably should in the shower, cranking the music up again and singing at the top of my lungs once more.

There are probably healthier ways to process emotion, but this works for me so I'm not going to question it. Music has always been an emotional outlet for me and I'm not about to change the habit of a lifetime.

By the time I'm done, dressed, and make my way downstairs, I find Indi sitting at the counter in the kitchen with Smithy, slurping on her milkshake, a plate of snickerdoodles in front of her.

"There you are, Miss Octavia. I was about to send out a search party," Smithy teases as I slide into the stool next to Indi. "Milkshake?"

"Sorry, I got a little lost in my own world." I give him a small smile. "I'd love one, please."

My stomach rumbles as I finish speaking and he quirks a

brow at me. "Dinner will be ready shortly, too. I do hope you're eating properly at school."

"Me eating isn't something you need to worry about. I eat plenty," I tell him, trying to reassure him. Because yeah, food isn't something I torture myself with. I make sure I work out plenty, but I am firmly in the camp of team food.

"As long as you are." He eyes both of us before sliding a milkshake in front of me. "I've got some things to get sorted, but I'll let you know when dinner is ready. Will you be joining us, Miss Indi?"

"I'd love to." She beams at him.

"Good, I'm making chicken parmigiana, so there will be more than enough." She groans at his words and rubs her stomach.

"Smithy, you keep talking dirty like that and I'll never leave."

"Indeed, Miss Indi," he says, shaking his head as he leaves the room, and she bursts out laughing.

"Dude, I think I just talked dirty to Smithy."

I shake my head, grinning at her before taking a sip of my shake. "Yeah, I think you did."

"God, I'm such an idiot when I open my mouth sometimes." She facepalms, and I snicker lightly. "We should probably just start studying so that I get something out of tonight other than just making an idiot of myself."

"You can be you here, there's zero judgement from anyone.

We love you just the way you are, goofy words and all." I wink at her, and she buries her face in her hands.

"I love you, too. Now, let's study before I die of mortification."

The night passes in a blur of working out standard deviations and interpreting the results for my presentation on Friday, and my French homework for tomorrow, while Indi groans about her upcoming Calculus test.

By the time she leaves, my eyes feel like they're going to fall out of my head. Not to mention we were so busy focusing that we had almost no time to actually catch up. Our only respite was dinner and I'm pretty sure Smithy didn't want to hear all of our dick talk over his delicious parma.

"I'm going to bed, do you need anything before I go, Miss Octavia?" Smithy asks, standing by the counter in the kitchen in his silk pj's and nightgown.

The old guy is freaking adorable. "I'm good thanks, just going to finish up this homework and then I'll be heading to bed too."

"Okay. Have a good night."

I smile up at him before jumping to my feet and giving him a hug. "Night, Smithy. Thank you for everything. I don't think I say that enough. Love you."

He squeezes me back, and gives me a croaky, "I love you too, Miss Octavia." He kisses the top of my head before padding out the other door in the kitchen toward the part of the house that has always been his. I've never even crossed that threshold.

I head back to my spot at the coffee table and drop down to the floor to finish my French homework, the words practically swimming on the page. I know people say that school is easy compared to 'real life' but honestly, I think adults just fully forget how hard shit can be at school.

My phone buzzes on the table while I finish writing my paper on music theory in French. Thankfully, French is probably the most fluent of the five languages I speak outside of English.

When it buzzes for the fourth or fifth time, I pick it up, sighing as I rub my eyes.

East

> I was thinking we could maybe continue our conversation from earlier

East

> Can I come over if you're still awake?

East

> V?

I smile a little at the messages, a wicked thought bubbling to the surface.

Me

> Want to go for a swim?

I bite my lip in anticipation. Maybe the best way to get him over the whole weirdness is to push a few more of his buttons. Plus, Maverick told me they're all aware of everything, so if they're good with us all messing around, why shouldn't I be?

I'm not about being put into a box with a label.

East

A swim?

Me

Sure. We can talk in the pool right?

East

You're aware it's January?

Me

I'm aware. Want to swim or not?

Sometimes his logic drives me insane, but I guess he is a Saint after all. Logic defies all, even in the face of emotion. Always has, always will. Harrison Saint was always that way when we were younger, too. Fiona had always been the emotional one in their house.

East

That isn't something I'm going to say no to.

I grin and hurry upstairs to change into my bathing suit, grabbing towels for us both, and thanking God that my pool is heated, otherwise this would've just been a really stupid idea. From the kitchen, I hit the control to remove the covering from the pool and take a deep breath, preparing myself for the cold hit I'm about to take.

It's fucking freezing when I step outside in just my black bikini, so I scurry across the flagstones and drop my phone and the towels onto one of the chairs. Once they're safe, I hurry into the warm water, ducking my head under the surface, and let out a deep breath once I come up.

I hear the clink of the gate between here and the Saints' and wait for East to appear from the shadows. He's in sweatpants and a hoodie, looking every inch the Adonis, even dressed like a hobo. He grins wordlessly at me when he spots me, kicking off his sneakers and stripping down to his boxers. I'm held captive by every delicious inch of him. He steps forward and dives into the water, staying under until he reaches me on the other side of the pool. Surfacing, he cages me between him and the side of the pool. "Late night swims are definitely a good idea."

His eyes heat as he speaks. His gaze, bouncing down before trailing back up to meet mine, leaves a scorching path where he looks at me. Releasing the side of the pool, I wrap my arms around his neck as he presses me back against the wall. "I thought we were going to talk."

"We could talk," I say before pressing my lips against his gently. "Or we could do this." I move to kiss him again, but he grabs the back of my neck, stopping my advance.

"You know I want you. I've made that clear. But if we start this, and I mean properly, not this half-assed whatever it is we've had going on, then I am all in. I know you have something going on with the others, and while I'd rather have you to myself, I won't make you choose. But I don't want you to think that I don't want you as mine."

His words stoke the embers inside of me and a fully fledged

inferno takes their place.

"We'll need to be careful until your birthday in the spring, and even after, until the school year ends. But even though I can't show you in public, just know that I'm in this, with every piece of me. I have loved you, Octavia Royal, for possibly my entire life, and I don't see that changing." He captures my lips with his as he presses me further into the wall, his dick pressing against me as I wrap my legs around his hips.

I have no words to say to him, I've never been one for pretty words, so instead I show him everything I don't know how to say.

I tell him how good he feels with each moan that falls from my lips. I make sure he knows how much I want him every time I press my almost-bare pussy against his cock. I plead with him to give me more with the tightening of my fist in his hair.

I may not have the words, but this... showing him what I want... this I excel at.

His big frame protects me from the chill in the air. The pool may be heated and California may not be anywhere near the North Pole, but the January temperatures are enough to make anyone think twice about being out here too long.

"You have no idea how long I've waited for this, Octavia. So fucking long."

His voice is deep in my ear, the tenor sending a trembling need down my spine and straight to my clit. "If you're not ready for this, really ready, I can keep waiting. I'd wait forever for you."

My heart pounds in my chest. He always seems to know exactly what to say to make me feel like I'm the only other person in his world.

I shake my head. "No more waiting."

Kissing him again, I try to show him just how much I mean what I say and he moans beneath my touch.

"You make me weak, Octavia Royal."

"More show, less tell." My words come out breathy and needy. I know he hears the pleading in my voice because I swear to fuck his cock grows even thicker than before as he pushes it against me.

He slides one hand down the column of my neck, across my collar bone, and down the length of my arm before he brings my own hand to my clit.

"Rub yourself nice and slick. Show me that you can be a good girl. I need you ready before I can fuck you exactly the way I've always fantasized."

His words make me shiver with unprecedented need.

I do as he says.

While obeying a Saint is never an easy feat, in this case it's an easy win-win.

With one hand still fisted in his hair, I keep the other alternating between my opening and my clit, his hand moving with mine as I keep myself nice and slick while the water tries to wash it all away.

No one ever told me that fucking in water was so goddamn counterproductive. Yet here we are, defying the odds and slaying it.

East showers me with kisses and licks and bites that turn me on even more. He's sexy and attentive. While the others might make my blood boil to warm me up, he has a whole different way about him. He is all man and I never knew being called a good girl by him would make butterflies take flight in my stomach, but I guess you learn something new every day, right?

When his hot mouth surrounds the hard peak of my nipple, my head falls back against the side of the pool as I enjoy each one of his torturous licks and sucks. It's like an electrified wire is linked from my nipple to my clit and every time he bites down just hard enough, I feel an orgasm begging to break through.

My ankles lock at the small of his back and my hips search out his cock all on their own. I don't even have to think about it. My pussy knows what she wants and it's got a Saint's name all over it.

It's when his hand takes over for mine that the pleasure amplifies to a level I never thought imaginable. Guiding my middle finger, he pushes inside me until both of our palms are rubbing over my clit as, together, we finger fuck my pussy. It's erotic in a way I didn't think was possible. I should probably be ashamed or some shit, but not even close. I'm practically breathless with the need to come.

"Can't wait much longer, V. If you're having second thoughts, now's the time to push me away." I almost laugh at the almost-gentlemanly undertones of his words but we both know I'm not going to push him away.

I slam my lips to his, slipping my tongue into his mouth and taking what I need

But when I release my grip on his hair and slide my hand down his chest and around his hip to push down his shorts, I feel the true girth of his cock as it's freed from its confines.

Fucking hell, I've landed myself the mother of all monster dicks.

"If you don't fuck me right now, East, I'm going to have to finish the job myself."

With a cocky grin I'm sure is responsible for many a spontaneous orgasm, East aligns the head of his dick at my entrance and whispers over my swollen lips, "I'm not going to lie, this might hurt."

A shiver of anticipation runs down my spine at his words, but I don't have time to respond because he pushes into me and I suck in a deep breath at the sweet sting.

East swallows every one of my cries, kisses the pain away as he pushes in and out, each time a little deeper.

"You feel so good, beautiful. So fucking good, like I always knew you would."

I almost laugh at his unintended rhyme but then the head of his cock is right there. Right fucking there and my entire body is shaking from the teasing of my g-spot.

"God, you're shaking. Are you cold?"

This time, I do laugh. A throaty, sexy sound I didn't know I had in me.

"If I were any hotter, I'd set this pool on fire."

He smirks at my words, and it's as if my words light something inside of him. He pushes me harder against the side of the pool, water splashing all around us with every thrust of his hips, East plants his big hands on each of my ass cheeks and squeezes hard enough to earn him a squeak from me.

The noise is like the strike of a match igniting the fuse within him and he fucks me like I'm all he'll ever need. Building my orgasm from a red-hot ember to a roaring flame of destruction.

His lips never leave me. He kisses me like he needs me to survive.

"Fuck, V," he groans into the crook of my neck before kissing me there too, biting on the lobe of my ear, pulling noises from me I've never made before.

He slows his rhythm, like he wants this to last forever.

"You're so fucking beautiful," he whispers against my lips before he loses control again, slamming his dick to the hilt and fucking me like he owns me while still worshiping me like I'm his queen.

"I'm close," I stutter, my nails digging into the flesh of his back. He sinks his teeth into the flesh of my collar bone in response, and just as he buries himself as deep as he can go, I lose every single piece of my control.

My nails dig further into his skin, I can feel it break under their violence, but it doesn't slow him down. He slams into me as I crest higher until a feral sound rips from him and he stills inside of me. Dropping his forehead onto my shoulder, I can feel the heat of his panting on my neck as we slowly come back down to earth.

"That was…" I trail off, and he laughs softly as he sorts himself out and pulls me back into his arms.

"It was." He shifts so he can carry me with an arm under my knees and walks us out of the pool. He puts me on my feet and wraps a towel around me before putting one around his own shoulders. "We should probably head inside, get you warmed up."

I nod, my teeth chattering from the cold air, and head inside with him close behind me. I put my finger to my lips when we enter the house—aware that it's probably a bit late to be worried about Smithy hearing—and re-arm the alarm before leading him upstairs. "Shower?"

"Sounds good." He smiles, almost bashfully. There is no way that he feels bashful after fucking me like that. Just no.

I take his hand and lead him into my bathroom, stripping out of my bikini, his eyes heating before he looks up to the ceiling. "You really are testing my self-restraint tonight, aren't you?"

I smirk at him, and he glances down in time to see as I drop my panties to the ground. "No one said you had to be restrained."

This week has been such a rollercoaster already and I didn't think it could get any more up and down. Boy was I wrong.

After Maverick kissing me on the steps on Monday and his general attention all week, the gossip has run riot like a freaking wildfire. So when Indi and I sit down for lunch on Thursday and everyone is staring at us, I think nothing of it.

"So, we're still on for tomorrow night, right? I so need some girl time, minus all of the homework." She grins at me before taking a bite of her chicken and avocado burger.

"Tomorrow night? What's tomorrow night?" Maverick asks as he slides into the chair beside her.

I look over at him, look him dead in the eyes, and say, "Nope. You don't sit here. Go back to your own table."

As I finish speaking, Finley and Lincoln drop into the seats on either side of me. "No, this isn't happening. Why are you three sitting here?"

Indi smirks at me from across the table and mouths 'kitty cat' at me, making me laugh, totally ruining my hard-ass façade that I need against the three of them.

"Didn't you hear, princess? You and I are hot tamales out here. We are officially the new 'it' couple, and your bitch of a cousin is spitting mad about it." Mav winks at me and I roll my eyes.

I look around at the others and no one else is smiling. "You're not kidding are you?"

He leans forward and steals a fry from my plate, grinning wide. "Why would I kid? They're not wrong are they? You and me baby, we're hot shit."

Indi giggles quietly as he wags his brows at me. "So, you two are cool with this?" she asks, her gaze bouncing between Lincoln and Finley before taking another bite of her burger. I grab my slice of pizza and take a mouthful because I am so done with this conversation already.

"Who cares what the sheep think?" Lincoln answers dryly. Except it's not really an answer at all. Unsurprisingly, Finley doesn't say a word, but I can feel the heat of his gaze on the side of my head, while I try to pretend that this isn't my life.

Sometimes I really miss tour life.

This is so… high school.

Sighing, I resign myself to the fact that this is, indeed, happening and say fuck it. Enough people saw Mav kiss me on Monday, there have been enough rumors flying around that I'm fucking them all—technically, that's just Mav as far as these guys know, too—so fuck it.

"Back to what we were saying earlier," I say to Indi, ignoring the other three despite the fact that Mav keeps stealing my fries, "Yes, I am so down for tomorrow night."

"What's tomorrow night?" Lincoln asks, and Indi smirks at him.

"Penis free, that's what it is."

I clamp my lips together trying not to smile. It's fun watching her slowly blossom into the badass I know she is deep down.

"I asked the same question, and got about the same response," Mav says with a shrug. "So if tomorrow night is penis free, then what are you doing Saturday?"

"Washing my hair," I deadpan, and Finley snickers beside me.

"You were asking for that one, man." He leans over and kisses my cheek before whispering in my ear. "Save Saturday night for us?"

A shiver runs down my spine and goosebumps erupt on my arms at his warm breath on my skin. I turn to face him and smile a little, then nod before leaning in and kissing him. If everyone's going to call me a whore, I have zero reason to try to hide whatever it is that's going on between us all. He tangles a hand in my hair, taking over the kiss, and I forget where we are as he burns through me.

"God damn," Indi says as I pull back, and she fans herself. "I think I need a smoke after that, and I don't even smoke."

Finley rewards her with a rare grin while I try to calm myself. The eyes in the room are all fixated on our table, but my fucks have officially disappeared.

I turn to Lincoln who raises an eyebrow at me, almost in challenge, and it riles me. But considering he has barely touched me since that night in the pool house, outside of rescuing me from Raleigh, I'm not about to push him. If he doesn't want to be anything but friends, I'm going to respect that.

The bell rings, ending my stare off with him, so I stand and look over to Indi, who looks like she's about to combust with laughter. "Walk with me to class?"

She stands, moving to grab her tray, but Finley puts his hand on it, along with mine. "I got it."

Indi looks up at me and shrugs. "I guess chivalry isn't completely dead."

Finley just looks at her and shakes his head. "Sweetheart, if you think that's chivalrous, you've been hanging with the wrong people."

# FIFTEEN

## OCTAVIA

I drop onto the couch in the theater room with a giant bowl of popcorn, putting it between Indi and me as she snuggles under the blankets we piled in here earlier. "Have I mentioned how much I love this room?"

"Once or twice," I say with a grin, and she sticks her tongue out at me.

Taking a handful of popcorn, she turns to me as I cross my legs on the giant couch. "So… boys… stop holding out on me and spill the goddamn tea."

I can't help but laugh at her as she flails her hands around.

"Okay. Tea… so uhm. I don't even know where to start."

"Maybe start with why Mav thought it was okay to kiss you at school on Monday and how you batted it back by making out with Finley yesterday?" Her grin widens as a blush spreads across my chest. "Also, zero judgement from the girl with three boyfriends, so tell me all the things."

And so I do. All about Lincoln staying pretty icy toward me despite Halloween, and Christmas. I tell her all about Christmas and the gifts from the guys, about Mav saving me after my first run-in with Raleigh, making out with Finn in here, and finally about East in the pool.

By the time I'm done catching her up her jaw is practically on the floor, so I flick a piece of popcorn at her.

"Dude, was it good? East totally looks like he can show a girl a good time."

I clamp my lips together, but a smile still pulls at the edges. "I mean, you could totally say that."

"God damn." She fans her face dramatically, making me laugh. "And you just know that Finley is going to be a scorcher too. All that tall and broody has to go somewhere."

"You are a little bananas. You know that, right?"

She grins at me and nods. "Oh I do, but Finley reminds me a lot of Dylan. He's quiet, but man that man's tongue is like nothing I've ever known. I mean, his dick is bomb, but his tongue…" She raises her hands like she's praising and I can't help but laugh, shaking my head at her.

"You still haven't told me much about them. They're Kings, right?"

She nods. "Yep… and yours are Knights."

"You know about the Knights?"

She bites down on her lip and nods. "Kind of. I mean, not really. Ellis told me some stuff. I know that they exist, that your guys are Knights. That most Knights are bad news."

I try to laugh, but it falls flat. "I don't know tons yet either, but yeah. That sums it up from what I've learnt. So you're with the Kings, and they're kinda like enemies with my guys? How did we manage that?"

She laughs before her smile drops a little again. "Yeah, I mean, Diego, their older brother, started the Kings. I don't know why, but it fucking terrifies me that they're so intertwined. If he goes to jail... well, let's not think about it. I don't know much about the thing between them and the Knights, but whatever it is, it's not good. Do you think Lincoln or any of them will tell you what's going on with it?"

I bark out a laugh, and then apologize. "Sorry, but Lincoln tells me jack squat. Though I have a plan to fix that, because I need some answers. They still haven't told me shit about my stalker either."

Her eyes go wide, and I realize I've not let her in on that little nugget yet either.

"Stalker?!" she squawks, "What fucking stalker?"

I tell her everything, the photos, the letters, that the guys have confirmed that it's not anything to do with the Knights. About the knife and the blood. Everything I hadn't realized I'd been keeping from her.

"Holy fucking shit, V. You need like a bodyguard or something. Can't Mac spare someone? Panda or one of the guys that you trust to keep you safe."

I frown, realising I left out one last piece of that puzzle for her. "Panda is a Knight."

*"What the actual fuck?"*

"I know," I say with a sad shrug. "Nothing quite like finding out everyone's been lying to you your entire life."

"Girl, I swear now, I will never lie to you. Ride or die." She puts her pinky out to me and I wrap mine with it. It might be a little childish, but it makes me feel better regardless. "Just promise me that no matter what goes on with the guys, enemies, frenemies, or whatever they become, it doesn't fuck with us."

"I swear it. They'll just have to suck it up and deal. Ride or die."

She practically leaps across the couch and hugs me, and I try not to get all emotional. I've never had a bestie before, but I think she might be the best bestie in existence.

"So," I say, wagging my brows at her once she's seated back on the sofa. "Tell me about *your* boys."

She blushes furiously and stuffs a handful of popcorn in her mouth. "They're boys," she says around it, and I laugh. "Movie time, right? Yeah, totally. You don't want to hear about the three-ways, and the er… other stuff, right?"

"Three-ways. As if you're holding out on me like that." I feign outrage and she looks at me with those big green eyes of hers, all puppyish, and I let it go. If she's not ready to share the details, I'm chill.

"I'll tell you one thing though," she says as she grabs the remote, "That twin intuition thing… definitely a thing. Oh boy, is it a thing."

"Any crossing of swords?" I ask, wagging my brows, and she blushes furiously again.

"Uhmmmm, I plead the fifth?"

"Yuh-huh." I grin. "One day you'll tell me, and then we'll both be living our best multi-peen lives."

"You think your thing with the guys could be serious?"

I shrug, and take another bite of the popcorn. "Not really. I think it's just some fun and I have no issue with that. East… well, he seems serious, but he's also chill with sharing. So for now, it is what it is."

"Do you *want* it to be serious?"

"I have no idea. These last six months have been a little insane. For now, I'm just going to enjoy myself and see where it goes. Are you and your guys serious?"

She nods. "As a heart attack. I was a little dubious at first, especially after they ended it over summer, but they seem to be all-in this time. I'm not sure what that means for any of us. Especially with them being Kings, with college, all of it, but that is a future me problem. For now, I'm going to enjoy being entirely loved up, and try not to stress about what the next few months hold."

I grab my can of soda and raise it. "Amen to that."

"You running with me today?" I ask Indi as I exit the bathroom and she groans, flopping back down onto my bed.

"Fuck you and your runs. What time is it even? The sun isn't even up." She flips me the bird and I bark out a laugh.

"Okay, drama. It's like six twenty-five, don't pretend you're not usually up at this time."

"Yeah, when I have school. It's a Saturday; this shit should be illegal."

I chuckle softly at her, drama and all, I wouldn't have her any other way. "Well, you can stay here and sleep, Smithy will fix you some breakfast if you want, but I have this weird anxious energy I need to burn off."

She flips over and sits up. "Are you okay?"

"I think so." I shrug. "Just feeling antsy. Running usually helps when it gets to be too much."

"You go run. I can chill with my man Smithy until you get back, then we can do breakfast before I head out. You're with the guys tonight right?"

"Finley asked me to keep tonight free for them, so I'm assuming so. I haven't really spoken to them much since then beyond Maverick hanging off me like a goddamn accessory on Friday."

She grins at me. "Yeah, I did notice that."

"It was hard to miss." I roll my eyes and drop down onto the bed with her before checking the time on my phone. Lincoln has been meeting me at the gate at six thirty to run, so I need to haul ass if I'm going to stretch out before I go. Asshole has been outpacing me ever since he started running with me two weeks ago, and I'm determined to sort my shit out so that I can put a stop to it. "I better go. Lincoln will be waiting."

"Wait! Lincoln runs with you? All that fine iceman man meat out there sweating with you, why on earth would you invite me to that? And now I'm considering my objections to running." She wags her eyebrows at me, so I reach back and swat her with my pillow.

"Iceman is about right. Egotistical asshole who is way too in shape is another apt description. If you're coming, you better haul ass, cause he's a stickler about being on time."

She leaps from the bed and runs into my closet. We're not super close in size, but fit wear is pretty universal. "Bottom shelf on the left," I tell her and less than two minutes later, she appears in my navy blue leggings and sports bra.

"Let's do this."

I shake my head because she's never this enthused about running. "We usually do about eight miles."

Her smile drops and I burst out laughing. "Eight fucking miles? Masochists, the pair of you. Come on, let's go before I change my mind. Maybe if we both pepper him with questions, he'll actually give us some answers."

"Don't bet on it." I grab my spare arm strap and hand it over to her. She slips it on, before rummaging through her bag and grabbing her headphones before we head downstairs. I call out a "good morning" to Smithy before we head outside.

We find Lincoln already waiting for us at the gate. He quirks a brow at Indi but doesn't say a word. Just taps his phone and motions for us to run ahead of him, same as he always does.

I know a lot of people might consider it strange that I trust him to have my six after everything that happened when I came back here, but I'm trying to take him at his word. He might not be sorry, but he was trying to protect me. In his own very fucked-up way.

I can't say if I was put in the same situation that I'd have done any different. I might have gone about it a little differently, but if my dad had been in danger... I can't say how far I would've gone to keep him safe.

I take off at a run, keeping my pace down for Indi because I know running isn't exactly her favorite pastime. We run the usual route, pausing at the pier for a water break like normal.

"You two are fucking insane. Are we done?" Indi pants and I smile, shaking my head.

"Do you want to tell her we're only halfway?" I say to Lincoln, the corners of his lips tugging up, he doesn't say a word as she flops down to the ground.

"Half way? Fuck you both all the way off. Stick a fork in

me cause I am done." She pants on the ground, and I can't help but laugh at her.

"Come on, you've totally got this. I'll even make Lincoln run up front so you have incentive to chase," I tease and she flips me the bird. Lincoln just raises his brows at me before looking back down at his phone. "I'll have Smithy make chicken and waffles when we get back…"

"Now *that* is the best kind of bribe," she says, heaving herself from the ground, "Let's do this!"

I look over at Lincoln who nods, wordlessly, and puts his headphones back in. "Are you okay?"

"Just stuff with my dad. I'm good." In those few words, he gives me more insight into him than he's given since I got back. So I run the risk of stepping up to him and wrapping my arms around him. He stiffens under my touch, but I squeeze him anyway before stepping back. He looks at me like I've lost my mind, but his eyes just look sad, and I wonder when the last time someone actually hugged him was.

"You're welcome to join us for breakfast if you want," I offer, but he shakes his head.

"I've got an errand to run this morning, but if Smithy wants to make lasagne tonight, I'm not going to say no."

I grin at him, thankful that he is a little bit human after all. "I'm sure he can do that."

He looks at his watch and puts his AirPods back in. "Come on, ladies. We're running behind."

I roll my eyes and turn back to Indi, who is looking down at her phone, giving us a minute. "Come on, we don't want to make him late."

"Awesome. Let's do this. Come on chicken and waffles."

I laugh as I put in my AirPods, and take off on the way home, trying to slow down a little for Indi, but the antsy feeling keeps ramping up because I'm not pushing myself.

I look back at Lincoln, silently questioning if he'll stay with her, and he nods as if he knows exactly what it is I need. So I pick up my pace until my muscles and lungs burn in that beautiful way they do, and the chaos and noise inside of me quiets a little.

Once the feeling starts to subside, I slow back down a little. It doesn't take long for the two of them to catch up and we stick together until we reach the gates.

Lincoln waves as he heads toward his own gates. "I'll see you tonight."

"I'll be here." I smile and open my mailbox before tapping in the code to the gate. I pull out the handful of letters and magazines in there, and as I do, a black envelope falls to the ground at my feet.

Lincoln sees it and grabs it before I do. The red seal is there, like always.

"What does it say?"

He opens it and scans it, a frown wrinkling his forehead. "It's the new date for the gala, along with a new venue." He turns the card and shows it to me, my stomach sinking.

"Gala? What gala?" Indi asks as she sucks in lungfuls of air beside me.

"The Knights," I tell her, and Lincoln looks at her questioningly.

His eyes turn stormy as his gaze bounces between us before he focuses back on her. "Do not say a word to anyone about anything you know."

I take the invitation from his hand, frustrated. "She's not going to say a thing. Don't be such an ass."

"It's for her own safety as much as yours," he counters and I roll my eyes.

She puts her hands up in the air, as if in surrender. "I'm not going to do anything to jeopardize V, my guys, or you and yours. You can chill."

He nods once before heading inside his own gates and storming up the drive.

"Sorry," I say to her on his behalf. "He's such an ass sometimes."

"He is, but I genuinely think he loves you and is just scared shitless. Sometimes you can see it in his eyes. The scared little boy who has already lost too much."

I gaze at his back as he opens his front door and ponder her words.

Why on earth would he think he would lose me when I'm not his to start with?

I head downstairs in my leggings and sweater, my big fluffy socks like a hug for my feet. I have no idea what the plans are for tonight, but comfortable and warm are on my to-do list. The smell of the lasagne from the kitchen makes my stomach grumble as I hit the bottom step.

Smithy sings in the kitchen as he cooks and I can't stop the smile that breaks out over my face. "Someone seems extra happy tonight."

He jumps when he hears me and blushes a little at getting caught. "Miss Octavia. Sometimes you are quieter than a mouse."

"I didn't mean to scare you. You should've gone into music," I wink at him with a smile as I slip onto a stool at the counter.

"Oh no, Miss Octavia. My life suits me perfectly well, thank you." He waves me off and turns his attention back to the stove as he builds the layers of the pasta goodness. "Now then, this is done, all you will need to do is heat it when you and your friends are ready to eat. I prepped some cheesy garlic French bread to go with it, which is in the refrigerator. Can you promise not to destroy my kitchen when you do that? I've left written instructions on the refrigerator door for you."

I belt out a laugh. "No, but I can promise to let East or Finley do the cooking. Taking a well-deserved night off?"

He turns to face me, looking more than a little bashful, yet excited at the same time. "I, Miss Octavia, have a date."

"A date?" I raise my brows and fold my arms. "And who, kind sir, is the lucky participant of your date?"

"You wouldn't know them, I'm sure," he stutters, and I smile.

"Fine, keep your secrets, old man. But I hope you have a wonderful evening."

He shakes his fist at me in that hilariously endearing way. "I'll give you old man." I can't help but laugh at him and wave as he heads down to his room, I assume to prepare for his big night.

Who would've thought?

I check my phone and shoot off a message to Indi, just to tell her I love her, before heading into the living room and getting comfy on the couch. It's been full radio silence from all of the guys since my run with Lincoln earlier, so I have no idea what time they're planning on coming over or if they're even still planning to show up at all. But I'm not going to build my night around them.

My night is all synced up for some hot-ass Dylan O'Brien on my TV, because his new film dropped today and this girl here is *so* ready for it. Grabbing the blanket from the back of the sofa, I lose myself in it, waving goodbye to Smithy when he leaves looking dapper as hell in his suit and wingtips, and fully lose track of time.

It's only when my stomach starts to rumble that I check my phone and realize it's nine.

Oops.

I bite the inside of my cheek, thinking about heating some of the lasagne that Smithy made earlier before remembering my promise to him that I wouldn't destroy his kitchen.

Still no word from the guys.

I head into the kitchen, chewing the inside of my cheek as I fret over breaking my promise, though I'm sure he'll be more furious if I just don't eat, so I turn the oven on and let it heat.

Snapping a picture of the lasagne, I create a group message with the four of them.

Me

I guess you guys miss out. More for me.

Passive aggressive? Hell yes. Do I care? Not even a little. I waited, got stood up essentially, so they can suck it. Here was me thinking that things were getting better, that we were moving forward, and now that stupid-ass nagging voice in the back of my head reappears, bitching about how this was all a ploy to lull me into a false sense of security. That I let them get too close after they were all—minus East—absolute fucking monsters to me. That I should've never let them in.

Once the oven reaches temperature, I pop the lasagne in and set a timer on my phone so I know when to put the garlic bread in.

I can't fuck it up if I stick to the times Smithy wrote down, right?

I put some music on, belting out the lyrics to *Burn It All Down* by PVRIS, realizing just how apt these lyrics are to my life sometimes. Burning it all down and walking away from the embers with just the few people and things I hold precious sounds like perfection.

Except... Could I really leave behind so much all over again?

The flames between me and the guys are there, flickering, and if I really looked inside my heart rather than ruling with my head, I know that I'm past everything. Except my brain is stuck on stubborn dumb bitch mode.

Problem is, she wants to have her cake and eat it too—personally the phrase never made much sense to me because who doesn't want to eat their cake—keeping them at arm's length *and* fucking around with them isn't going to work. Tonight being the perfect case in point. I try desperately not to be disappointed at the absolute lack of communication I've had from any of them. You'd think the least they could do is shoot me a text letting me know plans changed.

Though maybe it's a good thing, making me face exactly what it is going on inside of me when it comes to them. Introspection isn't something I've exactly made time for lately.

The timer on my phone pulls me from my thoughts and I pop the garlic bread in the oven, resetting the alarm so I don't burn everything to a crisp. The smell of the lasagne is enough to make my mouth water.

Instead of getting in my own head again, I grab my phone and do the only thing I can think of: Talk to someone with more sense than me.

Me

Do you have ten minutes for me to ramble at you?

Indi

Bitch, always. What's up?

Instead of texting back, I hit dial, and it doesn't even make it through the first ring before she answers. There's loud music, voices, and then a door closing, providing a sudden and impressive amount of silence. "What's wrong?"

I smile at her words. "Nothing is wrong. Well, not really. And did I mention today that I adore the freaking socks off of you?"

"Aww, I love you lots like gum drops too. Now what's wrong?" I can hear her smirk down the line as I lean back against the counter.

"Am I being a stick-up-the-ass, button-stuck-on-stupid bitch when it comes to the guys?"

She bursts out laughing, and I shake my head. Apparently she's not the only drama queen out here. "What, exactly, has you going down this particular path in your head?"

"Too much time to think and being stood up, probably."

"Those assholes stood you up? I swear to fucking Jesus, they make my job so hard sometimes." She pauses and confusion fills me as I wait for her to continue. "Back to your earlier statement. A little. Obviously I know what you've told me, and assuming that's everything, then yes, a little. I mean, Lincoln is the iceman, it's going to take him longer to thaw than the others, and it's not like they don't have some serious shit going on. But the others... they're trying—real hard—and as much as I love you, your walls are higher than *the* wall."

I let out a sigh. "See this is why I needed to speak to someone other than the voices in my head."

She laughs softly at me. "Hey, you've been through a lot. It's understandable that you'd be cautious, but the best things in life come with a risk. The greater the risk, the greater the reward right? So why not just try. Let them in the way you let me in. If you get your heart broken, I'll help you burn their worlds to ash."

"You're the best." I smile into the receiver. "I'm sorry for interrupting your night."

"You never have to apologize to me, V. Ride or die, remember? Anyway, this party sucks. The guys are too busy trying to find their asshole brother."

"Diego?"

"Yeah, he went on a bender last weekend, and nobody has seen or heard from him since. Chaos would be an understatement." I can hear the worry in her voice, and my stomach tightens.

"If there's anything I can do… anything you need…"

She sighs deeply and it makes me want to find Diego just to crack him in the nuts for making her worry so much. "Yeah, I know. I'll call. But for now, it's a waiting game. It's not the first time he's disappeared for a few weeks then reappeared as if nothing happened."

"I hope for their sake, and yours, that's all it is." But there's a niggle in the back of my mind that tells me something isn't quite what it seems.

"Me too. I should head back before they think I've disappeared too."

"Okay, I'll talk to you later." She says goodbye and ends the call just as the alarm on my phone goes off.

I rush around trying to get everything out of the oven before it burns, and I'm rewarded with the bubbling, gooey, cheesy pasta goodness. I drool a little, just watching it as it cools off a bit so I don't basically eat lava.

Once I've served myself a plate and plopped down on the sofa, I take stock of Indi's words. Maybe I do have my walls too high and I really should just take the guys at face value. Forgive, even if I can't forget yet. They've been upfront with me for the most part, so maybe it's time I pulled up my big girl pants and did the same thing.

I wake up as sunlight filters through the windows, blinking against the harshness of it. I groan as I move, realizing I fell asleep on the sofa. I'm too young to feel this achy from a single night of uncomfortable sleep. Fucking hell.

I stretch out, sounding like Velcro as I do. I run a hand through my hair, realizing it's come out of the braid I put it in last night, before checking my phone.

Smithy

Had car issues in the city. Getting a hotel for the night. I will be back in the morning.

Me

Sorry, I fell asleep. Hope you're okay!

I try not to be disappointed that the guys didn't reach out.

I know Indi thinks I should drop my walls, but they're making it really difficult. Just when I think I can trust them, that they won't let me down... they do something like this and I wonder if they can't do something so simple as communicate clearly, then how the fuck do we do the rest of this?

I let out a sigh, jumping when the house creaks. The house is quiet—too quiet—here on my own again.

I put my hair up in a messy bun and head into the kitchen, flicking on the coffee pot. The sound of the front door opening makes me pause, realizing I obviously didn't set the alarm last night after Smithy left.

Voices filter through and I realize who it is.

Hell no.

I lean against the counter with folded arms, an eyebrow raised as the four of them filter into the kitchen.

East at least looks a little sheepish as he comes to a stop in the archway. Maverick just grins at me while Lincoln heads toward the coffee pot like it's going to save his life, frowning when he realizes it's not ready, and Finley leans against the wall wordlessly.

"Hey, V," East says, rubbing the back of his neck.

"Hi." My voice clearly expresses just how unamused I am.

Maverick saunters toward me, smiling that cheeky as fuck grin of his at me. "Don't be like that, princess. We didn't mean to leave you hanging."

I blink at him. "You didn't mean to—"

"What he means," Lincoln says, ice dripping from his words, "is that something came up with the Knights and we didn't have time to speak to you."

I look up at East, wondering what his excuse is, since he's apparently not one of them.

"He was with us," Finley says as Maverick reaches me and puts his finger under my chin so I'm looking up at him.

"You're hot when you're mad, but just this once, please don't be mad?" What is it about them saying please that turns me into such a weak asshole? Maybe it's because I know they sure as hell don't say it to anyone else? Fuck knows. It's like he senses my weakness and kisses me right there in front of them all, again. His lips are soft as he tries to devour my anger with his kiss, stealing my breath right along with it. He smiles at me when he pulls back, like he knows I've already softened.

"So what was so important that not one of you could even send me a text?"

Mav grips my hips and lifts me onto the counter before standing between my legs. "I can think of far better things to do than talk about that."

It's then, when he's close to my eye level, that I notice the blood spatter on his neck. Just a fine dusting. I can't help but run my finger across it. "Do I want to know whose blood this is?"

He freezes and then grins again before walking out of the room. The slam of a door tells me he's gone to the downstairs bathroom.

My question hangs in the room until the front door opens and closes again. "Miss Octavia? Are you awake?"

Smithy's voice makes me smile, and I jump down from the counter. "I'm up. In the kitchen." He reaches the room before I'm even finished speaking.

"I am so sorry I was gone, Miss Octavia. Something to do with the spark plugs apparently. But we're all sorted now. Good morning to you all. Let me just get changed and I'll get breakfast started," he says in a flurry as he rushes through the room, dropping the mail on the counter.

"You really don't have to—" He cuts me off with a glare, and I close my mouth. Apparently he's dealing with breakfast.

"I guess you guys better get comfortable."

I take a seat at the counter, picking up the stack of envelopes since none of them are explaining last night to me and, apparently, I'm just supposed to be okay with that.

Sucking in a deep breath, I remind myself of Indi's words and make a conscious effort to drop my walls. They've already made it very clear that they think they're protecting me from this 'big bad' of theirs, so if the secrets make them feel better, they can have them.

Flicking through the letters, dismissing most of them as bills or junk, I notice a handwritten one to me.

I roll my eyes, whoever this is really needs to be more original.

Much as I don't want to see what the latest terror my stalker wants to inflict on me is, I tear it open and pull out the note.

*They think they can keep you safe.*
*They're wrong.*
*No one can keep you safe but me.*

I look down at the hair taped to the bottom and my stomach churns.

Is that my hair?

"Octavia, what's wrong?" Lincoln's voice pulls me from the horror settling itself into the pit of my stomach and threatening to lose last night's lasagne. I look up at him and can't know what he sees on my face, but he stands and comes around the counter to my side, gently taking the letter from me.

Panic and disgust war for a place in my stomach as I pull my hair from its ponytail. My trembling fingers slide through the strands, searching blindly for the piece of me that has been taken until I find it. I stare at the square chunk missing from the ends of my extensions for several seconds, numb and overwhelmed, before I launch myself from the chair and run for the bathroom, shoving past Maverick as he leaves it.

I only just reach the bowl when the contents of my stomach make an appearance. I retch until tears stream down my face.

Why is this my fucking life?

Once I've thrown up everything but my memories, I take a minute to compose myself, brushing my teeth, putting my hair back up in a bun, and splashing some water on my face before heading back out to the kitchen. I find the four of them staring down at the counter. Once I get closer I see the pictures of me from last night, asleep on the sofa.

I feel violated in a way that makes my skin feel like it's on fire.

"Why is someone doing this to me?" My voice comes out small, croaky and weak. I hate how weak I sound, but I'm not sure how much more of this I can take before I break. Finley doesn't say a word before heading past me toward the security room.

East moves to my side, and I let him usher me back into

my seat. "I don't know, but it's obvious whoever it is knew you were alone last night. Did anyone know?"

I shake my head. "Just you guys, and Indi. Though no one knew Smithy was gone. Hell I didn't know until I woke up."

"He hacked the servers and left us a present." Finley steps back into the kitchen and sets a laptop on the counter, hitting a button before spinning it around so the rest of us can see the screen.

The front door cracks open and a figure enters, clad in black from the mask over his face to the boots on his feet, and stares up at the camera for a moment. Then the bastard cracks a smile and waves, like he knows the guys would be here watching with me. "He's taunting us," I whisper, my voice so soft I don't know if anyone else hears me. The camera shifts from the entryway to the living room, and I gasp as the figure drops into a crouch in front of my sleeping body. The hair at the back of my neck stands on end and a shiver runs down my spine as I watch him run a hand down my cheek, brushing hair from my face before snapping the photo that now sits on my countertop, mostly forgotten.

"I think I'm going to be sick again." They all look at me, and Finley pauses the video. "I can stop it. You don't have to watch."

"No, I have to. I need to know. I'm tired of being in the dark with everything."

I jump as the door behind me opens and Smithy walks into

the kitchen. "Is everything okay?" His gaze bounces around us all until it lands on the screen. "What is going on?"

He looks up at East, his eyes steely. "Is this the trouble you told me about? I thought it was being handled." His voice is harsh, and he sounds more pissed off than I've ever heard him.

"You knew?" I ask before looking to East. "You told him?"

"Of course I knew. I'm your guardian. I can't keep you safe if I don't know." He looks at me like a disapproving father, and I look down at my hands in my lap. "Now then, I thought you boys told me this was handled. Obviously, that is not the case."

"We've got someone looking into it. A PI," East says, the others remaining suspiciously silent on the topic. Lincoln rarely lets someone else speak for him, so I glance up at him and find all of his attention on me.

East ushers Smithy into the other room, I assume to walk him through whatever they've already done and calm him down a little, leaving me with the others.

"You can't be left alone," Finley says so matter-of-factly that if I didn't know his voice, I'd think it was Lincoln that had spoken.

"I'm rarely alone. Lincoln already hammered that one home. Last night was a blip," I counter, because I really don't feel like having a bodyguard—let alone an entire squad of them. "A blip, I might add, that is entirely *your* fault. I wasn't *supposed* to be alone, remember?"

It was a low blow but, judging by the looks on their faces,

it struck home.

*Good. Fuckers.*

"We can take shifts crashing here. One night each, on rotation," Maverick offers, and I roll my eyes.

"Or not."

"It's not a bad idea. That way one of us is here at all times. To protect you *and* Smithy, should it be needed," Lincoln says as East re-enters the room.

"Is this just a ploy so that you can get back in my bed?" I ask, my arms folded and an eyebrow raised. I'm more than a little shaken about all of this, so my defense mechanisms are kicking into place and deflection has always been my go-to. From the looks on their faces, it worked.

Finn's gaze bounces between us and he opens his mouth to speak but Mav cuts him off. "I'm sorry, what the fuck did you just say?"

"Is that seriously what you guys are focusing on right now?" East roars, and the room stills. I guess he doesn't lose his shit often, but he looks mad enough to burn the world down right now. "Some fucking psychopath got into her house and took some of her hair, and you're focused on who has been sleeping in her fucking bed? Someone give me some goddamn strength to stop me from strangling the pair of you."

"You could try," Mav huffs, the challenge in his eyes is real.

"How about we dial this back a bit, gentlemen?" Smithy soothes as he enters the room, "Calmer heads make for better strategists. Let me sort breakfast, then we'll work out a plan to keep Miss Octavia as safe as we can. *With* her input. This is not the fifties."

I swear I could kiss that man. The others don't look exactly impressed, but they nod regardless and Smithy heads to the stove.

One argument down, Lord knows how many more to go. Maybe one of these pointless dick swinging contests will actually help us discover who this stalker is and my life can have some semblance of normal back.

I laugh out loud at myself.

Normalcy feels more like a fantasy with each passing day.

# SIXTEEN

## LINCOLN

Octavia Royal is going to be the death of me. There isn't a length I wouldn't go to, no trauma I wouldn't endure, no bullet I wouldn't take if it meant she got to come out the other side happy and healthy. Laying down my life to ensure she has hers isn't something I take issue with, because I'd gladly give her everything.

But this stalker of hers might be my kryptonite.

No one knows who he is. He leaves no DNA, no fingerprints. Not a fucking trace.

Finn can't even trace his hacker coding.

I don't know that I can survive this crushing sense of helplessness that has settled over the four of us.

At the very least, I'm going to need new teeth from all of the grinding they've been put through the last few months.

I slam my fist into the punching bag again and again until my arms feel like jelly.

This morning went about as well as Pompeii. Except Octavia lands more direct hits than Vesuvius did. I get that she doesn't want us with her all the time. After everything she's gone through, I can't blame her. But I'll be goddamned if I won't do everything in my power to keep this sick fuck, and the Knights, away from her.

I've loved the girl since the day I laid eyes on her and it almost fucking killed me when she left us. I cannot, *will not*, lose her again. Even if that means I keep my distance and give all of my focus to keeping her safe instead of keeping her happy. I've watched the others make their way back into her good graces. Let *them* worry about her happiness.

They can play Happy Homemaker if that's what they want. I'll do what I have to do to keep her alive and free.

Hopefully doing what I have to do involves finding this stalker and putting a fist through his chest.

Mother.

Fucker.

"If you hit that thing any harder it's going to split." I swing at the bag once more before turning to find Finley sitting on the stairs that lead down to my basement. I flip him the bird and grab my bottle of water. Sucking down the cold liquid like it might fix all my fucking problems. "Still pissed you haven't heard from Lucas?"

I glare at him. "No, of course not. I'm just chilling, kicking back. Can't you tell?"

He lets out a rare laugh and stands while I undo the wraps on my hands. "Have you talked to V?"

"No, why?"

He shrugs before leaning back against the wall. "You're the only one not trying with her. I know what you said, about not wanting to get close to her, but I think you're doing more harm than good."

"What the fuck does that mean?"

He rolls his eyes as I drop down onto the bench. "It means that you were apparently sleeping in her bed, you're looking into the stalker, trying to protect her from the Knights, yet you ice her out like you do everyone else. It's got to be confusing as fuck for her."

"She's a big girl." I shrug and head up the stairs. "Coming?"

He follows behind silently, but his words weigh on me. Octavia has enough on her plate, especially after this morning. She doesn't need me wading in and further complicating everything for her. It's better for everyone if I keep her at arm's length. *She's* better off without me getting too close.

I head straight for the kitchen and find East making lunch. "Sandwich?" He holds a plate out to me but I shake my head, so he offers it to Finn. After breakfast from Smithy, I've eaten plenty, and my stomach hasn't stopped churning over what could have happened to her. All because the Knights kept us busy chasing our fucking tails on their little errand.

I clench my fists at the thought.

We should've known it was a bullshit errand, but it's basically impossible to say no to them. They have all of us clutched in their death grip. Except for East, but even he happened to be with us, which meant he had to play by the rules too.

"Should we tell her about Diego?" Finley asks as he sits at the table. "Indi's probably already told her he's missing and you know as well as I do that she'll try to help."

I shake my head. "For now, Diego is safe. If she starts sniffing around, then we'll tell her what's absolutely necessary to keep her from getting any more involved. For now, the Donovans probably think he's just disappeared on one of his benders. I say we let them continue to think that. If we can't get him out safely, and we need more hands, then we speak to Ryker. If we can keep Octavia out of it, we do so at all costs."

He nods, taking a bite out of the sandwich East handed him just as East takes a seat.

"Where is Maverick?"

East snorts before answering. "He volunteered to stay with Octavia. You missed that part after storming out, all holier-than-thou earlier."

"I was not holier-than-thou," I snarl. "We were done talking, so I left."

"Keep telling yourself that, bro." I glare at my brother

before closing my eyes and taking a deep breath. Snapping at everyone isn't going to make me feel better.

Making some heads roll might. Especially if one of them belongs to whoever this stalker is.

"Hey, don't shoot the messenger." East holds his hands up in surrender. "You're the one who said you were done and stormed out. Just because you weren't the one calling the shots for a change, no need to get your panties in a bunch."

I try to smile at his teasing, but there's a part of me that very much needs that control he's ribbing me about. I zen out for a second, reminding myself that I might not be able to control my emotions, but I can control how I respond to them.

"Officially unbunched," I say through clenched teeth. "What else did I miss?"

"Not much," East offers while Finn finishes his food. "Just running through the basics of what we'd talked about before. Smithy confirmed he'd speak to his FBI friends to see if someone can take an official look into the stalker thing."

"His buddy is a Knight. I thought we wanted to keep them out of this."

"We do." Finn shrugs. "But there's only so much we can do alone. Since this is Smithy reaching out, it's not an official request, just a friendly one. It's as limited as we're going to get, especially if we want more eyes on her. She mentioned your morning runs too. You didn't mention you'd been running with her."

I shrug at them, not caring for the accusation in his eyes. "It's just a morning run. I go anyway and this way she's not out there alone."

"Are you sure that's all it is?" East asks, cutting his eyes to me.

"What else would it be?" I ask him, an eyebrow quirked.

He laughs, shaking his head. "You could've asked any one of us to go with her instead."

"Not all of us are just looking to get our dicks wet."

"Fuck you. You know it's more than that," he says, clenching the butter knife in his hand. Usually I'd laugh at the absurdity of the idea of him hurting me, but everything has been twisted since Octavia returned. I don't know how to get our dynamic back. Any of it.

"You run with her if you want. Why the fuck should I care?" I shrug and pull my phone from my pocket.

Two missed calls from Harrison. Fun.

"Of course it is," is all I can muster in response before I put my phone back in my pocket. "I'll catch you guys later. I need to shower and apparently Harrison wants my attention."

"You should talk to V," Finn says again before I leave the room, but I don't respond or react. He already knows it's futile. We've had the same conversation a dozen times since Halloween. If the rest of them want to chase what we know we can't keep, then I'm not going to stand in their way. But we vowed to keep her safe, and safe means out. Which means far the fuck away from here.

Far the fuck away from *us*.

I finish my shower and stalk across my bedroom, towel around my hips, as my phone rings on the nightstand. I pick it up, groaning when I see Harrison's name flashing on the screen.

"Harrison," is all I say when I answer, because I might not be able to beat my father in many ways, but I know it pisses him off when I call him by his given name. Petty maybe, but I'll take every jab I can get. Fuck knows he's gotten enough over the years—I have the scars to prove it. Mentally and physically.

"Lincoln, you know I hate it when you call me that. After I took care of your mess, too. You really should have more respect." I can hear his disapproval loud and clear for anyone to hear and roll my eyes. The days of me caring about his approval, or really much of anything, are long past.

I wait silently for him to speak again. He does the same. Except he called me, so if he expects me to buckle in this little game of his, he's got another thing coming. He taught me some shit too well and has no one but himself to blame.

He sighs as I drop down onto my bed, and I know he's going to give in. "It's time for you to repay that favor."

"What, exactly, does that mean?"

He huffs as if explaining himself to me is beneath him, especially when I owe him, but he obviously wants whatever it is enough to have been nice to this point. Well, nice for him. "It means you're coming to dinner with me tonight. We'll be dining with the Fontaines. Charles and his daughter are prospects for the Knights and we want them in. Charles wants a suitor for his daughter, Georgia. Someone of high ranking to establish their footing."

I bark out a laugh. He has got to be fucking kidding me. "So you're my pimp now?"

"Lincoln, you owe the favor. I could think of worse ways for you to repay it." His threat sends a shiver down my spine. "I will send you the details. Do not be late."

"How long am I supposed to maintain this charade? Are you sure East wouldn't be a better fit?" I sigh and hate that I can practically hear his smile at my submission to his will. It rankles me to give in, but I refuse to regret what happened to Raleigh. Not after what he tried to do. If this is the price, so be it. But of the two sons he has, East is more likely to woo some girl. I am not exactly the warm and friendly one.

"East is not a Knight," he hisses back at me before ending the call.

Awesome.

My phone buzzes seconds later with the name of a restaurant in the big city. I guess I had better get my shit together, because that's a few hours' drive and the reservation is at eight.

What a fucking awesome way to spend my Sunday evening: being some hooker for my father. I'll play along, but if he thinks I'm going to lean into his charade he has another thing coming. I might not be getting close to Octavia, but I have zero interest in anyone but her. Some whimpering daddy's girl is the last thing I want.

And isn't *that* just a kick in the nuts? Here I am, presented with the perfect opportunity to distract myself with some piece of strange, and the only thing I can think about is Octavia fucking Royal. She's so deep in my head I can't even entertain the idea of spending an evening with another woman, but I can't bring myself to spend a night with *her* either.

Fucking ridiculous.

I pick up my phone and pull up my group thread with Maverick and Finn.

Me

Tonight I pay the debt to Harrison. He wants me to woo some chick so her dad will join the Knights.

Finn

Guess it's a good thing you've kept your distance from V. Could you imagine trying to explain that?

Me

I could, and it wouldn't be pretty. Not that any of this means anything.

Mav

Yeah, and I'm sure she'd totally believe that. Where are you going?

Me

Chateau Pierre in the city. Reservation at eight. Keep yourselves out of trouble for one night?

Mav

Oh I intend to get into plenty of trouble. I'm still at V's. ;)

Finn

Let us know if you need anything. And fuck you, Mav.

Mav

Not you, buddy, but I'll sure let V ride me.

Me

I'll catch you boys later. Keep your phones on.

I drop my phone onto the bed beside me and flop backward on the comforter. What a fucking shit show this is going to be.

A knock is the only warning I get before the door opens and East enters my room. "You know I was only fucking with you earlier, man. We can't let this shit come between us. Not now. We need to stay focused. Get V free, then get you free."

He drops onto the bed on the opposite side and I sit up, turning to face him. "I'm the one staying focused. It's the rest of you who got distracted."

"Don't give me that shit. You might not have waded into the pool with her like I did, pun not intended, but you're just as in with her as the rest of us." He scoffs and I storm over to my closet to start getting dressed for this nightmarish evening.

"You can say what you want, but I'm focused. As focused as it gets. Octavia isn't clouding my vision. We get her free and the rest comes after," I tell him, not wanting to break it to him that me getting free is probably only going to happen when I die. When we made the pact I was much younger and way more naive than I am now.

Now… the Knights have shown me my place and, while I might fight it, I'm accepting that once you're in, you're *in*.

The only reason I'm hopeful for Octavia is that, technically, she's not in yet. She hasn't been through initiation. She can still get free.

I just need to figure out how.

But first, I need to deal with Harrison. I dress in my gray suit pants and a black shirt. Pairing it with a pair of black shoes, and my Breitling Navitimer. My hair is already dry, so I just run my fingers through it. It sits naturally and I decide that this is officially as much effort as I'm willing to go through. Showing up should be more than enough to please Harrison.

At least I hope so.

"Where are you off to?" East asks when I exit the closet.

"Harrison called. He wants me to join him at dinner with the

Fontaines. The daughter apparently needs wooing. I tried to tell him that I'm not the guy for the job, but apparently that doesn't matter." His lips twist at my words as he frowns, and I shrug. Not like there's anything either of us can do about it.

"Fuck him and his requests. Why are you even bothering?"

I cut my gaze to him, trying not to glare. It's not his fault I'm pissed off. "Because he called in his favor. This is the payment for dealing with the Raleigh mess. So essentially, it's for Octavia."

He nods, because we both know that's all the reason I need to do much of anything. Even if she has no idea the lengths I'd go to for her.

I grab my phone and drop the boys a message to let them know I'm heading out, then pocket it along with my wallet. Snatching up my keys, I take a deep breath.

I can do this. I have to do this.

"Let me know if you need a bailout," East calls as I exit my room. I nod, but we both know I won't take it.

If doing this means eyes off Octavia for a little longer, then I'm going to suck it up and do what needs to be done.

No matter how much I hate it.

I pull up to the front of the restaurant wishing I was pretty much anywhere but here. Handing over my keys to the valet, I head inside and the maître d' welcomes me. He ushers me to a table in the back corner, the best table in the house, and brings me a glass of whiskey without even asking.

Upside of Harrison owning the place, I guess. I might only be eighteen, but considering no one here is going to jail for serving me, there are perks.

I'm glad that I'm the first one here. It gives me a chance to prepare myself. The whiskey helps, too. It'll be the only one I have. I'm going to need to keep my wits about me tonight, plus I'm driving home.

The drive here wasn't enough to loosen me up. Even driving like my life means nothing, the adrenaline hit was minimal. It says something when nearly dying is pretty much the only thing to get the blood pounding. I guess it's easy to see why so many Knights fall into the depravity of life. Trying to find a new way to feel alive when you become numb to the more standard highs life has to offer.

Sipping the whiskey, I watch the people in the room, mostly to pass the time.

At eight on the dot, Harrison walks in, his booming laugh overpowering the room as he strides toward me with, I'm assuming, Charles Fontaine. The redhead that trails behind them must be Georgia. She's beautiful, in that model sort of way, but she looks like she lives with a stick up her ass. The resting bitch face she has on doesn't help. She kind of reminds me of Blair. All show, no substance. At least not until you dig real deep, and

I'm just not willing to put in that sort of investment here.

I stand as they reach the table, lifting the corners of my lips just enough that my father stops glaring at me.

He turns his fake charming smile back to his guests, and I resist the urge to roll my eyes. "Charles, I'd like to introduce you to Lincoln. Lincoln, this is Charles Fontaine and his daughter, Georgia."

I hold out my hand to Charles, who shakes it, before pulling back the chair beside me for Georgia. "Charmed, I'm sure."

She just glances up and down, taking in everything before her face transforms into a sultry smile. "I'm quite sure the pleasure is all mine." Her southern accent purrs in what I'm sure she thinks is a sexy way, it just does nothing to me. I smile tightly at her, waving for her to sit. Once she does, I push her chair in before taking my own seat once more.

"So, Lincoln. Tell me a little about yourself." She flutters her lashes, and all I want to do is laugh in her face. Does this shit really work for her usually?

Still, I keep my manners and give her my full attention, just as the favor calls for. I spend our time while we wait for the server to return to take our order ensuring she's entertained. She's older than me, but only just, and that doesn't seem to be an issue for her.

Apparently the allure of the Saint name is enough to keep her interested.

She's also way too fucking handsy for my liking, but I try

to keep it as polite as I can in my rebuffing. Especially since Harrison has demanded I woo her.

Unfortunately for him, I'm not his fucking whore.

My dick, my choice.

"If you'll please excuse me a moment," I say to Georgia and escape to the bathroom for a minute of reprieve.

I splash my face with water and take a long look at myself in the mirror.

This isn't who I want to be.

Or where I want to be.

The door to the bathroom slams open and Harrison storms in, all of his charming façade long gone. "If you fuck this up, boy, I'll come for that pretty bitch of yours harder than I have been. And I won't stop until she's as broken as you are. Do you hear me? You make that girl believe you're in love with her. I don't care what the fuck it takes, what you have to do, fucking do it. If we lose the Fontaines because of you, I'll make you regret ever looking at the Royal bitch."

His spit hits my cheek as he rants and I wipe it away with disgust, but I don't say one fucking word. He must really want the Fontaines on board if he's willing to threaten me this hard. He's mostly refrained from acknowledging that Octavia Royal is my soft spot, but if he's poking at it that means he's desperate. I tuck that little bit of knowledge away for later and just nod at him. He spins on his heel and smooths back his hair before leaving the bathroom, back behind the mask of the man he wants everyone to think he is.

I'll work out exactly what is so special about the Fontaines later, but for now, I need to be someone I'm not. I've always said I'll do anything for Octavia, so I guess we're about to see just how far I'll really go.

# SEVENTEEN

## OCTAVIA

I leave behind my Statistics class and head toward the cafeteria. This Monday morning can suck it. I am done. I know everyone complains about Mondays, but this is the Mondayest Monday in existence.

First, my car wouldn't start, then the garage gave me the news that despite all the repairs they've done on the Impala, it's, effectively, a dud, and I need a new car. Then we had a pop quiz in English, which I'm pretty sure I bombed, and Mr. Peters is back in Business after his sudden disappearance after Thanksgiving. Everyone was beginning to think he wasn't coming back, especially since no one knew why he was gone. I was starting to have hope that I wouldn't have to see his face ever again, but apparently I'm not that lucky this time.

Don't even get me started on Stats. I need some carbs, pronto. Preferably some chocolate too. It must nearly be that time of the month, because I've had an outbreak as well. I might not bleed thanks to my birth control, but that doesn't mean I don't suffer the rest of it. Bloating and cramps suck. Right along with the mood swings and bottomless pit of hunger that I become. I'm just feeling done.

I head into the cafeteria, spotting Indi already sitting at our table. I muster a smile and wave at her before stepping into the line for food. Mikayla shoulder checks me on her way out of the room, the rest of the bitch squad trailing behind her. Except for Blair. I close my eyes and take a deep breath, reminding myself that orange really isn't my color and those bitches are not worth going to jail for.

I grab an iced mocha from the machine and a tray. Piling it high and resisting the urge to do a dance when I grab the last chocolate torte, I pay and head over to where Indi is waiting for me.

I've just unloaded my tray onto the table and moved to sit when I feel the shove in my back.

Today is not the fucking day.

"Skank," Blair's voice snarks, and I see red. I grab the cleared tray and spin with it raised over my shoulder, ready to smack her with it, when someone catches my wrist.

I look up and find a smiling Maverick. "Woah there, killer," he says, stealing my tray, and turns to Blair. "What the fuck do you want?"

Usually I'd argue that I can fight my own goddamn battles, plus I could really use hitting something—the writhing rage inside of me is winning today. Instead, I drop into my seat and smile at Indi before taking a bite out of my chocolate torte.

"Bad day?" she asks with a sad smile, and I nod before tuning back into Maverick and Blair, who is stomping her foot in front of him. God, I'd laugh if I wasn't so pissed. Who the fuck even stomps their foot like that?

"You don't control me, Maverick Riley. I'll do what the hell I like. She ruined my family, so I'll see her ruined," Blair screeches and, while I have no idea what the fuck she's bitching about, I'm more than a little intrigued.

"How, exactly, did I ruin your family, Blair? 'Cause I'd really like to know why you hate me so much. All I did was come home and give your parents way too much of my fucking money." I sigh, leaning my head on my hand, looking far more relaxed than I feel.

"Don't act like a pretentious little bitch, like you don't know." She flicks her hair over her shoulder before narrowing her eyes at me. "I'll make you pay for it. Mark my words."

I roll my eyes, because apparently she's not going to tell me what it is I've supposedly done. "If you say so, Blair."

She squawks in frustration and spins around, stomping out of the cafeteria like a toddler having a tantrum.

"Well, it seems drama just follows you around, princess,"

Mav says as he drops onto the seat beside me. Leaning over and wrapping his arm around my waist, he pulls me into his lap. I squeak at the jolt of movement, but don't protest too much when he holds me tight.

Who would've thought the guy who held a knife to my throat would hug so well?

"She doesn't invite the drama, you know. You guys totally painted the target on her back. It just hasn't turned off yet," Indi says, and I can hear how pissed off she is, so I smile over at her while taking refuge in the hug.

He loosens his hold on me and pulls back so he can look at me properly. "People still haven't backed off?"

I shrug and Indi barks out a laugh. "Of course they haven't. You guys started something and you let it get out of control. Your hold is slipping. Blair keeps ignoring you all without consequence. No one knows if Raleigh was punished. People see them getting away with all of this with no retaliation from the kings of the school. So yeah... the order you guys once held is slipping."

As she finishes speaking, Lincoln and Finley arrive at the table. Lincoln looks exhausted. I thought as much earlier, but we didn't speak. He seemed to be in about as good a mood as I am. They sit without a word before he looks at me in Mav's arms then back at Indi. "What did you say?"

She repeats what she said, almost word for word, as I slip back into my own chair, despite Maverick's protests.

"We'll fix it," Lincoln says, before starting to eat. He spends the rest of lunch in a broody silence, but Maverick and Indi chat up a storm, more than filling the quiet created by the rest of us. I eat through my gargantuan lunch, feeling exactly zero shame at giving my body what it needs, and once some of the hangry slips away, I don't feel quite like I'm going to murder the entire student body anymore.

The bell rings and I groan, because how has time passed this quickly? The guys get up, Finn and Mav each kissing me on the cheek before they leave with Lincoln. I look over to Indi and smile apologetically. "Sorry, I totally spaced. Today is kicking my ass."

"You're good. Maverick was just telling me about his fight this weekend. We should totally go. It was fun last time, and if I remember correctly, you had a real good time after." She wags her brows at me and I bark out a laugh as we stand, clearing our food.

"Yes, yes I did. I'm totally down for that. You should invite your boys. Maybe we can make them all play nice." I grin and she nods.

"Yes, that sounds like a plan." She grabs her phone and shoots off a text before looping her arm through mine. "So long as they find Diego beforehand, it should be a good night."

"They still haven't heard from him?"

She shakes her head, biting down on her lip as we reach my locker. "No, not yet, which isn't exactly unusual, but it's starting to get more than a little tense with the Kings right now. Especially with the Knights sniffing around."

"Do you want me to ask the guys if they know anything?" Relief floods her face, and it hits me she's wanted to ask and just hasn't.

"Would that be okay? I don't like to ask—" I wave her off mid sentence as I swap over my shit in my locker.

"Don't even, it's fine. I'll ask. If I'd been thinking clearly, I already would've offered. Sorry, I'm such a shitty friend sometimes."

"You are not!" She swats at me until I smile at her. We head to her locker and then haul ass toward class. "I'll meet you outside French and we can head to Gym together?"

"Sounds good to me. Enjoy Spanish!"

"Oh yeah, it's a riot." She rolls her eyes and peels off down the hall while I laugh and head into French. I'm not sure what I did to deserve a friend like her, but I'll fight tooth and nail to keep her.

After a lousy start to the week, I'm finally smiling wide. It could be Maverick in his fight shorts, or the fact that I'm in the cage with him, but whatever it is, I'm not going to question it. When he offered to pick up my defense lessons so that I can actually defend myself if the occasion arises, I was not about to say no.

Especially not after seeing him fight already.

I had no idea that he owned a gym, but apparently he does. And when he kicked everyone out after someone wolf whistled at me, I just laughed.

Apparently Mav can share, just not with anyone who isn't inner-circle.

After one guy looked at my tits too long, I thought he was going to lose an eye with the vein that almost popped in Maverick's forehead.

So I'm here in my workout gear—which he groaned out his appreciation for already—in the octagon with him, pretending not to ogle his colorful chest and actually pay attention to what he's trying to teach me.

"Are you even listening to me, princess?" he asks, a smirk on his face as his gaze runs down my body.

"Not really. Focus is a little off," I say, poking my tongue out at him.

His eyes darken as his gaze narrows at me. "Do that again, and see where it gets you."

My heart rate spikes at the quiet words and I shake my head. This is not the place to be getting hot and bothered. I mean, it is, just not like that.

Instead, I bring up my hands like I've been shown a dozen times before, clenching my wrapped hands into fists, and prepare myself for what is likely going to be a shameful takedown if I don't focus and do what I need to.

"Okay, let's do this," he says, holding up the pads on his hands.

I work my way through the punching combinations he was showing me beforehand. They're simple enough, but my arms are burning by the time we go through them a couple of times. Apparently running isn't enough to keep me in tip top shape.

"Sweaty looks good on you, princess," he teases. I stick my tongue out at him again, a thrill running through me as his gaze darkens.

"I can think of better ways to get sweaty."

He closes his eyes and takes a deep breath. It's kind of fun being the one to push his buttons for a change.

"You shouldn't have let the others go. It'd be good to see if I can still fight off multiple offenders." My smile widens as his jaw tics. I shouldn't be getting off on this, but I definitely am.

The smile he gives me is nothing less than predatory, and a shiver runs down my spine in anticipation. "If you want more than my hands on you, princess, all you have to do is ask. I can get Finley here in a heartbeat."

"Promises, promises," I tease right back and lift my arms to protect my face again, except he shakes his head.

"Oh no, princess. I think you've graduated from the pads. I'm going to come at you, and you need to fight me off. I need to see just how skilled you are if I'm going to train you." His voice is a low purr, yet, it's impossible not to hear the threat in his tone. He lives for this game.

I tilt my head and jut out my chin in challenge. "Show me your worst."

His eyes flash and in a blink he's on me. He's got me in a lock from behind, his arm around my neck in a choke hold. I pull at his arm, but he's way stronger than I am. I claw at him, but that just seems to encourage him to hold tighter. "Come on, princess, I know you've got better skills than that," he whispers into my ear, and the threat to my oxygen intake almost makes me panic, which is ridiculous all things considered, but I never said I made any sense.

I need to focus, so I take as much of a breath as I can to try and clear my head, and think back to my training. Elbow, knee, balls.

So I thrust my elbow back into his gut.

As he hefts out a whoosh of breath I tilt the opposite direction, bringing my leg back and kicking at the back of his knee to topple him. Once he's on the ground, I hover my foot over his dick—rather than stomping it like I was taught—and smile down at him while I rub my neck.

"That was hot as fuck." He grins up at me and I laugh. Only he would think me taking him out would be hot. I offer him a hand up and he takes it, but instead of standing, he pulls me down and I fall on top of him. "I got you."

He rolls us over, caging me beneath him, and smiles again before capturing my lips with his. "You fighting me off really is hot as fuck," he says as he grinds his hard dick into me.

I can't help but smirk. "Apparently so, but aren't we supposed to be fighting, not fucking?"

He groans as I lift my hips and grind back against him. "You play dirty, princess, but yes, fighting not fucking."

I tangle my hands in the back of his hair and tug a little, bringing back that predatory smile. "Fucking does sound more fun though... except there's no one around. Can you keep it up when there's no risk of getting caught?"

Fire dances in his eyes at the challenge. "Oh, princess, you have no idea what I'm capable of when there's no one else around."

My heart thuds in my chest in anticipation of what's to come. This isn't how I saw my evening going, but I'm not exactly upset about it.

Just to fuck with him, I stretch my neck up to him so my lips are almost touching his and whisper loud enough for him hear me loud and clear.

"Oh yeah? Why don't you show me, tough guy?"

I barely have time to finish my last word when I find myself sprawled out on my stomach with a very heavy and very hard Maverick pressing down on my back. His mouth is at my ear, and I can almost hear the violence in his voice. That edge of danger that lives inside him is begging to escape and I practically give it the key.

"Do you know what happens to little girls who play with fire?" He grinds his hard dick into the crease of my ass cheek, almost like he's trying to get himself off.

"Orgasms?" I answer, my sass out for all to hear.

"Burns." I want to say he's joking or using some kind of metaphor, but Maverick is just this side of crazy to actually mean it. A thrill rushes through my veins at the prospect. What would it be like to feel that danger? The adrenalin from the fight, the attempt at flight?

*I guess we're about to find out.*

I poke the bear because I, too, am on just this side of insane, it would seem. Grinding my ass back so his dick is getting a good amount of friction, I hear his groan right down to my clit.

"Well, then, Mav. Let's see how hot you get me." I push my ass back again, in an attempt to get him off me but he's like a fucking wall, his weight a lead trap. It's as if he was expecting me to fight back. Then he lets up, giving me just an inch of leeway, and I pounce back with a good elbow to the gut. He doesn't whoosh air out this time, he seems to have my moves all figured out, but he does roll us over so that I'm lying back on his stomach. It's awkward for me this way but I still attempt to wriggle my way out of his hold.

My attempts are futile as he wraps his legs around mine and pins them down, immobilizing me at the same time his arm goes around my neck and I'm officially trapped. My hands immediately latch onto his arm, my instincts telling me to scratch him.

So I do. I go into fight mode but just as I'm drawing blood

from his forearm, I feel his free hand pushing my leggings down right along with my panties.

"What are you doing?" My breath is coming out in pants, and my blood is boiling with adrenalin.

"I'm going to fuck you, just like this, while you fight for your next breath."

If he thinks I'm going to give in so easily, he has another thing coming. And this is too much fun to quit just yet.

As I buck my hips to give him a solid ball busting, he shifts his weight and has me back flat on my stomach, my head turned to the side and my hair trapped in his fist.

"When will you learn, princess, that I get what I want when I fucking want it?"

"Never," I hiss. I'm not going to lie, feeling how hard he is, seeing how much he's enjoying the push and pull, spurs me on.

"Is this your fantasy, V? Getting fucked while begging me to stop? You want me to be your monster? You want me to make you come while you're screaming at me to leave you alone?"

That's not what I want. Is it?

With my face turned to the side I watch as the excitement flares in his eyes. Not just sexual, though. He's geared up for a fight. He's also geared up for more.

And I'm about to give him exactly what he wants.

Bucking back, I try to crawl away from him. I try to break free of his hold.

"Stone." That one word makes me freeze. My dad's name

from his lips at that moment is unfathomable.

"What?" My words are barely audible, the shock is so great.

"That's your safeword."

Again. "What?"

"Unless you say the word 'Stone', I won't stop."

Why the fuck did that one phrase get me even wetter? It doesn't matter because there is no fucking way I'm saying my father's name while Maverick is fucking me.

Why would he—

"You did that on purpose, didn't you? You know damn well I won't—" My words are cut off when I feel his hand push my leggings even further down than they were before. My ass is bared to him, but I refuse to let him win this easily.

I claw at the mat, using the little grip in my toes to push myself away from him but all I feel is his fist gripping tighter at my skull, the pressure pushing me further into the mat. There's just a second of rest before the pressure is right back.

"Don't fucking move, princess." I know we're role playing but, holy fuck, that tone he just used sounds really fucking real.

The smooth blunt head of his dick is now at my entrance. I want to just sink myself onto him, but at the same time I do not want to give up like this. Not so fucking easily.

With one last attempt to slink away from his monster dick, I heft myself up and try to gain an inch.

"Stop! Let me go!" The words rush out of me but not because I want to stop, I really fucking do not. Those words hurdle out of my mouth because this game is exciting me just as much as it is him. I can practically feel him vibrating with excitement. This whole thing is insane, and I fucking love it.

"You want my dick in your pussy, princess? You want me to make you cry?"

Now, the normal response to this type of question is "Fuck no" so I'm shocked when I hear the word "Yes" leave me in a breathy moan.

"That's what I thought, you dirty little whore. Now stop moving and give it to me. Give me that tight little pussy."

I don't stop moving. In fact, I fight even more until his dick slams inside my pussy and his weight pins me impossibly harder to the mat. My scalp stings from his tight grip and my legs are practically numb from the weight of him.

You'd think it would be fucking awful, but it's fucking amazing. His grunts fuel my fire. The friction of his pelvis against my ass is pushing me down and creating a delicious steady rubbing of my clit against the rough mat beneath us.

I'm already so close and he's barely been inside me for a minute.

Then I remember I'm supposed to be fighting him off, so I blurt out a weak, "Stop," but all it does is make him chuckle in my ear.

"If you come, I promise to stop."

Of course this makes me want to defy him, so I do what I can to fight back my swelling orgasm.

Maverick's free hand snakes beneath me and scoops up some of my wetness and like the little slut that I am, I rub up against him, taking advantage of his touch.

"Hmm, my little princess is a good little whore, isn't she?"

I want to cry out that yes, I am in fact a dirty little whore, but with his power of suggestion, all I can think of now is coming.

I need this fucking orgasm.

Like, right fucking now.

It's like he knows me better than I know myself.

Moments before my entire world explodes into tiny little pieces, Maverick motherfucking Riley pushes his slick, coated finger into my asshole and grunts in my ear.

"Time to fucking come, princess."

With my clit rubbing on the mat, his cock in my pussy, and his finger pushing deep inside my ass, I legit black out from the orgasm that hits me like a Mac truck.

My entire body convulses, I'm shaking and gasping and reaching for something to grab onto.

"That's it, baby, give it to me." That's when I feel the sting on my shoulder. The blunt ends of his teeth sinking into the flesh where my neck meets my shoulder.

I cry out, pushing my ass back into him as he fucks me even harder, rubbing my clit so he can get every last drop of this orgasm out of me.

Mav stills, pushing inside me one more time before everything around us disappears and I fall over the cliff once more.

There's no light.

No sound.

No pain.

Just the bliss of his dick buried inside my pussy, his finger deep inside my ass, and his tongue soothing what I'm guessing will be a very visible mark in the shape of his teeth.

He rolls off of me and pulls me onto his heaving chest. "Fuck, V, that was…"

"It was." My voice is a breathy mess.

"Are you okay?" he asks, tipping my face up to look at him. "Be honest with me. There's no room for anything else when we play like this."

"I'm more than okay," I tell him with a small smile. He kisses my forehead and just holds me on the floor of the octagon. I can't help but smile wider.

Maverick really does have a sweet side, even if he hides it from the rest of the world. I'm just glad I get to see all sides of him.

"Are you sure you're okay to give me a ride home?" I ask Finley as we head out of the school and make our way toward his car. Not having one of my own is a pain in the fucking ass.

He cuts his gaze to me and he rolls his eyes. "How many times do I have to say yes before you believe me?"

"A few more? It's on the opposite side of town from your place."

"It is, but Lincoln is busy and it's too fucking cold for you to go on Mav's bike. So you're stuck with me." He hits the fob on his keys and opens the passenger door of his Aventador for me.

"That isn't what I meant." I sigh as I climb in.

"I know," is all he says before he closes the door. He rounds the car and climbs in in silence. "Do you want to go straight home?"

"Did you have something in mind?"

He just stares at me, saying nothing. Typical Finley, but I'm not exactly ready for my day to be over, so why not? "Sure, let's do something."

He nods and starts the engine. The roar of the car sends a tingle through my body, and I grin as I buckle in. He peels out of the parking lot, and I cackle as he floors it. There is something about fast cars that just makes me feel alive.

He drives out to the beach and pulls up by the pier. "Wanna go on some rides? Like old times?"

I look over at him, and he looks at me so earnestly that I find myself nodding. I haven't done rides like this since we were kids. Theme parks were kinda off-limits when touring. Too many people, too many variables. I find myself grinning as he gets out of the car; this could actually be fun. I mean, the pier is reasonably limited, but there's still plenty of stuff to get the heart racing.

He opens the door and offers me his hand, which I take, because climbing out of this car, in this skirt, requires a 'degree in how to be a lady' if you don't want to flash the world. "Where to first?"

My stomach growls in response to his question, and the corners of his lips turn up just a little. "Soft pretzel? Or ice cream?"

"Both?" I shrug and he laughs softly before taking my hand and weaving his fingers through mine. It's a small thing, sure, but it's a small thing that makes my heart pound. Finley is an actions kind of guy, so this—all of this—means something. It's one of the things I adore about him. It's hard to misjudge him because he's as upfront as they come. If you know how to read him anyway.

We head to the ice cream stand and he gets a mint chocolate chip scoop, while I get a big ol' scoop of cherry with dark chocolate shavings and whipped cream. We walk the length of the pier in a comfortable silence eating the ice cream, and it's just… nice. It's calm, and I'm not sure the last time I had a moment of just feeling safe and calm, so I enjoy it for what it is.

A moment in time where we can just be.

I lean against the rail and stare out over the choppy water. "Do you ever wonder what life would have been like if I hadn't left?"

He drops onto the railing beside me, offering me a spoonful of his mint chocolate chip, and shakes his head. "No, I know what it would've been like. And as much as it hurt for you to go, for us to have basically no idea that you'd ever come back, I wouldn't change it. Because then you'd be broken too."

"We're all a little broken," I tell him, but the sadness in his eyes is almost my undoing. "You can tell me, you know? I'm not going anywhere this time. Even if I leave here, I'm not leaving you guys."

"You don't need to know my monsters, V. If we don't get you free, you'll have plenty of your own to keep you company." He lets out a deep sigh and looks back out over the ocean. "I went to see my mom over the weekend. I don't want that future for you."

"Your mom?" I ask softly, not wanting to poke too much. This is the first time he's really opened up since I got back, and the last thing I want to do is make him close back up.

"Yeah, she's in the city. At a care facility. I checked her in on my sixteenth birthday after I found her with her wrists in ribbons, lying in a bathtub.

"Oh, Finley," I gasp, reaching out to touch his arm, but he barely even reacts. "I'm so sorry."

"Don't be, it wasn't your fault. It was my father's. And the Knights'. This world is not made for the kindhearted. Anything good that comes here withers and dies. I'm not sure that my mom was ever good, she was with my father after all and that takes a special kind of person, but it got to even her. I don't want that for you. You've always been the light to our shadows.

Between mine and Mav's parents, Lincoln's dad… it was never a real surprise that Stone ran with you when he got the chance." He takes a pause, turning to look down at me properly and cupping my cheek with his free hand.

"Do you know why he ran? I mean, if the Knights are such a big deal, why run?"

He laughs softly, shaking his head. "I thought you'd have figured that one out. Stone might have been a shitty person, but he was always a good dad. He left, or ran as you put it, for you. He knew initiation was coming, and he didn't want that for you." He pauses, and I open my mouth to ask what the hell initiation is when he starts speaking again. "You always had this way about you, a strength, and your dad didn't want the Knights to have you. To break you. He made a deal with them to keep you free. I don't know what the terms of that deal were, if I knew I'd tell you, but I know that the last thing he wanted was to pass his legacy over to you. So if you get the chance, V, you run, and you never look back."

"I'm not going anywhere. My dad killed himself, Finn. I don't know why, maybe I never will, but whatever it was, he couldn't have wanted me gone from here so bad if he made it a part of his will that I return here upon his death." I sound bitter, and I kind of am, but that's for a different time and a slew of therapy bills that I'll rack up one day.

"I don't think that was ever his plan. I think that was maybe a part of the Knights contingency. Part of their deal. I get the feeling they never really let him leave, just gave the illusion of it. It's something they'd do."

"I know you guys want to save me from whatever this is, but did you ever think that maybe I'm strong enough to handle whatever it is the Knights want from me?"

"Of course we did. But we've also lived this hell for five years."

"Five years?" I ask, my eyes going wide.

He huffs out a laugh and drops his hand from my cheek, running it through his hair. "Yeah, Stone got you out just in time. The rest of us weren't so lucky."

"What happened to you, Finn?"

"They took us for two weeks. All three of us. We went through initiation. That's what they call it when they break you to see if they can remold you into what they want you to be. When they make you kill, and record it so you can never break free. And that… that is just the tip of the iceberg. So don't tell me you're strong enough to survive it, because no matter how strong you think you are, no one survives initiation. Not really."

My stomach drops and I feel sick. They were thirteen. "How… I…"

I have no idea what to say.

For the first time in my life I might actually be speechless, while my heart breaks for the three of them.

"Yeah," is all he says before picking up my dropped ice cream cup and putting it in the trash. "This isn't exactly what I had in mind when I brought you out here."

"I'm glad I know," I tell him quietly, still not able to look at him properly as guilt consumes me. Maybe if Dad hadn't saved me, it wouldn't have been so bad for them. Were they punished because I was freed?

"But now you think I'm a monster. That we're all monsters. I don't blame you. We are."

I look up, a fire blazing in my chest and grab his chin. "You listen to me, Finley Knight. You are not a monster. You are loyal, and love fiercely with every single part of you. You might hide those softer parts of you from most of the world, but those of us lucky enough to see who you really are know the truth. You're no more a monster than I am. None of you are."

He drops his forehead to mine, his eyes closed, and wraps his arms around me. "Thank you," he says so quietly that I almost miss it, and my heart breaks for him, for all of them, all over again. It's no wonder they were so fucked up about how they went about trying to get me out of here. Especially if that's what they think is waiting for me if I stay.

And just like that, any remnants of anger I was holding onto disappear. How can I not forgive them when this is what they were trying to save me from?

# EIGHTEEN

## OCTAVIA

Staring up at the ceiling, I try to pull myself out of the rabbit hole I've been in since I got home from school. For once, this week was pretty reasonable, and after my time with the guys I'm feeling more grounded than I have since I returned. But talking to Finley about his parents has had thoughts of my mom in the back of my mind since I got home last night. No matter how much I try to shut that voice down, it still plagues me.

Where is she?

How did she get out?

Why did she never come for me?

Do the Knights have her?

Is she even still alive?

And 'round and 'round on the carousel I go. It doesn't

matter that I know nothing good is going to come from pulling on that particular thread, I can't help but pull at it.

I've just about managed not to look too much closer at my dad's death since I found out all of this Knight bullshit, mostly because I don't think I'll be able to handle it if it was anything but what I know it to be.

All this being said, I don't have the first idea how to find my mom. I know Lincoln has a PI who's helping look into the stalker, but I don't really want to let anyone know that I'm looking for her. Especially if she did manage to escape the clutches of the Knights somehow, impossible as it seems.

Maybe she has the answers Finley's mom didn't. Or maybe at least answers she's willing to give that the others aren't.

I don't remember much about her, really. And Lord knows I was beyond oblivious to the shit going on around me. I was too young to really notice any of it, but it makes me question how much I missed. How much more there is that I don't know because I was too oblivious—too naive—to notice.

A lead weight in the base of my stomach tells me that there's a lot I still don't know, but I'm not sure how much of it I *want* to know. I've only just started to scratch the surface of what the guys have been through, and it already makes me so angry, so sad, that I just want to run away with them and never look back.

But Echoes Cove has its claws in me, and there's too much here that I couldn't leave behind now. Not to the point I could just disappear without a trace.

I can't help but wonder if Dad knew this would happen when he sent me back here. If this was what he had in mind.

I shake my head and sit up, trying to pull myself from the dark and twisty spiral that lies at the end of that train of thought.

None of this is productive, so I head downstairs and find the house empty. A note from Smithy on the fridge tells me he's out for the evening again, and a smile creeps over my face. I guess his date went well last week after all.

Pulling my phone from my pocket, I dial someone I know has zero connection to any of this crazy, but is likely to be able to help me.

I put the phone to my ear, and Jenna's cheery voice comes down the line. "Summertime Starlight! There you are! I was beginning to wonder when I'd hear from you again." I laugh at the eons-old nickname she calls me. I haven't heard that in years.

"Going back through old notebooks are we?" I laugh and she joins in.

"Maybeeeee. How you doing, girl?"

I let out a sigh, the last thing I want to do is kill her hobby with my bullshit. "Same old, same old."

"Are those boys of yours looking after you? I have to say, I never considered the poly thing, but damn, if I had four guys that looked like that chasing my tail, I'd play that game too, girl. Those boys are fire." She bursts out laughing, and I wonder if she's been drinking. She always gets super chatty when she's had tequila.

"They're not my boys. Not really. I don't think."

"Girl, if you say so. I saw the way they watched you. It was like you pushed and they pulled. I'm pretty sure if you told them to jump, they'd all ask how high."

I shake my head, envisioning me telling Lincoln to jump and him doing anything but glaring at me. "I have a favor to ask."

The music in the background turns down, and I hear the rustle of sheets. "Shoot, girl. What do you need?"

"Do you know any PIs? Good, but like, uber discreet?" I bite my lower lip as I ask, chewing at it while I wait for her to answer.

"Are you in trouble?" she asks, sounding as sober as I feel.

I can't help but smile. Jenna might not be Indi, but she's been a good friend of mine for a long-ass time. "No trouble, not yet anyway. I just need to find someone."

"Say no more. I got you, my friend. I'll shoot you Bentley's details. He isn't cheap, but he's good, and *very* good at discreet." She pauses and I feel my phone buzz. I check it and see the contact file on my screen. "If you need a place to hide out, or just somewhere to feel safe, you can always go to—"

"I know, thank you. You fucking rock. I love you."

"I love you too. Call me if you need anything, okay?"

"I will. Go back to your good time. I can't wait to come see you guys play again soon."

"We're actually not far from you tomorrow night. I'll send you the details."

"You're amazing. Love you. Talk soon."

"Love you too. Peace out."

She ends the call and I smile down at my phone, at what a beautiful human she is. Seconds later, details of the gig tomorrow are in my inbox. Pretty sure Indi will be down for a last minute road trip.

But first... I pull up Bentley's details and save them, trying to decide if this is really a good idea. The thought of not knowing is what spurs me on, because what if I could've had the answers all along, and I had my dumb bitch button stuck in the on position again and did nothing?

That alone is enough to spur me on to text the number Jenna sent me.

Me

Hi, Jenna B gave me your number. I'm in need of some help. Do you have any time to meet to go through it?

I drop my phone on the counter, not expecting a response straight away, so I jump when it buzzes.

Maverick

I have a fight tonight. You coming?

Shit!

I was supposed to be going with Indi. I scramble up the stairs and jump in the shower to freshen up. I rush through drying my hair, putting it up in a messy ponytail before looking at my closet. Fuck it. I dial Indi, and she picks up on the second ring.

"You almost ready? I'm leaving in ten."

"I'm currently staring at my closet, naked, trying to decide what to wear." She bursts out laughing and I grin. There's a lot to be said about not having to have a filter when it comes to your bestie.

"Considering the way your last fight night went, well, I guess it depends how you want the evening to end." I bite my lip at her words trying not to groan. My libido needs to calm the fuck down. She's been getting plenty, and yet, there's something about Maverick—about all of them—that makes me insatiable. I can't help but wonder what would've happened if Mav had called Finn earlier in the week when we were in the octagon. Or what it would be like to be at Lincoln's mercy, even though he hasn't shown any signs of wanting that.

What it would be like with both of the Saint brothers.

With all four of them.

"V? You there?" Indi's voice pulls me from my train of thought, and she laughs like she knows exactly what had me so distracted.

"I'm here, sorry, daydreaming. You make a good point, I think I know what I'm going to wear."

"Okay bish, I'll be there soon."

"See you soon!" I say just before she ends the call and I bounce into my wardrobe, pulling on some black lace and mesh undies before digging through my drawers for what I'm after.

When I find it all, I grin. This is one way to encourage Mav to win tonight, I guess.

I slide into the fishnets, cutoff shorts, pink tank, and mesh long sleeve top, finishing it off with knee-high Chucks. Sitting at my dresser, I do my makeup, reasonably subtle, except for the neon pink liner that highlights my eyes, framed with black. I pull a pink ribbon from my drawer and braid my hair with it.

Indi breezes into my room and whistles. "Damn girl, you sure know how to make those boys drool. You look hot as fuck."

I grin at her and take in her skater dress, with a tutu under the skirt, and Docs. "Girl, same!" She blushes, waving me off, but I love that she's embracing herself and sticking to exactly who she is, even with her guys chasing her again. "Did you pierce the other side of your nose?"

She nods, showing me each side of her face, the small gold hoops in each nostril.

"It looks cute as hell."

"Thanks. You good to go?" she asks, looking down at her phone. "Did I tell you Ryker and Ellis are coming tonight?"

I raise my eyebrows. "No, you did not, but I'm looking forward to officially meeting two of the boys coveting your heart."

"I'd tell you to play nice, but fuck it. They can sweat." She grins at me and I laugh.

"Damn straight they can." I snap a picture of myself and

send it over to Maverick, finally responding to his message.

Me

I am. See you soon.

Maverick

Fucking hell. Fighting with a hard-on isn't the easiest, but that's my reality tonight.

I laugh at his response and pocket my phone, slipping my wallet and keys in too before looking up at Indi. "Let's rock it."

It doesn't take us too long to find the warehouse again, but parking is a nightmare. We end up in the butt-fuck middle of nowhere, and it's dark as fuck.

"Ryker told me to stay in the car till he gets here," Indi says, biting her lower lip like she's trying not to laugh.

"Wow, he really is all kinds of protective, huh?"

She blushes and nods. "Yeah, just a bit. You cool just waiting a minute?"

"Yeah, I'm good. I can't imagine Maverick would be thrilled about me being out there in this darkness considering no one has a clue who my stalker is yet."

She pales at the reminder. "Yeah, that's true." She hits a button on the dash and the doors all lock. I try not to laugh. "Better safe than sorry."

It only takes a few minutes before her phone buzzes again.

"He's here. Didn't want to scare me."

"Aww, that's kind of adorable."

She unlocks the car and the door opens instantly as the tattooed wonder that is Ryker Donovan appears beside her. "Hey, baby." He grins at her like she is his entire world.

"Hey," she breathes before he kisses her, and I swear to fuck the entire car steams up with the heat of their kiss. I look down at my phone, giving them as much privacy as I can. "Ryker, you know V, right?"

"We knew each other once upon a time," he says, eyeing me suspiciously. I don't take it personally, he's a King. I'm meant to be a Knight. And while I don't know everything that's going on there, I know enough that he's not going to be my best friend.

"That we did. Time changes people though. Treat my girl right, and we're good."

"My girl," he growls, "and I could say the same to you."

I grin at them, while Indi rolls her eyes at him. "You're good. I'm never going to hurt her, and I never have." I quirk a brow at him and he nods.

"Touché."

"Let's get this show on the road, shall we?" Indi says, diffusing the tension. I drop Maverick a message to let him know I'm here, and that Ryker is walking us from Indi's car. Since we're in the middle of nowhere, I share my location with him at the same time. My stalker is still out there somewhere, and Ryker is about as likely to help me as he is to stick a knife in his eye.

I climb from the car, and we head toward the warehouse. The noise of the start of fight night reaches us, even all the way over here. I try to give them their privacy while not straying too far from them, but when a figure steps out of the darkness, I can't help but squeak. Ryker spins, gun out and aimed in my direction in a heartbeat.

"You better lower that gun before you find a bullet between your eyes, Donovan." Lincoln appears from the shadows, a gun of his own in hand.

"Lower the testosterone, boys. I'm a jumpy mess. No need for anyone to get shot," I say while Indi looks at me wide-eyed like she's about to freak the fuck out.

Lincoln doesn't move until Ryker lowers his gun, raising his hands in surrender. "No harm, no foul, Saint."

Lincoln nods at him before holstering his gun and pulling down his hoodie to cover it. It's only then, when the guns go away, that I take the time to take in the deliciousness that is a dressed-down Lincoln. Jeans, boots, and a hoodie topped with a leather jacket. Not exactly his usual attire, but hot fucking damn. I think my ovaries just went boom again.

"I'll see you inside, V," Indi says as Ryker steers her away from us, and I nod, giving her a little wave. I should probably try and smooth shit out with Ryker, just to make Indi's life easier, but I'll work on that later. Right now, I have an unexpected turn to my night.

"I didn't realize you were here tonight," I say to Lincoln, who motions for me to follow behind Indi and Ryker. He drops into step beside me, his hands in his pockets.

"I don't usually miss Maverick's fights, no matter how stupid they are. It's better for him to get his bloodlust out here than another way."

I nod at his words. I might not have Maverick all figured out yet, but it's impossible not to see that he enjoys dancing in the shadows a little more than the others. Not that that scares me. If anything, it intrigues me.

We continue in silence, the tension building between us with each step. "Thank you for coming to find me."

"I wasn't about to leave you out here with him. He'd probably leave you for dead if it meant Indi was safe."

I nod, because yeah. I'm at least sure enough that if I was in trouble, any of them would take the time to make sure Indi was safe too, purely because of how much she means to me.

Brownie points for each of them, I guess.

"Can I ask you a question?" I look over at him, blending into the shadows, but I catch the nod in the dim moonlight. "Why save me? You keep saying you were all trying to save me from the Knights, but if they're so vast, so powerful, why even try?" I don't really expect an answer, he doesn't exactly seem in the talking mood, but I figure it's worth a try.

He pauses and looks at me. "Some things in life are worth the sacrifice."

"You know that answer isn't an answer right?" I deadpan, and he just shrugs. Frustration builds up, but I let it out with a deep breath. Tonight is not the time, but at least I tried.

We head inside the warehouse without another word passing between us. He leads me over to where Finley and East are waiting with Maverick, who bounces on the balls of his feet in nothing more than his fight shorts.

I smirk at him when I see him, my gaze bouncing from his shorts back up to his eyes, and his grin matches mine. I know he's thinking about earlier in the week, just like I am. He pulls me into his arms, away from Lincoln's side, and kisses me until I'm breathless. My hands glide over his sweaty torso until my fingers tangle in his hair. He lifts me from my feet when Lincoln's voice snaps through our happy bubble. "Put her the fuck down, Maverick."

Maverick pulls back from me, putting me down and flips Lincoln the bird. "Don't be a jealous asshole. You could kiss her if you wanted to."

I suck in a breath at Maverick's challenge and catch Finley's eye over Maverick's shoulder, not daring to look back at Lincoln. Finley takes my hand and pulls me toward him, saving me from the testosterone showdown happening between the two of them. "Hey, you."

"Hey." I smile up at him as East moves to lean against the wall beside him.

"You two should leave the fighting for the ring," East says

to the other two while I nuzzle into Finn's chest. Enjoying the warmth of him.

"You look beautiful, in a rave, party girl kind of way," Finn whispers in my ear, and I smile.

"Thanks." I pull back and East smiles at me. I don't get butthurt about the lack of affection from him. I'm very aware that crossing boundaries in private with him is one thing, but in public… well, I don't want him to go to freaking jail for getting handsy. He's here and that's what's important. "Do you guys know where Indi is?"

"She's with the Donovans," Finn says, pointing across the room.

"Thank you. I'm going to go get a drink and talk to her for a minute. What time is your fight, Mav?"

The guy in question grins at me like a crazy person.

"You called me Mav. I knew you were softening to me, princess." He winks and I bark out a laugh. "My fight is in thirty; you've got time. Just make sure you're back here to kiss me good luck."

I sashay over to him and stretch up on tiptoe to whisper in his ear. "I've got something better than luck for you. Win, and you can stay at my house tonight."

I drop back down and the wolfish grin he gives me is enough to send a shiver down my spine. "Oh, I was going to win anyway, princess, but that is way too good of a prize to let go."

I head to the bar and grab a bottle of water before elbowing my way through the crowd to where Indi is standing with her guys. Someone grabs my ass and I use the technique Maverick showed me to twist his arm, so if he moves too much his wrist will snap. "Do not fucking touch what isn't yours."

The asshole whimpers, nodding, and I release him, pushing him back into the crowd. Another point for Maverick tonight, 'cause he ran through that hold with me so many times I thought I was going to scream. I hear a whoop from across the room, and find Maverick looking in my direction, laughing hard. "That's my girl!"

I laugh, shaking my head before continuing through the crowd until I stumble into Indi. "There you are!" she exclaims. "I was going to try and rescue you from that jack hole, but I saw you had it covered, and these idiots wouldn't let me go anywhere." She points over her shoulder, and I find Ryker glaring at me while Ellis smiles.

"Is that Dylan?" I ask her, motioning to the other guy standing with the twins, and she giggles, nodding.

"That's him," she confirms, and I hug her.

"Damn, girl, Ryker might be a bit of a jerk, but they are fire. You deserve no less. I stick by my earlier words though. I'm happy to remove certain appendages if they fuck you over again." She giggles at me again and squeezes me tight.

"Oh, I'd let you, too, but I think we're good now. Is Mav ready for his fight?" she asks, and I look over my shoulder to where I know he's watching. She waves at him and he nods. Just like that, her guys are at her back. "Will you guys chill? They're not going to do anything to me. They all want V's kitty cat too much for that."

I burst out laughing at her, but I'm inclined to agree. Except for Lincoln. But he won't hurt her anyway. He might not want me like the others do, but I know he wouldn't hurt me like that.

"They already had your car jacked," Ryker growls, and as much as I hate to agree with him, he isn't wrong.

"They won't hurt her again. You have my word on that. No one will touch her because of me," I tell him, holding his gaze. I'm not sure how many people dare take on Ryker Donovan in a battle of wills, but I'm not about to back down. He might be dangerous as fuck, but I'd lay down my life for my girl, Indi. That includes going up against her guys if that's what's needed.

"Oh, I like this chick," Dylan says, distracting Ryker, and I smile over at him. He's taller than the twins, his floppy blond hair falls into his green eyes, and his t-shirt shows off every single muscle he's sporting. I stand by my earlier assessment. Hot fucking damn.

"Nice to meet you," I say to him with a grin.

He steps forward and bundles me into his arms. "Oh, girlie, we don't say hello like that. Not 'round these parts. And don't worry about Ryker, his bark is worse than his bite." He winks at me before releasing me. Indi's eyes go wide, and I let out a sigh as soon as I feel their heat at my back.

"Calm down. He was saying hello," I say to Mav, whose

eyes flare as he steps up behind me, all territorial.

"Nice to see you again, Dylan," Finn says, sounding calmer than Mav looks.

"You too, man." Dylan smiles, and I look at Indi. Two down, the rest to go. "Good luck with your fight tonight, Maverick. That asshole deserves a beatdown. Did you hear what he did to the Erikkson sisters?"

Mav shakes his head and the three of them break off to talk about whatever that is, leaving Indi and I with the Donovans and the Saints. Not even a battle of wills going on here or anything. Here was me thinking after Halloween, that there might be a tentative peace, but apparently I was wrong.

"Well, this isn't awkward at all. Will you guys dial back the testosterone please?" Indi sighs, looking at the Donovans, while I look at East and Lincoln.

"What she said."

"Do you know where Diego is?" Ryker asks, ignoring us both and looking straight at Lincoln.

Lincoln puts his hands in his pockets and shakes his head. "No idea. Should I?"

Most people would miss it, but I see the tic in his jaw. He's lying. I don't say anything, but he's got another thing coming if he thinks I'm going to leave that alone. I won't do it here in front of the twins and Indi, but I know how worried she's been, so there's no way in hell I'm going to let that lie.

"If you say so," Ryker snarls while Ellis pulls Indi back so her back is flush with his chest. She sighs, relaxing into him.

"We should go. Mav's fight starts soon," Finley interrupts as the three of them rejoin us.

"Sure thing. I'll see you in a bit?" I say to Indi who nods and mouths a 'sorry.' I shake my head, she has nothing to apologize for, but if the guys want anything more than a quick fuck from me, they're going to have to get on board with the Donovans. I don't care what their history is; I won't consider one damn thing if it's going to fuck with our friendship.

Not a fucking one.

I let Finley lead me back over to where they were standing before, Maverick, Lincoln and East following behind. I wait until we're standing back by the wall before I turn to Lincoln. "You were lying. You know where he is."

His eyes go wide before he locks down his features. "I was not lying."

He turns his back on me and heads to the bar, and I try to swallow my frustration down as East follows him.

"Fight time!" Mav announces, bouncing in front of me. "Kiss me good luck, princess."

I step forward and kiss him, pouring every ounce of heat and frustration into it, while I try to lose myself in him. He pulls back grinning. "Don't think I forgot my reward for winning, either."

"I didn't imagine you would." I smirk. "Now go get him, killer. Make him bleed for me." I wink and he groans.

"Just you sounding all bloodthirsty is enough to make me want to forfeit and just take you to my bed instead."

"Blood first, fuckery later," I tease, and he stalks toward the ring.

"Thank you," Finley says as he pulls me back against his chest. "For not pushing Lincoln, and for being here for Mav. He'll never admit it, but he focuses better with you here. He keeps his head a bit more. You're good for him, so thank you."

"You don't have to thank me," I tell him as I lean my head back on his shoulder, and he slips his hands in the front pockets of my shorts. "I wanted to be here. Lincoln, however…"

I trail off and he kisses the side of my neck. "Be patient. He struggles."

"I wasn't asking much," I counter, and I feel him smirk against my skin.

"You were asking more than you think," he says, and I relax a little further. "He's coming around, but… well, he's Lincoln."

"Don't I know it." I sigh as the bell rings, announcing the start of the fight, and I turn my attention to Maverick and the fucking behemoth of a man in the ring with him. "Umm, should Mav be fighting that guy?"

"You doubt he can win?" Finn asks, his chest vibrating against my back as he chuckles. I like this side of him. I wish he relaxed like this more often.

"I mean, have you seen that other guy?"

"Have a little faith," is all he says before Mav flies through the air, fist raised as he bounces from the ground, and smashes his fist into the guy's cheekbone as he comes down.

Holy shit. It's like something out of a fucking movie. I grin as the crowd cheers, and Maverick winks over at me momentarily before focusing back on the guy in the ring.

I guess I'm not sleeping alone tonight.

When I get back from my run with Lincoln, who didn't say a word on the entire route, Maverick is still sleeping in my bed. I grin as I stand in my doorway, the white sheet tangled around him, bunched down at his hips, leaving the rest of him bare for my eyes to feast on.

"I can feel you watching me, princess," he murmurs, half asleep, lifting his arm to cover his eyes. Of them all, I definitely didn't expect Maverick to be the one that I warmed to the fastest, to get to this point with first, but there's just something reckless about him that makes me want to join him in his abandon.

"I can still feel you inside of me, so that makes us even," I counter and he groans. I grin at the sound as he grabs his dick through the sheet.

"You coming back to bed?" he asks as I start to undress. I glance over at him and catch his predatory stare following my movements.

"I need to shower. And then I need to speak to Indi about a

gig tonight in the city," I tell him as I shoot Indi a message to see if she's around today.

"I could always join you in the shower," he grins at me, an odd mix of lascivious and dangerous, ripping a sharp laugh right out of me.

"You could, but I have a feeling, Maverick Riley, that if I let you do that, the rest of my plans for the day are going to get derailed."

He feigns indignation, scoffing at me. "Why, princess, must you always think the worst of me? I was merely offering to wash your back." I stick my tongue out at him, and his eyes darken as he sits up.

"Sure you were." He grins at me wickedly.

"You know me so well, princess, because by washing your back, I totally meant your ass... with my dick." I roll my eyes at him, trying not to laugh at how he goes from playful to Maverick in zero-point-two seconds.

"Exactly."

Sliding out of my leggings, I put them in my laundry hamper before padding into the bathroom and starting up the shower. "If you let me shower quickly, we can have breakfast before I need to head out."

"I can make it go faster if you let me have breakfast in the shower," he says as he enters my bathroom, stark fucking naked, dick standing to attention, wagging his brows.

I finish undressing and let down my ponytail. "Well, I guess it would be rude of me to make you starve like that…"

His eyes drag down my body, stopping on each and every mark he left on me last night. From the bruises on my hips to the teeth marks on my tits, amongst the various others scattered across my skin. "You look good wearing me," he growls as he steps toward me. I swear that growl alone is enough to make me fucking wet. "Ass on the counter. Now."

"But I just went running," I whine. "I should shower."

He quirks a brow at me and folds his arms across his chest. "Do I look like I give a fuck? Ass on the counter. Now, princess."

I let out a breathy moan but do as I'm told as he sinks to his knees, pushing my thighs apart. He bites the inside of my thigh and I jolt forward a little, but that just makes him grin harder against my skin. His tongue laves over the stinging flesh as his fingers dig into my thighs. That's going to leave yet another bruise and I'm totally good with that.

"I didn't think you were such a tease," I groan in challenge, and his eyes flash as his gaze meets mine, need and determination written all over them.

I cry out as he thrusts two fingers inside of me, circling my clit with his tongue, teasing every nerve ending inside me. There's a steady, mind-blowing rhythm to his actions and my entire body reacts to it all at once.

With every push and curl of his fingers, his tongue flicks my clit. Over and over again until my brain can't take it anymore. I'm a panting, writhing mess with one hand clutching the side of the counter while the other fists in his hair, encouraging him to send me over the edge.

His movements slow and I whimper.

"You wanted me to be a tease." He winks at me like this is a game and I'm his personal puppet, but the moan that escapes from my lips tells us both that I'm loving every second of his torturous ways.

"No, no I didn't," I pant as his fingers move in and out slower, curling to hit that magical spot inside me, pushing hard when he hits it, sending shivers through my entire body. "Please, Mav."

He pulls back and stands, looking down at me as his fingers continue their slow torture.

"Oh, I like it when you beg, princess. It's almost as good as when you fight me."

His words spur me on and instead of begging I change up my tactics. I want him to drive me wild and make my world spin. So, I raise my hand and slap him across the face. He grins down at me sadistically, catching my wrist in his free hand. "Oh, princess, you want to wake the beast?" A shiver runs straight up my spine and I'm not sure if it's from a tiny bit of fear or a whole lot of thrill.

Probably both.

He withdraws his fingers, watching me intently as he licks them clean. Pulling me from the counter, he pushes me into the shower and presses me up against the cold tile. I hiss as the chill hits my skin, but I'm trapped and barely able to breathe as he uses his entire body to keep me pinned. He takes my wrists and binds them in one of his large hands above my head. "You remember your safe word?"

I nod, barely able to make the movement, crying out as he thrusts into me and bites down on my shoulder. I welcome that sting of pain, crave it, even. With his dick fully seated inside me, I'm whole again. Needing everything he has to give to me.

Mav's dick is a relentless piston fucking me without abandon. In and out, he owns my body and has no qualms showing me exactly who's in charge. His body shields me from the hard sting of the shower water—muting its sound—and all I hear is the musical rhythm of skin slapping against skin. It's raw and carnal. It's crude, but it's us. It's everything I never knew I needed.

One hand snakes around my waist and slides down my lower belly until his middle finger flicks at my clit. A hoarse cry rips out from my throat at the bittersweet sting of pain, but he doesn't stop. He doesn't let up or even acknowledge my reaction as my orgasm flashes through me without warning. "That's it, princess, come all over my dick."

He fucks me until I wilt then pulls his still very hard dick out before turning me to face him. "Kneel."

I do as I'm told, his hand fisting my hair until it stings, the warm spray on my back.

"You're going to look so pretty with me painted all over

you," he says, stroking his dick so hard the veins on his forearm pop out deliciously. It's when he taps the head of his cock against my lips that I take my cue and push my tongue out, earning me a groan so hot it makes me wet all over again. "Fuck, princess."

That's all the warning I get as he sprays his cum all over my lips, my cheeks, my throat. I keep my mouth open until he's done, licking up and swallowing down what little ends up on my lips.

"You really do look hot as fuck with me on your face." He smirks at his cheeky remark and it makes me laugh despite the intense moment we've just experienced. Tilting my head back, I close my eyes as the spray from the shower washes away all remnants of his cum from my face. I don't even bother trying to stand, my legs probably can't hold me up anyway.

"I suppose I really should scrub your back for you now, huh?"

I laugh as he lifts me to my feet and kisses me until my toes curl. "Probably should, yeah. I'm going to need to wash my hair now, too. You don't have to stick around for all of that."

"Pssh," he hisses and grabs my shampoo from the rack. "Turn around, princess, I got this."

I smile up at him, kissing his chest before doing as I'm told. He's so gentle with me after he fucks me. He washes my hair, massaging my scalp as he does, putting in the conditioner before scrubbing me head to toe with my loofah. Once he's done, he washes himself quickly before jumping out and grabbing towels. He wraps himself up before turning off the water and wrapping my hair in one towel and my body in another, carrying me through to my bed when he's done.

"Thank you," I say quietly when he crouches in front of me. "You didn't need to do any of that."

"I don't need to do anything," he says, capturing my chin in his thumb and forefinger. "But I wanted to look after you. Now let's get dressed and get that breakfast, shall we?"

My stomach rumbles in response and he chuckles at me.

"Come on, princess. Can't let you go hungry now, can I?" He winks at me as he starts to dry off, and I go through the motions of getting ready for my day. This wasn't exactly how I saw my day starting, but I am far from mad about it.

# NINETEEN

## EAST

"**L**inc—"

The slam of the door cuts me off and I let out a sigh. Good to see his mood has improved a ton since last night. I knew going there with V was a bad idea, but trying to stop any of them when they had something in mind is like herding fucking cats. He's been a grumpy fucking asshole ever since she called him out last night. Pretty sure Maverick spending the night over there didn't help either.

She might be safer with him there, and Lincoln might still be resisting being close to her, but I know my little brother. There are very few things in life that can fuck him up like this, but every single thing about Octavia Royal has him tied in knots.

Denying himself of her isn't helping either, but I don't know how to break through that thick skull of his and convince him that he won't lose her. Not if we all work together to keep her safe, Knights or not. Between the four of us we can shield her from the worst of it. Even if I'm not a Knight. Maybe even *because* I'm not a Knight.

I head downstairs and find Betty in the kitchen. Our housekeeper hates it when I call her Mrs. Potts, so I try to respect her wishes as much as I can. Especially since she's been more of a mother to Lincoln and I than Fiona has ever been.

Hell, Fiona hasn't even tried to contact us for nearly five years. She left not long after Stone and V did. I'm not sure if Lincoln even knows why she finally left, but I was older. It wasn't hard to see the way she looked at Stone; to see how depressed she became once he left. I'm pretty sure it's one of the reasons my dad hates V as much as he does.

In fact I'm pretty sure it's one of the reasons he allowed Stone to leave with her in the first place, to get her out. Because at least then he wasn't being humiliated by his wife fucking around with the guy next door. Someone who was, once upon a time, higher up on the Knights' food chain than he was, what with Stone having been the Regent before he stepped away.

"Morning, Easton. Would you like some breakfast?" Betty asks as I sit at the table, "Eggs? Pancakes?"

"Morning, Betty. Yes please. Whichever is easiest for you," I tell her with a smile. Really, I'm old enough and capable enough to make myself breakfast, but she'd chase me with a fucking spatula if I told her as much.

"Blueberry pancakes it is, I know how much you like those. I got some fresh berries from the market this morning too. Will Sir Grumps-a-lot be joining us?"

I chuckle at her description of Lincoln. To say he struggles with the whole affection thing is an understatement. Our parents really did a number on him, and it shows. "I doubt it, but I'll text him and let him know what you're making. He might come down."

I shoot off the text to Lincoln, giving him the option to ignore it if he wants to. He's already spent hours in the gym in the basement this morning, apparently that wasn't enough to sort out his funk. And that was *before* he went on his morning run with V.

My phone buzzes on the table, and instead of seeing Lincoln's name, I see my dad's.

"I'll just take this outside," I say to Betty and head out the back. No one else needs to bear witness to the joy that is me speaking to him.

"Father," I say as I answer the phone, more to piss him off. Lincoln refuses to give him the title and it infuriates him, but he wishes I wouldn't. "What can I do for you today?"

"What the fuck are you and your brother up to?" he hisses down the line, and I let out a deep sigh.

"I don't know what you're talking about."

"I'm not fucking stupid, Easton. This is all about the Royal girl isn't it? Of course you'd both fawn over the Royal bitch."

"Harrison—" I start, but he cuts me off.

"Don't take me for a fool, Easton. I will kill her and be done with it if you make things difficult."

I swallow the lump that rises in my throat. I have no doubt he would, too.

"What can I do for you?" I ask, trying to remain non-combative. He already holds too many of the strings to my life in his hands.

"You can fucking disappear, that's what you can do. Stop filling Lincoln's head with ideas that he'll ever be anything like you. You and I both know you're fucking nothing. I never should've let you stay at the house with him."

I grind my teeth together. How much he enjoys poking at me… but I refuse to stoop to his level. Unfortunately, I have to live with the grace of his mercurial mood. "We had a deal."

"That deal isn't working for me so much anymore." He pauses and I hold my breath. I don't want to beg him, but if that's what it takes to protect Lincoln, even in such a limited capacity as I am currently capable, then I will.

"What do you want?" I ask again, trying to sound as pliant as possible.

"I want Lincoln to be focused on the Fontaine girl. Not Octavia. I don't care how you do it, but get it done. Otherwise this little deal of ours is done and you'll be out of that house, and out of The Cove, so fast your fucking head will spin."

How the fuck am I supposed to do that?

I take a deep breath, pinching the bridge of my nose. "I'll do what I can."

"You do that. You might have the protection of the Knights as per our deal, but that can easily be pulled, and all of those advantages you've existed on will quickly disappear. Including that little side job of yours." I hear a voice in the distance and he barks something out to them before speaking again. "I have to go. Do not fuck this up, Easton. You're living on borrowed time."

"Yes, sir." I sigh, resigned to the fact that, despite everything, he still has more control over me than I ever wanted. The sacrifices I've made to keep my brother safe aren't something I'll ever regret, but sometimes I wish I would have just run with him when I found out the truth.

Kidnapping a minor wasn't exactly something I wanted on my rap sheet though, even if I was still a minor at the time too, Harrison still would've locked me up and thrown away the fucking key.

I wait until he ends the call and lean back against the wall. Fuck my life.

I've been trying to push Lincoln toward V. I know that's where he'll find his happiness, and now Harrison is shitting all over my plans. That's not really anything new, but fuck.

Maybe I should just tell Lincoln the truth. Maybe then he wouldn't resent me so much for the position he's in. I've let him, and I haven't held it against him. It was part of the deal I made with Harrison. I thought it would be easier for him not to know… but I'm beginning to think I was wrong.

Fuck this is way too much for a Saturday fucking morning.

I head back into the kitchen and find Lincoln sitting at the table while Betty fusses over him. I can't help but smile. He might be a grumpy asshole, but he's our grumpy asshole. And even though he can't stand the fussing, he still lets her do it because he also understands that she's the closest thing to a real mother we've ever had.

"All okay?" she asks, looking up as I take a seat again. I just nod, and she heads back to the stove where the griddle is heating for the pancakes.

"You okay?" I ask Lincoln, who is focused on his phone. He drops it onto the table and sighs. The bags under his eyes make me worry. He never sleeps enough. There were a few weeks where he slept okay, and now I know that that's when he was sneaking next door and sleeping with V.

This is exactly why my father's wishes are so hard to follow. Octavia is good for him, even if he won't admit it himself. There is something about her that settles the storm that lives inside of him. All I want, all I've *ever* wanted, is for him to be happy. As much as I love V, if I knew it would make them both happier for me to step back, then I would.

"Just Harrison. He wants me to take Georgia—the Fontaine girl—to the gala." He looks so fucking sad, it guts me. It's also how I know he's so fucking tired. He wouldn't usually show this much emotion. Even here. Even to me. "Except... I think Octavia is going."

"I didn't think she was going to go..." I'm shocked. Balls aren't exactly her thing.

He shakes his head before running a hand through his hair as the smell of the blueberry pancakes fills the air. "I'm not sure she has much of a choice. We've been distracting them from her as much as we can, but whatever the shitstorm was that they were dealing with over Christmas is finally clearing up. They're focusing again. I just wish I knew what they wanted from her. They don't usually go back on a deal, so for them to try and get her back, after freeing her in the deal with Stone... it has me all kinds of fucked up."

"We'll keep her safe."

He slams his hand on the table and hisses. "I can't keep her safe if I have to keep my attention on this Georgia chick. And you're not even invited."

"V has a plus one though, right? I can go with her, then she doesn't need to be officially linked as attending with any of you. And the three of us can keep her safe while you do what you need to do." I try to reason, and when he nods, I try not to let my shock show. He really must be tired if he's agreeing with me. My brother is a lot of things, but agreeable is not one of them.

Betty places the pancakes in front of us both, a smiley face on them made from extra berries and whipped cream. I can't help but laugh and even Linc smirks a little. "Eat up. You boys don't eat enough."

"Yes ma'am." I grin at her as I pick up my fork before looking back to Linc. "We'll get it all sorted out, and I'll help you where I can."

He nods, the sadness flickering back into his eyes. "Thank you."

He doesn't say anything else. My brother, the guy who usually has all of the words, reduced to two words that I know don't come easy for him. I don't focus on it anymore, but I make a mental note to speak to Finley, and to V.

We need to help him, and if I can do that, I will. Even if Harrison does renege on our deal. Some things are more important than his dirty little secret.

A secret that happens to be an entire human being.

A secret that happens to be his eldest son…

A secret that happens to be… me.

*I stride into the house, having just dropped Lincoln and the others off at football practice. It might be my sixteenth birthday, but some things never change. Including the argument my parents are having in the family room. I'm glad Lincoln isn't here. He might turn thirteen in a few months, but he's still too young to listen to this shit.*

*I've protected him from it most of his life, but that's what big brothers are for. I wasn't able to protect him when V left without a trace, but this? This I can protect him from.*

*I try to tiptoe past the doorway, but pause when I hear my father.*

*"There he is. The waste of space in question. Get your freeloading ass in here, oh son of mine."*

*Awesome, I guess he's been hitting the whiskey already.*

*"Harrison!" my mother shouts at him as I enter the room.*

*"What, he's old enough to know now, don't you think?" he says, staggering a little as he drops onto the sofa.*

*"To know what?" I ask, even though I'm pretty sure I don't want to know.*

*"The reason that you weren't my legacy. I know you had to have had questions," he slurs as he sloshes his drink in his glass. I look at Mom, but she looks about as sober as he is. Though I'm not sure she's been sober since Stone left. Just another thing I probably shouldn't know, but do.*

*"The Knights?" I ask. Yet another thing I probably shouldn't know but do.*

*Harrison barks out a laugh. "You're astute, I'll give you that. Yes, the Knights."*

*"I didn't realize I wasn't your legacy," I say with a shrug, trying not to feed his drunken delusions.*

*He throws back the contents of his drink before throwing his glass at the wall. I duck and it just misses my head. Some people think being a Saint is everything in life. That we want for nothing. Little do they know what goes on behind closed doors.*

*"Oh you, bastard of mine, will never be my legacy. Happy fucking birthday to you and surprise."*

*I look between him and my mom, who cries softly as she sits in a mess on the floor.*

*"Bastard?" Shock runs through me. He can't be serious.*

*"Yes, your cheating whore of a mother got knocked up just after we got married, but it wasn't mine. You didn't think* Stone *was her first dalliance. I know you pay far more attention than that. You might not be mine in blood, but I taught you better than that." He says it like he's proud, but his words are at odds with his tone.*

*I take a deep breath, trying to process all of this. Happy fucking birthday to me, indeed.*

*"Who is my father if it's not you?" He just laughs and I look down at my mother, realizing she's not going to be any use. "What does this all mean?"*

*"It means that you will never be a Knight. That mantle will go to your brother, who is actually mine. And it means, that you can get the fuck out of my house."*

*I stagger back and slide down the wall. "No. You can't do that to him. I know what happens… initiation. You can't put him through that."*

*"You're too fucking weak for it anyway," he spits at me. "You don't get a fucking choice in it."*

*"I'm not leaving. You can't make me. The last thing you want is everyone to know you raised a bastard son," I argue, trying to stuff down the emotions raging inside of me. I can't leave Lincoln here alone with them. They'll ruin him.*

*"You won't breathe a word of this to any-fucking-one," Harrison shouts, lumbering toward me. Sucks to be him right now, 'cause he's fucked up and I'm not. He might be intimidating, but I've spent my entire life learning how to defend myself against him.*

*"Try me," I argue, and his face turns beet red. I guess he wasn't expecting an argument. "You try to get rid of me, kick me out, separate me from my brother, I'll tell the fucking world that the Saints aren't the picture-perfect family that everyone thinks they are. Or I stay, I keep my mouth shut, and no one ever has to know."*

*What I don't say, is that I'd love to get the fuck away from here, but I'm not leaving, not without Lincoln. And there's no way Harrison will give up his one true heir. I could run off with him, but I don't want to rip him away from everything he's ever known when he's still reeling from V leaving.*

*But if we stay... and he goes through initiation... I don't know that I could ever forgive myself for not saving him from that.*

*"And Lincoln doesn't go through initiation," I say, trying to save him the only way I know how.*

*Harrison just laughs at me. "Oh boy, you've got some big*

*balls, I'll give you that. But you don't get to say shit when it comes to the Knights. You know I could just kill you and be done with it?" My mother screeches at his words, and while they make me think twice about speaking out, I'm not that shocked. "If it wasn't for your brother, I probably would. Except he's going to be a Knight, and the last thing I need is him focused on you disappearing, or using resources to find you. I'll think over your terms. We'll finish this discussion tomorrow, but you don't breathe a word of this to anyone. Not even your brother. If he finds out, no deal." He waves his hand, dismissing me from the room. I head straight to my bedroom on autopilot. Once I lock the door and lean back against it, I try to suck in a breath. A lump builds in my throat as I try to process all of the emotions running through me.*

*He's not my dad.*

*I should be relieved.*

*I should be free.*

*I should be so many things, but instead I'm devastated. More for my little brother. Harrison not being my dad doesn't mean much. He's never been much of a dad anyway. But the fact that this means Lincoln will be inducted... that I can't spare him that.*

*Fuck.*

*A sob works through my chest, and I bite down on my fist to try and stop it from escaping.*

*This can't be happening. I was prepared. I've been prepared since I was thirteen. I know that's when initiation usually happens. Harrison was right about one thing: I do pay attention. I know far more than I should. But I was ready to face the horrors that come with initiation.*

*I should've known something was off. But there's been so much going on over the last few years, and my dad—Harrison— has been drinking more and more... I just chalked it up to that. That was why my initiation was delayed.*

*I never wanted to be a Knight, I just wanted for Linc not to have to be.*

*There has to be a way around this.*

*I can't help but wonder who my father is. If he's a Knight too. If he has more power than Harrison. Maybe he can save Lincoln. There has to be a way. Stone took V away, she's not being initiated. I heard my dad talking to Mr. Riley about it last week. It was the only upside to her leaving.*

*There has to be something I can do.*

*I slam my head back against the door before sinking to the floor.*

*Happy fucking birthday to me.*

After breakfast, I tell Betty I'll deal with the dishes and she heads back home to her family. It's the weekend, and I am more than capable of looking after Lincoln and myself. I hate that she spends so much of her time here rather than with her grandkids.

Harrison might not care, but then, he doesn't give a fuck about much of anything outside of the Knights anymore.

Not since Mom left.

Lincoln retreated back to his room after he finished eating. He didn't say anything about my call with Harrison, but I know he called Lincoln during breakfast too. Lincoln ignored it, but it was impossible to miss how tense he got watching the call ring out.

This is everything I wanted to save him from, and I failed.

Now all I can do is run as much interference as I can and just be here for him. Even if he resents me for not taking the mantle with the Knights. Even if he blames me for the shit he goes through. I'm not going anywhere when he needs me.

The thing is, he needs V. And as much as I know he's in love with her, has been his entire life, he's a stubborn pain in the ass.

But I have to try.

If he would just speak to her—God knows he won't speak to the rest of us—then maybe, just *maybe*, some of that weight that he carries can be shared. Lincoln is the leader of their little group, and while I sit on the outskirts, I'm still a part of them. Always have been, always will be.

I weigh going to speak to him and suffering his wrath against letting him spiral some more and decide that him being pissed at me is worth it. Especially if it helps him.

It doesn't hurt that it will help V too, but I'm trying not to factor that into my decision. As much as I love her, Lincoln has to stay my priority. Even when he's up to shit I don't agree with, my end goal is still getting him free. Even if it means the end of me. Saving her, saving him. It's all likely to end the same way.

Climbing the stairs, I rack my brain, trying to find the right words, but when I hear the smash in his room, I pick up my pace and burst through his door. He's seated on the opposite side of the room on the floor, back against the wall. His phone is in pieces on the ground by my feet.

"Bad call?" I ask, trying to make light of it and he gives me the finger.

At least he's still him I guess.

"Harrison wants me to step up my game with Georgia. Apparently just taking her to the gala isn't going to cut it. I swear, he'll make me marry this girl if it suits his needs." His fists clench at his sides, and I hate what this is doing to him.

He's eighteen. His biggest worries are supposed to be girls, exams, and college applications.

Not this bullshit.

I head over to sit beside him, sliding down the wall as I do. "I'm sorry, Linc. What can I do?"

"There isn't anything anyone can do. I'm the heir, remember?" I take a deep breath, the venom in his words twisting the knife, but that's nothing new. "Will you ever tell me why you left the legacy to me?"

The vulnerability in his voice guts me.

"When I can," is all I say.

He barks out a dry laugh, void of any actual happiness. "What does that even mean?"

"It means exactly what I say. When I can tell you, I will."

"You didn't pick this did you?" he asks, and I just shake my head. Technically I'm not saying a word, so my deal with Harrison is still in play. He sighs and runs a hand through his hair. "It's so fucked up. I wouldn't really wish this on you anyway. Just sometimes…"

"Sometimes you wish it wasn't you," I finish for him and he nods. "You should speak to someone, Linc. Someone who isn't me, or the guys. Someone you can just be you with."

"You want me to speak to Octavia, don't you?" He sounds like such a broken kid when he says the words.

"Yeah, I do. She gets you, she always has. You never had to pretend with her. I don't know why you've been pretending with her since you decided not to run her out of town. The only people you're hurting are you and her."

He drops his chin onto his folded arms balanced on his knees. "I don't get to keep her. I'll never be free, and I wouldn't wish this world on her. It's the last thing I want for her."

"Did you ever think that maybe, just maybe, you could both get free? Or that if we can't get her free, that life might just be easier with her in it?" I counter, and it takes him a second, but he nods.

"I've thought of little else since I realized that she's stronger than all of us. That she'll probably survive this world without breaking as bad as the rest of us have." He takes a deep breath and looks over at me. "But how do I tell her that I'd rather wade through the cesspit of life with her at my side, so that she can save me, rather than let her be free?"

# TWENTY

## OCTAVIA

After Maverick left, I got another delivery from the Knights Society. Apparently my attendance at the gala next weekend is not optional. I'm going to have to speak to the guys, because I have no fucking idea what's in store for me when I get there, or how any of this shit works. I really hate being dictated to, but I'm almost more pissed that I have to fucking dress up.

I finish my laps in the pool, the air not quite as cold today, so I figured why the fuck not. My run this morning with Linc wasn't enough to get the antsy feeling out of my system. Since I can't run alone, and I haven't sorted out a proper gym at the house yet, the pool is all I have.

It takes a few minutes to psych myself up to get out of the warm water, but once I do, I haul ass, grab my towel, and run inside. It might be warmer outside than it has been, but it's still fucking January.

Rushing through another shower, I decide to spend the rest of my day relaxing with a movie since Indi can't hit up the gig with me tonight. I know I could go alone, but I'm trying to be smart about the whole stalker situation, so that's a real big no. I slip on a pair of leggings, a tank, and my hoodie before going back downstairs.

"Miss Octavia!" Smithy exclaims as I slide across the tiles in my thick socks, and I grin up at him.

"YOLO?"

"Indeed. I am going out for the evening again, do you require anything before I leave?"

"Smithy, you old dog, you. Are you on date number three?" I ask and he stammers a little so I hug him. "I hope you're happy."

"Thank you, Miss Octavia. It is making me very happy."

"Do I get to know who it is you're dating?" I ask hopefully, and he blushes a little.

"Maybe in time. Now is there anything you need?"

I shake my head and pull back. "No, I'm good. I *do* look forward to finally learning who this secret suitor of yours is, though. You have a good time. Will you be back tonight?"

"We're heading into the city, so I got a hotel room so I don't need to rush back. Please set the alarm when I leave."

I hold up three fingers and grin at him. "Scout's honor."

He shakes his head, laughing. "Very well. I'll let you know

when I'm leaving."

"Okay, I'm going to make some popcorn and head to the theater room."

"I'll sort your popcorn, just please make sure to eat something more substantial for your dinner. I have a lasagne in the oven, all you need to do is heat it. I figured since you didn't burn the house down doing that last time, it was a good idea." He grins at me and I stick out my tongue.

I mean, he's not wrong, I did manage not to burn the place down, and it was some real good lasagne. "Thank you, I appreciate it. You sure you can manage the popcorn? I totally don't mind."

"Go," he says, shooing me toward the theater room. I laugh and pad my way down there, trying to decide what movie to watch, or if I'm just going to hardcore binge some TV. It's not usually something I do, beyond crime documentaries, but I have the urge to watch something mindless and full of drama. A bit of a distraction from the anxiety about next weekend.

This fucking gala is going to suck.

Especially since I have zero idea what I'm walking into. It's done up as a charity fundraiser, but after everything I've been told, I'm pretty sure that it's a way for the Knights to feel me out. With what little insight I have into how it all works, I can't help but be a little nervous.

On the upside, I might finally learn what it is they want from me.

It could be nothing, and the boys have been freaking out for no reason.

A girl can dream anyway.

I decide to watch the new Battle Royale TV show Indi has been going on about for the last few weeks, and get it all lined up. The door opens and I turn to thank Smithy. I find Lincoln standing in the doorway, holding a giant bowl of popcorn instead. "Smithy asked me to bring this to you and told me to tell you he's leaving."

"Oh, umm. Thanks," I say, shuffling around on the couch to make room for him among the piles of blankets. "Did you want something?"

Why the fuck does this feel so awkward?

He pads forward, and I try not to smile when I see he's in sweats and a hoodie. Another first for me, seeing him like this. He seems wound too tight for such chill clothes.

"I wondered if you had a minute or ten to talk…" He trails off, noticing the screen. "But if you're busy, it can wait."

"Don't be silly, come sit." There is no way I'm passing up on him actually talking to me. Getting anything from him these days is like getting blood from a stone.

He takes a seat, handing me the giant bowl of popcorn. I pop some of the buttery kernels in my mouth to stop myself from speaking. He's here to talk, so I'm not going to push. Lincoln Saint wanting to talk to me, willingly, about anything, is basically unheard of. So I'mma shut my mouth until he starts.

"I wanted to talk to you about next weekend…" he starts, running a hand through his hair. "The gala. I know we haven't talked much lately, but I wanted to try and prepare you a little better. The only upside of my dad being who he is is that sometimes I have extra information. Except that when it comes to you… he doesn't tell me a goddamn thing."

"It's okay, Lincoln. I don't expect you to have all the answers. I don't expect you to save me or whatever grand notion it is you have. Whatever it is that they want from me, I can take it."

He looks at me like I've lost my goddamn mind. "I thought Finley explained to you—"

"He did. A little anyway, but the fact is that I've been through a ton of shit and come out the other side. This isn't going to be any different. Except for the fact that I'll have you guys with me this time." I try to be as open and as raw with him as I can, because I can see how much it's fucking with him that he can't save me from the clutches of the Knights. "Who knows? Maybe the deal my dad made still stands, and they don't actually want anything."

"Maybe," he says quietly. We sit in silence, the previews for the show playing lowly in the background while I give him a minute. He's obviously not finished yet, but I'm not about to rush him. This might be the most vulnerable I've ever seen him. "They initiated us when I was thirteen. They held us for two weeks… and every single day I didn't think I would survive.

But I pretended. I faked it, because Maverick and Finley were just as fucking scared out of their minds. All of our deepest and darkest secrets were laid out for each other to see."

I practically hold my breath, not wanting to interrupt him. He sounds so broken, yet so removed from whatever it was that happened. I know Finley told me some of this already, but if he needs to talk, then I'm not about to stop him. Even if my heart is breaking for him.

"Handing three thirteen-year-olds guns, and telling them that one person isn't leaving the room. That we had to decide between us who wasn't leaving…"

Oh my fucking God. I want to crawl across the sofa and hug him, but he keeps talking and I know if I do, he'll stop.

"Do you know how long it took me to decide to put the gun to my head and pull the trigger to save them?" He looks at me, his eyes glassy as I swallow against the lump in my throat for the boy before me who will literally take on the world for the people he loves. "Thirty seconds. I thought it would be better for them if I just made the decision. If I didn't make them pick. Thirty seconds to decide that their lives were more important than mine. After I found out everything else they'd already suffered through, at thirteen, I decided it was my turn to take the hit."

"Linc—" I start, but he talks over me.

"The gun was filled with blanks. They all were. It was then that the Knights realized the bond between us wasn't going to be broken by them. That each of us would sacrifice for the other. That's when they changed their tactics. We went through hell for two weeks, and then they told us that you were going to be killed if we didn't kill the three men they put us in a room with. Do you know how long it took each of us to lift the guns we were given? Seconds. We didn't hesitate. Not when you were at risk. Maverick was twelve and he didn't even blink when the guy's brain splattered across his face. Twelve."

He takes a deep breath and finally looks me in the eye. "Do not think that you can beat them, because there is no winning. You are either free because they don't want you with them, and trust me, they *do* want you, or you're dead."

I take a deep breath and try to push down all of the warring emotions inside of me and fail. My heart pounds so loud that I can practically hear the blood whooshing in my ears. Panic seizes me at the thought. I get that he's being honest, and trying to scare me at the same time, which he is fully fucking succeeding at, but if I just lie down and cower in a corner, what use am I to anyone?

"There's really no way out?" I ask, and he shakes his head. I hate how beaten he looks. I've never seen him look like this. Lincoln is a force of nature, an oncoming hurricane that tears through everything in his path. He was always the strong one, the cunning one, the vicious one even, so the rest of us didn't necessarily have to be, but I'm beginning to think I'm going to have to become all of those things if I want to survive, despite my words of bravado.

"Maybe, if we work together, we could find a way out. For all of us. My dad did it, right?"

He laughs at me, straight up laughs. "Your father must have had something they wanted. And still, look at how that ended up."

My eyes water from the sting of his words. I'm still trying to wrap my head around the fact that my father was one of these people. That he made young boys do such awful things in the name of what? Power? My father wasn't that guy... was he?

"There's still a chance, right? That's why you've tried so hard to protect me."

"There could be. The sky could also be pink." I roll my eyes at him and get comfortable. At least he can still laugh, I guess. We sit together in silence while I try to process it all and after a while, he tips his head back and stares at the ceiling "My dad wants me to woo some girl, to convince her dad to join the Knights."

My eyes go wide in horror. The punches just keep coming and I'm at my limit of 'stuff it all down and put it on a shelf'. "He's pimping you out?"

"Fucked up, right?" He shrugs his shoulders. "Just another day in the life, I guess. Everything about the Knights is fucked up. The worst part... I'll do it, even though I hate it. Even though the thought of touching her gives me hives. Because while he's focused on them... he's not focusing on you."

"Linc…" I start, scooting toward him. I don't even know what to say.

"Don't. I don't deserve you. If you knew all of the things I've done, you wouldn't look at me like that, say my name like that."

My heart breaks all over again for him, because how could he ever think something like that? "Is that why you've kept your distance? Because you thought you didn't deserve me?"

He just clenches his jaw as he balls his hands into fists. I put the bowl of popcorn on the table and move to straddle him. I have exactly zero right sitting on him like that, but I'm pretty sure, despite the fact he is always the one with the right words, nothing but action is going to show him the truth of anything right now. I grip his jaw in my hands and make him look at me. "We all have monsters inside of us, but those monsters help us survive. I would never judge you for your monster. Never."

"You can't say that—" he starts but I cut him off, kissing him and pouring every piece of myself into it. I already knew he wouldn't believe my words, but despite the fact that he's kept himself withdrawn, I know he understands just how hard it is for me to lie with my body. His hands glide up my back before he pulls my hair out of my ponytails and his hands tangle in my hair.

He matches my fire with his own, and I'd happily burn with him like this forever.

When I run out of air, I pull back, and rest my forehead on

his. "Don't tell me what I can and can't do."

He pulls on my hair, tipping me back as he leans forward, so I have to look up at him. "You can't save me, V. All you're going to do is drown alongside me if we start this. Because if I'm in, then I'm in, and I'm never going to let go. I can't lose you again."

My chest heaves as I try to breathe around everything he's telling me. "You can't lose me if you don't have me, Lincoln. But if you're in this, then I'll happily drown alongside you. Just don't underestimate my ability to keep my head above water."

I move to stretch out in bed but pause when I feel the heat of Lincoln wrapped around me. For a minute I thought last night had been a dream, but apparently it was very real. He's sound asleep, so I lie still and let him sleep. The bags under his eyes yesterday were more than a little prominent, and while I'm sure he wouldn't exactly appreciate me saying anything, or attempting to take care of him by lying here and letting him sleep, that's exactly what I'm going to do.

Lincoln spends all of his time looking after everyone else, but I'm not sure he's ever really let anyone look after him. God knows Fiona was never really a great mom, and Harrison is a giant bag of ass. He definitely isn't winning any father of the year awards.

With everything I've heard about all of their dads, I'd happily light the three of them on fire and dance as they burn for the way they've treated their sons. And I'm sure I've just started to scratch the surface.

Hearing what they did to the three of them in initiation… I just… I can't even begin to fathom how much that fucked with all of them. It makes everything they've done make a lot more sense. I wouldn't want someone I cared about going through anything like that. It also explains why they were so fucking extreme. They live life so far in the extreme with the Knights that their scale of what's, ya know, *normal,* is totally fucked.

"You think really loud," he murmurs, his arms tightening around me. "Are you okay?"

I glance at the time on my phone then snuggle back against him. "I'm good, go back to sleep. It's still early."

"Are we running today?" he asks, kissing the top of my head, burying his face in my hair.

"No, we don't have to. Sleep. You're tired."

He lets out a deep breath before kissing my head again. "Okay, let's sleep. We'll run when we wake up."

He falls back asleep almost instantly, so I close my eyes and enjoy the heat of him. The fact that he's trying. I know what he said yesterday, but a part of me half expected him to run the minute the sun came up. For yesterday to have been a blip. That we'd go back to the way it was before.

Some would call me greedy, selfish even, to be with all four of them and still hope that they only want me. Hell, it sounds conceited even in my own head, but it is what it is. As long as they're all as okay with this as they've made out.

I end up dozing back off, waking when Lincoln extracts himself from the bed and heads to the bathroom. I stretch out, groaning as I do. Nothing feels quite as good as that early morning stretch. I open my eyes and find Lincoln smiling at me from where he's leaning against the door frame in nothing but his boxers. It's really not fair that he gets to look like that first thing in the morning, and then there's me, likely looking like I got dragged backward through a bush with epic morning breath.

"Morning."

"Morning," I say with a small smile. Is it weird that I feel a little like a kid with a crush right now? 'Cause that's exactly what happens when he looks at me like that. Butterflies take flight in my stomach and my heart races. "You sleep okay?"

"Better than I have in weeks." He moves toward me and sits beside me on the bed. "You want to run?"

I think about it for a moment and nod. I really should. Though, the thought of just getting back under the covers with him is sorely tempting.

"Okay, I'll slip back home and get changed then meet you back here in half an hour?"

I smile up at him and nod again. "Sounds good to me."

He leans forward and kisses me gently before putting his

sweats and hoodie back on. "I won't be long."

He jogs out of the room, and my phone buzzes a minute later as he disables the alarm. I climb out of bed and watch like a creeper as he jogs across the backyard to the gate then disappears onto his side of the fence.

I pad over to my closet and get dressed for the run, going with the black and navy leggings and sports bra combo, grabbing the matching jacket before putting my hair into a ponytail and making my way downstairs. Smithy isn't back yet, but it's only like nine in the morning, so I'm not overly surprised.

I head to the kitchen and grab a granola bar and a bottle of water before turning the dishwasher on to clean the mess from my dinner with Linc last night.

My phone buzzes on the counter, and I smile when I see Indi's name.

Indi

Hey bish, I hope you had an awesome night in the end. Sorry I couldn't make the gig.

Me

My night definitely took a surprising turn for the better, so no sweat. I hope you had fun with your boys.

Indi

Oh I did. We went paintballing. I have paint in places it has no business being.

I burst out laughing. I love her way too much.

Me

That sounds like fun for sure.

Indi

Wait, why was your night surprising?

Me

Lincoln.

I don't say anything else, I'm pretty sure I don't have to. She gets it better than most.

Indi

I expect more info on this tomorrow, but Ryker is er... demanding my attention.

Me

Go enjoy the D. Talk soon

I laugh as I drop my phone back onto the counter just as the back door opens and Linc strolls into the kitchen.

"Ready to go?" is all he says.

It still amazes me that a guy who exudes so much charm can sometimes be so short, but that's just a part of who he is.

I nod before finishing the water and taking the last bite of my granola bar. "Let's do it."

We run our usual route and he pushes harder today, so I push too. We might be... well, whatever the fuck we are, but I'm still not about to lose to him.

When we get back to my place, I'm laughing because he runs like an absolute dork, arms pinwheeling, his legs flailing, being a total goof for the last hundred feet and *still* beats me back. It's nice to see him a little lighter, a little more carefree. Apparently a good night's sleep does wonders for him. Who would've guessed? I grab the mail from the box as we head inside, and once we reach the kitchen, I drop it on the counter and flip on the coffee pot.

"Octavia…" Lincoln says, and I turn to find him holding a manilla envelope that has my name scrawled on it in Sharpie. That's new. "Do you want me to open it? You don't have to see this shit."

"No, I can see it. You don't need to protect me from everything." I smile at him and he nods, handing me the envelope even though I can tell he doesn't really want to.

Taking a deep breath, I open it and pour the contents onto the counter. A ton of photos spill out, except this time, they're not just me.

It's the guys.

It's Indi.

It's her guys.

All with a crosshair over their heads.

*I think I'm going to be sick.*

Lincoln picks up the note and reads it before turning it to me.

*They can't keep you safe. I told you.*
*You're mine.*
*Not theirs.*
*Don't make me prove it to you.*

"This is out of fucking control," I say, gripping the edge of the counter. "I wish I had even a fucking hint of a clue as to who this is."

"Smithy hasn't had any luck with his fed contacts?" he asks, and I shake my head.

"Not as far as I know. I'm not sure that a stalker who hasn't actually done anything is that high up on a priority list though," I tell him, biting the inside of my cheek. Why is this my fucking life?

"I'll get Lucas to link up with Smithy's contacts, and if it wipes my entire trust fund to find him, I don't give a shit. I'm tired of this sick fuck messing with you."

Riding into school with Lincoln now that he's all in is definitely something. I really should buy a new car, but finding the time hasn't exactly been the easiest.

I glance over at him and open my mouth before closing it and looking away. I don't know that I want to ruin whatever this is between us right now by asking questions, but if I don't I'm going to feel like a shitty friend.

"Just ask your question, Octavia. Your nervous energy is making me edgy." He doesn't even take his eyes from the road, but I should've known he would pick up on it. Lincoln is nothing if not astute.

I wring out my hands, but decide to bite the bullet. "Do you know where Diego is?"

His jaw ticks as his knuckles go white from the death grip he now has on the steering wheel. A few beats pass in silence before he glances over at me. "I can't tell you."

"So you do know, you just can't tell me where. Or you can't tell me whether or not you know?" He nods and I sigh in frustration. "I thought we were past the whole keeping me in the dark thing, Linc."

He lets out a deep breath and glances at me again, his body seeming to relax. "Compromise?"

I nod and wait for him to continue.

"I know where he is, but I can't tell you where he is. But he's alive, and while he might not be well, he's not close to death either."

It's not much, but it's something, and I'm going to take it. I might prod for more again later but for now, I'm going to take the win. I lean over the center console and kiss his cheek. "Thank you."

We ride the rest of the way in silence, the tension in the car as his palm is splayed across my thigh is so thick I could cut it with a fucking knife, but that has nothing on when we pull into the lot.

He comes around to open the door for me, pulls me from the car, his hands on my waist, and holds me against the door, kissing me like it's all he's wanted to do his entire life.

"It's about goddamn time, bro," Mav calls out as Linc pulls back from the kiss so hot that my panties now definitely need replacing. Mav claps his hand on Linc's shoulder, despite the fact he's still pressed up against me, having basically just claimed me publicly.

"You have got to be fucking kidding me!" I wince at the screech. Ah Blair, always with her perfect timing. She storms over to where we're standing as Linc lets me down to my feet and I push my skirt back down. "You're seriously all fucking her? What the hell is wrong with you?"

"I thought you were with Raleigh?" I say, feigning boredom. Sometimes I think that's the best way with her. "Why would you care who I'm fucking if you have him?"

"Shut up, you stupid fucking skank whore."

"Blair, speak to her like that again, and see where it gets you," Lincoln growls, stepping in front of me, while Maverick barks out a laugh. "Do not fucking test me. Not with her. You, more than anyone, should know fucking better."

I peek around him, and Blair looks like she's going to cry. I have no idea why. What could I have possibly done to make her hate me this much?

She stomps her foot and flicks her straight blonde hair over her shoulder. "This isn't how this was meant to go, Lincoln. We had a deal. You know what's at stake for me."

Her voice cracks, and I go to move in front of Lincoln, but Maverick weaves his arms around my waist and pulls me back. "Not yet, princess. She needs to get with the program."

"Blair, I don't give a fuck. I told you to back off and you didn't. I told you I'd still help you, but you just kept pushing and that's on you. You're on your own. I won't help you anymore, and that's not on Octavia. That's on you for being a desperate bitch. And just so you know, he really did try to rape her. He would have, too, if we hadn't shown up. So maybe you should think twice about just how much the fact that your world is about to crumble around you is your own fault."

"Please," she whimpers, a tear slipping down her cheek before she swipes it away. "I can't... I don't have any other options."

"I said no, Blair. You made your bed, now go fucking lie in it."

She glares at me over Lincoln's shoulder before turning and storming away, just as Finley pulls into the space beside us, followed closely by Indi in her Wrangler.

"What did I miss?" Finley asks as he climbs from his car and Blair screams at some unfortunate soul who dared get between her and the front doors of the school.

"I have no idea," I tell him, before he looks at Lincoln.

He shrugs and just says, "I called it a day." Like that explains everything.

"What he's not telling you is how he claimed our girl right here for all to see," Maverick says, laughing as Indi rounds the car, eyes wide.

"He did what?" she asks, handing me a cup of coffee.

I wrangle myself from Maverick's hold and smile at him before linking arms with Indi. "Girl, we have a lot to talk about," I murmur to her before taking a sip of the nectar. "I'll see you guys in a bit." I blow them a kiss and leave them standing there, watching me go, making sure to put an extra sway in my hips, just for giggles.

"You're telling me we have a lot to catch up on. I know you said Lincoln was your surprise, but I didn't think it would be quite *that* much of a surprise. Hot damn. Did you and your kitty cat have fun?"

"He didn't come near my kitty cat," I tell her, laughing. "But we had a nice time regardless." I fill her in on my weekend as we sort all our crap out before heading to English.

"Hot damn, I turn down one concert, and all the puzzle pieces fall into place for you." She laughs as we slip into our desks.

"Did you have a good weekend?" I ask, wagging my eyebrows.

"You could say that. I swear, I still have paint stuck in places. It's like fucking glue." She groans before sipping on her drink. "But they definitely made it up to me. Around searching for Diego, anyway."

"He's still not back?" I ask, biting the inside of my cheek, cringing on the inside. I totally spaced on asking Lincoln more about it, but I move it to the top of my list. I hate how worried she looks. It's not like I can tell her Diego is alive, because then I have to explain it, and we want the guys to get on, not start a goddamn war.

She shakes her head. "Not yet, and if he doesn't come back, or is in jail or something, Ryker has to step up as his second. It's totally fucked. I'm kinda head over heels for him, but I'm not sure I fit in their world."

My heart breaks for her a little. "I'm sorry. But maybe love can conquer all?"

She shrugs, turning to face the front of the room as the bell rings and Miss Summers floats into the room. "One can hope?"

# TWENTY ONE

## OCTAVIA

I stare at myself in the mirror, and I almost don't recognize myself. I look way older than usual. My dark, smokey eyes, my long hair a cascade of curls with tendrils pinned back from my face.

And this dress.

The sweetheart neckline, snowy white, with a halter that buckles behind my neck, so light, it feels like it might not be there at all. I step forward, the thigh slit revealing my entire golden leg, extra bronze from the shimmer spray Indi insisted I add, and my white stilettos that ribbon halfway up my calves.

It's almost Grecian, and so freaking beautiful, but so far from what I'd ever usually wear.

Yet another delivery from the Knights.

Apparently the first dress wasn't suitable for tonight. I move back over to my bed and pull the lace mask from the box that arrived this morning.

A masquerade ball.

The white mask is beautifully intricate. The lace inlaid with pearls and what I'm really hoping are just little crystals. It shimmers in the light of the room, captivating.

For an organization that's supposed to be terrifying, they sure have good taste. I wonder, not for the first time, how they had my measurements. How this dress could fit so perfectly. How the shoes feel as if they were made just for my feet.

It's uncanny.

I grab the only white clutch I own, putting my lipgloss and eyeliner in it because you never know when you'll need a touch up. My phone buzzes on the bed, and I take a deep breath when I see Lincoln's name.

Lincoln

Are you ready?

Me

As ready as I'm going to be.

Lincoln

Good. I'm heading over. We need to finish our conversation from before.

I can't help but chew on my lip. There was me thinking that we wouldn't have to discuss this again, but considering everything that's happened in the last week, how he has very much claimed me… I'd been wondering how tonight would go. Especially with everything Harrison expects of him.

Smithy is away for the weekend with his new beau, and I couldn't be happier for him. I'm also secretly glad that he's away because if anything goes wrong, at least he isn't here to suffer the consequences.

Not that I'm expecting anything to go wrong, but everything the guys have told me has me on edge.

I make my way down the stairs, glad that I've worn heels often enough that the slight tremors running through my hands and knees aren't making me worry about staying upright.

The front door opens as I glide down the stairs and I pause, taking in the sight that is Lincoln. Black suit, black shirt, black tie… the mask in his hand is different from mine: a solid half face mask, also black.

"You look…" he looks at me, eyes wide, and shakes his head as if he's unable to speak.

"Thanks," I say, a blush spreading across my chest. "You too."

I reach the bottom of the stairs and he holds out a hand for me, which I take, and gasp as he sharply pulls me into him. "Honestly, you look fucking exquisite."

"I mean, you don't clean up so bad yourself. Is the car here already?"

He shakes his head and takes a step back. "No. We've got some time. I just… I know that you're aware of Harrison's manipulations, but tonight, I don't get to be myself. Tonight I am nothing more than his puppet. Which means I will be with Georgia for the evening."

That destructive, nagging self doubt rears its head inside of me again. Was this last week just more of his games?

It can't have been right?

No, of course not. He wouldn't do that.

Would he?

He must see it all written all over my face, because he steps toward me and cups my cheek with his hand. "You know I don't want her, but I have to do this tonight. If I don't… well, it isn't worth thinking about. This thing between us, it can't—"

I sigh at his explanation, and while none of it makes complete sense to me, mostly because I still have a ton of things I need to know, my heart hurts a little at the thought of him attending tonight with someone else. You'd think having the other three with me would be enough, but no. "You don't need to explain yourself to me, Lincoln. You already told me what your dad wants of you. I get it. You have to be who they want you to be, and that means that whatever this thing between us is… was… it doesn't get to be more than it has been. I just wish you'd trust me enough, respect me enough, to let me help you."

"Octavia, must you really always be so obtuse." I quirk a brow at him. He really is just full of compliments tonight.

"What is that supposed to mean?"

"It means that you are infuriating and exasperating, and

still, you're the only thing I want." I suck in a breath, trying to process what he's saying. His eyes blaze as he looks at me, like a thunderstorm that's about to unleash havoc on the world.

"The only person I've wanted in my entire life is you, but I am no good for you. So I keep my distance. You don't need my mess raining down on you. So for you, I stay away. It isn't about me trusting you, or respecting you, it's about what is best for you. Except that sometimes… Sometimes I can't help myself. Like when I'd hear your screams in the middle of the night, and I'd come to you. I am only human, and sometimes, even I break."

"Is that why you had those other guys paw at me in the pool house? Because I'm the only girl you've ever wanted. Your words are pretty, Lincoln, but actions speak louder." The words spill from my mouth, just the tip of the iceberg of the things we should've said to each other before now. I don't know if I can keep doing this with him. It hurts too much.

"Actions speak louder? Like me sending them away, because I couldn't stand to see anyone's hands on you but mine? Like when I dropped to my knees in front of you, because I wanted to replace their touch with my own? Like when I made you come on my face because the thought of anyone else making you come was like fire in my heart?"

I suck in a breath at his words, taking a step back with each declaration. He stalks toward me until my back hits the wall.

"Octavia Royal, there has only ever been you for me. No

one besides my brothers gets to ever touch you again. The only person I truly belong to is you. And I'm going to prove it to you. It might be her body my hands are on at this farce, but it's you I'll be wearing." He drops to his knees in front of me, mirroring the movement he did so long ago, except this time he pauses, looking up at me, waiting for permission.

There is something heady about the power of having someone like Lincoln Saint on his knees before me. Waiting for my yes or no. I nod my head just once, untying the buckle behind my neck that holds the dress in place. It floats to the floor, nothing more than a puddle at my feet, leaving me in my white silk panties and white heels. I step out of the dress, lifting it while he watches in rapt silence. I drape it over the back of a chair and move back to stand in front of him.

That's all the permission he needs.

He traces his hands softly up my legs, until he reaches the white silk panties that barely cover me. Curling his index fingers, Linc slowly, to the point of torture, drags the thin fabric down my legs until the only thing between my pussy and his lips is thin air.

I don't touch him even though my hands are itching to sink into the mass of his perfectly combed hair.

Placing both of his large hands to the back of my thighs, he pulls me closer and closer, until my core meets his open mouth.

A shiver courses through my body at the first lick of his tongue. It's hot and warm and everything I need right now.

"Hmm," I moan as he repeats his languorous teasing. Sliding his hands from my thighs to my ass, he digs his nails into my flesh right before he circles his tongue around my clit, flicking it at irregular beats. Keeping me on my toes.

I choke out a mixture between a grunt and a moan, spreading my legs wider and leaning further against the wall to avoid falling flat on my face.

"Linc, God, yes."

His fingers slide from my ass to between my thighs and straight to my pussy where he opens the lips wider still to give himself more access.

My head falls back, my eyes fixed on the ceiling. I probably look like I'm praying. Maybe I am. To the gods of orgasms.

Linc's tongue stops teasing my clit, heading straight from my opening where it spears inside me and stays there until he does this curly thing at the tip and holy mother of God, it touches something in there that I didn't even know existed until this very moment.

Looking down, I see his entire face buried between my legs, his lips and tongue devouring every drop that I give him. His arms are wrapped around my thighs, his fingers contributing to my impending orgasm.

"What the fuck was that?"

He doesn't answer. He can't, what with being busy eating me out and all, but I can almost hear his smirk.

Smug bastard.

My legs shake with his every lick and suck. I'm barely able to stand at this point. Thank fuck for the wall.

Linc backs up just an inch and looks up at me with eyes so sincere I can't help but believe every word he said earlier was unfiltered truth.

He wants me.

He'll kill for me.

He *has* killed for me.

Without a second thought, I raise my leg and drape it over his shoulder, opening up for him even more. His slurps and moans are like a gift; I lock them up in my heart for future need, like when he's being a complete and total dickhead.

With the top half of my back still leaning on the wall, I thrust my hips at him, searching for more friction, more skin on skin, more… just more of him.

That's when he slams two fingers inside my pussy and rips a scream from my throat in the process. Steadily, he fucks me with his fingers while his mouth is sucking on my clit.

"Of fuck, don't stop, please do not fucking stop."

He doesn't. He just keeps building my orgasm up to its peak until I say fuck it and do exactly what I was trying to avoid all along.

I bury my fingers in his hair and push his face deeper into my pussy, grinding on him and spreading my juices all over his clean-shaven face.

I should be ashamed or some shit, but I'm not.

I'm fucking his face, completely out of control, pushing at his back with the heel of my foot. I need him closer, I need him deeper, I just *need* him.

Linc pulls back barely long enough to blow a gust of breath across my hypersensitive clit and I bite down on my lower lip hard enough to break the skin. I can taste the coppery tang of my blood but I don't have time to care because at that moment, Linc thrusts his fingers impossibly deeper inside me and rubs his entire face all over my wet-as-fuck pussy.

I am vindicated knowing that every time Lincoln is close to his date, she'll be able to smell where he's been.

All over me. That's where he's been. All the fuck over my wet pussy.

Linc may be prancing around with her, but he's mine.

*All fucking mine.*

That single thought and the slight bite of his teeth on my clit rip the climax right out of me like a lightning bolt through my bloodstream.

I rub myself all over him, making sure my scent is imprinted on his skin as he gives me one last lingering lick before he looks back up at me with a smirk that would disintegrate my panties right off. If I still had them on, of course.

"With any luck, my scent will be the perfect repellent," I tell him, rubbing my thumb over his bottom lip before bringing it to my own mouth and sucking on it.

Lincoln darts out his own tongue, licking my orgasm right

off his mouth.

"Hmm, delicious." He pockets my panties but I steal them back from him, because hell no. Just as I slide them back into place and put my dress back on, the front door opens, and East is standing there, wearing the exact same thing as his brother.

"The cars are here," he says, smirking as he takes in the scene before him.

Linc climbs back to his feet and straightens his tie. "I'll see you both soon." He turns and leaves without a backward glance as East steps in, shutting the door behind him.

"You okay?" he asks and I nod, my heart rate just about going back to normal. "Okay. We should probably give him a minute and then go out to our car. Are you ready for tonight?"

"As ready as I'm going to be," I tell him, mentally steeling myself after the rollercoaster that has been the last twenty or so minutes.

He fixes his mask in place, and I do the same before he offers me his arm. "Then let's get this show on the road, shall we?"

I nod and loop my arm through his. "Let the games begin."

The car pulls to a stop in front of the mega mansion on the outskirts of the city, and I can't help but take in the beauty of it. The driveway, if you can call a three-mile road a driveway, has a long pond running down the center, evenly spaced fountains spraying delicate arcs of crystal-clear water into the night sky. The clean, white stone of the water features glistens warmly in the glow of the underwater lights, providing a welcoming sense of warmth and safety and *just* enough light to navigate the long, straight road to the house.

The giant building looms ahead of us, pure stately glamour. Stone columns rise from the top of a wide, stone stairway, illuminated in the same warm light as the fountains. Massive double doors stand in stark contrast to the white marble façade of the structure, dark and sturdy, prepared to stand the test of time and probably withstand a small militia. Every window visible from the front of the house is lit and glittering against the inky black sky as people slowly make their way up the front steps and slip through the doors.

I'm not normally one for obscene displays of wealth, but this place screams old money. "Whose house is this?" I ask, looking back to East, who has been pretty quiet the entire drive.

"This place belongs to Harrison's father. The old man keeps the place for occasions like this, but it usually sits empty, except for the staff."

Huh. Yet another thing on the long list of shit I didn't know but probably should have.

"Do you know everyone here tonight?" I ask, cursing myself for not peppering him with questions on the drive here. He seemed pretty nervous, so I didn't want to make it worse.

He nods, taking my hand as we wait for the car to pull to the front of the line. "Yeah, I've been around this world long enough to know most of the players. Though some are a mystery to all of us. Some people here aren't Knights at all, they're just rich enough to warrant an invite or they're actually nice people, here to help the fundraiser."

"It's an actual fundraiser? I thought that was just a stupid front."

He laughs at the shock on my face. "It's an actual fundraiser. How do you think they all uphold their ridiculous public façades of being decent humans? Every seedy underbelly has a shiny exterior to keep the darkness hidden from the masses. Despite the reach of the Knights, at its heart, it's still a secret society—one that's growing—but a lot of people don't even know they're dealing with the society. They just think it's rich assholes ruling their lives. Oh, to be so blissfully ignorant."

"So who do I need to be wary of?" I ask as butterflies take flight in my stomach.

"Everyone," he says somberly. "I'll do my best to point out who is who for you, and when Maverick or Finley can free themselves up, they'll likely do the same. Just keep your guard up unless there is more than one of us with you. Even then. This place might look beautiful, but the darkest of minds hide in the most beautiful of places."

I nod, and adjust my mask yet again, my hands shaking just a little at the prospect of stepping outside of this cocoon of safety.

"I've got you. You won't be alone at any time tonight, okay? No matter what happens, one of us will be with you at all times." He takes my hand and squeezes it just as the door beside him opens. He steps out and buttons his jacket before offering me his hand. I take it, because climbing out of this car in this dress while keeping my modesty... yeah, that requires assistance.

"Thank you," I say to the man who opened the car door. He's in a gray suit, with a gray mask. His eyes go wide behind the mask, like he didn't expect me to speak to him, let alone thank him. He closes the door to the car before scurrying to the next in line.

What is this place?

"He's a pawn," East explains, and weirdly that makes sense to me in this setting. Not that any of this makes sense complete to me, the whole pawn, prospect, rook, regent bullshit. Who thought a secret society named after a chessboard was a good idea?

It was definitely part of the penis parade.

So fucking pretentious. Then again, everything about the whole secret society thing is beyond pretentious, so at least it fits.

We climb the stone steps that seem to go on forever up to the ornately carved wooden double doors that wait for us. There are two security guards on the doors, so I pull my invitation from the clutch and hand it over. "Good evening, Miss Royal. Who is your guest?"

"Easton Saint." I quirk a brow, daring either of them to say a thing as they look at one another like they're unsure if he should be allowed to enter. I still don't understand the whole thing between Easton and his dad, and him not being a Knight, but I'm also not about to push him on it. If he wants to tell me, or it becomes need-to-know, he'll tell me. That much I trust.

They step aside and let us into a small room where four further guards are waiting. We wait for them to usher us forward. One of them takes my clutch, and before I get a chance to object, he says, "No phones."

"You have got to be kidding me." I look at East who is handing over his phone, which is put into a small plastic pouch with his name scribbled on it.

"Fine, fine." I take my keys from the purse along with the eyeliner and lipgloss, slipping them in East's pocket. "You might as well keep the damn thing. Saves me holding it."

The guy looks at me like I've lost my damn mind while East coughs to cover his laugh. What sort of stupid rule is no phones? Once they've waved their security wand things over us, they allow us entry into the actual gala.

I gasp when the doors open. This place might be a place of darkness where the depraved come out to play, but it sure does look pretty. Twinkle lights are strung up all over, the only actual source of light in the giant foyer. There's a bar set up to the right in front of the sweeping staircase, and there are way more people in here than I thought there would be.

"Drink?" A server asks as they pass us with a tray of what looks like champagne. I look at East and he declines the drink, so I do the same.

"Don't drink anything you can't see being opened," he warns and I nod. Good to know that the same rules apply here as at any high school party. His warning hits a little too close to home, though I learned my lesson well enough at Halloween.

We head through the foyer, and I try to see if I recognize anyone, but the masks make it pretty hard. All of the women are in white with lace masks like mine, the men in black with the solid half-face masks that East has on. All of the male servers in gray, with gray masks, and the females in red, I guess to show the difference of status, but who the fuck knows? It's a very fucking strange set up.

We go to move through the room when someone steps into our path. "Octavia, how nice of you to grace us with your presence."

It takes me a second, but when East stiffens at my side, I know instantly who it is. "Harrison. Good to see you."

"Indeed," he says, swallowing the champagne in his glass, the fake smile that graced his face no longer present as he looks at his son. "Easton, I see you wormed your way in here."

"You asked me to keep Lincoln focused, how better than this?" I look at him, a little shocked because I have no fucking clue what he's talking about.

Harrison barks out a laugh. "Well, at least you're good at

following orders. Better than nothing, I guess." He looks down his nose at his son, and I want to kick him in the shins with my pointy shoes.

What a jackass.

"I'll come and find you later, Octavia. But next time we invite you to something, maybe bring better company." He saunters off into the crowd like he didn't just snub his oldest kid.

"Are you okay?" I ask East, who just nods once.

"Nothing I'm not used to."

I bite the inside of my cheek, not wanting to pry. I *do,* however, want to stab my stiletto into Harrison's eye for being such an ass. "Anything I can do to help?"

"It's fine. Let's see if we can find the others before the auctions begin," he says, taking my hand. I let him pull me into the masses, because despite Harrison's obvious distaste for East, he still knows this world and its players far better than I do.

I just hope I can learn the rules of the game fast enough that we can all survive it.

The night passes in a blur of faces, talking to people who very much know who I am, but I still have no idea who most of them are. East is the perfect escort, because he seems to know almost everyone.

We've danced so much that my feet are starting to hurt, and

despite the circumstances, he's had me laughing so much that my cheeks ache.

Thus far, the Knights seem to have left me alone, and I even bid on a weekend retreat in the auction and won. I might have paid too much for it, but since the money is for orphans, I figured why not.

I've barely seen the rest of my guys tonight, and I know they warned me that would likely be the case, but I can't help but worry that something's happening while I stand here oblivious to it all.

My world could be crumbling and I'd have no idea.

The song finishes and East leans forward, whispering into my ear, "Water?"

"Sure," I nod and let him lead me across the room to the bar. While we're standing there waiting, a pair of arms wrap around my waist.

I stiffen until "Princess" is growled into my ear. I look back and find Maverick staring down at me. He looks like a man starved, and I'm the only food in sight. "You look good enough to fucking eat."

I turn in his arms, relaxing against him. "Hey, stranger. Busy night?"

"Frustrating night," he says when I notice the red on his collar.

"Bloody night?" I ask, and he grins.

"Nothing major, just someone getting a little too big for their britches. Nothing for you to worry about." He leans forward and kisses me chastely. "How has your evening been? East looking after you?"

"Yeah, he's been a perfect gentleman." I smile up at him, happy that he's okay.

Maverick looks up at East and grins that wolfish grin of his. "Lincoln was looking for you." He tilts his head, motioning across the room. "I've got our girl."

East looks at me and I nod. "I'll be fine, go see what he needs."

"Okay, I won't be long." He stoops to kiss my cheek before he leaves. I watch him cross the room and spot Lincoln, his arm around the waist of a redhead, whom I assume must be Georgia. A spike of jealousy runs through me at the smile he wears for her. Her hand rests on his chest.

He must feel me watching because he looks up and catches my gaze, holding it for just a second, his smile dropping before he puts his puppet mask back on and turns back to her.

"Don't worry, princess. It's all just a show," Maverick murmurs in my ear, "Now that I've got you alone, we should quit this party and have one of our own." He wags his brows at me, making me laugh.

"If only. I get the feeling leaving early isn't exactly an option," I say as I glance around the room at the shut doors, and the security standing in front of them.

He shrugs, pulling my attention back to him. "Maybe not,

but I'm sure we could still have some fun."

"Maybe after, we can all head back to my place and relax?"

"Oh, princess, I like your style."

I laugh again, because that totally wasn't what I meant, but of course he went there. "Have you seen Finn?"

He nods, and points across the room. "He's with his dad."

I follow where he's pointing and find my blond, brooding god looking about as happy to be here as I've ever seen him. "Is he okay?"

"He's with his dad," is all Maverick says, like that holds all the answers. East returns in that moment and says something to Maverick.

"Best get back to the party, princess. I'll catch you in a bit." He quickly kisses me again before disappearing into the masses.

"Everything okay?" I ask East, who nods and takes my hand, leading me toward the stairs at the back of the room. "Where are we going?"

"You'll see," he answers as we begin the climb to the mezzanine level. It's quieter up here somehow. There are only a few people wandering around, and it's nice to be separate from it all. It's like I can breathe again without worrying about who is around us.

East jerks me into an alcove, and I come face to face with Lincoln.

This isn't where I saw this going when he dragged me away from the party.

"What—" I start, but Lincoln puts his finger against my lips to stop me from speaking. He pushes my mask up off my face and it flutters to the ground at my feet. East's chest pushes against my back until I'm flush against Linc, sandwiched between them. "I don't understand," I whisper, moments before Lincoln captures my lips with his.

I whimper under the heat of it. His lips on me as East's hands roam my body, teasing me in the most excruciating of ways.

"He needed to feel you," East whispers to me, his dick digging into my ass as Lincoln's presses against my stomach. Images of them both fucking me, both of them inside me, flash through my mind, sending shivers across my skin.

Holy shit, this is so fucking hot.

"So I brought you to him," East finishes, his hot breath dancing across my skin before his lips work down my neck, his tongue darting out and teasing. I clasp the lapels of Lincoln's blazer as his teeth latch onto one of my breasts through the fabric, his fingers slipping beneath the thigh slit of my dress, feeling just how fucking wet I am right now.

His groan reverberates across my skin as East unclips the buckle of my dress, letting the top fall down exposing my chest fully, while their bodies pressed against mine hold the rest of it in place.

"Does he make you feel good?" East asks, as he tweaks one nipple while Lincoln's mouth continues its magic on the other, biting down hard when I don't answer.

A breathy "Yes" escapes my lips before East captures them just as Lincoln's fingers slide inside of my pussy.

"We don't have too much time, so come nice and quick for him," East orders, all while Lincoln doesn't say a fucking word.

Forcing my head to turn to the side, East swallows my moans, his hand around my throat as Lincoln fucks me with his fingers while lavishing his attention on my tits.

"Quiet, V," East commands, and I whimper as Lincoln pushes me over the edge, flicking his thumb over my clit. The world bursts into color as I come for him for the second time tonight. He brings his head up and readjusts himself, before nodding to East. He kisses me once more, with so much need it makes my toes curl, then puts both of his masks back on and leaves without a word.

"What in the—" I start as East helps me reclip my dress into place.

"He's having a bad night. He needed you, so I offered some assistance," he says with a smirk, but I am not about to complain.

"Oh," is all I manage to say, and he chuckles before holding his arm out to me.

"We should probably head back," he says, a dark laughter lighting his gray eyes. "Mask back on, Miss Royal."

I pick my mask up from the floor where I dropped it and he ties it back into place for me. "Back into the depravity we go."

When my feet ache to the point that I don't want to stand any longer, East takes pity on me and we head out onto the balcony of the mezzanine level. It looks out over the expanse of land in front of the house. Beneath the starlight, lit up like it is, it's just breathtaking.

"We should be able to leave soon, right?" I ask him, and he checks his watch.

"Yeah, I'm not sure why they haven't opened the doors yet. The auctions and fundraisers are done. Dinner is done. It should be winding down by now."

An icy drop of dread runs down my spine at his words. If that's the case, why the fuck are we still here?

"It should be, but we wanted a word with Miss Royal." I turn at the voice and find myself basically pinned in by five men, all in the black on black suits, all with black masks, but set apart from the others by a navy-blue pocket square.

I don't recognize the voice. I try to place the face, but the mask makes it impossible. "And who," I ask, "is 'we'?"

"East, I suggest you give us five minutes with Miss Royal."

The words are more of a command than a request, but I take his hand and jut out my chin. "I think I'd rather he stayed."

One of the men laughs. "She's got balls, I'll give her that."

"No need to be so hostile, Miss Royal," the first voice says again, "This is merely a welcome chat, an invite, as it were, extended by the conclave to you, to join the Knights Society."

"An invite?" I ask, quirking a brow and trying not to laugh.

The man looks me in the eyes, his irises as dark as the night sky; the soulless eyes of a monster. A shiver runs through me as I hold his gaze. "Yes, an invite."

"Well, I'm flattered, but I think I'll decline. I'm very happy with my life as it is, thank you." I sound more confident than I feel and East squeezes my hand. I'm not sure if it's in encouragement or warning, but I'm just winging it and hoping for the best.

Lincoln said there's no escaping them, but if I don't become one of them, then they have no hold on me.

Right?

"You might want to rethink that," the man says, his voice low and menacing. The others stay quiet, watching and assessing my every move.

Nothing quite like feeling like I'm on show.

I take a step forward, keeping my fingers linked with East's. "If that was all, gents, I think I'll be heading home. It's been a long night."

I pause, waiting for them to let me pass, but the man who has been doing all of the talking grabs my upper arm and squeezes so tight, I know I'm going to have a bruise. "I will be seeing you again, Miss Royal, and next time, I might not be so nice."

I hold my ground and lift my gaze back up to his before

trying to tear my arm from his grasp. "Maybe next time, I won't be so nice either."

I have no idea how my voice isn't shaking, because on the inside I'm a fucking mess. Each and every one of them looks at me like they want me dead. They probably do.

"Father, you should probably let her go." Maverick's voice rings out in the silence, and I suck in a breath. That's his dad?

How did I not recognize him?

I officially hate masquerade parties.

"Maverick, it's fine. We were just having a nice chat with your friend," Mr. Riley says as he releases me.

Maverick saunters over, standing at my side, flanking me with East. "I'm sure you were. But I'm also pretty sure she said she wanted to leave. I didn't realize tonight was a hostage situation."

"You should watch your words, boy," his father hisses, but Maverick barely flinches. If anything, he stands taller.

"Maybe you should keep your cool, old man. There're a lot of people here after all. God forbid you besmirch the Riley name," Maverick counters, and I swear I hold my breath, waiting to see how this goes down.

His father barks out a laugh and clasps Maverick's shoulder. "Indeed. Run along, children. I'll be seeing you soon, Miss Royal."

Maverick wraps his arm around my waist, my opposite

hand still intertwined with East's, and we walk away from the Conclave.

I think I'm going to be sick.

"We should get out of here," Maverick says quietly, and East nods.

"I'll get the others and meet you by the cars," is all he says before he darts off, leaving me with Maverick.

I look up at him as he guides me down the stairs, into the safety of the crowd. "How much trouble am I in?"

He looks down at me, looking more somber than I've ever seen him. "I'm not sure, princess, but it's not good. The Conclave doesn't corner people like that. We need to get you out of here and speak to the others about it all."

My stomach rolls at his words, and the severity of the situation hits me.

I might just be royally fucked.

# TWENTY TWO

## MAVERICK

After spending the night at V's, I kind of dread heading home. Last night did not go to plan, and we still have no fucking idea what the hell the Knights want with her, beyond them wanting her in their ranks.

The way they cornered her last night… it's just not usually how they do things, and it reeks of desperation. No matter how much I rack my brain, I can't think of a reason as to why they would want her so badly, other than her being a legacy.

Sure she has money, but that's not something the Knights are exactly short on. And if it was just about legacy, we already offered them Blair and Nate, which they refused.

Which means it has to be something about her specifically. Something she has, or something she can give them.

We were up most of the night going over what it could possibly be. Not exactly how I pictured our first group sleepover going. Definitely not as fun as I'd hoped it would be either.

I tiptoe into the house, hoping that my dad is still asleep. Mother dearest wasn't at the event last night, so fuck knows where she was, but after the way it ended last night, I'm pretty sure my dad is going to try and beat my fucking ass.

Won't be the first time, but seeing his hands on V had me seeing red.

The stair creaks as I hit the first step and I curse internally, pausing in the hope no one is around.

"There you are, I wondered when you'd make it in." My dad looks down at me from the top of the stairs, before heading toward me. I take a step back, into the main foyer, and prepare myself for whatever is to come.

For V, I'll take whatever this asshole has to dish out.

"I spent the night with the guys."

He barks out a laugh as he passes me. "And with your little whore."

I clench my hands into fists and take a deep breath, that dark pit inside of me firing up. No one gets to call her that. Not even him.

"Don't look so angry, Maverick. I just call them as I see them." He pours himself a glass of scotch from the decanter, offering me one too, but I shake my head. "Your loss. It's the evening somewhere in the world."

He shrugs before coming to stand back in front of me, still in his suit, minus the blazer and tie. Glass in one hand, the other in his pocket. "I assume you all spoke about the Conclave last night?"

I don't make a move as he swigs back his drink, his dark eyes pits of nothingness as he watches me.

"You need to bring that little bitch to heel. And if you don't, it won't be just her that suffers. I can't, and won't, save you from the Conclave if you go against us," he says before turning his back on me, moving to where the decanter sits on the opposite side of the room. He pours himself another drink and takes a seat, calmer than I've seen him in a while.

He must've taken his anger out on some poor girl already.

"What do you want with her?" I ask, since he seems to be almost reasonable right now.

That was my first mistake. Thinking that the monster was dormant. He launches his glass at my head and I duck. It barely misses me before it shatters on the wall behind me. "That, you little fucker, is need-to-know. Don't think that I've forgotten you stood beside her instead of with me last night. It didn't go unnoticed. If I lose my seat because you're an ungrateful little shit… well, maybe I'll take that out on your little whore too."

I grind my teeth together, trying not to lose my shit. "Do not call her that."

"Well that's what she is. I assume she's fucking all of you. Just like her mother. Always up for a good time. I didn't say there was anything wrong with being a whore. Women aren't good for much else beyond what's between their legs." He shrugs and leans back on the couch while I practically vibrate with rage.

We stay frozen like this, a stalemate, for what feels like hours before he finally leans forward, watching me, and rests his elbows on his knees, almost taunting me. "What's wrong, boy? Angry? Think you can finally take me? I fucking dare you to try."

I take a deep breath, trying not to let the rage consume me.

"You're just like me. You might try to deny it. You might think you're better than me, but the apple doesn't fall far from the tree, does it?" His eyes flash with amusement while I stand there, unable to say a fucking thing. I hate how paralyzed he makes me. Give me any other monster, and I'll take them on without thought.

But him?

He'll always be the monster that hides in my closet.

The one that makes me tremble with fear.

Because he's more than just words and threats like Harrison. He enjoys it when you scream. He fucking gets off on it.

Maybe he's not wrong. The apple doesn't fall far from the tree.

But I'd never do to my kids what he's done.

He stands and strides toward me. He moves so quickly I almost don't get a chance to duck when he rears his fist back and swings at me. "I'll teach you to fucking defy me."

His fist grazes my cheek bone, as I manage to move just in time, but I don't see the follow up before it's too late, and he knocks the air from my lungs with a fist to the chest. I crumple to the floor, trying to suck in breath, but nothing comes.

His fists rain down on me in a flurry, until he gets bored and starts to kick me, stomp on me. By then, I'm too injured to move.

"Edward! What are you doing? You're going to kill him!" my mother screeches as she flies down the stairs. One of my eyes is basically swollen shut, but I can just about see her as she kneels in front of me.

"Little asshole deserves to die. He disrespected me last night, in front of fucking everyone. He's lucky I don't flay his little bitch and make him watch."

I groan, anger burning through me at the thought of V in his clutches. And he laughs. He fucking laughs before he spits on me. "He's nothing more than a dog; one who needs to be taught who his master is."

He kicks me once more while my mother screams at him, before walking away in the direction of the basement. I hear a scream as the door opens, but I can barely fucking move. Not that I've ever helped anyone in his basement. I've never gone down there, and I never will. That probably makes me a shitty human, but I have other things to worry about.

"Oh, Maverick, when will you learn?" My mother sighs.

"Let me call an ambulance."

"No," I croak, "I'll just call Finn."

She pulls my phone from my pocket and dials, putting it on speaker.

"What's wrong?" is how he answers. I swear he's fucking psychic sometimes.

"Finley, it's Lenora. Maverick and his father... well, they had a bout. He won't let me call an ambulance."

I hear a car start and the line goes quiet. A door slams before he speaks again. "I'm on my way. And Mav? Pack a fucking bag."

The line disconnects and my mom looks down at me like she might cry. "He's right. You probably shouldn't stay here right now."

Usually I'd try to argue, but if this is the start of things to come, then I'm not about to stick around for it. My mother should leave too, but she's as bad as he is most of the time. She must be sober this morning. This is the most mothering she's done in a few years. I'm not expecting it to last.

She helps me stand up, and I grind my teeth so as not to cry out. My ribs are definitely bruised, if not broken.

Finley enters the house just as I manage to stand alone. "Fuck, man."

I nod, groaning as I grip the bannister to stay upright.

"You stay there, I'll go grab you a bag, and then we're out of here." I nod and he jogs past me, heading up the stairs. I should probably worry about the screams that came from the basement, or leaving my mom here with my dad, but I don't think about any of that.

All I think about is, if he's willing to do this to me, what the fuck would he do to V if he got his hands on her?

The thought alone is what keeps me standing until Finn reappears with a few duffels of my shit.

"Let's go," he says, putting an arm around me and helping me hobble from the place I've always called home.

I'm not sure when I'll be back here, and I'm not sure that I give a fuck.

After Finley takes me to visit his private doctor, we head to Lincoln's. My ribs are wrapped, I've got a full script of painkillers that I probably won't touch, and one of my eyes is entirely swollen shut. The worst part is the headache. Even just opening the one eye I'm able to hurts.

Doc said I probably have a concussion, but I'm not about to go to an actual hospital to get checked out further. The last thing I need is someone asking more questions.

I already told Finley about everything that happened with Dad and his insane interest in V. He's smarter than me, so maybe he'll figure out what the fuck it is they want with her, because God knows it's not likely to be me that pulls the rabbit from the hat.

We pull into the Saints' drive, the gate closing behind us with a loud clang that I swear has me seeing colors, and find Linc waiting for us when we pull up.

Finn hops out of the car, and I'm just glad he didn't bring the Aventador, 'cause fuck getting out of that right now. Lincoln opens the door and I slide down out of the Range Rover, groaning when my feet hit the ground.

"What the fuck happened?" Linc asks and I try to grin at him, but wince when the split in my lip pulls.

"My dad wasn't too thrilled about me taking V's side last night rather than standing with him."

He curses before slamming the car door closed. "This is bullshit!"

"It cool if I chill here for a few nights, till he's cooled down?"

Lincoln looks at me, and the bags in Finn's hands. "Usually, yes. But Harrison is home, and we both know he'll kick you out if Edward breathes a word to him."

"Well, fuck," I hiss, resigning myself to the fact that I'm heading back home to that nightmare.

"What in the fuck happened to you?" I look up at V's screech as she tears across the space between us.

I let out an *oomph* as she tries to hug me.

"Sorry, sorry. What happened?" She looks at the others when I don't say a word. "Someone better tell me what the fuck is going on and why he looks like he went ten rounds with Wilder."

Goddamn she's hot when she's pissed. "Just a little disagreement with dear old Dad, princess. Nothing for you to worry about."

"Your dad did this?" she asks, taking a step back, her eyes wide in horror. "Because of last night? Because you stood up for me."

Well, no one ever said she wasn't a smart cookie.

"It's all good. I'm still alive and kicking."

"Maverick Riley, don't you dare downplay this," she scolds. "I am so sorry."

I look to the other two for help, but they're whispering between themselves. "You've got nothing to be sorry for, V. This isn't your fault."

"Have you seen a doctor? Is there anything I can do?" she asks, tracing her fingers down my face.

"Well, you could let him crash with you for a few nights," Linc pipes up, and as much as I want to glare at him, also, hell yes. Unfiltered access to my girl? Not something I'm about to turn down.

She looks between Lincoln and I, a little shocked, but I watch as she makes the decision and it takes root. "Yeah, of course, whatever you need. Smithy will be happy to have more people in the house. Do you have everything you need? I'll go tell him you'll be staying. He was supposed to be away for the weekend, but came home early this morning."

She pulls away but I grab her hand, wincing at the sudden movement, and she looks at me, disapproving, but it melts away when she sees I'm in pain. "What's wrong?"

"Nothing, just didn't want you to go yet." I try to smirk at her, to hide just how fucking vulnerable I feel right now.

She wraps her arms around me gently and places her head on my chest. "You don't have to. Come on, let's get you settled in."

Pulling back, she glances at the others. "You coming too?"

They look at each other and nod. "Yep, we'll be over in a second. I'll bring his bags," Finn says. I have no idea what the two of them are up to, but I'm sure they'll fill me in soon enough.

V pulls on my hand gently and tugs me along behind her. We walk in silence over to her place, and Smithy is in the kitchen when we arrive.

"Oh, Master Riley! What in the... are you all right?" He clucks around me while V tries to explain that I'm okay, and that I'll be staying with them for a bit. "Yes, of course. I'll make up the guest room. Not a problem at all. You get comfortable on the couch. Do you need a doctor? I can call a friend of mine to take a look at you."

"Thanks, Smithy, but I already saw a doc. I'll be fine. Just need to take it easy for a few days."

He glances over me and his worry is obvious. "If you're sure."

"I swear it," I say to him, trying not to grimace at the ache in my ribs. He hurries out of the room, muttering about the Knights, but I don't quite catch what he says. "Can we sit?"

"God, yes, sorry!" V exclaims and helps me over to the couch, where I lie down. I groan with pleasure as I get off my feet. The ache in my ribs is still there, but nowhere near as bad as it was when I was standing. "Do you want a drink? Something to eat?"

"Stop fussing, I'm okay," I tell her playfully as she sits on the coffee table watching me.

"I've never seen someone look as fucked up as you do right now, so excuse me for fussing. I'm so sorry, Maverick. If I'd have just accepted their invitation…"

She trails off but I shake my head. "Then you'd be in as deep as we are, and God knows what they'd have you do for initiation. Not gonna happen. My dad probably would've found another reason for this anyway. It's one of his favorite games. How far can he push before I die?"

She gasps, her eyes wide, and I realize what I said.

Fuck it. Can't take it back anyway. There's no point in lying to her about who my father is. If we can't find out what they want from her, she's going to find out at some point anyway.

"There are worse things in life than death, trust me," I tell her before getting comfortable on the couch. I'm saved from the questions in her eyes as Lincoln and Finley enter the room.

Thank fuck for that. Her puppy dog eyes slay me. I'd tell her every fucking secret I know if she hit me with them. Linc would probably kill me for it too.

"All sorted?" Finn asks as he drops my bags at the side of the couch. He steps forward and scoops V up in his arms, sitting in the chair with her in his lap.

Lucky bastard.

I might get to live here, but I'm severely out of action.

Though I'm pretty sure if she went on top, I could totally still get down with that.

"Yeah, Smithy is sorting him a room," she says as she snuggles into him. He smirks at me and I give him the finger. Asshole.

"I'm sure he'll work his way into your room soon enough," Linc snarks as he drops onto the couch by my feet, "But for now, this setup works. Shame you don't have room for Finn too."

"I mean, I do," she says with a shrug before looking up at the guy in question. "You can stay here if you need to."

He squeezes her tight before kissing her and I groan as she whimpers against him. I do love to watch, but fuck me. All I ever want to do with her is play.

"I might just take you up on that." He nips at her lip, and I look up at the ceiling. Only I could be this fucked up and still lie here with a fucking semi.

"Well, let me know," she says all breathy, and I swear I can fucking taste her.

"Please, for the love of my soon-to-be blue balls, take it down a notch," I plead, and Finn belts out a laugh.

"Fuck you, man. You deserve some blue balls."

I launch a cushion at him, gasping at the burning sensation that tears through my ribs and remembering at the last second that it's more likely to hit her than him, but he grabs it before it does.

He's about to tear me a new one when I'm saved by the Smithy.

"Your room is all made up, Master Riley. Please let me know if you need anything at all. Will you all be staying for dinner?"

V jumps off Finn's lap and hugs the old man while I give Finn a shit-eating grin, because I'm not the only one with a semi.

"Thank you, but you don't need to cook. We can just order pizza."

He scoffs at her in horror. "Wash out your mouth, Miss Octavia. I think not! We have guests. I'll make pizza if you would like pizza." He looks across at the rest of us, and I just try not to laugh. One: it totally won't be appreciated, and two: the idea of laughing right now makes my ribs scream, let alone actually doing it.

"Pizzas it is," he says, extracting himself from her and heading into the kitchen.

"Well, I guess you're all staying for dinner."

She smiles, leaning on the arm of the chair, when Finley pulls her back into his lap. He whispers in her ear and she laughs gently. "Nowhere else we'd rather be."

# TWENTY THREE

## OCTAVIA

It's been almost a week of having Maverick in my space… and, oddly enough, it hasn't been weird at all. We seem to have just kind of fallen into a routine. Not that Maverick went to school for the start of the week, but I've driven in with Lincoln every morning, and either come home with him, Finn, or Indi.

Though, study night with Indi was definitely interesting with Maverick here too. They've developed this love-to-annoy-each-other thing, which was funny as fuck to watch, even if it was distracting as hell.

"You got much planned for this weekend?" Indi asks as we get changed after Gym.

I think over my plans and my eyes go wide. "Shit! It's Mav's birthday tomorrow."

"Oh hell," she groans. "You forgot?"

"I did, we've had so much going on that I totally spaced. I need to go shopping." I can't believe I forgot his birthday. His eighteenth.

Fuck.

"Maybe just go to like Six Flags or something? Or take him skydiving. He's the adrenaline junkie type, right? And he's on the mend, so why not? Or head out to the mountains for the weekend and go snowboarding. He seems the type."

"You, my friend, are a freaking genius." I swear I could kiss her. That's a great idea. Now to get the others on board, because there is no way I'm doing a weekend away with just Maverick. "And while I remember, I won a spa retreat weekend away for next weekend at the gala, if you're up for it."

She grins at me, nodding her head. "Massages, pampering, and time away from this place? Hell yes I'm in."

"Has everything been okay with you lately? I feel like a shitty friend. I've been so wrapped up in my bullshit that I feel like we've barely spent any time together since the start of the year."

She scoffs before closing her locker. "Girl, we've both been juggling, but you are far from a shitty friend. Plus, now we have next weekend. As for everything going on with me, it's fine. It's all Kings related. The time away from the insanity will be nice."

"Let's just hope the crazy doesn't follow us," I joke and then wince.

*Way to jinx yourself, V.*

"Fingers crossed. I've gotta jet; I've got a date with three very surly Kings. They have a meeting tomorrow, and if Diego isn't back… well, I have no idea what's going to happen. All I know is this stress is making me gray. Do you have any idea how many times I've had to touch up the roots of this purple? I'm honestly tempted to just go silver and save myself some time."

"I mean, you'd rock the silver. Why the fuck not?" I close my locker and head through the halls toward the parking lot with her.

Lincoln, Finley, Maverick, and Easton are all standing by the Porsche, which just happens to be next to Indi's Wrangler and has been all week.

"They're all a little protective, huh?" She smirks, nudging me with her shoulder.

I sigh, shaking my head. "I'd say you have no idea, but, well, I've met Ryker."

She bursts out laughing, drawing the attention of my guys. "Yes, yes you have. He's not usually so assholey, but this whole Diego thing has him on hyper alert. Plus, he really doesn't like the Saints."

"Yeah, I got that much. They'll come around, but we can worry about that later. I'll drop you the details of the retreat later?"

"Sounds good to me." She hugs me and breaks away to

head to her Wrangler while I head toward the guys, who go suspiciously quiet as I approach.

"Talking about me?" I ask, an eyebrow quirked.

Maverick saunters over and wraps his arms around me, smirking at me in that cheeky way he has. "About you, princess? Us? Never. Do you really think so little of us?"

I plant my hands on his chest, swatting him a little, mindful of the bruises that still stain his inked skin. "Not at all, but if you think I'm not aware that you all still have a ton of secrets, you're kidding yourself."

His smirk grows to a fully fledged wolfish smile before he leans down and whispers, "Some secrets are better kept hidden." He pulls back a little before capturing my lips with his, biting my bottom lip as he ends the kiss.

"Do you have any plans for tonight?" Finley asks, and my cheeks heat a little as I turn to the rest of them. You'd think I'd be okay with it by now, but it's too easy to get wrapped up in each and every one of them.

"Not yet," I say cautiously. "Why?"

Maverick tightens his hold around my waist, dropping his chin onto my shoulder. "Well, you might have forgotten, but it's my birthday tomorrow."

"Had not forgotten," I tease. "What did you all have in mind?"

"Well, since he's still recovering, we were just thinking a movie night, the five of us. Smithy is still out tonight, right?"

Lincoln asks and I nod.

"Yeah every Friday, like clockwork. He's nothing if not a man of routine," I confirm and East grins.

"Perfect. Then let's head to your place. I'm thinking tacos?"

I let out a whoop. "That, right there, is why you're one of my favorites."

"Hey," Mav whines. "It's my birthday. How come I'm not the favorite?"

I turn in his arms as the others pile into Lincoln's car. "I never said you weren't. I said favorites. The *S* is vital."

"Good." He nips at my lips again before Lincoln hollers at us from the car. "We should probably do as his Saintship requests."

I giggle at his nickname for Linc. "And here was me thinking you weren't one for following the rules," I tease, "But yeah, we probably shouldn't rile him up too much."

I take his hand and lead him to the car. He jumps in the front, riding shotgun thanks to his injuries. Finley is leaning against the side of the car, door open, waiting for me. "Thanks," I say as he takes my bag so I can climb in. I scoot over to sit in the middle since, despite all my curves, I'm still the smallest one of the five of us.

Finley splays his hand across my thigh as we drive back to my house, and I give Lincoln the code so he can just pull into my drive rather than go to his first.

We pile out of the car and into the house to find Smithy

singing in the kitchen. It's so nice to see him so happy. He has definitely had a pep in his step since he starting dating whoever this mystery person is. I'm just excited to meet them. Though I wouldn't mind doing a deep dive into whoever it is' past, because, well, life in the Cove has made me more than a little cynical and untrusting.

"Afternoon all, having a night in?" he asks as we pile into the kitchen. "Milkshakes?"

"Smithy, you truly know the way to my heart." I sigh as I slip into one of the stools at the counter.

He grins at me, hand on his heart. "I try my best, Miss Octavia. I made some salted caramel earlier for a cheesecake, so how does salted caramel and dark chocolate sound?"

I salivate at the sound of it. "Yes, please." I nod and the others all agree.

"Don't worry, Master Lincoln. I've got strawberry in here for you too."

Lincoln smiles as he sits opposite me. "You're too good to us, Smithy."

Smithy's chest puffs out as he goes about making us milkshakes, and we talk about school shit until he's done. "Hot date again tonight?"

"Indeed, Miss Octavia. I'm heading out shortly. My cheesecake and I have plans." He winks. "Do you need anything before I leave?"

"Nope, I'm sure between the five of us we will survive."

He frowns at me. "Do not burn down my kitchen, Miss Octavia. I'll forgive you murder, just not murder of my kitchen."

The guys all start laughing. My lack of culinary genius is well documented at this point. "I promise not to touch a thing. Finley and East can both cook, even if the rest of us can't. If all else fails, I know there's still lasagne in the fridge."

He nods and heads back to his rooms, I assume to get ready. I turn to Maverick, who is slurping down his milkshake like someone might steal it. "So, since it's your birthday weekend, what are we watching?"

He grins while Linc and Finn groan. "Why don't you pick, princess? I'm sure I can get on board with whatever you choose."

"Maverick Riley, who knew you were such a cutie?" I laugh and his eyes darken.

"Just racking up favorite points."

I can't help but laugh at him. "No points needed. I don't pick a favorite anything. Them's the rules."

"Speaking of favorites…" Lincoln starts, stealing my attention. "We wanted to speak to you about this thing between us all."

I swear my heart stops in my chest. While I'm aware they've all spoken about it before, and Mav told me all casual that they're all good with it, we've not had 'the talk' and I am so not ready for it.

"Oh?" is all I manage to squeak out under his intense gaze. "What about it?"

"We wanted to lay down some… rules."

"Rules?"

"What Sainty is trying to say," Mav interjects, "is that we're all chill sharing you. As long as it's just us. No outsiders."

My eyes go wide. I hadn't even considered anyone else. The four of them are more than enough to juggle. "Okay…"

"And while it probably doesn't need saying." Lincoln pauses for a moment, sighing. "We aren't interested in anyone else. So it's just the five of us."

"What about Georgia?" I kind of hate myself as the words fall from my lips, but it's out there, so I hold my breath as he shakes his head.

"Georgia is nothing. I'm not interested in her. I'm doing what I must to repay Harrison for the favor I owe him. Nothing more, nothing less."

"But what happens if that favor means taking things further with her? You already told me your dad has zero lines that he won't cross for the Knights."

Lincoln leans back in his chair while the others just watch us both like we're the goddamn movie. "What exactly are you asking me, Octavia?"

"I'm asking if you're going to fuck her."

God, I sound so needy, and I hate it. It's selfish. I don't even know why he owes Harrison, but the thought of him touching her like that… it makes me sick and pissed off all at once.

He moves forward, leaning his forearms on the counter. His

eyes darken as he narrows them at me. "The only person I intend on fucking anytime in the future is you, Octavia."

Sweet baby Jesus.

"Okay," I say, nodding, unable to tear my eyes from his.

"Well, now that's settled," East interjects, "Tacos anyone?"

I burst out laughing. Thank fuck for him. "Yes, please. I am so here for tacos."

"You, sweet girl, are on lettuce duty because Smithy won't forgive me if I let you near his stove." He kisses my cheek as he passes me on his way to the refrigerator.

Smithy appears seconds later dressed in jeans and a sweater, and I swear to fuck my jaw hits the floor. He owns something that isn't a suit? Well, damn.

"Smithy, my man, you look fly as hell." Mav grins at him.

"Why, thank you, Master Riley. Are you sure you don't need anything before I leave?"

East shakes his head. "Nah, I've got this. You've got taco boats in the pantry right?"

Smithy smiles and nods. "I run the house for Miss Octavia, of course I have taco boats."

I let out a cry of fake outrage and he laughs at me. "I will see you all on Sunday. Please try to behave."

"We'll be on our best behavior," Lincoln tells him, and Smithy gazes at me like he doesn't quite trust it, but turns to leave regardless.

"Have fun!" I call out as he leaves before focusing back on

my guys. At least tonight should be fun, even with the conversation from earlier hanging between us. Well, for me at least. The rest of them start helping East prep tacos while I don't even end up with the goddamn lettuce.

Apparently I can handle a gun, but chopping food in the kitchen is too dangerous.

Not that I'm complaining. Watching the four of them be all domesticated is hot as shit.

Sometimes it's fun being me.

After the movie ended, Linc and East went back next door, but Finn decided to avoid home for the night, so he's crashing here with me and Mav.

"Someone needs to be able to protect you if your stalker comes knocking. Mav's still down for the count," Finn teases while Mav scoffs.

"I'm more than able to fight or fuck thank you very much."

I sit on my bed, more than a little amused as they bicker back and forth. Who would've thought that these two would be the ones that squabble like an old married couple.

"Prove it," I challenge, and they both still before turning to look at me. What can I say? I've thought about it enough, and since they all laid everything out on the table I'm feeling a little... bold.

They look at each other, a silent conversation happening in front of me, before they turn back to face me.

"Are you sure you're good with this?" Finn asks as I scoot further back on to the bed.

My gaze bounces between him and Maverick. This might not have been how I saw our evening going, but I am definitely not complaining. "What is there to not be good about?"

"That's my girl," Maverick says excitedly as his heated gaze roams over my body. I take off my blazer and push myself back against the pillows on my bed. I'd be lying if I said I hadn't thought about playing with more than one of them at once, but I haven't even fucked Finn yet.

"Are you good with this?" I ask Finn, because Mav is clearly fine with it all, and Finley just laughs.

"Yeah, V. If you're good, I'm good." I bite my lip from the heat in his stare. I've never done this before, so I'm hoping to God one of them is going to lead this thing, 'cause if they're waiting on me, it's all going to go to shit.

Propping myself up on my elbows, I watch, in awe, as Maverick reaches back behind his head and pulls his t-shirt off in a move so fluid it's hypnotizing.

But when my eyes fall on his chest—with its array of colors and designs—my mouth waters at the sight of him, even with the extra bruises.

The sound of Finn's groan breaks my stare and I dart my eyes to him, my teeth trapping my bottom lip, sinking into my flesh.

Fuck, I wish I were biting something else… some*one* else.

"I told you she's fucking gorgeous when she wants to get fucked." Mav is being crude because he knows it turns me on.

"Don't be crass, asshole. But yeah, she's fucking perfect." Finn doesn't look at him when he speaks, he only has eyes for me and, damn, that makes me so wet just thinking about it.

With a scoff, Mav unbuckles his belt and unbuttons his jeans, slowly sliding the zipper down, one frustrating tooth at a time. "The dirtier the better, Finn. Trust me on that."

"You two need to stop talking about me like I'm not here." Cocky assholes.

Cocky—gorgeous, hot as fuck, and infuriating—assholes.

"Spread your legs, princess, show Finn just how wet your pussy gets when I talk to you like my favorite little whore." I almost wish he were wrong, but he's not and I have zero shame about just how hot he gets me.

Who needs shame when you can get orgasms?

As I spread my legs wide enough to give them a clear view, my skirt falls down my thighs until it rests at my waist. The only thing sitting between my pussy and Finn and Mav's view are my soaked panties. Judging by the impressive, if not scary as fuck hard-on Finn's sporting, he's definitely enjoying the view.

"See that? The perfect wet spot on perfect little silk panties covering a perfect little pussy." My gaze goes back to Mav at his words and, with a purr in my voice, I give him what he craves. A fight.

"Maybe you're just the appetizer today, Mav. I think I'm hungry for more than you can give me." I grin at him, the defiance in my stare fueling his fire to dangerous levels.

"Hmm, princess wants to play." Not a question, a statement of fact.

Darting my gaze to Finn I drink him in as he pulls his monster dick out of his pants, palming it as he settles on the big chair by my dresser. I have them both in my sights, one behind the other, as I spread my thighs just a little bit further apart.

When Mav pulls his dick out too, all joking and playing are out the door.

He bends over and places both of his hands on the bed between my open legs—his dick bobbing against his bare stomach—as his gaze sweeps over my pussy and up my torso until he reaches my hungry eyes.

"You know what happens when you fight me, princess? I bite back." Without warning, he almost launches himself at me and in half a second his mouth is attacking mine with a kiss so hungry it short-circuits my brain a little. He's all tongue and teeth and punishing fingers digging into the flesh of my thigh.

And I fight right back. I fist his hair with my hand, clutching hard enough to make him growl and bite his lower lip as he tries to retreat.

Fuck that, I'm not done with him.

With eyes like lava rocks ready to incinerate me, Mav— slowly and methodically—swipes his thumb across his bleeding lip before he sucks on the digit with a snarl that should scare the fuck out of me.

It should, but instead… instead it lights a flame inside me that burns like nothing I've ever felt before.

"I told you, brother, she likes it hard and dirty. That's why she's perfect. For all of us," Mav tells Finn over his shoulder, all the while staring right at me with pride and danger written all over his face.

"Are we going to fuck or are you going to wax poetic all fucking night?" I'm having too much fun right now pushing all of Mav's alpha buttons, but I may want to dial it back a bit or else my body is going to be painted in bruises all over again.

Not that I'm complaining.

"Careful, princess." That's all he says before his mouth is on mine again.

When he moves his kisses down my neck, I look over his shoulder to see Finn stroking his dick. He looks at me, eyes blazing, and I cry out as Mav bites the side of my neck. The sound seems to encourage Finley on. Hot fucking damn.

This moment is so fucking hot. Feeling Mav all over my body while watching Finn rub his own cock and wishing he'd let me touch him instead.

The thought makes me moan and writhe under Mav's ministrations.

"You want him too, don't you, princess? You want to touch him and taste him while my dick is fucking you, don't you?"

Looking back at Mav's expectant gaze, I nod. I'm almost afraid of his reaction but then I remember who I'm speaking to, and I know it's fine. Mav is down with anything as long as he gets to have me.

Which he will.

Fuck yes, he will.

Maverick's mouth moves down my chest and with an ease that surprises me considering his injuries, his fingers latch onto both lapels of my shirt and pulls hard enough to send all my buttons flying across my bedroom.

Holy fucking shit, that was hot.

His eyes flash, and in a blink, his mouth is on my nipple, licking and sucking and biting until I can't form a coherent thought.

Instinctively, I grind up on him, silently begging for more.

When he reaches my stomach, Mav takes the zipper at the side of my school skirt and drags it down, exposing my skin to his hungry tongue once more.

I think he's going to take my skirt off, but he doesn't. He leaves it bunched up at my waist, making his way directly to my pussy.

"Please don't r—" The sound of tearing fills the room and I know I'm a second too late.

My panties no longer exist, Mav has ripped a hole right in the center and pulled it apart so that nothing stands in the way of him and my pussy.

"If you want to save your underwear, next time don't wear any." He kneels up, his hands gripping my waist, and pulls me further down the bed. Darting his gaze my way just long enough to smirk that delicious smirk of his, he turns his attention back to my bare pussy. Licking his way down my slit and across my clit in long, torturous strokes of his tongue until I gasp out his name. He murmurs something I can't hear but feels intimate nonetheless.

My view of Finn is now unhindered. His strokes slow down but he's still so fucking hot that I can't help but stare at him. Him and his giant cock. The girth alone should scare me but it just makes me want him more.

"I don't know what you were just thinking but fucking hell, V, think it again. I'm only just getting started."

"Mav?" I don't look at him as I speak, my eyes are fixated on Finn and every one of his calculated moves.

"Yeah, princess?"

"I want to suck Finn's dick."

The whole room freezes.

Mav's mouth is motionless, just hovering over my clit. Finn's closed fist is frozen midway up his cock as he stares right back at me. Me, I suck in a breath, afraid I've said the wrong thing.

The moment is broken with Mav's low chuckle and a long lick up my slit to my clit.

"You heard our girl. Give her something she can suck on,

brother." Just as he finishes talking, he thrusts two digits deep enough inside me that I can feel the curl of his fingers. I buck against him, and he chuckles again, but not once have I let my gaze fall from Finn. I can practically see the wheels turning in his head before a calm washes over his features and he finally rises to his feet. His hand still on his cock, languorously moving up and down his shaft. With measured strides, he makes his way to us and stops at the side of bed where I'm sitting up against my pillows.

"You sure about this, V?" he asks again. His voice is low, almost a growl.

"Yes." It's one simple whimper, but it changes everything.

While Mav fucks me with his fingers, making me cry out as I buck into him, begging for more, Finley moves closer.

Placing a knee on the bed, I feel the weight of us shift. Mav comes up for air long enough to smirk at Finn as he scoots his way to the side of my face, his strokes long and even.

"Open your mouth, princess," Mav orders and I do as I'm told, no questions asked.

Obedient, I push my head back just enough to get comfortable and wait expectantly for Finn to give me what I want.

He doesn't move. Not even an inch. My gaze goes from Finn's dick to his face and frown.

"What's wrong?"

Mav stops eating me out right before he lets out an exasperated sigh. "Fucking hell, man. Really? I was nice and comfy all up in my girl's pussy."

Confused, my gaze bounces between the two of them.

What the fuck?

Mav rises to his knees and gently takes what's left of my panties off—leaving my skirt at waist—before turning me on my stomach with so little effort it takes me a minute to catch up. "He prefers it when you're on your hands and knees," Mav explains like it's the most natural thing in the world.

Okay then. I look up at him from all fours.

Finn's dick is just mere inches from my mouth, teasing me like an ice cream cone on a hot summer day. Mav's behind me, his dick gliding up and down the crease of my ass with shallow dips into my pussy.

"Open your mouth, princess." Again I do as I'm told, waiting to finally taste Finn's cock.

Finn's hand lands at the back of my head, fingers tight on my scalp, and he angles my head exactly as he wants it while Mav lines up the head of his cock at my pussy.

As if a silent command goes between them, they enter me at the same time and I whimper at the fullness of it.

Finn holds my head at the perfect angle for his cock to slide in and even though it stretches out my mouth to the point of pain, I don't pull away as Mav thrusts inside my pussy in a punishing rhythm.

I gag for a second as Finn pushes too far but instead of pulling back, he whispers, "Breathe through your nose."

I do as he says and little by little I accept the sheer size of him all the way to the back of my throat.

When I'm not sure I can take much more, Mav reaches forward and palms my throat. "Fuck." His groan fills the room and he fucks me even harder.

Finley grips my hair tighter, fucking my throat so slowly, I'm not sure how much longer I can keep it up.

"You. Are. So. Fucking. Hot." Each word Mav says is punctuated with a thrust that sends Finn's dick a little deeper inside my throat.

"There they are." I barely acknowledge Finn's words, I'm so concentrated on not gagging on his giant fucking dick.

"Fuck yeah. I love it when she cries."

He pulls out and I close my eyes as Mav removes his hand from my throat and moves it to my clit. Finn licks a hot path up my cheek with his tongue, and I realize that he's licking my tears away.

"That's it, do it again. She's digging it, brother. She's fucking soaked." The slapping of skin on skin behind me is hot. Mav's words are hot. Finn's dirty tongue and gentle touches are hot.

My entire body is on fucking fire, and I've never been more willing to burn.

"You wanna come, don't you, princess?" Mav pinches my clit with two fingers while his other hand digs into the flesh of my hip as he fucks me like a man possessed.

Finn is more controlled as he slides his dick back into my

mouth, holding me down with one hand and fucking my mouth in careful, measured thrusts.

It's only when I look up at him and see the blazing fire in his eyes that I lose all semblance of control. Finn darts his eyes back to Mav and it's like an electric current flows through the three of us.

Finn growls as he comes down my throat, holding my head in place while I swallow him down. Mav thrusts one last time, burying himself inside me, the move tearing an orgasm from me so powerful I nearly choke on Finn's dick. He instantly pulls out just in time for me to cry out my ecstasy.

Mav follows closely behind me with a shout before we collapse onto my bed together. I close my eyes as I come down, hearing Finley as he pads across the room. "Gimme two seconds, princess," Maverick says as he untangles himself from me.

I can barely nod, feeling used in the best kind of way, and just lie in my bliss.

Mav reappears and helps me clean up before snuggling with me on the bed. "Where's Finn?" I ask, almost absentmindedly, but a little concerned too.

"He had to go, but he's okay."

I frown, but he holds me tighter. "Are you sure? Did he not want to—"

"Don't even think it, princess. It has nothing to do with you, I promise."

I nod and kiss his chest. "Are you okay?"

"I am more than okay." He chuckles softly as he holds me, and I start to give in to sleep.

"Happy Birthday, Mav," I murmur, and he kisses the top of my head.

"Best birthday ever."

# TWENTY FOUR

## OCTAVIA

I wake up splayed across Maverick's chest, our legs tangled together, cocooned in his embrace. I really don't want to wake him up, but if I don't move, I'm going to have to do the pee dance, and that isn't exactly conducive to him sleeping either. So I kiss his chest in the hopes he stirs enough to release me, so I don't have to fully struggle-cuddle my way out of this.

He mumbles in his sleep, moving just enough that I manage to slip away and dash to the bathroom.

Once I'm done and freshened up, I grab my phone and pull up a group chat with the other three.

Me

Morning, how does everyone feel about a night in the mountains for Mav's birthday?

Finley

> He'd love that, but he already asked to have the day with just you.

I bite my lip because, well, that's adorable. I also can't help but wonder if that's why Finn split last night. I mean, I doubt it. Mav has never had issues sharing, but who the fuck knows?

Lincoln

> If he's changed his mind, we're up for whatever, we had the weekend cleared.

East

> I'm good with whatever he decides to do, just let me know. Surprised you fuckers are all awake already.

I laugh softly, because it is the ass crack of dawn still.

Me

> Okay, I'll speak to him and let you guys know.

I pull up my thread with Finley separately and drop him a quick message too, since I didn't get to speak to him last night after everything.

Me

> Mav said you had to leave. I hope you're okay, that I didn't push any boundaries.

Finley

> It wasn't you, pretty girl. Just some of my own shit. We're good. Let me know what the plans are for today, and if he's down for sharing you on his birthday, I'm in.

Staring at the screen, I can't help but wish I'd never left The Cove. Maybe then I'd have more of an idea what haunts each of them. But if I'd stayed, who knows what any of us would look like right now?

I shut off my screen and pad back to bed, dropping the phone on the nightstand before slipping in next to Mav.

"There you are, princess. Running away from the big bad wolf?" He smiles sleepily at me, and I brush some of the hair from his face.

"You're not the big bad wolf. You're the birthday boy."

"Hell yeah I am." His smile widens and he pulls me into his arms.

"What did you want to do today?" I ask, which feels a little like putting him on the spot, but if the mountains are out, I still really want to celebrate with him. Being the last one to turn eighteen sucks, but I love doing birthdays. I'm pretty sad I missed Linc and Finn's over the summer.

He smirks at me and wags his brows. "You."

I burst out laughing. "You're a cheesy fucker sometimes, you know that right?"

"Only with you, princess."

"Now that I believe." I sigh happily. "Now what do you really want to do for your birthday? Skydive? Snowboard? Theme park? The world is your oyster."

He shrugs, and sadness flickers in his eyes. "Birthdays haven't really meant much to me since you left."

My heart hurts for him. Initiation must have messed with him more than he lets on. I shouldn't be surprised, he was only twelve for fuck's sake.

My phone buzzes on the nightstand, but I ignore it until he picks it up and answers it. I look up and see it's a video call with Indi.

"Morning, assface. Where's my girl?" Indi says with a smirk, and I bury my face into his chest to stop the snort laugh that threatens.

"*My* girl is riding my dick," he answers, and her laugh makes mine worse.

"Must be a shitty dick if I can't even hear her," she retorts, and he flips her the finger. I pull his arm down and wave at her on the screen. "Oh, there she is, haiiiii bestie."

"Morning." I smile. "Everything okay?"

She nods and blows a bubble with her gum. "Yep, I just wondered if you guys had decided what you were doing with your day yet?"

"Not yet, why?"

I hear voices in the background, and Dylan appears on screen with her, kissing her cheek.

"We're heading paintballing and wondered if you guys wanted to come," Dylan says with a smirk. "Us versus you guys."

"A chance to shoot at Ryker's cranky ass and not get fucked up? I'm in!" Maverick whoops beneath me and I shake my head.

"I guess we're in. Drop me the details and I'll let the others know."

"Sounds good, sweet cheeks. We'll see you soon."

"You will, maybe this time you won't end up with paint in unspeakable places." I wink at her and she scoffs, sticking her tongue out before ending the call. "I guess we're paintballing for your birthday."

He grabs my hips and pulls me up to straddle him. "Hell yes we are. This is the most I've looked forward to a birthday in ages. But first, I'm hungry."

"Then let's get food."

He leans forward and kisses me until I'm breathless. "I didn't mean food, princess."

Getting geared up for paintball has been hilarious. I've never been, but it seems like a more painful version of laser tag. The body armor and mask I'm wearing definitely point to the whole painful thing, but fuck it. Maverick is so excited, a little pain is worth it.

Lincoln was not as excited as Mav at the prospect of shooting at the Donovans, but we're all here, and there seems to be a tenuous peace created by Dylan and one of the other Kings they brought with them, Thomas, and Finn and Mav. East and Linc haven't said a word to the Donovans yet, but the day is young.

"You think this might work? Getting them all to kiss and make up?" Indi whispers as we load our guns with the paintballs. She managed to convince the guy that she needed just purple balls for her and her guys, and we ended up with blue, which made Maverick laugh, because he definitely isn't suffering blue balls at the minute.

"It could. Maybe they just need to shoot at each other without, you know, killing each other, and get some of that testosterone out. Boys usually sort shit out by hitting each other, so it could work." I tighten the strap on my vest and grab my helmet.

"Why didn't we offer to be the stupid flags?" she squeaks. "I can deal with being taken by the opposing team and recaptured... being shot at is going to suck."

Dylan appears as she finishes speaking and lifts her over his shoulder. "Don't worry, Shortstack. I got you. I won't let these assholes shoot my girl."

"Put me down, you big oaf!" She squeals and he slaps her ass in response.

"Don't worry, we chose the easy option for you girls. Just

have to capture the flag, no having to return to your own base with it. To start with anyway. We'll go easy on you," he explains, still not putting her down, but it does make me feel a little better.

"See you out there, Octavia." He winks at me and walks off with Indi. She pounds his back, but he just laughs as he heads toward Ryker, Ellis, and Thomas. I head over to where my guys are huddled together.

"This looks very serious," I tease as I infiltrate their huddle. "Want to let me in on your super secret spy plans?"

Lincoln rolls his eyes at me, but that just widens my grin.

"Why so serious?" I quote and then burst out laughing, Mav along with me. "I'll stop, I'll stop. So seriously, what's the plan? Or is this just a free for all?"

Finn grins at me and Lincoln scoffs. "There is no way we're taking on the Donovans without a plan."

"You get that this is supposed to be fun, right?"

"Winning *is* fun," Linc responds, his eyes alight. "All you need to do is worry about not getting shot. Because you are our secret weapon. I've seen you shoot. They haven't."

I laugh, because of course that's his plan, but they all look so excited that I'm totally here for it. Even if the bruises are going to suck tomorrow.

I salute him, with a "sir, yes sir," which just makes him smirk again.

"That's more like it. Let's do this." They do a weird boy grunt thing and head out the same way Dylan carried Indi, and I trail behind them wondering if this is either genius on Indi's part or an absolute disaster waiting to happen.

We hike out into the wooded area where the purple flag is planted in the ground, and without even speaking, Finn and Mav break off from Lincoln, East, and me. It's like they're a well-oiled stealth machine.

Not going to lie, I'm kind of looking forward to seeing them Hulk out a little. Paintballing gear shouldn't be hot... but on these four... well hot damn. Apparently a guy with a gun and glorified football pads is hotter than I thought it would be.

Then again, these four could probably wear one of Indi's tutus and I'd still salivate.

"You'll be with us. You are going to capture their flag, and we'll cover you," Linc says as we crouch in front of our flag, waiting for the air horn.

"We're leaving the flag open?"

East chuckles under his breath. "You think he'd leave that to chance?"

My gaze bounces between the two of them and I shrug.

"Finn is currently climbing a tree to take the high ground, he'll act as cover for the flag." East whispers. "Maverick... well... he'll do what he does best."

"Just remember, we need them to think you're helpless until we're closer," Linc adds.

I nod as the air horn goes off, and the air gets real tense. Lincoln locks eyes with his brother and nods. They pull down their masks and stand in unison. It's freaking uncanny watching them move together like this. I make sure my gun safety is off, pull down my own mask, and follow behind them.

Their guns are raised, sweeping as we move through the bush, when I hear the *pop* of a gun in the distance.

Hopefully that's Maverick taking someone out, and not the other way round.

The two of them move through the woods like they've done this a thousand times, but considering East isn't a Knight, I'd be surprised if they have. I try to focus on where I'm going so as not to trip and become a liability, but this is all new to me.

Stealth and tactical advantages aren't exactly things I was schooled in on the road. I have no idea how East is so good at it, but Lincoln looks like he could wage wars single-handedly and come out unscathed. I might not be able to see his face beneath his mask, but he moves like this is second nature for him.

For all I know, it could be.

I see a flash of purple ahead, and tap East's shoulder, pointing in the direction I saw it. East peels off from us, as if to flank whoever it is ahead of us, and I stay with Lincoln.

"Their flag is going to be across the field, planted in the opposite wooded area. Unless they're carrying it."

"They might, Indi did say something about being the flag," I tell him and he nods.

"Let's do this."

He starts moving again and I raise my gun this time, trying

to help if needed. We're near the edge of the tree line when I hear a squeal pierce through the air.

"Maverick, you ass hat! You shot me in the ass!" Indi cries, and I can't help but laugh.

East appears from the left and stands on my other side. "Ready?"

"Let's move," Lincoln says, and we haul ass, sprinting across the field, the two of them in front of me trying to protect me from any incoming fire. Maverick appears, bringing up the rear. Crazy asshole has his mask lifted and barks out a laugh as he runs.

He winks at me before he pulls it back down when the Donovan twins appear before us like fucking forest wraiths. Lincoln grabs me and spins me to the right, leaving East and Maverick to deal with the two of them. I want to see who wins, but I try and stay focused.

Who would've thought paintball would be enough to bring out my competitive side?

I see the flag in the distance and change direction, heading straight for it. It's only when I see Thomas I realize they laid their own trap.

Unfortunately for them, they don't know me.

I raise my gun and let off three rounds which hit him squarely in the chest, and I let out a whoop and keep running. I hear shots to the right where Lincoln was, but I don't let myself get distracted. I head straight for the flag and yank that sucker out of the ground when I reach it, setting off the alarm.

Lifting my mask, I do a little jig on the spot, because I feel like a fucking badass, even if this is only round one. Maverick appears and picks me up, spinning me around, before he starts dancing with me.

The others appear in the wooded area as we continue to dance, and Indi laughs at me. "You might've won the battle, but you haven't won the war." She cackles as Ryker steps up behind her.

He looks me square in the eye and smirks. Heart be still, the grump smiles! "We know your secret now, Royal. Game on."

We spend all fucking day running around, and I swear it's like I have a giant neon arrow above my head that says 'shoot here'.

The upside to the day is that Maverick is smiling wider than I've ever seen him and even Lincoln is smiling. Probably because we won.

The other upside is there seems to be an almost tenuous truce between the Donovans and my guys, which helps me breathe a little easier. Lincoln and Ellis are walking together as we head to the parking lot, while Maverick is talking shit with Ryker.

Me, I'm just hobbling along, enjoying the moments of peace and hoping they last.

We gather at the cars and I lean on East, laughing at Indi getting a piggy back from Dylan across the lot. "Today was actually more fun than I thought it would be."

East puts an arm around my shoulder, chest shaking as he chuckles. "Yeah, me too. Who would've thought the Donovans had a sense of humor."

"I heard that, Saint," Ellis shouts, pointing at us, but still has a smile on his face as he and Lincoln join us. "We're great fun when we're not surrounded by assholes."

"You know what they say about assholes," Indi chimes in. "Everyone's got one, some are just more full of shit."

Dylan's laugh booms around us, and even Ryker cracks a smile.

"Now if we just knew where Diego was, we could've had the full Donovan team," Ellis says, and while it's not with malice, the tension goes from sixty to one hundred in a heartbeat.

Indi sighs, tapping Dylan's shoulder to let her down. "I thought we spoke about this?"

"We did," Ryker answers for his twin, and my heart pounds a little faster at just how tense this feels. "Ellis isn't accusing anyone, are you?"

"I'm not. You asked us to play nice, so we're playing nice. Today has been fun. I just wish Diego was here too. That's all I meant."

I let out the breath I'm holding, especially because I know Lincoln knows where Diego is.

"We'd probably have lost harder if he was though," Dylan adds, laughing and breaking the tension. The guys keep up their smack talk, and Indi comes to lean on the car with me.

"That was close," she sighs, resting her head on my shoulder. "I thought all hell was going to break loose."

"Me too." I nod. "I'm glad it didn't. This was a good idea, thank you."

She grins and takes my hand, interlocking her fingers with mine. "It was, I'm glad we did it. And if they can start this without killing each other, maybe there's hope for them actually being friends."

Paintballing yesterday was fun, but fuck me, I am sore as fuck. I finish my run with Linc, trying not to whimper from the aches and bruises that cover my body.

We might've won yesterday, but it was close, and once the Kings knew I could shoot, they targeted me like a bunch of dick bags. I might be able to shoot, but tactical advantages really aren't my strong suit.

"You okay?" Linc calls out as I drop onto the lawn once I'm inside the gates. I put my hand up in the okay salute and try not to groan into the ground. He drops down next to me, and I roll onto my back. "What hurts?"

"Everything?" I say and he laughs softly.

Lincoln fucking Saint laughs.

Of course it's at my pain.

"I'd offer a massage, but bruises and massages probably aren't the greatest of ideas."

"I mean, I'm not about to turn down a massage, but you're probably right." I sigh. "At least today I have nothing on my to-do list but a long soak in a bubble bath."

He looks down at me and frowns. "Actually, I was going to see if you wanted to go car shopping. I know the Impala is down for the count, and you can ride with all of us, but I think it'll be safer if you have your own car."

"I can always use Dad's Range Rover if I need it," I tell him with a shrug. "You guys just didn't want me alone because of the whole stalker thing, so I figured riding with you was easier."

The lines on his forehead sink deeper as his frown grows. "We don't know who's had access to it. I'd rather we get you something new, something safe. Preferably bulletproof. Better safe than sorry."

"I'm pretty sure I don't need a tank, Lincoln," I say, rolling my eyes. "I have a stalker, not death threats."

"I don't know, those last round of images looked pretty much like death threats to me," he deadpans.

I sit up and shrug. "I mean, technically, they were against you guys. Not me."

"Octavia."

One word is all he needs to scold me, and I sigh. "Fine, fine. I was really looking forward to that bubble bath, you know."

"You can have your bubble bath after," he says with a shrug.

"I'll be back here in thirty to grab you."

"Okay," I say as he stands.

He pulls me to my feet and I brush down my leggings before heading toward the house. "Oh, and Octavia?"

I turn at his words and he captures my waist, pulling me into him before wrapping my ponytail around his hand. "If you're good, you might even get rewarded."

A shiver runs down my spine at the growl in his voice before he leans down and kisses me. My fingers curl in his t-shirt as our tongues battle for dominance. I let out a whine as he tugs on my hair and wins the battle of wills. He pulls back, his eyes hooded as he looks down at me. "See? You do know how to behave."

He kisses me softly again before releasing me. "Thirty minutes. Don't keep me waiting."

I shake my head and haul ass inside. I mean, if that's what happens when I'm good, I'm looking forward to finding out what happens when I'm bad.

Shutting down the alarm, I run up the stairs and rush through a shower. Ugh, boys will never understand how long it takes to wash, condition, and dry hair as long as mine. I swear these extensions make it take even longer to dry too. Thankfully, they fall as wavy as my natural hair once they're dry.

Once I'm ready, I throw on a pair of jeans, my boots, a tank, and a blazer before heading back downstairs. I fire off a text to Smithy to let him know I'm out with Linc and grab my purse and keys before locking up. My phone buzzes and Bentley's name pops up on the screen.

Bentley

> Hello, Miss Royal. I'm sure I can help you out. I'm free Thursday evening if you want to meet and discuss your requirements.

I run a hand nervously through my hair, trying to decide if finding my mom is a good idea, then kick myself for going into dumb bitch mode. Again.

*It's better to know and not use it, Octavia.*

I drop him a response to let me know the date and time then head over to the Saints'.

I know he said he'd come over here, but somehow I have five minutes to spare. When I get there, the back door is open so I let myself in and find Mrs. Potts in the kitchen. "Oh, morning, Octavia dear. Lincoln is just upstairs, he mentioned he was popping out with you."

"Thank you, I'll just head up." I smile and make my way through the house. It's been a minute since I was over here, but it's exactly how I remember. I head up the stairs, going straight to Lincoln's bedroom, hoping he hasn't moved rooms.

I knock before I enter, but there's no answer so I let myself in. It's empty. That's when I hear the running water and notice the door to his bathroom is slightly ajar.

"Lincoln," I start, pushing the door open and find him in the shower, his hand wrapped around his dick. He locks eyes with me, but doesn't say a word or stop what he's doing. He strokes his dick, the look on his face almost daring me to look away, but I couldn't if I wanted to. Everything about him is fucking mouthwatering, and his dick... well fuck.

His eyes close as he leans his head against the glass, his cum coating his hand as he moans my name.

I lick my lips at the thought of wrapping them around his dick, having him at my mercy.

He clears his throat, drawing my attention back to him, and smirks. "I'll be out in a minute."

"Erm, yeah, sure, I'll just wait out here." I can feel my cheeks heating as I manage to stumble through my words. After everything I've already done with him, with the others, you'd think I'd have more composure at seeing him get himself off, but apparently not.

God, I'm an idiot sometimes.

I drop onto his bed, trying not to look as off-kilter as I feel. Car shopping with him after watching that is going to be... intense.

My mind wanders back to him in the shower until he appears in nothing but a towel, smirking at me. "I thought it'd take you longer than thirty minutes."

"So did I." I shrug. "Who knew I could get ready so quickly?"

"I'm just going to get dressed. Try not to let your curiosity get the better of you this time." He heads into his closet, and I give him the finger behind his back. Asshole. Taunting me like that is just asking for me to go in there, but I keep my ass where I'm seated and wait him out.

I can hear him laugh in the closet, but I just take a deep breath and pull my phone out, scrolling through the news, because well, how else am I supposed to kill time?

He reappears in a black t-shirt and jeans, grabbing the hoodie and leather jacket combo from fight night, and it's all I can do not to drool over him. "Ready?"

I tuck my phone away and smile at him like I didn't just see his dick. "As I'm going to be. Just promise me no tanks."

His eyes light up as he shakes his head. "Not going to make promises I can't keep."

I let out a deep sigh and stand. This is going to be interesting for sure.

# TWENTY FIVE

## OCTAVIA

I try not to think back to the sight of Lincoln yesterday as he drives us to school in his Porsche, his hand on the bare skin of my thigh. Maverick stayed with Finn last night, he didn't give me a reason, but I'm also not his keeper, so I didn't question it. I know they're all still a little hesitant about telling me stuff to do with the Knights, so I let it go.

Car shopping with Linc was unsuccessful. I'm not that surprised as we don't exactly see eye to eye on a lot of stuff. He wanted safety, I wanted something not fucking hideous.

Not that I mind being without a car a little longer, because riding to school with him isn't exactly a hardship. Except for the fact that I kind of want to jump his bones. He's just so goddamn restrained, I know that I'm unlikely to push him over the brink before he chooses to take that leap himself.

Frustrating as hell, but I'm not about to push him. It's just not who I am.

We pull into the drive-thru to grab coffee, and I drop Indi a text to let her know I'll grab her one too.

Once we have the five drinks, we head to school, just the low sound of You Me at Six playing in the background. Definitely not what I pictured him listening to, but then, he could have just put it on for me. He's perceptive like that, and it's such a him thing to do.

It's also freaking adorable, but I'm not about to call him out on it either.

He sips on his coffee, handing it back to me as we pull into the parking lot. Indi is standing with the others and grins at me as Lincoln turns off the engine.

"I'll take them," he offers, taking the coffee trays from me once he's unbuckled.

"Okay, thanks." I hand them over and grab my bag, taking my cup back before jumping out of the car.

"My ass still hurts, assface." Indi nudges Maverick who barks out a laugh as I approach. "Good to see you all aren't as battered and bruised as I am."

"Speak for yourself," I huff. "Your boys got me good." Lifting my skirt I show her the purple spread on the top of my thigh, and Lincoln's eyes darken.

"You didn't tell me you had that."

I wave him off, because protector mode is not warranted. "It was paintball, and apparently I bruise easily there. It's fine."

He raises an eyebrow at me, but I just grab Indi's coffee, handing it to her before looping my arm through hers and heading into the school. "You have a fun Sunday?"

"Nope, my cousins flew in on Saturday, unbeknownst to me, and we had family freaking dinner. Dylan got invited in because he dropped me off at home. My family are a fucking nightmare, V. He basically got the Spanish Inquisition. Could you imagine if they knew I was dating three guys? Jesus fucking Christ, they'd lose their minds. Poor Dylan took it like a champ though."

"Well, that's good news at least. I bet he loved it, really. He seems like a people person," I say with a shudder. "Gross."

She barks out a laugh as I open my locker. "Yeah, he actually likes peopling. It's weird, but I love him just how he is."

"Aww, you're adorable. Were they bad losers about Saturday?" I ask as I sort my shit out before closing my locker.

"Nah, they took it okay. It was nice to see them all getting along, even if it was full of snark and jabby comments."

"It was. Maybe there's hope for them yet. Any news on Diego?" I ask, kicking myself for forgetting to prod Lincoln further still. I'm the fucking worst.

"Nothing. But they've put feelers out. They've officially given up on the theory he's out on a bender." She shrugs before opening her locker. "I just hope they find him alive."

"You think they might not?"

"Anything is possible. They work with some really fucked-up people."

I want to ask what they actually do, but the bell rings, stopping the words from forming. "Did you get your assignment done for Miss Summers?"

"Fuck, no. Fuck my life, how did I forget that?"

She grimaces as she closes her locker. "Because we didn't have an actual study night this week. It's fine, I'm sure she'll give you an extension. She's awesome like that."

"Ugh, I cannot let myself get behind again this semester. It was too stressful before Christmas. I have a study night with Lincoln tomorrow to finish up our Business project."

"Has Mr. Peters been gross again?" she asks as we walk to our seats at the back of the room.

I shake my head as I sit down. "No, thank God."

Blair and her bitch squad slide into the room as the second bell rings, all glaring at us. Shock. Horror. Thankfully they take their seats without saying a word. I guess whatever her and Lincoln talked about the other day has finally sunk in.

Maybe I should go over to her house. Try to work out exactly why she hates me so much, use the excuse of picking up the stuff she said I'd had delivered there. It's not that I want us to be besties, but I don't have much family left—she's pretty much it—and the fact that she hates my existence just for breathing, or so it seems, rankles me.

Miss Summers pulls me from my train of thought as she starts class, talking about the differences between the expectations of modern publications and those of classic literature in line with our next choices from the reading list. I'm not going to complain too much, this is by far my favorite class, so if I need to read and compare three texts in depth, and compare them to how I think they'd be perceived if they were released in today's market, then I can do that.

Text analysis is something I'm weirdly good at when it comes to literature.

The class passes in a blink, just like always, and before I know it the bell is ringing.

"Don't panic, leave your things where they are and head out to the fire evacuation point," Miss Summers shouts above the noise. It's only then I realize it's not the bell. It's the fire alarm.

I tap my pockets, making sure my keys and phone are on me. I don't mind leaving my books, but after everything I've been through lately, I'm not leaving my personal items lying around for anyone. We head outside to the evacuation point, everyone complaining around us. It's only when we're outside and I see the black smoke that I freak a little.

I can't see Lincoln, Maverick, East, or Finley.

I have a really bad fucking feeling, and my fingers start to tingle in anticipation as panic seizes me like a hand around the throat.

I scan the crowd as people pour from the building, trying not to freak the fuck out when I see them come around the corner of the building. My heart stops for a second as I acknowledge they're okay, and I try not to question why they're coming from that direction together.

What the hell is going on?

After the chaos at school, and basically getting no explanation from the guys, the day was cut short. Lincoln and Maverick had somewhere to go, and East had stuff to do with the school, so Finley offered me a ride home.

Except somehow, we ended up at his place instead.

It's been a long time since I've been in Finley's room, but it's entirely him. It's a different room from the one he had as a kid, and it's done in dark royal blues, white, and black. The giant bed is framed in dark wood, and light barely filters in through the thick curtains.

"So your dad is away?" I ask as I drop onto the bed.

He loosens the tie around his neck as he closes the door. "Yeah, he's gone all week. It's like a fucking vacation."

I can't help but smile. Knowing what I do about his dad, which is still very little, I'm sure that what he's saying is entirely true. "Why do you still live here?"

"Part of the deal. I might be eighteen, but my inheritance from my grandfather doesn't hit until I'm twenty-one. Same as my inheritance from my parents. I have basic access to funds, but nowhere near enough to survive without them. Just the way my father wants it." I bite my lip, contemplating my next words. "Is that really what you want to talk about?"

His eyes darken as his gaze roams over me sitting on his bed. My lips curve up, because no, I can think of much better things to do than talk right now. He's been so restrained with me until now, but I want to see him. All of him. All parts of that beast he keeps caged inside of him. I'm sure there's probably something wrong with me, that I want to see it. The thrill at the thought alone should be enough to set off red flags, yet... it changes nothing.

I watch intently as he starts to unbutton his shirt, but then he stops, as if realizing I'm in here too and lets his hands drop to his sides.

"Take it off, Finn. Show me."

His eyes dart to the side, the uncertainty clear in his eyes, but when he looks back at me it's like he's made a decision.

Pulling his tie from around his neck, he takes two steps closer to me and holds out his hand, waiting expectantly. I blink, unsure of what exactly he's asking of me.

"Give me your hands, V."

Our gazes lock and I hold out both of my wrists, watching, rapt by him, as he takes my arms and loops his tie around my wrists. It's mesmerizing watching him do it, almost as if it's instinctive, second nature for him because he never once looks at what he's doing.

He watches me the entire time instead, and being the target of his attention is almost heady. In those few seconds I become his prisoner, but as I study his features it feels like he's becoming mine too. I've never been more willing to be held captive.

"There are things you don't know," he says as he adjusts the tie. "Things I've told only my brothers." He tightens the knot and makes sure it's not stopping the blood flow to my fingers.

"You don't have to—" I start but he cuts me off with a shake of his head.

"I do." Those two little words hold so much weight, I can feel them on my chest and it's almost hard to breathe.

"Okay," I whisper with my hands out like an offering. I don't dare move for fear of breaking this moment. He doesn't speak much, so the chance of him finally opening up... I don't want it to disappear.

He looks around the room in a quick scan, moving to his dresser drawer and pulling out another one of his ties.

This one is a soft pink, almost the same shade as my lip gloss, which is fitting since he presses the largest end to my mouth then fastens it behind my head.

His outdoorsy scent surrounds me, his heat seeping into my flesh, overtaking my senses. He's everywhere without even touching me.

"No touching. No speaking. Those are the rules. If it gets too much, your safe word is kiwi. Nod if you understand."

A thrill runs through me, but I can't help but question his commands. I'm down for the big dick energy he has going on, but he never lets me touch him and I don't know why. Regardless, I nod and the relief on his face is palpable.

He moves me into a position of his liking, and I remain pliant. Straddling me, he scoots up to my chest and pulls my tied wrists up to his headboard. That's when I notice the hooks.

All along the top of his massive headboard, he's got evenly-placed hooks and he latches the tie to the one directly above my head.

It occurs to me that I'm not the first one he's had tied up here, but I push the thought away. We all have pasts. But I can't help but wonder if he's ever let *anyone* touch him.

Once he's satisfied with my position, he crawls back and admires me, eyes roaming me from head to pelvis.

The corners of his mouth tug up into a small smile, and I mewl under his intense gaze.

"There are things about me you don't know…" He reaches back for his shirt and slowly pulls it over his head, ruffling his gorgeous, thick hair.

"There are things no one needs to know." He keeps his shirt close to his chest long enough to bring his gaze back to mine.

"But you, V? You deserve it all. All of me for all of you."

When he discards his shirt to the side, somewhere on the floor, I see it.

I see them.

The scars. Dozens of them scattered haphazardly across his chest, his nipples, his stomach.

He's covered in past wounds inflicted on him throughout his lifetime. Years and years of suffering.

My muffled gasp doesn't surprise him. I try not to react, because he's finally showing me parts of himself that he's obviously self-conscious about, but the sight before me is shocking and cruel. It's abuse at the most profound depths of depravity. Burns, cuts, and things I can't decipher. A map of what he's survived, that led to who he is today.

Alone and closed off.

My shock dissipates and quickly turns into a burning rage. Who the fuck did this to him?

"Don't." One word and my focus is back on him. He's right, this isn't the time to get emotional about his past.

I push down the anger and settle back down onto the plush pillows, letting myself relax as Finn places both of his hands on the outside of my thighs. He runs them slowly up until he has palms full of my ass.

He hasn't taken any of my clothes off but I have a feeling he's taking his time with me. When he reaches the top of my skirt, he pulls the tab of my zipper down and with one expectant look, and a tap on my ass, he asks me to help him.

This is definitely a game I can play, so I raise my ass, a shiver running through me as he pulls it down my legs and tosses it across the room.

Once it's gone, he moves his focus to my shirt, unbuttoning it slowly, methodically, and my anticipation ratchets up.

I watch him intently, every move he makes is so precise and in a few moments my shirt is wide open, leaving me in just my underwear.

"You're stunning, you know that?" I can't answer. I'm pretty sure it's a rhetorical question anyway.

Curling his fingers around the lace cups of my bra, he pulls both down at the same time, exposing my tits, and places the fabric below them.

One thumb grazes my hard nipple, then the other. He's gentle, almost reverent, as he touches me exactly the way he wants to.

Bending down, he captures almost half my tit in his mouth and sucks hard enough to elicit a muffled moan from me.

He repeats the action with my other breast before he pulls back and gets up. I feel the cold where his heat had been just a second before.

Standing at the foot of the bed, Finn unbuckles his belt and pulls the leather strap from the loops before he lets it fall to the floor at his feet.

He undoes the zipper of his pants and my mouth waters. As they drop to the ground, I realize he doesn't have boxers on. He's been commando all fucking day. He bends down and places his pants neatly on the back of his desk chair. When he turns back to me, the fire in his eyes burns white hot and my heart pounds in my chest.

I want to lick my lips but this damn tie is holding my tongue hostage. I want to reach out and grab him, to feel the smooth skin of his cock, but again, I'm captive to his will.

With one hand stroking his cock, Finn places a knee on the bed and his free hand on my thigh.

"Open."

I obey, bending my knees and spreading my legs as wide as they'll go to allow for the sheer size of his body to nestle between my thighs.

He hasn't taken my panties off yet and I wonder if he's like Mav and believes they shouldn't exist, or if he prefers knowing there's an extra layer between me and the rest of the world.

Palming the back of my thighs, Finn places my legs over his shoulders and slides his hands to my ass cheeks before he bites into the lace fabric at my center, ripping it right off like a possessed animal.

It's hot as fuck and, judging by the satisfied grin on his face, I'm certain he knows it. But what is with these guys and ruining my fucking underwear. I'm going to need to go shopping again if this keeps up.

Using two fingers, Finn rips away the rest of my underwear until there's nothing left but two tiny strips at my waist. Then the heat of his mouth is on me and my hips buck against him. His tongue is fucking magical and he uses his fingers to open me up, curling upwards to push against my g-spot. I swear I almost see fucking stars.

He plays my body like an instrument he's mastered his entire life.

He builds me up slowly, biting gently on my clit as his fingers fuck me to a rhythm only he hears. It's the most exquisite kind of torture, and I want more. *Need* more. But this is his show and I'm just here for the ride.

Whimpers spill from me as he pushes me to the edge, and when he uses his other hand to pinch one of my nipples, it's like my entire body lights up as I fall over the edge. But he doesn't let up, pushing me through my orgasm like he's chasing a second.

And just when I think I can't take any more, I come all over his fingers again.

He pins me with his stare as I try to come back to earth and traces a hot path of gentle kisses up my stomach, my torso, each nipple. Reaching the hollow at my neck, he darts out his tongue and licks just enough to tease me.

That's when I feel the head of his cock at my entrance. My pussy is a greedy little bitch, because I'm practically panting for him. Thick and velvety, I yearn to have more—feel more—of him inside me.

He smiles at me, like he knows just how crazy he's making me and he loves it.

At a slow and torturous pace, Finn kisses his way up the column of my neck as his dick pushes inside me. I gasp at the size of him, but he takes his time, giving me a chance to adjust, because holy mother of monster dicks.

He continues to worship me with his kisses as he pushes in, the most delicious of stings ringing through my body as he does. I close my eyes as he pushes in further and feel his lips gently touch my lids, one, then the other, when his cock almost bottoms out.

It's only when I feel the blunt head hitting my most desperate spot deep inside me that Finn rips the tie from my mouth and slams his lips against mine, owning me with this desperate kiss like he can't hold back anymore. And I am more than here for it.

He lets his body tell me all the things he never has with words.

He fucks me like he's waited his entire life for me; hungry, and almost desperate as he drives me out of my goddamn mind. His dick slams in and out of my pussy with ardent fervor and his tongue lashes out all of his emotions, a fiery kiss filled with unspoken words.

Finn's body coils with every thrust, his muscles almost trembling above me when he bottoms out. The energy in the room is a living, breathing thing that burns me from the inside. What started out as calculated is now a series of hard, slamming thrusts and I'm convinced that Finn controls absolutely nothing right now.

Not a damn thing.

Except maybe his words.

He slows his thrusts and looks at me, like he's at war with himself. He leans back, removing my ankles from his shoulders before he unhooks my hands and releases them.

"Are you sure?" I ask, knowing, even though I don't understand why yet, that this is huge for him.

He nods. "I trust you."

I run my hands through his blond hair, stroking his cheeks, accepting this moment as a momentous one.

"I won't ever hurt you," I tell him, and his eyes close. He stills as I run the tips of my fingers gently down his shoulders and arms. He trembles beneath my touch, and I hate how much he seems to struggle with the touch, but love that he trusts me enough to allow me this moment with him.

I sit up and, without saying a word, he moves us so he's sitting where I was, and I'm straddling his lap.

"Are you sure?" I ask again, and he nods.

"With you, I'm sure."

I trace my fingers along his scars, following with my lips, wishing I could heal them, take them away, but I wouldn't change one part of him. Kissing him, I try to tell him all of this before sinking down onto his dick, his hands tightly gripping my hips as he trembles beneath my touch.

I bring my forehead to rest against his, our eyes fixed one on the other as our breaths dance with each of our gasps.

The thickness of him feels different, more meaningful maybe, in this position. I can feel every hard inch of his cock as

I rise and sink onto him, his fingers digging deep into my flesh like an anchor to his aching soul.

"Fuck, Finley, you feel so good. So fucking good." I don't need to speak out loud, we're so close that my words travel in whispers from my mouth to his ear.

Releasing one hip, he brings his hand to the back of my neck and fists my hair at the nape, hard enough to elicit a sharp breath.

"More." He gives me one word and it lights up every fucking nerve ending in my body.

Suddenly, we're not moving slowly anymore. We're not making some kind of fucked-up love. With that one syllable, Finley went from loving to animalistic before I could even register the change.

Fucking me from underneath me, he slams his hips upward—hard—holding me against him by the hip and neck. I may be on top, but I'm no longer the one in control and I have exactly zero issues with it.

Our breaths become gasps, our moans become cries. Our foreheads no longer touch as Finn pulls my hair hard enough to give him access to my neck where he bites and licks and no doubt leaves marks of his own.

I'm okay with that. I want to look in the mirror tonight, or tomorrow, or the next day and see that he's been there.

Although, I'm sure my sore pussy will be all too happy to remind me.

With every bite, he bottoms out and with every lick, almost pulls me right off of him. Over and over again, he pummels my hungry pussy, taking everything he needs and giving me everything I've ever wanted.

He shifts his body a little lower, causing my already-sensitive clit to rub against his pelvic bone and I lose my shit.

The bolt of electricity that runs from my clit to every other nerve ending in my body makes my entire body shiver. The low growl that shakes his chest tells me he felt it and it makes him just as hungry as I am for this impending orgasm.

Speeding up his thrusts, Finn fucks me with abandon; not measuring his strength, just giving me pleasure like it's an Olympic sport.

His hand is back on my hip, allowing me to wrap my arms around his neck and meet him thrust for thrust. I'm breathless, chasing this massive climax that may ruin us both.

With his mouth at my ear he murmurs, "Give it to me, V. Give me everything you've got."

I break at his words. My body goes still, my breath locked in my throat. I squeeze him tight around his neck and let the blanket of pleasure envelop me with every rush of dopamine that invades my bloodstream.

Finn's hands slide up my back and latch onto my shoulders, pushing me down, as he halts his thrusts and spills deep inside me.

The only sound in the room is our breathing; rapid-fire

bordering on wheezing.

I think he broke me.

I may have broken him, too.

Or maybe, just maybe, we mended each other.

I still for a minute, coming down from all of that and he adjusts us until I'm lying on his chest.

I could almost purr in satisfaction as I lie in his arms, trying to catch my breath as his fingers trace up and down my ribs. "You really aren't repulsed by the scars are you?"

I turn in his hold to look up at him. "Why would I ever be repulsed by any part of you?"

He takes a deep breath, tucking me back under his arm so I'm not watching his face. "Because you don't know how I got them."

"You don't have to tell me." A shudder runs through his body and my heart breaks for him, because whatever it is he has to tell me is obviously something difficult for him to talk about.

"This isn't exactly how I saw myself telling you, but I don't want to keep hiding from you. Until you know everything, it feels like there's this wall between us." He pauses, but I stay quiet. I'm not about to rush whatever this is. "I was eight the first time my dad brought his friends over and offered me to them. I didn't understand it, I just knew I didn't like it. That it hurt... but it didn't matter how much I cried or begged... the friends kept coming around."

I suck in a breath as I try not to cry for the horrors he's

obviously endured.

"Each time I tried to hide or escape, my dad made sure I'd regret trying to stop it from happening the next time. When their tastes got more… bloodthirsty, the cutting and burning started. My mom… she just pretended it wasn't happening."

"Finn—" I start, but I feel him shake his head so I stop.

"I'm not telling you this for you to pity me, the last thing I want from you is pity. I just need you to understand that sometimes…sometimes I can't be touched. Sometimes I need that control over what's happening. Otherwise I just can't."

Anger burns through me and I vow to myself to make his dad and his friends suffer for every single mark. Those on his body, and his soul.

"This doesn't change anything," I tell him softly. "To me, you're still Finn. Scars or not. Past whatever it is. It's who you are that I care about, and despite the horrors, you are one of the kindest, most loyal people I know. You love fiercely, and you protect the people you consider family. I don't need to know anything else to know I love you."

He tilts my chin up, finally letting me see him. His eyes are glassy, and I kiss him softly, trying to show him just how much I mean what I say.

"I love you too," he breathes, holding me tightly against him, like he's scared I'm going to run away. But I'm not going anywhere. Not now, not ever.

I might've planned to escape The Cove when I returned

here, but that was before I knew everything that was waiting for me, and the only way I'm leaving now is with all of them at my side.

After an intense few days, I'm more than ready for my girls' weekend away with Indi. But first, I have to pack… and I have my meeting with Bentley. I still haven't told the guys I'm searching for my mom. I'm not exactly sure why, but it seems like a fool's errand and I don't want to look like that pathetic little girl chasing the parent who didn't want her.

Regardless, I still want to know what happened to her. I need to know that she got out of this world in one piece. That Lincoln might be wrong and there is hope for us all to get free.

I'm not stupid enough to go alone, stalker alert and all that, so Indi coaxes Dylan into coming with us to the diner I'm meeting Bentley in. Which is exactly why I'm in the back of his car, butterflies running riot in my stomach, as we head out of The Cove.

"You sure this is a good idea?" he asks, glancing at me in the rearview mirror.

I shake my head and laugh dryly. "Not at all, but better to have all the information available, right?"

He quirks a brow at me and Indi pokes his ribs. "Don't judge her, mister. I thought you'd be the most chill one of you idiots to bring with us, especially since you don't hate her on principle."

"No judgement here, shortstack, but all things considered, from what you've both told me so far, this is a risky move."

I blow out a breath and nod again. "It is, which is why I'm not going alone. And as much as I know the guys want to protect me from everything, this is something I need to do. I have memories that don't quite make sense with everything I've learned since I came back here. My mom is probably one of the few people who has answers."

"Now that I understand. Don't worry, secret's safe with me. And if shit gets out of hand, I'll get you both out as safely as I can."

"I don't see it going that way. My friend gave me this guy's details; he should be solid. It's more the stalker thing." I shrug, like it doesn't totally skeeve me out. "Safety in numbers, right?"

He laughs. "Something like that, yeah."

He turns his focus back on the road, and Indi turns up the radio when a Midnight Blue song starts playing. She bounces around in the passenger seat to it while I try not to get lost in my thoughts.

It isn't long before we pull up to the diner in the next town over, and Dylan scouts the place out before coming back to the car. "Looks chill, like a little mom and pop diner. Smells fucking delicious, but no one looks too sketch. Let's do it."

He opens the door for Indi while I climb out of the car, trying not to let my nerves take over. I have no idea why I'm so fucking nervous, but I think this stalker thing is finally starting to hit me fully. It's also the first time I've been anywhere lately without one of my guys, and if anything happens they're going to be so pissed.

Rightfully so too, and I'm aware that this probably isn't the smartest idea I've had, but here I am. I did at least grab a gun from Dylan when he picked up Indi and me. It's small, a .22, but it doesn't need to have a big bang to do its job. My hands don't exactly work with a .44.

I head in with them, moving to a booth in the back, and they take one by the door like we agreed. The server comes to my table, an older lady who looks like everyone's favorite nana. "Afternoon, dear, what can I get you? I recommend the apple and blackberry pie, but I'm a little biased." She winks at me with a warm smile, and I instantly feel at ease.

"I'll take the pie." I smile back at her. "And a coffee please."

"Sure thing, sweetie. I'll get that right out for you." She wanders over to the counter, bringing my coffee and slice over before heading to the other tables. I take a bite, closing my eyes as the flavors burst across my tongue.

Pie is good enough to almost forget my nerves.

Almost.

I scarf it down. I hadn't realized how hungry I was, though it could be nervous hunger, then fidget with my coffee while I wait for Bentley to arrive.

It doesn't take too much longer before a man slips into the

booth opposite me. "Miss Royal, it's good to meet you."

"Bentley, I assume?"

"The one and only. Jenna said you're good people, so I'll be straight with you. My fees aren't cheap, but I'm good at what I do and I don't rest until I find what I'm after."

My nerves settle a little. I like how to-the-point he is, I can do this.

"Good to know, and money isn't really an issue."

He nods as the server appears again, topping up my coffee and grabbing him a mug before disappearing. "So who is it that you want found?"

I take a sip of my coffee before meeting his brown eyes. "My mother. She left when I was younger, and I haven't seen or heard from her since."

"Is she definitely alive?" he asks, and I bite down on my lip.

"No idea. As far as I know, yes."

He nods, and I tell him everything I know about her, about when she left, but really I don't have that much information to give him.

"Okay, that's a good place for me to start. It might take me a week before I have anything even remotely worth mentioning for you, but I'll check in next weekend and let you know what I have, if anything." He slides me a card, tapping the top of it. "These are my account details. Transfer over the starting funds, and I'll get to work right away. We'll assess the fees as we go if money really isn't a problem."

"It's not," I confirm, and he smiles before standing.

"Well then, Miss Royal. I'll be seeing you." He leaves, and I let out a deep breath.

I'm not sure what I was so worried about, but I feel better already. Indi bounces across the diner to me, and sits in the spot he just vacated, Dylan not far behind her.

"All good?" she asks, sipping on the milkshake she brought with her.

"Yeah, I think so. Thank you guys for coming with me."

"Anytime." She grins around the straw of her shake. "Also, don't tell Smithy, but this cherry milkshake is the fucking bomb."

I bark out a laugh and mark a cross over my heart. "Secret's safe with me."

"Well, if we're done, I should get you guys back before anyone notices you're missing," Dylan says, draining his mug. I nod and do the same as Indi groans about having to sacrifice the last of her shake. He takes her glass over to the counter and the lady behind it pours it in a to-go cup.

"He's so good to me." She sighs as we slip out of the booth.

"He better be." I grin at her and loop my arm through hers as he ushers us out of the building. "You ready for tomorrow?"

"So freaking ready! Massages, hot tubs, and facials are calling to me."

"Still can't believe you won't let one of us come with you," Dylan grumbles. "Need an escort to a coffee shop, but not a freaking spa weekend."

"Don't pout," she teases. "It's a spa retreat, what's the worst that could happen?"

I groan at her words, because if she just jinxed our weekend...

No. I won't even think it.

It's going to be nothing but bliss.

Nothing but goddamn bliss, dammit.

# TWENTY SIX

## OCTAVIA

I slide into the driver's seat of my dad's old Range Rover—which Lincoln insisted on having Finn check over before I was allowed to drive—as the valet loads our bags in the trunk. This weekend was everything I needed it to be. Relaxing, quiet, zero stress, and just happy times with my girl.

The early morning sun might be shining outside, but I'm kind of sad that it's over already. "We should do this more often… or go away over the summer."

"Yes!" She whoops as she buckles herself in. "I am so down for a summer vacation. The world is our oyster, right?"

"Hell yes it is." I pull on my aviators and grin at her. "Anywhere in the world, my jet can take us. You name the place, or places, and we're there. And if they behave, we can bring the guys too."

She giggles nodding. "Imagining all of them on your jet is too funny. The sheer amount of brooding would maybe be too much."

"You're not wrong." I grin as I start the engine. "They can get their own damn jet."

"Preach!" she exclaims as she sets up the playlist on my phone and I pull away from the retreat. "Just in future, let's not make travel plans where we have to get up at the ass crack of dawn. Please?" I laugh at her as we leave the resort and head onto the long winding roads. We're a few hours from home, but I don't even care about the long drive. I kept in touch with the guys all weekend, as promised, and had my location shared with them in case anything went wrong.

I'm beginning to think that all of this drama is just that. That maybe my stalker is harmless. That the Knights aren't after me.

A girl can dream, right?

We spend most of the drive singing at the top of our lungs, laughing about stupid shit the guys have said or done, and just enjoying the last of our bubble away before school and everything else comes crashing down around our ears.

I check the rearview and spot a black truck that's been behind us almost since we left the retreat. I bite my lip, trying not to be dramatic, because it can't be following us, right?

"What's up?" Indi asks, looking at me wide-eyed.

"I'm sure it's nothing," I tell her, checking the mirror again, changing lanes on the freeway just to see.

The car doesn't follow, so I let out a breath.

"I'm being a jumpy bitch. Ignore me," I tell her, and she glances out the back before turning back to face me.

"Are you sure?"

"Not entirely, but pretty sure," I admit, signaling for our exit. We're nearly home, so at least if I'm not being dramatic, help is close by. "Am I dropping you home?"

She shakes her head and smiles softly. "Nah, take me to the twins' if that's okay?"

"Course," I respond, taking the exit that will take us to that side of The Cove rather than toward home.

It doesn't take long to get to the twins' house, and I hug her tight. "Thank you for coming away with me."

"Always, bish. You're my favorite. Just don't tell Ryker." She laughs, winking at me.

"My lips are sealed." I make the zipper movement across my lips and she laughs.

"And that is exactly why you're my favorite. I'll see you at school in the morning. Do you need a ride or is Lincoln still happy giving you a ride?" She barks out a laugh at her punny before jumping from the car.

"I'm good, I can ride in with Linc. Saves you coming out of your way."

"Okay! I'll grab my shit and head in." She grins as Ryker appears at the front door. He stalks over to the car, motioning for me to open the trunk, so I hit the button and he heads straight to the back of the car. I wave to Indi as she closes the door and skips towards Ryker as he slams the trunk shut, banging the back of the car to let me know they're clear.

I pull away from the curb and decide to grab a coffee before heading home. I pull out of the drive-thru and spot the black truck again. So, rather than heading straight home, I detour toward the beach, just to see if I'm being a paranoid bitch, but when the truck follows me with every twist and turn, I realize I'm not.

So I do what I should've already done.

I call Lincoln.

The ring sounds through the sound system, each ring feeling like a lifetime, as my heart hammers in my chest.

"Hey, you almost home?" Lincoln sounds almost relaxed when he answers, and I feel bad dropping this in his lap.

"I am, but I think someone's following me. No, I know someone's following me."

"What do you mean?" His tone changes in an instant, fully alert.

"I thought I saw a black truck follow me back from the retreat, but then it didn't turn off to The Cove, so I thought I was imagining it. But the same truck is following me through town." I try to keep my hysterics to a minimum, but I am freaking the fuck out.

"Head straight home. The boys are here, we'll wait at the gate for you. But do not drop this line, Octavia."

"Okay." My voice shakes as I answer him, my eyes darting between the road before me and my rearview mirror.

"You can do this. Just try to drive like normal." His voice is calm, that soothes me a little, but I can hear him bark out to the others, and the sounds of movement come down the line.

"Do you think it's him?" I ask, my hands trembling as I clutch the steering wheel.

"It could be, but you're going to be okay." I know he's trying to reassure me, but holy fuck.

I pull onto my road, and I can see the four of them standing at the end of my drive, the gate already open. I try to drive like nothing's wrong and pull through the gate. It closes behind me once the guys are in.

The truck slows as it passes then speeds back up, disappearing. I end my call with Lincoln, and rest my forehead against the steering wheel, trying to take a few deep breaths to settle myself down. I've been in worse situations than this, so why the fuck is this messing with me so much?

Fuck my life.

The car door opens and I squeak, jumping at the movement.

"It's just me," Lincoln says as I turn to face him. "Are you okay?"

"Yes?" I try to smile, but I'm pretty sure all I manage is a grimace. Sometimes I feel like such a badass. Then shit like this happens and I become very aware that I am very much not a badass.

"Come on, let's head inside. Smithy isn't back yet, so Mav is just checking the house." He lifts me from the car and holds me against him until my hands stop shaking.

East grabs my bag from the trunk, handing it to Linc, and jumps in the car. "I'll put this away and meet you inside."

"Thank you." I smile at him just as Mav appears at the door.

"Coast is clear," he shouts, jogging down the few steps and stealing me from Lincoln's arms. "You okay, princess?"

"I'm better now," I tell him as I nuzzle against his chest. "Where did Finn go?"

"He got the plate; he's having Lucas run it to see if we can get an idea of who the fuck it was. Let's head inside and we'll run you through everything we've worked out so far," Lincoln says before heading through the front door. Mav leads me indoors and I spot Finn already in the living room on the phone. I close the door as East appears from the door to the garage.

"Hey, sweet girl. I'm sorry your weekend took a turn for the worse."

"Thanks." I shrug. "Just another day in my insane life, I guess?"

"We'll get it figured out. Nothing's going to happen to you while we're around." He steals me from Mav who grunts in response, but I've never felt more treasured than I do now being passed between them.

We head to the living room where Finley finishes up his call and curses. "It was a fucking rental. Lucas is looking into it now, but I think we were right: it's too neat and tidy."

"What do you mean?" I ask as Maverick pulls me into his lap on the couch.

"We're pretty sure your stalker is a Knight," Linc says as he paces back and forth in front of the TV. "It's the only thing that makes sense. We can usually find anyone. Trace them, get something. But there is *nothing.*"

My eyes go wide as his words filter through my chaotic mind.

"Do you have any idea who?"

"Not yet, but we're working on it. It explains why Lucas and Smithy's friends haven't been able to find anything. He can cover his tracks too easily. But I'm also not convinced he's working alone."

"Holy shit." I try to take a few breaths to keep from hyperventilating, but it doesn't work. I climb from Maverick's lap and start to pace.

"V, we're not going to leave your side. This twisted fuck isn't going to get to you," Maverick says vehemently and I pause, looking at them all, when it hits me.

"I'm not even worried about me, but what if whoever it is hurts you guys? Hurts Indi. Just to get to me? I couldn't live with myself if that happened."

"We've survived hell and come out the other side," Lincoln says, moving toward me while Finley stares at me intently. "We'll survive this too."

I take a deep breath just as the lights cut out. "What the—"

I don't manage to say anything else before all fucking hell breaks loose. I scream as the door bursts open behind me, followed by the smash of glass as people crash through the windows behind the guys. Gunfire pops around us and I try to move when an arm wraps around me from behind, and a cloth is placed over my face.

I try not to breathe in; I know that smell, and I do not want to pass out right now.

"Octavia!" I hear Lincoln cry as I'm dragged backward. I try to struggle against the giant body moving me backward, but my lungs burn in my chest from trying not to breathe and my vision starts to blur.

I see Lincoln try to run toward me, but more gunfire cracks across the room and East dives toward Lincoln.

I suck in a breath, unable not to anymore, and scream when I see the blood.

"No!" I kick and flail but it's no use. My arms grow heavy as my eyes start to flutter shut.

The last thing I see are the Saints on the ground in a pool of blood.

# TWENTY SEVEN

## FINLEY

I don't even count how many bodies I drop as I try to get through them to get to V. Watching the door close as she's dragged out makes my blood run cold, so I fight harder.

The sound of screeching tires reaches me and the few bodies left standing do a fucking runner, except for the one Maverick's still fighting off. That's when I see Lincoln and East on the ground.

"Fuck!" I yell, pulling Maverick's attention. There's another *pop*. My attention swings to Maverick as the guy opposite him drops to the ground, the back of his head splattered on the wall.

Running to the brothers, I see the blood pouring from East's back. "Call an ambulance," I yell at Maverick as I try to move East off of Lincoln and put pressure on the wound.

He's still breathing so there's still hope.

This cannot be fucking happening.

Maverick has the phone to his ear as he drops to a crouch opposite me and checks Lincoln's vitals. "He's breathing, just a nasty gash to the head."

I nod, focusing back on East.

He can't fucking die.

"How the fuck did this happen?" I growl to no one in particular. Lincoln starts to stir, fighting off Mav who tries to keep him lying down. Lincoln is about as good at taking orders as his father. Which basically means he sucks.

"East!" Lincoln's voice is almost hollow as he takes in the picture before him. "Fuck!"

He runs a hand through his hair, blood dripping down his face as he rises to his knees. Putting his hands over mine, he sways a little. "I've got East. You two go get fucking Octavia."

I glance at Maverick, who is pacing the floor, and nod. "Okay, call us when you get to the hospital."

"This was the Knights. No one else would've coordinated an attack like that. We should've seen it coming. We were too distracted by her fucking stalker." Anger rushes through me at the thought but now is not the time.

"We'll head to The Cage. If they're going to initiate her, that's where they'll take her," I say, climbing to my feet and wiping my bloody hands on my jeans. Looking over at Maverick, I nod. "Let's go."

I move, almost on autopilot, out to her garage, grabbing the keys to her Range Rover and sliding into the driver's seat. I peel out of the garage and through her gates like my life depends on it.

Except it's worse, because *her* life might depend on it.

For once, Maverick is silent and tense beside me as the miles to The Cage speed past. I'm breaking every fucking speed limit that exists, but I'll be fucked if I'm going to let them just take her from us.

If she doesn't agree to their terms, they'll kill her. It's what they do.

Rage pools in my stomach, at war with the fear in my heart.

I can't lose her.

Not like this.

My phone rings and Maverick answers it, putting it on speaker phone.

"We're at the hospital, he fucking flatlined on the way in."

My heart sinks. If Lincoln loses East *and* V… he'll lose all of his humanity. I'm pretty sure East is the only thing that kept him human the last few years.

"Keep us up to date. We're nearly there."

"Let me know when you have her," he says before the call ends. I glance at Mav who looks as worried as I feel.

He has to fucking survive.

The car slides as I turn onto the dirt road, dust and stones kicking up all around us as we hurtle towards The Cage.

I slam on the brakes when we reach the entrance, making sure the safety is off of my gun. This might not be the smartest move, but it's all we've got. "You ready?"

"Let's get our girl back," is all he says in response as we climb from the car. I try to act normal, like we're just going to The Cage as if it's any normal day, but my heart beats so hard in my chest, I swear I can hear it like a fucking drum.

We enter the elevator and I push the button to take us all the way down. The ride feels like forever, and when the doors open, my heart sinks.

*She's not here.*

# TWENTY EIGHT

## OCTAVIA

**M**y entire body aches as feeling starts to come back to me. The brain fog is so fucking thick it's all I can do to remember to breathe—which has never fucking hurt so much before. It feels like someone sandblasted my esophagus. My fingers and toes prick with pins and needles as sensation returns and I whimper. It's as if someone turned every nerve ending in my body up to ten.

I drag in a few deep, painful breaths to try and clear the nausea and my eyes flutter open for a moment before slamming shut against the harsh, bright lights. My brain feels like it's moving through gelatin as I try to work out what the fuck is happening.

That's when it comes back to me.

Lincoln.

East.

The break-in.

Shit.

Fuck.

My breathing speeds up, and I try not to panic as darkness presses in at the edges of my vision.

"Oh good, you're awake."

I stop trying to breathe. I know that voice.

Pain lances through my body as I struggle against my bindings. I'm tied down to a table of some sort, but I'm vertical.

What the hell?

I open my eyes again, blinking as they fill with water in response to the harsh light and hope this is all a very fucked-up nightmare.

Then I see him.

This can't be happening.

The world swims as I take in my surroundings and fear claws its way up my throat, burning and acrid. I don't know if it's the pain of the bile tearing into my throat or the terror his words evoke, but my brain finally succumbs to the darkness and my vision goes dark. I hear him, but he sounds far away, distant and echoing. Even my barely conscious brain registers the threat of his breath on my cheek though.

"I told you they couldn't protect you. And now you're mine."

# ACKNOWLEDGMENTS

So… This is where we are… and I'm sorry.

Thats a lie. I'm not sorry at all LOL. But, I do want to say thank you for reading and sticking with me and V this far!

When I say this book took a village, I really freaking mean it.

Imma start with a HUGE thank you to my noodle loving besties. You know who you are and I wouldn't have finished this book without you… or at least without a mental breakdown without you. Who thought so many words could pour from these fingers!

The MVP of the book is by far Elisabeth Crowl, who without, this book wouldn't exist because my life would be chaos. She makes my squirrels into ducks and I adore her for it. So thank you Elisabeth, for fixing all the things, and a special shout of to Steph for plotting evil things with me, designing all my merch, and going off on tangents with me when Elisabeth wasn't looking muahaha.

To my alpha & beta teams, you guys are freaking rockstars. Lisa, Zoe, Megan, Kiera, Jeni, Lauren & Jessi. Thank you for your priceless feedback, and for loving these characters as much as I do.

To David, Sarah & Sam for making Octavia sparkle and shine. You guys pulled this one out of the bag, right down to the wire and you'll never know just how much I appreciate it.

Finally, to you the reader, thank you. For taking a chance on an author you've probably never heard of. For picking up a new book. For running the gauntlet with us. Just thank you.

Book 3 won't be long, so I guess I better go dive back into the book cave.

Peace out

xoxo

# ABOUT THE AUTHOR

Lily is a writer, dreamer, fur mom and serial killer, crime documentary addict.

She loves to write dark, reverse harem romance and characters who will shatter your heart. Characters who enjoy stomping on the pieces and then laugh before putting you back together again. And she definitely doesn't enjoy readers tears. Nope. Not even a little.

If you want to keep up to date with all things Lily, including where her next book is out, please find join her reader group, Lily's Wild Hearts, on Facebook.

# ALSO BY LILY WILDHART

### THE KNIGHTS OF ECHOES COVE

*(Dark, Bully, High School Reverse Harem Romance)*

Tormented Royal

Lost Royal

Caged Royal

Forever Royal

### THE SAINTS OF SERENTIY FALLS

*(Dark, Bully, Step Brother, College, Reverse Harem Romance)*

Burn